D0357855

DAVID VS. GOLIATH

Once more, the foes are poised to strike.
Who will win this time?

On David's side: Robert Miller, the American journalist tracking Judas; Colonel Marc Ram, the legendary one-armed Israeli intelligence chief; Major Falid, a courageous Jordanian policeman; Gina, an Italian beauty torn between Christianity and Communism; and Eli Abraham, the dashing young Israeli Prime Minister.

The forces of Goliath: Rostov, the KGB mastermind who, with Judas, has given Italy its first Communist government; Mundt, a mortar expert with his sights on the Church of the Holy Sepulchre; Ayad, a handsome young Palestinian terrorist; Sonia, the Russian Jew blackmailed into the deadly plot; . . . and Judas, the cold-blooded British assassin dedicated to destroying the first American Pope.

GOLIATH
A conspiracy of terror.

It could happen tomorrow.

GOLIATH

W. J. Weatherby

A Quicksilver Book

GOLIATH

*A Bantam Book / published by arrangement with
Quicksilver Books, Inc.*

Bantam edition / April 1981

All rights reserved.
Copyright © 1981 by W. J. Weatherby.
Cover art copyright © 1981 by Bantam Books, Inc.
*This book may not be reproduced in whole or in part, by
mimeograph or any other means, without permission.
For information address: Bantam Books, Inc.*

ISBN 0-553-14593-2

Published simultaneously in the United States and Canada

*Bantam Books are published by Bantam Books, Inc. Its trade-
mark, consisting of the words "Bantam Books" and the por-
trayal of a bantam, is Registered in U.S. Patent and Trademark
Office and in other countries. Marca Registrada. Bantam
Books, Inc., 666 Fifth Avenue, New York, New York 10103.*

PRINTED IN THE UNITED STATES OF AMERICA

0 9 8 7 6 5 4 3 2 1

Goliath is a story of the near future. Anyone familiar with the European and Middle Eastern settings will soon spot the changes I have made in the present picture. Based on what we know now, these predictions seem quite justifiable.

W.J.W.
New York City

January, 198—

It is 7:20 on a cold winter morning thirty miles north of
Rome. The grape fields are white with frost. A faint mist rises
among the pine woods.

Suddenly the roar of high-powered engines shatters the
early morning stillness.

Birds flutter wildly out of the pine trees as three armor-
plated cars come speeding down the driveway of a large white
villa. Formidable-looking Maseratis, they are specially built
to absorb considerable punishment and yet still execute bootleg turns and high-speed escapes. In a cloud of dust, only a
few yards apart, they turn onto a narrow country road and
head for Rome.

People having breakfast in several of the nearby villas
catch only a fleeting glimpse of the Maseratis—and of the fat,
little, tousled-haired man in the back of the middle car.

His name is Alberto ("Papa") Tolloni, fifty-five-year-old
leader of the Italian Communist party. He is on his way to a
9:00 A.M. meeting at party headquarters. The armored escort
is to insure that he gets there alive.

Tolloni swallows an indigestion tablet and settles back to
read a newspaper. A headline about the coming general

election catches his attention. The ruling Christian Democrats are running scared. The Communists have a chance to win this time. The latest polls show the party short of an overall majority by only three percent. Tolloni could be the next prime minister, the dream of his life ever since he began as a young party organizer in Sicily . . .

He yawns. His heavy country breakfast has made him sleepy. Before he closes his eyes, he glances out at the two Maseratis flanking his car front and rear. All three cars are moving at nearly seventy miles per hour. He is as proud of them as of the white villa he has just left. Armored cars are a new status symbol in Italy, and his three are the latest models—two-inch thick, armor-plated bodies, bullet-resistant glass, high-powered engines. The Maseratis give him a great feeling of security. Surely he can afford to relax. His eyelids droop, and soon he is dozing with his mouth open, snoring loudly.

The three Maseratis are now speeding down a bumpy country lane between two distant farms. The deserted, wintry fields flash by. The drivers, all trained at the Counter-Terrorist Driving School in Rome, watch the road, but notice nothing wrong. There is a broken stone wall, a high hedgerow . . . Beyond the hedge they can't see . . . their eyes pass on . . .

There is no warning of any kind.

One moment the scene is peaceful, the next destruction transforms everything.

With lightning speed, a heavy grenade shatters the leading Maserati and blows it across the road into a ditch. It is hit directly in such a way as to avoid any collision with the second Maserati carrying Tolloni.

The explosion rocks Tolloni awake. Barely conscious, he rubs his eyes in bewilderment when there are two more explosions, one after the other, only seconds apart. The armored car at the rear explodes with a great roaring flash—a direct hit in the center of the roof leaves it a smoking ruin at the side of the road. The other explosion demolishes the hood of Tolloni's car, killing his driver, but only showering the party chief with broken glass. Once again a grenade has been used skillfully to insure Tolloni's survival.

He is thrown to the floor of his car, gasping for breath. His only injuries are a few minor cuts on his fat, fleshy face. Blood trickles down his chin. His head slowly clears, and he begins to realize what has happened.

His impregnable mobile fortresses, his beloved Maseratis, are impregnable no longer. His security has been totally destroyed. He is left defenseless on a deserted country road. His eyes narrow with fear. Who is out there? Which of his enemies? Bellini? . . .

The answer comes swiftly. Tolloni's car door is wrenched open, and rough, violent hands grab him, pulling him out onto the hard, cold ground. Tolloni's short fat legs fail him. He stumbles and falls, losing consciousness before he can recognize the face bending over him . . .

PART ONE

ASH WEDNESDAY

1

Dublin . . .

Snowflakes as big as silver dollars were falling on the Irish capital as Robert Miller hurried to the old pub hidden away in the back streets.

The tall American journalist cursed himself for not taking a taxi from his hotel. His dark blue raincoat was already turning white. But he had needed a walk. He'd had a frustrating twenty-four hours since arriving in Dublin, and he was the kind of man who had to release his feelings in action or explode.

Seven inches of snow were expected by nightfall. Already streets signs were hard to read, and the few people who passed like ghosts were in too much of a hurry to stop and give directions. Luckily the hotel doorman had drawn Miller a detailed map, and at last he found the narrow side street leading to the old pub.

Brushing the snow off his raincoat, Miller pushed open the heavy oak door with glazed glass panels. Immediately loud talk and laughter engulfed him. Behind the door was a thick black curtain to keep out the cold. He pulled this aside impatiently and found himself in the main bar. He stared round eagerly, looking for the man he had come to meet.

The old Dublin pub was crowded with lunchtime drinkers. Obviously the snowstorm hadn't affected business. The long bar and the plain Victorian decor reminded Miller of a Blarney Stone in New York, but the atmosphere was more cheerful. Dubliners seemed less uptight than New Yorkers.

He examined the lively Irish faces, trying to spot an obvious cop—or an Englishman. But no one stood out in the noisy groups filling the big high-ceilinged room.

Making sure the *Irish Times* under his arm was easy to see, Miller moved slowly through the crowd toward the long bar. Several faces turned to stare at him, trying to place him. He was obviously an American, but just as obviously not a tourist. With his unruly, reddish hair and strong-boned, open face, he had a lot of Irish in him, but he didn't look as if he'd come to trace his roots. His manner was too aggressive, too impatient. Miller's frustration still showed.

Two burly young Irishmen, holding mugs of beer, blocked his way. They eyed him casually, noting his powerful shoulders, broken nose, and the challenging look in his eyes. They stepped aside.

Miller leaned against the bar, aware of being watched. He put the *Irish Times* down on the stool beside him. That was to identify him. But no one came over. He turned and faced the door, waiting for the Scotland Yard man to come through the curtain. His inquiries so far had got nowhere. Superintendent Thomas Milligan of the Counter-Terrorist branch of Scotland Yard was his last hope.

The Superintendent kept him waiting for nearly half an hour. Miller had four empty pint beer glasses on the bar in front of him by the time the Scotland Yard man at last came through the curtain, brushing snow off himself. Miller recognized him at once. It wasn't his bloated, beery English face or his tweed topcoat so much as the sharp, detached way he surveyed the pub crowd and immediately spotted Miller. He could only be a cop. The Superintendent was in charge of the British side of the investigation into the recent assassination of Jeremy Sampson, the British Home Secretary. Sampson had been shot while on a visit to Dublin. It had been done at long range, and no one had been caught—yet.

"Sorry I'm late," Superintendent Milligan said briskly.

Keen brown eyes deep in the bloated face, like raisins in dough, examined Miller. "I was delayed by the news from Italy. Alberto Tolloni, the Italian Communist leader, has been kidnapped."

Miller was immediately alert. "By political terrorists?"

"Too early to say yet," the Superintendent replied cautiously. He bought himself a pint of beer and another for Miller. They took the big, foaming glasses over to a table in a quiet corner. "The kidnapping only took place early this morning. It was superbly well organized—as smart a job in its way as the assassination here."

"Could they be connected?"

"On the surface, it seems unlikely, and yet . . ." Superintendent Milligan stared at his beer as if the pint glass were a crystal ball. A man came to sit at the next table. Milligan leaned forward and spoke more quietly. "Our political branch at the Yard thinks I'm obsessed. But I've been convinced from the beginning, Mr. Miller, that the assassination here wasn't a local job. I believe the same people were responsible who assassinated the West German Foreign Minister in Munich last month. This Tolloni affair may be their work, too. But this time apparently it's a kidnapping, not a simple assassination. Tolloni's body hasn't been found yet . . ."

It was a moment Miller was familiar with—when a hunch was confirmed by someone at the scene. Superintendent Milligan was thinking along the same lines as Miller's boss, Bruce Carl Vaughan, the Pulitzer Prize-winning editor of the *New York Mirror*.

Miller was the *Mirror*'s top investigative reporter. Three days ago Vaughan had recalled him from a ski vacation in Colorado. The *Mirror*'s editor had learned from a reliable contact that the Central Intelligence Agency believed the recent political assassinations in Europe were the work of one tightly organized group. Vaughan told Miller: "The CIA's investigation is top secret, but apparently the agency's theory is this: The group's aim is to influence the international political scene by killing key leaders. The CIA doesn't yet know what they're after, who's the brain behind it, or who the next target is—which leading politician. Miller, I want you to find the answers." Robert Miller had flown to Dublin the next day. After inspecting the small square that was the scene of the first assassination, he had talked with the Irish investigators. All their leads had been exhausted. But the Scotland Yard man had now given him the confirmation he needed. Vaughan was on to something big.

"Professional assassins often sign their work like great artists," Superintendent Milligan said thoughtfully as Miller bought him another beer. "I see the same signature in both these assassinations. Look at what happened. The Home Secretary was shot in a moving car from several hundred yards away, a very difficult shot. The West German Foreign Minister's plane was hit by a short-range missile soon after taking off from Munich, a neat trick even for an army. There was the same brilliant organization, split-second timing, shrewd exploitation of the local scene, and great technical skill. And the killers escaped without a trace in both cases. Slick work, indeed. The early reports of the Tolloni kidnapping suggest the same kind of planning. Tolloni's armored cars, travelling very fast, were wrecked by mortars, without apparently harming Tolloni himself. Not an easy operation for trained commandos, and brilliantly carried out. And again the killers have escaped. My hunch is the same people are behind it. The idea of a highly organized international group has often been rumored, but nothing more important has been uncovered than haphazard, amateurish collaborations between the Irish and the Palestinians, the Czechs and a few other small foreign groups. Nothing more . . . until now. I sense one mind behind both the assassinations and the kidnapping. This could be the beginning of what we have long feared . . ." The bloated face looked grave.

When Robert Miller returned to his hotel, the late editions of the evening papers already had the Tolloni kidnapping on their front pages. It was big news in Dublin. The Irish, tragically divided over rival faiths, identified with the Italians' Catholic-Communist struggle. Alberto Tolloni was the leader of the wrong side, but as a true Eurocommunist on bad terms with the Soviet Union, he was the kind of rebel the Irish liked.

Miller watched the early TV news reports. Tolloni's wrecked armored cars were shown in films from Rome; they reminded Miller of Vietnam. "The whole of Italy—the whole of the world—is now wondering where Alberto Tolloni is and what is to be his fate," said a TV reporter dramatically in a soft Irish accent. "And how will his kidnapping affect the forthcoming Italian general election?"

Miller was reaching for the yellow pushbutton phone by his bedside to call New York when the phone buzzed softly.

"Is that you, Miller?" asked a familiar brisk voice. Vaughan had beaten him to it. "I want you to fly to Rome immediately. We may have found the next target . . . Alberto Tolloni."

2

It was impossible to fly out of Dublin immediately because of the snow. Great drifts blocked the runways, and the airport had to be closed for several hours. By the time planes could take off, Robert Miller's frustration was close to the boiling point. He flared up at a barman who gave him wrong change. Anything to relieve the tension. Precious time was being lost; this trail could go cold on him, too.

When he landed at Fiumicino Airport, the Italian government had already received a message from Tolloni's kidnappers. They offered to exchange Alberto Tolloni for three right-wing activists who were in a Roman jail for blowing up Communist information centers. The immediate public reaction was relief. It seemed as if Papa Tolloni might be safely back home in his white villa within a few days.

Miller had a sense of letdown. Maybe the Tolloni kidnapping was going to have a happy ending and his instinct was wrong. Vaughan's, too, and Milligan's. He went into an airport bar to decide on his next move, in time to watch the government's reply to the kidnappers on television. He knew immediately from Prime Minister Ignazio Silvieri's grim expression what the reply was going to be. "The government cannot make a deal with kidnappers," said Prime Minister Silvieri, the silver-maned Christian Democrat leader. "Where would it all end if we did? More and more kidnappings would occur, and then there would be complete chaos—the end of Italian democracy! We cannot risk ruining the nation for the life of one man, not even the distinguished General Secretary of the Communist party."

This last remark was greeted with grim chuckles in the

airport bar because Silvieri, the Christian Democrat, and Tolloni, the Communist, had been lifelong political opponents. The kidnapping wasn't nearly as simple as it seemed, Miller thought, reassured. Superintendent Milligan had sensed that. At least a happy ending was postponed. Miller decided to stay on.

He went out to the white villa to hear Tolloni's wife appeal to the government to change its mind. On the way, he passed the scene of the kidnapping—the wrecked armored cars were still there. Mama Tolloni, a small buxom woman dressed in black, spoke to the crowd of reporters in the villa's big courtyard under a canopy of eucalyptus trees. It was at least ten degrees warmer here than in Dublin. The pale winter sunlight through the furry leaves gave Mama Tolloni's face a sickly greenish hue as she bitterly attacked the government. "They will do nothing because they don't want my husband to win the election," she cried.

As he watched her, Robert Miller was aware of the complexity of the Italian situation, of motives and pressures and relationships behind this case that he knew nothing about. Miller's blunt, aggressive approach had been extraordinarily successful in uncovering scandals back home. He felt he knew the American scene and this gave him great confidence in his instinct there. But here . . . well, Italy made even the feuding in Ireland, the land of his fathers, seem comparatively simple. It was lucky that he had learned some Italian for a Mafia series, without that he would have been lost, but he was unsure how to adapt his style to suit the Italian temperament. He wondered for a moment whether his trusted method of ruthlessly following his hunches would work here. And then, characteristically, he shrugged the whole matter off. Facts were facts, Miller reminded himself, and even this labyrinth of ancient Italian rivalries must lead somewhere—perhaps even to the international connection he was looking for.

When he phoned the New York office, Vaughan had only one instruction: "Don't tread on the toes of the Rome bureau." Miller pretended not to know what he meant, and Vaughan snapped, "A little competition among fellow staff members is healthy, Miller, but you always carry it too far. The Rome bureau is especially sensitive. Go easy. I don't want to referee any more brawls."

Miller's reputation for being difficult had been made ten

years before, when he was twenty-three, and had written a series on the Texas oil companies. He had been involved in a near brawl with the head of the Houston bureau, and Vaughan had been called in. But it was Miller's first big break, and he had saved his job by producing a series that was vivid, unbiased, and powerful. Miller, in his wholehearted pursuit of a story, was seldom diplomatic, but then a diplomat wouldn't make a good investigative reporter, and at thirty-three Miller had developed into a top-notch one. And he knew it. He filed Vaughan's warning away to forget. He had no intention of going near the Rome bureau unless his story took him there.

The kidnappers' next message repeated their offer and identified them as members of Il Duce, a far right, fanatical group of Mussolini admirers whose aims included the restoration of the monarchy and the outlawing of the Communist party. Italian counter-terrorist experts Miller consulted were astonished that this group had been capable of such an expert operation. All the Il Duce members had accomplished up to then was to disrupt a few Communist public meetings. "Such a complex operation so perfectly carried out is beyond them," one expert told Miller, "unless they had outside help."

Outside help . . .

Could this be the group he was looking for?

Miller spent a lot of time with the Rome police, looking for an answer, but they were running around in circles. The kidnappers had covered their tracks very successfully. Just as the killers had in Ireland and in Germany.

The government must have been worried about the Italian people's reaction because Prime Minister Silvieri went back on television to explain again why the kidnappers' offer had to be rejected. The kidnappers' answer this time was immediate and much more threatening. They warned the government that Alberto Tolloni would be "executed" unless their offer was accepted, and they circulated pathetic letters from Tolloni to his wife and to the government, pleading for his life. These letters had a big effect when they were published in the papers, because Tolloni was very popular, even among people who hated Communism. He was often critical of Moscow and was regarded as an Italian first and a Communist second. Italians also identified with his engaging human qualities—his huge appetite, his earthy jokes, his devotion to his family, even his pride in the luxury of his white villa. And now they identified with his great fear conveyed in the pathetic letters. "My dear wife, I write to you in a spirit of desperation. They tell me they are going to kill me . . ."

Miller read and re-read the letters. There was something puzzling about them, something he couldn't pinpoint. His instinct told him something was wrong. What had reduced the great Tolloni to this—or rather *who* had? Miller waited impatiently for the kidnappers' next move.

The attempts to bargain with Tolloni's life dragged on for several weeks. There were more pathetic letters, more government explanations, more appeals by Mama Tolloni. She even asked the Pope for help: "You and my husband have different faiths, but you respect each other as fellow Sicilians, as fellow Italians. Save him for me and for Italy!" Old Pope Alfredo made a personal appeal to the kidnappers to release "this devoted family man." He even offered to take Tolloni's place. But the old Pope made no mention of the kidnappers' offer. Mama Tolloni, who had hoped he would persuade the government to accept, was bitterly disappointed. "If my Alberto had been a Christian Democrat," she told reporters at the white villa, "the Pope would have saved him."

By this time, public sympathy for Tolloni was so great that hardly anyone believed the kidnappers would dare to kill him. The election was too close.

"It would be like giving the Communists a million extra votes," the shrewd veteran right-wing Italian journalist, Mario Lepecci, told Miller. "Italy's already in the mood for a change. Many Italians feel the way their fathers felt just before Mussolini's rise to power—they long for a strong leadership to restore national pride. The Communists are always a big temptation, but never bigger than in this coming election. Tolloni has already humanized their image. The Il Duce group daren't make a martyr of him. They'll find some face-saving trick to release him."

The Italian journalist—handsome, grey-haired, tall and graceful—looked more like a distinguished politician than a reporter. Miller had first met him in Washington when Lepecci was covering the Watergate hearings. Gradually the two men developed what was for Miller a fairly close professional relationship—which meant occasional drinks, occasional dinners, and endless shop talk. Miller tended to avoid

most of his fellow reporters; he was just too competitive to
relax around them. But he made an exception of Mario
Lepecci. Partly it was because the Italian wasn't competing
with him, was foreign to the New York scene where the
gossip, the incessant name-dropping, the flip cynicism rubbed
Miller's midwestern sensibility the wrong way. But also—and
perhaps this was more important—the Italian's age put Miller
at his ease: Lepecci was nearly old enough to be his father
and, in fact, took a fatherly interest in his young American
colleague. Miller had been married in those days to a New
York model, and when Lepecci found out, he insisted on
meeting his wife. The Millers' marriage was already on the
rocks and their divorce followed soon afterwards, but their
dinners with this gentlemanly Italian journalist were like calm
oases in the desert of their final months together. Lepecci, a
great family man himself and a firm believer in the Catholic
sacrament of marriage, had a way of making the couple feel
as if everything would work out in time. Miller wanted to
believe it, he loved Eve with a kind of unreflecting intensity—
when he was with her. But ultimately he had to admit she was
right. He was obsessed with his work. That always came first.
Once Lepecci was gone, they lost forever the moments of
simple joy in companionship. They were too seldom together.
He was continually away on assignments—it was as if
Vaughan were deliberately helping to break up the marriage.
No wonder Eve hadn't liked the old man. She called him The
General.

Lepecci didn't know about the divorce, but when Miller
told him about it, all he said was "It may not be permanent,
my friend. Perhaps just a temporary separation. We'll see."
Miller shrugged. Catholics were all alike, he thought, always
trying to foist their faith on you. It was all over with Eve. It
had taken him long enough to face the truth—that it was her
or the job, and he'd chosen the job—and he didn't want to
talk about it with Lepecci. It was the story that was important. That was his justification. He had come to get the
Italian's help in sorting through the tangles of the situation in
Rome. He usually found Lepecci's political judgment reliable,
and he listened intently as the Italian journalist elaborated on
his analysis of why Tolloni would be released. The right wing
simply couldn't afford any Communist martyrs before election day. His reasoning seemed right, but as it turned out his
conclusion was not.

Shortly before ten o'clock the next morning, a body was discovered in a stolen Alfa Romeo parked on the Via Michelangelo Caetani near the Communist party headquarters. When Miller glimpsed it over a policeman's shoulder, he understood why the body hadn't been immediately identified. It looked very different from the fat, voluble little man the public had known from television and newspaper pictures. The body of Alberto Tolloni had lost about thirty pounds and had a shrunken, wasted look. He had been shot once in the head.

"It doesn't make sense," Mario Lepecci said as they watched the police photographing the body. "The Il Duce crowd have bungled it badly."

Miller looked again at the wasted body. No wonder Tolloni had broken and written those pathetic letters. He had been starved into submission. But it didn't seem like the work of bunglers. It was too calculated, too well-planned, too ... ruthless. Miller had a sense of the mind behind it, and he shivered slightly. Someone capable of anything. Someone totally amoral. With a consuming hatred—but for what, for whom? The treatment of Tolloni had gone far beyond cold calculation. It had been systematic torture by a mind that must enjoy such pain and humiliation. A sick mind, but not a bungler's. Just the opposite. No, there was something wrong, very wrong, about the whole scene. But Miller couldn't pinpoint what it was—yet.

It seemed to Robert Miller then that the final stages in what became known as the Tolloni affair had an eerie inevitability, almost as if they were part of a prearranged plan.

The funeral was held the day before the election. Mama Tolloni refused to allow any government representatives to attend. Sandro Bellini, her husband's successor as General Secretary of the party, sat beside her. Bellini had none of the popular human qualities of Tolloni. A sallow-faced man with an aggressive chin, he was a Marxist bureaucrat, a former engineer trained at Moscow University, and slavishly loyal to the Moscow line. Mama Tolloni had never cared for him, and her husband had never trusted him, but now she embraced him as an ally in her war against the government that had let her Alberto die. She held one last press conference at the white villa—to appeal to people to vote Communist.

And the appeal worked.

Next day the stunning news went round the world: REDS WIN IN ITALY.

A great outpouring of sympathy had swung enough votes to the Communists to give them a narrow victory.

For the first time in Italy's history, the Communist party was empowered to form a government . . . and the Tolloni Affair was given the credit. Miller kept thinking of that mind behind it. The mind of a brilliant puppeteer, a brilliant manipulator, yet the result had been bungled and had helped to overturn the existing order—the opposite of what the Il Duce group wanted. It didn't make any kind of sense . . . as others were beginning to suspect, too.

"Italy has played with fire for years," tartly observed the Vatican's newspaper, *L'Osservatore Romano,* "and now it has jumped into the fire. In reacting to the murder of Alberto Tolloni, who was above all an Italian patriot, Italian voters have elected Sandro Bellini, a professional Marxist and Soviet lackey."

Much of Italy suffered a deep psychic shock. The unbelievable, a nightmare for years, had actually happened. The Communists were in power! "Many people," Robert Miller told Vaughan, "look as if they expect to wake up at any moment and find it's not true." Miller himself felt much the same way. Communism was taking over an ancient ally, though God knows there had been a long enough warning. Yet somehow—until the Tolloni affair—he had assumed the canny Italians would continue their longtime compromise, trying to get the best of both sides.

He found himself continually returning to the Tolloni affair to try to explain what was happening, to find the key. More than ever he felt the sequence of events had the inevitability of something prearranged. It was as if there had been a stage manager, a manipulator behind all that had happened since Tolloni's kidnapping. He argued this view so strongly with the editor that Vaughan told him: "Let the Rome bureau handle the new government and current developments. Stick with your own inquiries. If your instinct's right, that could be the big story. Keep me closely informed."

The Italian situation was worsening hour by hour. The election results meant that those Italians who had prided themselves on being half-Catholic and half-Communist, able to live with both, now had to take sides. Miller watched Catholics turn out for morning mass in greater numbers than

ever before, and many fights were reported in the streets. The
division between the Vatican and the new government was so
deep, political commentators said, that perhaps Italy was on
the verge of a civil war . . .

The civil war nearly broke out when Sandro Bellini went to
pay his first formal visit as Prime Minister to the Quirinale
Palace, the symbolic center of the Italian Republic and
official residence of the President. The President, Italy's
ninth, had been a compromise choice two years before. The
Electoral Assembly had elected the candidate acceptable to
both Christian Democrats and Communists—Guiseppe Moltani, a sixty-four-year-old veteran of the Socialist party. In
theory, the President was the most powerful man in Italy for
his seven-year term, able to dissolve parliament and call new
elections, as well as being head of the armed forces, but in
practice he generally functioned as a figurehead, saying and
doing nothing without the consent of the Prime Minister. It
was already rumored that Bellini, as soon as his government
was securely established, intended to pressure Moltani into
resigning to make way for a Communist president.

Opposing groups of supporters and critics of the new
government had massed outside the palace. In the back of the
government limousine, a dark blue Fiat, Prime Minister Bellini
stared uneasily at the faces that peered in at him. Some
people cheered him, others booed—the crowd was deeply
divided and obviously in an emotional mood.

As the Fiat limousine crossed the wide pink piazza toward
the palace gates, where a line of guards in ceremonial uniforms waited, a grey-haired man broke through the police
line and beat on the thick, bullet-proof window closest to
Sandro Bellini. The man then held up a large board with a
handwritten message for Bellini to read. Robert Miller was
standing in the crowd on the far side of the limousine, so he
couldn't see what the message was. It seemed to infuriate the
Prime Minister. He spoke rapidly to his bodyguard sitting
beside the driver. The limousine slowed, and the bodyguard
opened the door and struck the man with a loaded cane. He
was slightly built, quite frail-looking, and Miller saw him go
down with blood on his face. Police grabbed him; they
seemed to be beating him on the ground. The limousine drove
on through the palace gates.

Miller pushed through the hostile crowd, his big body like

a battering ram, enjoying a sense of release in this simple physical action. By the time he reached where the man had fallen, two thick-set *Carabinieri* in military police uniforms were carrying him away on a stretcher. They had put him face down so no one could see what they had done to him; the back of his grey head was stained dark with blood. He looked dead to Miller. Lying on the ground were the remains of the board with the handwritten message. It couldn't be read. The *Carabinieri* had made sure of that.

Miller noticed a plainclothes police type holding back a youngish woman who struggled to reach the stretcher. The man held her until the stretcher disappeared into a police ambulance. The woman stood watching the ambulance drive away, tears rolling down her pale, pinched face. Miller asked her if she knew the identity of the man on the stretcher.

"A nobody named Luigi," she said bitterly. "But his son— my husband!—was Alberto Tolloni's driver. My Pietro was killed when Signor Tolloni was kidnapped."

Robert Miller suddenly had the feeling of getting close to the heart of the matter.

"What was on the board he held up?"

She looked strangely at him. "It said: WHO KILLED TOLLONI? Luigi only did it because of me. I repeated to him something my Pietro said. Alberto Tolloni once told my Pietro that it wasn't the Catholics he feared. It was his enemies in his own party. And that was why he got armored cars!"

"Did he mention Bellini?"

"Yes," she cried fiercely, anger replacing her tears. "He said Moscow wanted Bellini to take over as leader of the party."

"And that's just what has happened," Miller said.

He went to the *Mirror's* Rome office near the Via Veneto, feeling very disturbed. What the woman had told him had changed his way of looking at the Tolloni Affair.

It hadn't been bungled; it had achieved exactly the result intended from the beginning.

Miller remembered Bellini's rage when he saw the message through the limousine window. The bodyguard's reaction under orders had been excessive.

WHO KILLED TOLLONI?

Why should that worry Bellini so much unless . . . ?

But if the Prime Minister was involved, that meant the new government was, too. And behind them . . . the Russians.

Miller's mind boggled at the possibilities of what he was getting into—and the dangers.

He had to talk to Vaughan.

He found the *Mirror* office deserted. Everyone must have gone out to lunch or for a siesta. He phoned Vaughan at home—it was about seven A.M. in New York—but Vaughan wasn't there or at the office. Miller left a message, wondering how long it would take to reach Vaughan.

Miller chain-smoked Camels and stared out across the Roman roof-tops at the distant dome of St. Peter's Basilica. He came from a small Illinois town where anything a hundred years old was valued as an antique: It was Hicksville compared to this ancient city. Centuries of complex family intrigue, nurtured by such experts as the Borgias and Machiavelli, had formed this society, the society of Tolloni and his murderers.

The phone rang, shockingly loud in the silent office.

It was Vaughan, sounding very clear and confident. The message had taken only eleven minutes to reach him.

Miller gave him a quick summary of what had happened, with his conclusions. The *Mirror* phones were probably tapped; the Communists no doubt were listening in on all foreign calls. He talked very guardedly and Vaughan understood at once. The editor had worked with army intelligence in World War II and still enjoyed cloak-and-dagger techniques. He seemed impressed by what he heard.

"It means we're on the right track, Miller. Maybe even bigger than we imagined. Watch your step from now on. Keep digging, but don't take any damn fool chances. You could be in danger after this call." Vaughan's usually cool editor's voice sounded anxious, unsure whether to risk saying more. He added very rapidly: "In the future, you better contact me through a Colonel Crane at our Embassy. He's a . . . cultural affairs officer." That was sometimes a CIA cover. "He has . . . er . . . safer means of communication than our Rome bureau. Remember the name—Crane. Okay?"

"Okay," Miller said.

Talking to the old man had cleared his head of useless introspection. He was ready for his next move. He had to go for broke on this story. He felt a personal commitment creeping into his professional attitude. He might never completely understand the Italian temperament, but he had to find out the truth about the Tolloni affair ... whatever the cost.

3

A late-morning mass was coming to an end in a side chapel of St. Peter's huge Basilica. Many of the people there had ash marks on their foreheads.

The day was Ash Wednesday—the start of Lent, the traditional Christian period of penitence, of sweating fat off the soul. It was always a strange time in Rome, coming toward the end of winter when the sun-loving Romans were beginning to feel stir-crazy. And this year the mood of the Eternal City was intensified by a deep feeling of uneasiness as everyone waited to see what the new Communist government planned to do.

Shafts of sombre winter light from the great windows cast an unearthly pallor over the rows of kneelers. Several people with ash-marked foreheads stirred restlessly, but then quietened down as a final prayer was said for the recovery of Pope Alfredo.

The old Pope's illness was one of the current mysteries of Rome. The Vatican press office had issued a series of vague and contradictory reports. The Pope had a bad cold, said the first announcement. He was "indisposed," said the second. Then a public audience was cancelled and the rumors began.

L'Unità, the Communist party's newspaper, claimed the Pope had had a heart attack when he heard the election result. The Vatican's *L'Osservatore Romano* countered with reports of meetings the Pope had held in his apartment on the top floor of the Papal Palace. Although "indisposed," he was well enough to attend to pressing Vatican business, it was stated. The Holy Father hoped to meet representatives of the new Communist government soon. "Their small majority does not give them any mandate for radical social change . . ."

But still the rumors that the Pope was seriously ill persisted. His doctor was said to be visiting him twice a day now. He was only semi-conscious . . .

No explanation preceded the prayer in St. Peter's. The priest merely prayed for the Pope's recovery "from his recent indisposition." But the priest's voice had a grave resonance in the giant marble surroundings that seemed to hint of bad news, to confirm the rumors. The congregation prayed loudly with him. The old Pope was very popular, a comforting symbol of stability in these uncertain times. His illness made them very uneasy. What a time to be ill when he was needed most!

Immediately the prayer was over, there was a rush to get outside. Heels clicked over the marble floor as people took a shortcut across the great central nave. It was like being in the womb of a giant. Those pressing to leave felt like dwarfs under the massive dome. Outside, they faced the Piazza San Pietro, another immensity.

A dark-haired, pretty young woman hurrying out across the great square ahead of the crowd hardly noticed her famous surroundings. The Piazza, like St. Peter's, was familiar in every detail, she had seen them all her life. She was also bundled up in her winter clothes, her eyes almost hidden between fur collar and fur hat, and she was worrying about the time, whether she'd be late returning to her office. Praying for the Pope certainly wouldn't be an acceptable excuse . . .

A sudden squeal of brakes cut through her thoughts. A black Mercedes limousine had stopped just about a yard from her. She felt little stones and dust sting her legs.

"Are you all right?" a uniformed chauffeur cried.

Shock made her angry. "You nearly killed me!"

An old priest with white hair opened a rear window. "Are you hurt, my child?" he asked gently, smiling at her youthful, very Roman face.

She noticed the Vatican's white and yellow flag on the roof and cooled down.

"I'm fine," she said more politely. "It was my own fault." She smiled back.

The old priest had a deeply-lined, gaunt face, and his white hair was cropped short like a monk's. An ash mark stood out on his forehead like stigmata, and there was a large *SD* across

the chest of his trim, blood-red cassock. She wondered what
the letters *SD* stood for.

"Take care, my child," he said, making a quick sign of the
cross over her. "Always look where you're going, especially in
Rome. Even Julius Caesar complained of the traffic here."
Then he turned to the chauffeur. "Drive on." His voice
sounded urgent.

The black limousine shot forward and roared down into
the tunnel of the Arch of the Bell—deep into the Vatican.

Remembering the Pope's illness, the young woman was
suddenly worried. That chauffeur drives like a messenger
with bad news, she thought. I hope *Il Papa* isn't any worse.

And then she noticed the helicopter with the red, white and
green markings—the colors of Italy. It was a government
helicopter. High overhead, it was slowly circling away from
the Vatican, away from the Piazza San Pietro and back
toward the Tiber river. It occurred to her that the helicopter
had been following the limousine. Now what was so important about that old priest? she wondered.

There were security delays along the route to the Pope. The
tension of the city as a whole was reflected in the Vatican.
Usually relaxed and easygoing, the small independent state
was tense now, incredibly so, aware of being the symbol of
opposition to the new government. The Vatican's mixed
security forces had been on duty along the black limousine's
route—the Swiss Guards and plainclothes civilian security
corps formed recently by Pope Alfredo. Several men saluted
the old white-haired priest, assuming he was a VIP, but the
black limousine was stopped twice for routine checks. There
was a long wait each time.

Beyond the rounded rear of St. Peter's, medieval arches
with overhead spikes led down into another long tunnel, and
then the limousine emerged into the marble splendor of the
Belvedere courtyard in front of the Papal Palace. The palace
was a biscuit color, its blinds drawn to protect the fading
frescoes from the light.

The old priest stepped quickly out of the limousine, as
erect as a professional soldier. The Swiss Guards at the
entrance to the palace looked curiously at the *SD* on his
blood-red cassock. They knew what the letters stood for—
Servus Dei, Servant of God, the most militant of the monastic
brotherhoods. *Servus Dei* members worked exclusively in

poor parishes, usually in industrial slums, and frequently clashed with the Communists. They were seldom seen at the Vatican.

"Don Paolo is to be taken to the Holy Father immediately," said the chauffeur.

"No visitors are allowed," replied one of the Swiss Guards. He insisted on checking Don Paolo's identity, then phoned up to the papal apartment for clearance. He returned much more respectful. "They're waiting for you," he told Don Paolo.

The Pope's apartment on the top floor used to be the servants' bedrooms. There was a modest reception room with fine high marble walls and medieval tapestries, but very little furniture. Most of the people waiting to see the Pope had to stand. Cardinals, bishops, priests, nuns and laymen talked in hushed voices, aware of being only one thick marble wall away from the Pope's living quarters. A tall Swiss Guard, in the ceremonial orange, blue, and yellow uniform that Michelangelo designed, stood stiffly at attention outside the door to the inner rooms.

Don Paolo came slowly into the crowded reception room and looked around, shy and uneasy. He was still bewildered by the sudden summons of the night before. He had been hearing confessions in his parish church in faraway Palermo when one of the lay brothers called him to the phone. He was about to reprimand him for interrupting confessions, he should have taken a message, when the lay brother told him it was a long distance call—from the Vatican. He grabbed the phone. A distant man's voice, hard to hear, told him the Holy Father wanted to see him at once. "Why?" he asked, greatly astonished. The voice didn't know. But he must be on the first available plane and a Vatican limousine would be waiting for him at Fiumicino Airport. It was very urgent.

A plump, middle-aged man in a grey business suit, who had been talking to a cardinal, came over.

"You must be Don Paolo. I am Orlando Moravia, the Holy Father's secretary. I was the one who phoned you. Come, he has been asking for you."

"How is he?"

The plump secretary looked grave. "The news is not good. He has had a massive intestinal hemorrhage. The doctor administered coagulants, blood plasma, morphine. The bleeding was brought under control, he has rallied, but I'm afraid I must tell you it is only a matter of time. Come, this way."

The secretary pushed his way toward the Swiss Guard. Some people looked indignant when they realized Don Paolo was being allowed in ahead of them. A tall, grey-haired cardinal grasped the secretary's arm.

"Signor Moravia, I have to discuss urgent affairs of state that cannot wait. We have a Communist government at the gates, remember. We have important decisions to make—decisions vital to the future of the church. No one can take precedence over me."

"Please, Cardinal Garonne, I am only obeying the Holy Father's instructions."

"But is he still clear-headed, still rational?"

"Perfectly." Signor Moravia sounded annoyed. He gestured for Don Paolo to follow him.

The Swiss Guard stood aside for them to enter. The first very frugal little room was where the Pope ate his meals with only his pet parrot for company. The parrot usually sat on his shoulder, chattering happily, but now the big colorful bird perched in a corner of its cage, looking miserable and refusing to speak. The room's evidence of papal humility made Don Paolo feel proud.

The Pope's bedroom was even smaller and as plain as a monk's cell. The curtains were drawn, and the only light came from a flickering candle on a low table near the bed. Two nuns with rosary beads knelt by the bedside. Between their bowed heads, Don Paolo saw the old Pope lying on a simple iron bedstead, a white sheet drawn up to his chest, and he knew at once that his old friend was dying. It was five years since he had last seen him. The Pope then had been a big, jolly-looking man, full of vitality, but now he had a wasted look as he lay back exhausted against a pile of pillows, his eyes closed. His white cassock was too big for him now, and his head was skull-like. For a moment, Don Paolo's iron self-control slipped and his eyes filled with tears. It wasn't the Pope who lay dying before him at that moment, but his old boyhood friend he had known all his life.

"Alfredo," he murmured emotionally and made the sign of the cross over his dying friend.

At the sound of his voice, the Pope's eyes fluttered open, and at once Don Paolo controlled himself, choking down his tears, and knelt to kiss the gold Fisherman's seal ring, with its gem stone depicting St. Peter as a fisherman, on the Pope's outstretched hand.

"At last you have come," the Pope murmured in a faint but firm voice, his alert eyes looking at Don Paolo with great relief. He had been waiting patiently for this moment, conserving the little energy he had left. His deep-set, dark eyes moved to the two nuns. "Please leave us."

The nuns rose obediently and left the room. Signor Moravia hesitated and then followed them out.

The Pope waited for the door to close, then he whispered urgently, "The crucifix—examine it for me." One of his hands had risen feebly from the bed and was pointing at the large ebony crucifix on the plain white wall facing him.

Don Paolo was bewildered. The ebony crucifix, he remembered, had belonged to Alfredo's mother. Alfredo had had it ever since his student days.

"What do you want me to do?" he inquired softly.

"Do what I say." The Pope's voice was very low as if someone might overhear. "Examine it." Don Paolo obediently took the heavy crucifix down from the wall. "Now run your hand over the back of it . . . Look under the Christ figure . . . Do you find anything concealed? Anything suspicious?"

Don Paolo suddenly realized what he was being asked to do. Alfredo wanted him to search for hidden listening devices. Surely, he thought, no one would dare to eavesdrop on the Holy Father. Alfredo must be mistaken. Perhaps his mind was a little confused by his illness. Alfredo also had the added burden of the Communists in power—they must be haunting his last hours.

"There is nothing," Don Paolo said gently. He replaced the crucifix on the wall. "Don't worry about such things. It is impossible here."

The old Pope sighed. "Ah, my old friend," he murmured, "you do not know the world if you say that . . ." He paused to gain more strength. Through his wasted body, the flame of his intellect and his great determination still burned, keeping him alive. "I used to wonder why you, who have the better character, were not made Pope instead of me." He rested again for a few moments. "But you are *too* innocent. Our world has changed—even here in the Vatican. This used to be a sanctuary, but technology has taken over . . . No one's privacy is safe now . . . not even our secrets." His voice developed a slight tremor. "I cannot be sure whom I can trust . . . That is why I have sent for you, my old friend." The Pope's fingers touched Don Paolo's hand. "I know I can trust *you*. We have not met for a few years, but that is not my fault." He panted for breath. "You refused all my offers of high office here in Rome . . . You didn't want me to be accused of favoritism . . . But did you never realize I needed someone I could trust, someone I had known since we were boys together in Sicily?"

The mention of his boyhood seemed to revive him, and he continued in a firmer voice: "I was a few years older, but that made no difference. I was the older brother you never had . . . Do you remember that day in Palermo, in the outdoor market when we were unloading the fruit trucks, how we swore to help each other *always?* Do you remember, my old friend?"

"I remember."

"That is good because . . . because I need your help now."

"I am ready, Alfredo."

"It may not be easy."

"I will do anything . . . *anything*."

"It is a very important mission," the old Pope whispered. "It is of the utmost importance to the future of the church . . ." His breathing became very labored.

"Rest for a few minutes," Don Paolo told him. "Save your strength, Alfredo."

"No . . . there isn't time . . . I haven't long in this world now, and this must be accomplished before I die . . . for the future safety of the church in case anything happens here in Rome. You must remember we live in very dangerous times, my old friend. The church has many enemies and it needs your help against them."

"Ask anything of me, Holy Father," Don Paolo said. "I am ready to serve you in any way I can."

The old Pope glanced around the room as if still unsure whether he was being overheard.

"Come closer," he whispered, and his hand clutched Don Paolo's wrist with great urgency. "Nobody must know," he panted. "Secrecy is essential. A great deal of harm could be done to the church internationally if this secret matter was revealed prematurely." His lips trembled as he went on. "Forget your innocence of this world for once, my old friend, and trust nobody. *Nobody*, you understand . . . Powerful enemies will try to stop your mission if they learn about it." His hand crept up and touched Don Paolo's face. "My old friend, you could be in *danger* . . . I wouldn't ask you to run such a

grave risk if the mission wasn't so important . . . But we
haven't much time left now . . ."

His deep-set, dark eyes stared up at Don Paolo with great
compassion, and Don Paolo began to appreciate the seriousness of what he was being asked to do.

"What is my mission, Alfredo?"

"I want you to go to . . . *Jerusalem*."

4

Robert Miller's meeting with the widow of Tolloni's driver
had opened the door to the truth. Now he only had to find
it.

He went back to police headquarters to talk to the investigators in the Tolloni case. He hadn't been in touch with them
since the election. He found they were no longer on the case.
A new investigator had been brought in from Milan and was
much less cooperative with reporters. Miller had to wait
nearly an hour at the Ministry of the Interior before he was
shown in to meet him—Inspector Scaglia.

"Scaglia?" Mario Lepecci had frowned with dislike when
Miller asked him if he knew the inspector. "A real Communist bastard. The party planted him in the *Carabinieri* and
then succeeded in getting him in the special counter-intelli-
gence force. The Christian Democrats were that dumb. Scaglia did his best without losing his job to wage ruthless war
against all enemies of the party—Catholics, Christian Democrats, liberals, Fascists, right-wingers like me, *everybody* who
wasn't a Communist party member. Since the election of
course, he's been able to surface completely. He's going to get
a big job in the government's reorganization of the police,
maybe in charge of domestic surveillance here in Rome.
They've probably given him the Tolloni investigation in the
meantime as a way of silencing criticism. Look, we've put one
of our best people on it! Or it could be a cover-up. There's no
more profit in the Tolloni Affair unless it can be used against
some of the government's enemies. And Scaglia is an expert
on them."

Miller said thoughtfully, "You don't think such a dedicated Communist wants to track down Tolloni's killers?"

"You must be joking, Roberto. Scaglia is a Bellini type, a Moscow man. Tolloni's kind of Eurocommunism wouldn't appeal to him. You'll know what you're up against as soon as you meet him."

Inspector Scaglia was slim, hard-eyed, and middle-aged, with the short haircut and formal dark suit favored by the new government. Large photographs of Prime Minister Bellini and such safe dead Communist heroes as Lenin and Togliatti were on his plain green office walls. When Miller mentioned the Tolloni case, the Inspector showed little interest.

"Inquiries are proceeding," he said in a cold, bored voice. "That's all I can tell you, Signor Miller. The fascists will eventually fall into our net unless the previous reactionary government let them escape from the country."

"You're satisfied it was a right-wing operation?"

The hard eyes examined Miller more carefully. "That has been established, I believe," he replied.

"Then it was bungled."

"Of course. The fascists don't understand the people."

Miller tried to sound casual. "Is there any chance some other group was involved—with a different aim?"

"Signor Miller," the Inspector said impatiently, "I understand your tenacity as a reporter, your need to find sensational news, but in this case you are flogging an already dead horse. There is no more sensation, only hard investigative routine."

Miller tried a more aggressive approach. "The original investigators were taken off the case. Why?"

"The new government in its wisdom thought a fresh mind was needed," the Inspector said smoothly. "We shall continue to pursue the fascists with all the considerable means at our disposal—unless, as I have already mentioned, the previous reactionary government let them escape."

"You think the Christian Democrats were involved?"

"That's a political question. I'm a mere policeman. We're informed," he added with a knowing smile, "that some of Tolloni's neighbors saw a strange priest in the area the day before he was kidnapped. What that means we aren't sure, but we have our . . . suspicions." Inspector Scaglia stood up. "The interview is now over."

Well, Miller thought as he left, I've at least served notice I'm not satisfied. Let's see what they do now. It was a calculated risk.

Lepecci phoned to get his impression of Scaglia.

"I think he's been brought in to bury the case or to find a scapegoat among the Christian Democrats. Tell me what you think, Mario."

Lepecci didn't want to talk any more on the phone. They met at a bar on the Via Veneto. Mario was in a gloomy mood.

"What does it matter now what I think, Roberto? Like all my right-wing friends, I wait to discover if I have any future in Italy now. As a journalist, I am very visible. I am on their list—maybe on Scaglia's personal list. I can't afford to pursue any story that might upset the government and make me even more unpopular at the Quirinale. Remember, I am a foolish old man with a young family to support." Lepecci, now in his middle fifties, had married late and had three young sons, aged seven, six, and five, who were the joy of his life. "You investigate it, Roberto. You and your beautiful wife are no longer together." He gave Miller a rueful glance. "You have no children, and you're an American. The worst they can do to you is throw you out of Italy, tell you to go home to America. Me, they can imprison for life and ruin my family. That's why right now I'm more interested in the Pope's health. Is the old man really ill or is he foxing to avoid having to deal with the government? That's what I call a safe story."

Miller felt impatient with Lepecci's caution, and yet he had to admit he had none of the Italian's responsibilities. He was alone now; he could afford to take big risks. He sensed again his growing personal involvement with the story.

"You know how much I respect your judgment, Mario," he said. "What's your *personal* opinion of the Tolloni affair? And I promise not to quote you."

The Italian journalist looked down the bar to make certain no one was listening. "All right, Roberto, I'll tell you. I think it stinks to high heaven."

Next, Miller tried underground sources.

He had researched a long series on the Mafia two years before, and so he phoned one of his Mafia informants in New York's Little Italy for some introductions in Rome. Through this informant, he met the same afternoon with an old man named Sergio Fruttero, who had the grey, withered look of a Godfather. They talked over thick espressos at a small cafe near the Stazioni Termini, Rome's main railway station. Robert Miller told the old man he was interested in contacting the Tolloni kidnappers. Fruttero showed no reaction; it was impossible to tell if he knew anything.

"You spend money?" he asked.

"For the truth—yes."

"The truth . . ." The old man spat on the floor and made the Sicilian two-fingered sign of the *malocchio*, the evil eye. "It was a personal satisfaction to me when Tolloni got killed. They call *us* gangsters. Those Red bastards got no souls!"

"The truth might hurt them—the whole government."

Fruttero's shrewd eyes examined Miller. "How much are you willing to pay?"

"I'll pay real money for a real lead."

"You'll be hearing from us," the old man told him.

Miller expected to hear nothing for several days, but late that same night, after a long leisurely dinner at the famous Hassler Roof Restaurant with Mario Lepecci and his beautiful young wife, he received a mysterious phone call in his room at the Cavalieri Hilton. Someone must have been watching in the lobby for him to go up.

"Signor Miller, the American journalist?" It was a man's voice, and he sounded nervous.

"Yes, I'm Miller."

"Listen carefully then. At midnight, you must be at the Via Silone on the south side of the city. At the end of the street, there is a small overgrown field. Beyond the field there is an abandoned railway tunnel. Be at the mouth of the tunnel at midnight." The voice quickly repeated the instructions. "You understand?"

"Tell me who you are." Miller tried to keep him talking, but the man was too nervous.

"*Arrivederci*, Signor Miller." He hung up.

The Via Silone was in a poor section of Rome. Boarded-up houses, vacant lots, teenagers huddled at street corners, old men playing cards on broken marble steps—it reminded Robert Miller of run-down parts of New York, except that even here there was that sense of a very ancient culture and the unique sun-burned colors of Rome.

The field at the end of the Via Silone looked very dark

under a cloudy midnight sky. It was certainly overgrown, as
the man had warned him. The grass came up to Miller's
thighs, and he felt big thorns tear at his trousers.

Slowly he tensed up. He knew the risk he was running in
this half-abandoned area—even the police had probably given
it up. He was an easy target for anyone wanting to stop his
inquiries. The phone call could have been just setting him up.
He remembered his meeting with Inspector Scaglia—maybe
that had been a mistake. But he had to take chances, to put
pressure on people, and sometimes you had to pay for it. He
still had a scar on his chest from a shotgun blast, fired from a
passing car while he was trying to interview a black share-
cropper family in Mississippi. And in the last year of the
Vietnam war, when he had just arrived in Saigon as a
correspondent, he was jumped one night by a Vietcong
guerilla and stabbed deep in his left shoulder. It had been a
very dark, cold night . . . like this one.

Miller put his hand on the .44 in his sports-jacket pocket.
If someone was waiting for him out here, he was ready. His
father had pressed the gun on him after the incident in
Mississippi. He hadn't wanted it then because it came from
his father—his macho father who was always goading him to
compete, always forcing him to prove himself—but he had
practiced regularly with it and become a crack shot. The cold
metal was certainly a great comfort as he forced his way
through the high grass, feeling he was being watched.

He found the old railway tunnel quite easily, the directions
had been precise. A single rusty railway track stretched out
of the darkness and disappeared into the high grass. Miller
stood at the mouth of the tunnel, peering into the darkness,
seeing nothing. He felt very vulnerable. Then suddenly, from
quite close, a man's voice whispered: "Step into the tunnel
so we can talk without being seen." It was the voice on the
phone.

Miller moved cautiously forward, trying to avoid the railway line. He heard the man move to his side. They stood near
each other in the darkness. Miller was ready for anything,
then he heard the man's quick breathing from nearby, and
told himself, *He's as nervous as I am.* He relaxed his grip on
the gun.

"We mustn't stay here long," the man whispered. "There is
a nightwatchman now. We must do our business quickly. I
understand you want to buy information about the Tolloni

kidnapping. How much are you willing to pay for information about the organizer, the man who killed Tolloni?"

"How will I know the information is genuine?"

A hand gripped his. "Come with me," said the voice. Miller was led farther into the tunnel. He felt tall grass brush against his legs. The ground was uneven, and he stumbled several times in the darkness. They reached a rough stone wall.

"Lower your head. There's an opening."

The man's hand guided him through a hole in the wall. He felt the man stretch upwards and a naked electric bulb flashed on, revealing a small room with bare brick walls and a wooden table. It also revealed the man. He was about forty, tall, heavily built, with receding dark hair and worried eyes. He wore an old army jacket and worn blue jeans. He was the kind of man Italian movies would have cast as a garage mechanic. He looked too nervous to be a successful kidnapper.

"Take a look in here."

The man opened a plain wooden door leading to another small room, the only furniture a single bed with an old, stained mattress.

"That was where he kept Tolloni—the poor bastard. It used to be a storeroom when the tunnel was in use."

Miller stared round with more interest. This was where Tolloni had waited for his death all that time. This room could tell him all he wanted to know. But could this man?

"Okay," Miller said. "What are you selling?" He tried to sound casual. Any sign of the excitement he felt would put up the price.

"Nothing about me or anybody else except him—the organizer. I'll tell you what I know about him. How much is that worth to you?"

"Two hundred dollars."

The man laughed nervously and sat down on the edge of the bed. "You must be joking. Look, I'm putting my life on the line. If he finds out what I'm doing, I'm a dead man. Is my life worth only two hundred lousy dollars? I'm only doing it to raise cash to leave the country. Italy is finished now that the Communists have taken over. I want to reach somewhere safe from them. I need at least three thousand."

"Tell me more about what you're selling."

"I'm going to tell you about . . . Judas. That was his code name."

Judas. Miller remembered Tolloni's wasted body. It was a good name for him.

"Okay, two thousand." Miller felt he had to get closer to the man's price. Vaughan had allowed him unlimited expenses—within reason.

"Three thousand—no less."

"Twenty-five hundred."

"Three thousand or no deal. That's cheap for a man's life."

"Okay, three thousand." It wasn't his money.

They met the next morning to make the exchange. The man didn't want to meet at the same place. He was too scared—not of the Communists but of the mysterious Judas. Miller rented a car for the day and they drove north beyond the city. Miller took the main Autostrada, turning off at Valmontane. He wanted to take the man past the scene of the kidnapping in case it helped his memory. At first the man was worried all the time that they were being followed. But when they reached the outskirts of Rome and no car stayed with them, he began to relax. Counting the money also made him feel better.

"Now tell me what you know," Miller said, impatient to hear about Judas.

The man cleared his throat nervously. "I'm a member of the Il Duce group. You've heard of us?"

"That came out at the time," Miller said. "You're an underground fascist group named after Mussolini."

"We're anti-communist, conservative, and we believe in the Church and the Monarchy."

"And you believe in violence."

"Against the Communists. An eye for an eye."

"And your group admitted kidnapping Tolloni."

"We took the credit for it, but we were really just a back-up group. We were given a blueprint and we helped to carry it out. An outsider came with the plan worked out to the smallest detail—the exact place on Tolloni's route where the attack should be made, the range and blast effect of the grenades—everything. It was brilliant. Our leaders agreed to carry out the plan."

"You had gone underground. How did he find you?"

"Through contacts in West Germany. He had previously planned an operation there." Ah, proof of a connection at last! "He came with the highest recommendation from several West German groups."

"He is German?"

"I don't know his nationality, except he's not Italian. One of our leaders thought he was English, but I can't say, I don't know the English. He spoke Italian with a foreign accent."

"What does he look like?"

"Tall, blond, always wearing sunglasses that cover half his face. Very self-confident, very ruthless."

"Why do you say that?"

"His plan was ruthless. He killed all Tolloni's drivers and bodyguards. Then he starved Tolloni and broke his spirit so he would write those letters."

"He thought the letters were very important?"

"Oh, yes. He forced Tolloni to write them."

"Yet they only won sympathy for the Communists. What was his idea?"

"To persuade the government to change its mind. That's what he told us. But I knew it was useless after their first rejection."

"Yet he persisted?"

"Yes. That was when I began to suspect something."

"What did you suspect?"

"Why do you think I am willing to betray him? For the money alone? No! It is because I believe he betrayed us."

"You have proof?"

"I know it, I tell you. I allowed myself to be blinded because my younger brother was one of the three in jail to be exchanged for Tolloni. But it never happened." There was a sudden silence—the man realized he had given away enough to identify him. "I tell you too much. No more! I give nothing more away. I tell you about him, not us."

They were on the narrow country road where it happened. There were no armored cars left now. Miller recognized the place only by a break in the hedgerow. He stopped the car.

"Show me where you fired from."

"We were back here, beyond the hedge. Judas had examined the ground for several miles and had chosen a flat stretch. He even knew the average speed favored by Tolloni's drivers, and the likely wind speeds for the day. I know my business so I could check on him. He had prepared the whole attack in detail. His thoroughness is *fantastico*. That, too,

blinded me to his real aim. The man is brilliant, only he has
no heart, no feelings at all." They walked into the grape field,
across the hard wintry ground. "We set the grenades up here,
you can see the marks still, and we waited for the lookout to
tell us when the armored cars came into view. We hit them as
accurately as if we were in a shooting gallery." The man
stared bitterly across the field at the road as if he could see
the armored cars again. "He knew from the beginning that
the government would never agree to the exchange. They
would never weaken as long as the other parties backed them.
Not even the Communists, Tolloni's own party, put any real
pressure on the Christian Democrats. It was all a game on
Judas' part. He even warned us by calling himself Judas. That
was as good as telling us he was going to betray us."

"Why did he do it?"

"He wanted the Communists elected. Everything he did
was timed for the election. He killed Tolloni so the funeral,
the emotional highpoint, would be held on the eve of the
election."

"Why? Who's he working for?"

"I don't know. You must understand I wasn't one of the
group leaders. I never talked politics with him. I never got
close to him. I was merely one of the grenade launchers.
When he arrived, he was very down on the Communists. He
sounded like one of us. Our leaders were taken in. They still
won't admit they were fooled. That's why the group is
finished."

"And you were fooled, too?"

"At first, yes, but no more. He wanted me to work with
him again. He knew I was good with the mortar, had a
natural feel for it, but I turned him down."

"What was the job?"

The next target!

"He didn't say. I don't think he'd worked out all the
details. He's a great detail man."

"Where was the location?"

The man hesitated.

"Come on," Miller pressed him. "You promised to tell me
everything about him. Earn your three thousand bucks. It's
slim pickings so far."

"This, he would surely kill me for." There was deep fear in
the man's eyes.

"Tell me!"

"He said he would be there the first week of Lent—he often used Catholic terms. He told me he was brought up a Catholic and then gave it up. Whatever he was planning would take place sometime during Lent before Easter Sunday, but he would pay a first visit at the start of Lent—sometime this week."

"Where?"

"He said he was going to . . . Jerusalem."

5

Miller went immediately to the U.S. Embassy.

Colonel Crane, a small balding soldier from Iowa, didn't need to be told why he'd come. Within ten minutes he was in a small sound-proofed room talking to Vaughan. The old man was so interested in Judas he didn't even grumble about the three thousand dollars.

"*Judas*," Vaughan repeated thoughtfully.

"At least he's got a sense of humor," Miller said.

"No," Vaughan told him, "it's arrogance—the arrogance of evil. The same arrogance the Nazis had." The old man was on his hobby horse. "You better talk to Marc Ram in Jerusalem, Miller." Colonel Ram was a well-known Israeli intelligence expert. "If anyone knows about Judas there, it'll be Ram. Call him and mention my name."

"I already have. He clammed up. Would talk only face to face in private."

"Then fly to Jerusalem."

Miller grinned. He'd outsmarted the old man this time. "All flights are booked. I've arranged to fly to Tel Aviv and then drive over. I'm seeing Marc Ram at The Knesset this afternoon."

The rented blue Fiat began the final ascent to the Holy City. Robert Miller felt a growing sense of excitement as the car roared up the eroded, terraced hills that seemed unchanged since Biblical times. It was a fine, evocative approach to one of the oldest cities on earth, but Miller's excitement was due to much more than the extraordinary view. Here in Jerusalem, the city of Jesus and David and Mohammed, he hoped to find the man known as Judas. And then he would learn the truth. Who was behind him? What was his aim?

Rusting army trucks and tanks lined part of the beautiful ascending road, mementoes of the 1948 war when Jerusalem was cut off and threatened with starvation. Then suddenly the Holy City lay before Miller in all its glory, a honey-colored Jerusalem in the early afternoon sun, under a pale blue and white sky. Flocks of goats and sheep grazed on the fenceless slopes. As the dusk filled the valleys between the barren hills, the local limestone would turn golden, almost luminous, glowing against the background of deep browns and greens and purples on the wooded Judean slopes.

Robert Miller was surprised how much the scene affected him. He had given up going to church at nineteen when his mother died, and yet he felt as moved by the Holy City as if he were still a believer. It was similar to the intense feeling that Rome gave him—perhaps it was no more than a small-town Illinois boy's reverence for genuine antiques, he thought wryly. Yet he knew it was much more personal than that. His reaction to this ancient city was closely related to his feeling about the story he was covering. It was not only potentially the biggest, the most important story he'd ever reported, but he had a feeling about it he had never had before about a story—that it was important to his own life. Usually he avoided any personal involvement: "I'm just a reporter," he'd tell people who tried to get him to take sides. But this time he felt different, almost as if he had assumed Vaughan's attitude, which he had once scoffed at, and was taking part in a struggle between good and evil. A memory of Tolloni's withered body came back to him: Judas *was* evil, as evil as any of the devils who had struggled for the soul of this land in Biblical times.

It was easy to have such thoughts before the timeless Holy City, but Miller told himself he was being sentimental, his romantic Irish side was getting out of hand. What he needed now was a reporter's tough, realistic attitude. He knew whom he was after: Like a hound sniffing out a fox, that should be all that he had on his mind. Evil was for the birds, it belonged back in his Catholic boyhood or on psychiatrists' couches. The Judas he was after wasn't a treacherous disciple of Christ

two thousand years ago, but merely a contemporary assassin
... or was there much more to this Judas than that?

He began the last part of his journey. The Fiat skirted the
weathered Turkish walls enclosing the Old City and its great
Christian, Jewish and Moslem shrines. Robert Miller
glimpsed a distant, rounded cap of gold that dominated all
the cluttered rooftops—the fabulous Qubbet es Sakhra, the
Dome of the Rock, from where Mohammed was said to have
ascended on his winged white horse into the presence of
Allah. Not far away, but out of sight from the Fiat's windows, were the Church of the Holy Sepulchre on the site of
the Crucifixion, and the Western or Wailing Wall, that colos-
sal fragment of Herod's Temple, the lodestone of Judaism,
also respected by Moslems as the place where Mohammed
tied his steed. The congested Old City, with its enclosed
narrow, bustling streets and its oriental atmosphere, was a
bazaar of three different cultures.

Then the new buildings—the New City beyond the Old—
stretched ahead, all in matching local stones, and there at last
was Miller's destination: The Knesset. He recognized it at
once. Israel's modern parliament glowed like a peach in a
complex of government and museum centers on the high
ground overlooking the Valley of the Cross.

A young Israeli soldier in a beret, holding a squat Uzzi
submachine gun, stopped the Fiat in front of The Knesset.
He told Miller to get out.

"I have an appointment with Colonel Ram," Miller said,
not moving. He held out his passport through the open
window.

The soldier gestured impatiently with his Uzzi. Miller got
out reluctantly and followed the soldier into a small office
where several other soldiers were standing, chatting among
themselves, with submachine guns at their feet.

Miller brushed back his unruly reddish hair impatiently.
"I'm short of time," he said gruffly. "I have an appointment
with Marc Ram."

The soldier behind the desk was no more impressed than
the other soldier had been. He slowly looked through Miller's
passport and phoned Colonel Ram's office to check about the
appointment. Miller then had to enter a curtained booth
where another soldier searched him for weapons, felt the
lining of his grey sports jacket, and touched his legs, pockets
and sides. The soldier even examined his cigarettes one by

one. Miller was relieved he had left his .44 in the car. At last
the soldier was satisfied and opened the door leading to the
open plaza in front of the parliament building.

After being searched two more times, Miller was finally
allowed to enter the press box overlooking the public session.
Marc Ram had said he would meet him there. Ram hadn't
arrived yet, but about a dozen journalists were busily taking
notes. Miller sat at the back, where he could watch all the
120 members of The Knesset down below. The abstract
design and furnishings reminded him of the United Nations
building in New York.

Miller looked for the young Prime Minister whose tanned
handsome face had been on the covers of most of the
magazines back home. At forty-six, Eli Abraham was the first
prime minister of the new generation. He was a Sabra, as
native-born Israelis are called; his roots were in Israel, not in
Europe or America like the older generation. His proving
ground had been the Israel-Arab wars, not the European
holocaust. A former pilot in the Israeli Air Force, Eli Abraham had been shot down in the 1973 Yom Kippur war and
had spent several months in an Egyptian prison camp. Returning home a war hero, he founded a new, more pragmatic
liberal party that combined many of the minority groups of
the past. Israel was going through one of its periodic fits of
disillusionment with its politicians and was ready for a new,
young, fresh face. Eli Abraham certainly stood out among the
older faces of The Knesset, Miller thought, spotting the
Prime Minister down below. He was sitting with his cabinet
members at a horseshoe-shaped table facing the speaker. And
he was plainly bored and impatient as only a vigorous man of
action can be listening to long speeches. Miller watched him
doodle on the margin of an official report as a debate on
inflation dragged on. Suddenly one of his aides hurried in
with a note and the doodling was quickly pushed aside. Miller
saw him tense as he read, and then he rose abruptly to
interrupt the debate. It was the first time Miller realized how
tall he was. The Prime Minister was over six feet, and his
athletic build made him look even taller.

"I wish to share with you a message I have just received
from Rome," he said gravely in Hebrew. Miller grabbed the
earphones at the side of his chair to listen to the English
translation. "It has just been announced at the Vatican that
the Pope's illness is now very serious." He glanced down at

the note he had been handed. "The Pope's doctor stated that
his condition suddenly worsened when he suffered a massive
hemorrhage. His mental condition remains lucid, but his
pulse and cardio-circulatory system are weak. The medical
report holds out no hope." The Prime Minister looked up at
the hushed Knesset as if uncertain how his next remark
would be received. "I wish to put on record the government's
sorrow at this news and to send a message to that effect to the
Vatican. I trust I have the agreement of all members."

He glanced around briefly, seemed satisfied, and was sitting
down when a shout broke the silence.

"No! A thousand times no!"

The Prime Minister appeared startled. All the heads in the
press box craned forward to identify the voice.

A Hasidic-looking man with a black beard, sidelocks and
dangling fringes had risen and was gesturing angrily at the
Prime Minister.

"It is hypocritical to record such sentiments!" he shouted.
"The Church of Rome has never accorded diplomatic recognition to the state of Israel. It has always been on the side of
the Arab extremists. It has accused us of putting Jesus Christ
to death many times in the past. It has not changed. I say *No!*
A thousand times *No!* We must not be hypocrites, whited
sepulchres!"

The Prime Minister, frowning angrily, stood up to face
him. It was obviously not the first time they had clashed. Eli
Abraham had already introduced several controversial
changes, notably in improving relations with the neighboring
Arab state of Jordan, that had been vigorously opposed by
some of the older members.

"Who is he?" Miller asked an Israeli journalist sitting in
front of him.

"Bellowitz. He's a traditionalist. He's against anything that
doesn't agree with the traditional values of Judaism. A real
thorn in Eli Abraham's side." The Israeli journalist grinned
and turned back to listen to the Prime Minister's reply.

"We are all aware of the Vatican's diplomatic problems in
the Arab world. It has many members there, whereas it
cannot expect many converts among us Jews." There were
low, grim chuckles of agreement. "But the present Pope has
been friendly to the state of Israel. He has encouraged a
Jewish-Christian dialogue and the development of the Inter-
faith Movement. In time, he would have done more, drawn

closer to us. This I know. We are losing a friend, a good friend of our country. I trust our fellow member will withdraw his objection so it can be recorded that The Knesset was unanimous."

"Never!" the bearded man, Bellowitz, thundered. He began to repeat his objections, calling on other minority members to support him. No one else rose to speak.

Miller was so involved in the drama below that he heard nothing behind him until something gripped his shoulder—it felt like the talons of an eagle. He turned round quickly and saw a black gloved hand and then the man behind it.

"Mr. Miller?"

It was Colonel Marc Ram of the Mossad Aliyah Beth, the senior Israeli intelligence organization, and the Prime Minister's adviser on all counter-terrorist warfare. Colonel Ram had lost his left arm and right hand in the fighting over Jerusalem in the 1967 war. The left sleeve of his dark suit dangled emptily, but he had an artificial right hand concealed by a black glove. His grip suggested the hand was made of steel, but he never took off the glove. A large cheerful man in his mid-fifties with deceptively mild blue eyes, he never referred to his war wounds and still played several strenuous outdoor sports—when he had the time. As a young man, he had been one of the leaders of the Irgun Zvai Leumi, the Jewish underground group; the British had once listed him as their most wanted terrorist. Since then he had made use of that experience to track down terrorist teams against Israel. He was credited with more than one hundred successful manhunts. It was Marc Ram who had succeeded in sealing Israel's borders against Palestinian terrorist attacks in the sixties and seventies.

"Follow me, Mr. Miller." Colonel Ram glanced down at The Knesset members. "Or maybe you want to hear that guy to the bitter end?" Bellowitz was still talking.

"That's not why I'm here, Colonel." Miller prided himself on his physical alertness. When he was home, he went to a local gym every day. His reflexes had saved his life a couple of times in Vietnam. So he was annoyed he hadn't heard Marc Ram come up behind him. He had allowed the older man to take him. He wanted information the Colonel might not be willing to give, and that meant he should be pressuring Ram. But Ram was a tough, dedicated man, very hard to corner. Never even been married, Miller recalled, and he wondered if Ram's wounds were the reason, or whether the Colonel was a confirmed bachelor, married to his work. *Like me,* Miller thought, and he remembered the painful analysis of his character Eve had delivered to him when she announced she was getting a divorce. "I feel more like your mistress than your wife," she had told him. "I know you love me, baby, but I need a little bit more than the odd Sunday and a flying kiss. Robert, don't you see how you're *exactly* repeating the pattern of your father? You're a workaholic just like him . . ." Eve was right and he knew it. He *had* inherited his obsession with getting a story at all costs from his father, who was a news photographer until his death in a plane crash in Cambodia ten years before. His mother had divorced his old man when Miller was in his teens, and for much the same reasons that Eve had stated on divorcing him.

"This way, Mr. Miller." Colonel Ram led the way down a long corridor.

"The Prime Minister's announcement certainly received an angry response," Miller said, angling for the Colonel's opinion in the hope of learning more. There was something about the drama in The Knesset that worried him, that aroused his reporter's instinct. Something the Prime Minister had said about the Pope. *In time, he would have done more, drawn closer to us. This I know.* How did he *know*—unless something was happening behind the scenes?

"Just one man, and he's a fanatic," the Colonel said contemptuously. His loyalty to the young Prime Minister was well known. It was almost a father-son relationship.

"Israel and the Vatican haven't always been friendly," Miller pressed him.

"Too many of us live in the past, Mr. Miller." Unconsciously the Colonel's black-gloved hand tensed, the steel fingers bent like claws. "We have to accept change. We in Israel depend on it for our continued existence. The old order *has* to change. Come, I take you to my private office. We have private things to say."

Two workaholics together, Miller thought, but Ram's even worse than I am. People said Ram had had no personal life at all since he lost his hand, that the psychological wound had been worse than the physical loss. Miller wasn't sure he could believe this now that he was face to face with Ram. There was too much vitality in the man, and a certain deep longing detectable at odd moments in his blue eyes. He must have a beautiful Sabra hidden away, Miller decided.

The Colonel led him to a small, windowless, soundproofed back room, situated so the entrance was private and no one could witness who went in. There was a steel desk—bare except for a pushbutton phone—two straight-backed wooden chairs, and a photograph of a British army officer on the wall. The Colonel noticed him looking at the photograph.

"Captain Orde Charles Wingate," he said with an almost affectionate tone. "One of the great British eccentrics of the Middle East, in the class of Lawrence of Arabia. He taught us much of what we know about guerilla warfare and how to combat terrorists. His favorite lesson was from Joshua's conquest of Canaan." Marc Ram grinned, showing a chipped gold tooth at the front. "He knew how to talk to us Jews, even the Haganah, our militia in those days. Always take your examples from the Bible, then we listen!" He sat down at the desk, his black-gloved hand flat on the top. Miller tried not to stare at it. "Now," the Colonel said briskly, "what do you want from me?"

Move One, Miller thought. He said carefully, "I'm researching a series on international terrorism."

The Colonel made an impatient gesture with his gloved hand. "I know that, Mr. Miller, and if that were all, I would have arranged for you to speak to one of my assistants in charge of press inquiries. I agreed to see you myself for one reason. On the phone, you mentioned a name."

"Judas."

The Colonel stared at him, and the mild blue eyes were suddenly much sharper, more penetrating.

"How much do you know about . . . Judas?"

"I've come to find out what you know, Colonel." Move two.

"No fencing, Mr. Miller. What I tell you will be determined by what you know already."

Miller immediately decided to change his tactics. It had to be a trade. "Okay, I'll tell you what I've learned so far. I began in Dublin. I wanted to study the assassination of the British Home Secretary. Foreign terrorists were rumored to have been involved in that. But the second day I was there, Alberto Tolloni was kidnapped. So I flew to Rome. But I got nowhere with official sources, either before or after the election."

"The Communists infiltrated the Rome police long before the election," the Colonel grunted. "They had their own people in the key positions. The *Polizia,* the *Carabinieri,* the Italian intelligence service—we never trusted any of them for the last year. Nothing concerning the Soviet Union, the Eastern bloc, was shared with them. If they hadn't won the election, we expected some kind of coup eventually when they felt strong enough. Instead the Tolloni murder did it for them."

"The Tolloni murder certainly backfired against the right wing."

"They were only pawns in a Communist game."

"You believe they were used?"

"I'm asking the questions, Mr. Miller. How much do you know?"

"Know or suspect?"

"Know."

"I know the Tolloni kidnapping was organized by an outsider—Judas—but I don't know if he was working alone or through an international network."

"How did you learn about him?"

"It cost me three thousand bucks," Miller said. He described his two meetings with the disillusioned member of Il Duce and what the man had told him.

"The poor devil realized he'd been used," Colonel Ram said quietly. "Okay, I'll be as frank with you, Mr. Miller, as you've been with me. We reached the same conclusion as you about the Tolloni case. It was a phony. Everything points to its really being a brilliant trick to win sympathy for the Communists in time for the election. But who was behind it? Tolloni's enemies in the party, Moscow—or is Judas some kind of loner we don't yet understand? We haven't a clue we can recognize as to his motivation or his identity."

"From what the Il Duce man told me, it seems pretty clear he was involved in the assassination of the West German Foreign Minister."

"The style was similar. The Foreign Minister's plane was hit by a ground-to-air missile just after takeoff, remember. The planning was incredibly meticulous, with split-second timing."

"Like the shooting of the British Home Secretary in Dublin," Miller said.

The Colonel nodded. "We don't have enough proof to satisfy a court of law, but we're pretty sure Judas was involved in that, too. Three big jobs in as many months—and in as many different countries. Fantastic! One detail will interest you. The assassin's code name for the Dublin operation was Delilah—you'll remember Delilah in the Bible was mixed up with Samson, and the British Home Secretary's name was Jeremy P. Sampson. The code name for the West German operation was Cain, no doubt because the Foreign Minister's name was Herman Abel. Presumably no Biblical connection could be found for Alberto Tolloni, and so Judas was used to describe an operation that was essentially a betrayal."

"At least we know he's fond of biblical allusions," Miller said. "If we could find out what the code name is for his operation here, then maybe we'd be getting somewhere. Why do you think he's selected Jerusalem? Ireland, West Germany, Italy . . . Jerusalem. What's the connection?"

"We can only speculate, Mr. Miller. There may be no connection, merely a pattern. In each place, he has used an assassination to change the political picture. The British Home Secretary, an Irishman himself, had successfully brought both sides to the conference table. His removal has ended a period of good will. His successor is a hard-liner. Similarly, the West German Foreign Minister headed a movement for the reunification of the two Germanys, West and East. Without him, the movement is already drifting and will soon collapse. We've seen what killing Alberto Tolloni achieved—Italy's first Communist government."

"And who is his target in Jerusalem?"

"That's the question I keep asking myself—who?"

"The Prime Minister?"

The Colonel's black-gloved hand clenched into a tight fist. "It's possible. He's always a potential target. Judas—or whatever you want to call him—seeks someone whose removal will upset the status quo. At present Israel and the more moderate Arab leaders are drawing closer together. You can now even phone Jordan from here without any problems, and we have routine police exchanges. That kind of normalization is a step on the right road. But those who want to keep us divided would like nothing better than a terrorist assassination in our capital here that could be blamed on the Arabs. There would then be terrific pressure here to go back to a warlike stance; all normalization would cease. Jerusalem has become a symbol of our coming together—Jew, Arab, and Christian. Judas, for his own crazy purposes, or for whatever master or god he serves, no doubt wants to keep us apart by some big divisive action, some major incident that would capture world headlines. Publicity is always one of the major aims today, propaganda around the world via television. And the man is clearly capable of doing anything—he is extremely dangerous. And we're in a weak position against him until we know more about him."

"Doesn't it seem likely he's either a dedicated Communist working for Moscow or part of an international terrorist network?"

The Colonel brooded about his answer; he was being very careful. "The Russians' relations with terrorist groups are very ambivalent. They're afraid of getting too closely involved with fanatics they can't control. They try to make use of them from a distance—through one of their satellites, usually Czechoslovakia—but their aims are rarely the same. The Soviets often seem too conservative to the terrorists. As for being part of a network, the terrorists rarely agree among themselves. A network really needs a common cause to last, and their backgrounds and aims vary so much from country to country."

"But Judas has apparently been able to work equally well with several very different foreign groups."

"That's what makes me sure he's a loner, unattached, even though, as in the Tolloni case, he sometimes does Moscow's work for it. I don't think he could work internationally so successfully if he was committed, if he was attached to any one group. The Baader-Meinhoff gang in West Germany, the Red Brigades in Italy, the Irish Provisional Republican Army or IRA, the more extreme Palestinian groups, the Japanese Red Army—as you know, they've all tried to work together, but it's not been very successful on a long-term basis. Their differences often got in their way, their lack of a real concrete unifying cause. If they ever found such a binding cause, then they would be internationally very dangerous—a real threat. An international team has so many more resources to call on. The murder of our Olympic athletes at Munich showed how easy it can be for a team of determined assassins to penetrate normal security. I know something about that kind of work firsthand, Mr. Miller. I was on Menachem Begin's staff in the Irgun Zvai Leumi in the forties. We were an underground, but we used some of the same techniques as the terrorists. You need great planning down to the last detail—as well as a willingness to die."

"If Judas is a loner," Miller said, "at least all these international facilities will be available to him—weapons, training camps, false documents, money."

"He will need a team to work with him. He can't do everything himself." Marc Ram suddenly looked grim. "He'll recruit them elsewhere and bring them in with him."

"All then we know for sure is that he's supposed to be here this week."

"He's probably picking his target right now," the Colonel said. He rubbed his chin with his gloved hand. It was a habit, Miller thought, from the days when Ram had a real hand. "How big a play do you intend to give this information, Mr. Miller?"

"It'll be the lead, the angle of my series—*The Search for Judas.*"

"When will you publish it?"

"As soon as possible. Maybe within a couple of weeks if I'm lucky."

The Colonel's expression became less friendly. "That timing would be bad for us, Mr. Miller. Very bad. We don't want to alert him to what we know. Publicity would also give him more authority, more prestige, among other terrorists. If he wants it, let him get it himself, and to do that, he'll have to reveal himself. No, I must ask you to delay your series. Take that as an official request by my government."

"It's impossible, Colonel. It's a story that won't wait."

The Colonel leaned across the desk, irritated. "Let me be frank, Mr. Miller. I could try to stop publication at the highest level. The Prime Minister personally could phone Bruce Carl Vaughan. But I know you journalists. That would only enhance the value of your story. It would get an even bigger play. And by then too many people would already know about it. There would be a much bigger risk of leaks. Tell me this, Mr. Miller, are you open to a deal?"

"I'll listen." Move Three.

"My offer is this. Hold off for seven weeks and I'll share

everything we get on Judas with you, every stage of the hunt."

"Why seven weeks?"

"You'd never win our Bible quiz, Mr. Miller. That's the period of Lent plus a few days to clean up. We know he's going to do it—whatever 'it' is—by Easter. Didn't Jesus fast for forty days and forty nights in the desert to prepare for his crucifixion and resurrection? Isn't that what Lent's based on? Tell me. I'm not a Christian."

"That means I lose five weeks," Miller said impatiently.

"Yes, but you'll have a much better story."

"I risk another journalist breaking the story first."

"Very unlikely. On our side, very few people know. Only people at the top. They won't talk. Any leak would have to come from Judas' own side."

"It's happened once already."

"It won't happen again. Judas will make sure of that. He can't afford not to."

"He doesn't know about it."

"Don't underrate the guy." The Colonel's black-gloved hand stretched out flat on the desk—it told a lot about his feelings, Miller thought, if one only knew the sign language. "Anything on Judas internationally is going to be routed right here, Mr. Miller. I'm bound to know if any other journalist starts poking around and making inquiries. I'll promise to tell you immediately and you can publish your story ahead of them. What do you say, Mr. Miller? Do you accept my offer? It might make all the difference between trapping Judas and letting him get away with yet another murderous terrorist act. You must give us the time to stop him."

Miller pretended to look thoughtful. His decision mustn't seem too easy, even though it was. His story was still too sketchy, too speculative, his research incomplete. He needed to know much more about Judas. What was the connection between the Tolloni case and Jerusalem? He thought of consulting Vaughan, but since it was about lunchtime in the States, Vaughan might be hard to find. He said slowly, as if very reluctant, "Okay, I agree. I'll hold off until Easter in return for the full story—being kept fully informed along the way."

"Good man. I'll keep you as fully informed as I can and then hand over everything on a plate at the end. As soon as we have a psychological profile of him, I'll let you have a copy, but so far the data is very incomplete. I assume sharing information is two way—that if you find something we haven't got, you'll let us have it. Our people in New York tell me you're usually ahead of the game."

Miller nodded. It was a fair trade. "Is there any religious angle? Judas is fond of biblical allusions, he or one of his group dressed up as a priest apparently for the Tolloni kidnapping. At least a strange priest was seen near Tolloni's villa—unless the Italian police are lying."

"It was probably part of Judas' complex scenario for making it look like a right-wing plot. A disguise as a priest would be an equally good trick in Jerusalem," the Colonel said grimly. "We don't know enough yet to say what the important clues are. All I know is we've got to trap him. Judas must be stopped. Jerusalem is too important to the peace of the Middle East and, therefore, the world. What we need to know first is . . . his target."

The pushbutton phone buzzed.

"Yes?" the Colonel grunted, annoyed at being interrupted. Then he listened with close attention. "Zion?" he murmured, glancing at Miller to check if he was listening. "It's risky. Let me go in your place. I know you promised, but security comes first . . ." Ram listened again. "Okay, okay, I can tell you've made up your mind. Nothing will change it. But at least let me follow you. You better not go there alone. Remember, he could be here in Jerusalem right now." The Colonel looked at Miller as he spoke, and Miller pretended to be reexamining the Wingate photograph on the wall. "Okay, I'll do that. But watch your step all the way. Don't take any stupid chances." The Colonel sounded very anxious.

He banged the receiver down and stood up. "I have to go, Mr. Miller." He paused with his hand on the door knob. "You can trust me to keep to our agreement. And if you don't"—his hand curled in a pincer movement—"I'll have your balls."

Miller came out of The Knesset into the large open plaza, relieved to get away from the tight security and the tension inside. The late afternoon sun was low in the sky and its golden rays were slanting across the great bronze menorah. Darkness wasn't far off.

As he was unlocking the car door, a small black Pontiac came out of the official Knesset parking lot and passed him at a fast speed. He just had time to recognize the driver. It was the Prime Minister. Now that doesn't make sense, Miller thought. They make The Knesset as hard to get into as a besieged fortress, and yet the Prime Minister drives out by himself, unguarded—and at the very time Judas could be in Jerusalem. He remembered the Colonel's conversation on the phone: *You better not go alone.*

On an impulse, he decided to follow. His reporter's instinct was aroused. Where was the Prime Minister going all alone and in such a hurry? Already the Pontiac was a mere black dot in the distance on the highway. The Fiat swung round to pursue it when suddenly, appearing from up the hill, a long green Jaguar cut in and blocked the way. Annoyed, Miller stuck his head out of the window—and stared into the smiling face of Marc Ram.

"Mr. Miller, there's something come up I thought you should know about." The Colonel spoke slowly as if he were in no hurry, while Miller seethed with impatience. The Pontiac was disappearing! The Colonel grinned, and then Miller realized he was deliberately delaying him. The Colonel didn't want him to follow the Prime Minister. And there was nothing he could do to get away. This was the Colonel's turf. "We've just had a report from Rome, Mr. Miller, that one of the Il Duce group has been found shot." Miller's heart missed a beat. "Pinned to the body was a note, 'Thus die all traitors,' and the note was signed 'Iscariot.' "

Then entered Satan into Judas surnamed Iscariot, Miller thought guiltily. The man had been right. The three thousand bucks had cost him his life.

"The Rome police, I understand, have suppressed the note," the Colonel added. "They don't want to do any explaining to reporters. More of the Tolloni cover-up."

"Then that means Judas is still in Rome—"

"Not necessarily. The police received a note in the mail directing them to an abandoned railway tunnel where they found the body in an old storeroom. The body had been dead at least twenty-four hours—ample time for anyone to get here. No, he's here in Jerusalem. I know the city's vibes, Mr. Miller." The Colonel stared down the highway, the way the Pontiac had gone. "I can *feel* him here now."

"He must have killed him soon after I saw him the second time. But how did Judas *know?* We met in secret, we weren't followed."

"You sure?"

"That was what he was scared of. He was satisfied he wasn't followed."

"Apparently he also contacted the Tolloni widow to try to raise some more money. Perhaps it came out through her."

"But how? He must have taken the same kind of precautions he did with me."

"Maybe she told someone, someone she thought she could trust. It wasn't a professional matter to her. She was dealing with one of the men responsible for her husband's death. God knows what her reaction was. Revenge, maybe. At least we can learn a little more about Judas. It's very important for him to keep the loyalty of each foreign group he works with. Any traitor must be punished as an example. It's another piece for our psychological profile." The Colonel stared grimly down the highway. "Take my word for it, Mr. Miller —he is *here* now."

The Colonel saluted and the Jaguar purred away down the hill. Miller sat, momentarily stunned. It had all come much closer to him. He remembered the man's quick nervous breathing in the darkness of the tunnel. The man had been right to be nervous, scared. What had he said? "If Judas finds out what I'm doing, I'm a dead man . . ." But how had Judas found out? They had both been very careful. Had Judas been watching them? He had a feeling of Judas' presence now, unseen, but watching, threatening. He decided it would be worth talking to Signora Tolloni as soon as he returned to Rome. She might be able to tell him something that would lead to Judas . . .

A young soldier with an Uzzi submachine gun stood guarding the exit to The Knesset.

Miller pointed the way the Pontiac had gone.

"Where does that lead to?" He remembered the phone conversation Ram had had. "Zion?"

The soldier nodded. "Yes, you can get to Mount Zion that way."

Mount Zion!

6

The great wheels of the El Al Israel 707 touched down on the Jerusalem runway two hours after leaving Rome. Don Paolo immediately unfastened his seat belt and stood up, impatient to complete his mission.

He had changed into a plain black clerical suit, with only a small red badge in his lapel to identify him as a member of Servus Dei. There were several other priests on the plane, and at first the people who had come to observe his arrival—agents of at least three countries—had difficulty in spotting him. But his gaunt appearance and his fast, erect walk soon drew attention to him. He marched forward like a soldier, leaving the other priests behind.

Don Paolo had never been to Jerusalem before, but the instructions he had been given were very precise, and he was a highly disciplined man, used to the military obedience of the monastic brotherhood. He was soon through the passport check, and he had no luggage to be examined. He hurried through the crowded arrival hall of the shining new King David International Airport, ignoring the noisy groups of pilgrims arriving for Lent, and made straight for a taxi.

The idea of being in the Holy City moved him greatly, but he had no time to visit any of the shrines. The only concession he allowed himself was to ask the taxi driver to point out the Church of the Holy Sepulchre as they passed close to the ancient stone walls of the Old City. He couldn't believe it when he saw the shabby dome in the distance. He had expected a sight as imposing as St. Peter's Basilica. Italy would have created something much more impressive over the site of the Crucifixion! He realized how far away from home he was when he saw some of the narrow, crowded streets with donkeys and Arabs in flowing headdresses. The sense of being in such a strange, foreign environment made him uneasy for the first time. He remembered the Pope's warning. *You could be in danger . . .*

The taxi left him near the Zion Gate, one of the seven

gateways to the Old City, and he walked the rest of the way up to the tomb, up a series of steps and then an easy path that climbed slowly. The way ahead was deserted. It was too late for anyone to be on duty at the tomb. He was alone now, and yet as he walked up Mount Zion, Jerusalem's broad western hill, he felt eyes were watching him. But that was impossible, he told himself. Extraordinary precautions had been taken to make sure no one knew about the meeting. King David's Tomb had been agreed on not only because it was common ground for Christian and Jew, but because it was so private, so secluded, late in the day. His nerves were playing him tricks. He was too old for this kind of mission, maybe he'd even caught some of Alfredo's suspicions. *I cannot be sure whom I can trust . . .*

He was close to the tomb now. The bullet-scarred Dormition Abbey with its black conical roof and towering belfry—where, he remembered, the Virgin Mary "fell into eternal sleep"—was already behind him, and the tomb was somewhere up ahead among the shadowy rocks and cypress trees. The weathered, honey-colored limestone glowed like markers along the way. Far below was the Valley of Hinnom—or Gehenna, the Place of Eternal Torment—and he turned away with a sudden shiver, childhood memories overcoming his self-discipline. When he was a boy in Sicily and his mother, who knew the Bible even better than the priest, wished to punish him, she always threatened to send him to Gehenna. Her graphic description of the torments down there had terrified him. The Jews associated the valley with Hell; you were cast into Gehenna to a depth equal to your sinfulness. Somewhere down there in the wasteland was the tree from which Judas had hanged himself, and also the "field of blood" bought with his thirty shekels of silver, his reward for betraying Jesus.

The great heat in the valley sent up a cloying odor—the odor of evil!—and even on a clear, cold day like this one, he seemed to catch a strong whiff of it. He wished now another place had been chosen for the meeting. He hadn't been in Jerusalem long enough to be used to famous biblical places as everyday sights. You were supposed to be able to shrug off the closeness of Gehenna as if it were no more than a decaying valley . . .

He stepped back and almost collided with a fat, balding

man in a grey sweater and blue shorts, who had come soundlessly up the path.

"I beg your pardon, Father." The man had a soft American accent. "I didn't mean to startle you." He beamed and seemed eager to talk. "I was just studying the layout here on Zion. It means the Jewish homeland, you know, also Utopia— Heaven! Up here, Heaven and down there is the valley... Hell."

The fat man had a map in his hand, and a camera and binoculars slung round his neck. He looked such an obvious American tourist, too obvious in every way, that Don Paolo's suspicions were aroused. He was about to walk quickly away, when the fat man clutched his elbow.

"Let me introduce myself. Name of Cousins, Francis Cousins, archaeologist and biblical scholar. Over here on a sabbatical." He giggled nervously. "You know, Father, somewhere down in Gehenna is all the proof that people like you and I need. If Hell is real, so is Heaven. So is the whole works." He leaned closer as if confiding secrets. "We learn about Christ from the Anti-Christ. Show me not where Jesus was crucified, but where Judas killed himself—Aceldama or The Field of Blood. The reverse, the anti, the other side of the coin, the dark side of the moon—that's what we need to explore. You follow me, Father?"

Don Paolo, even more suspicious now, said curtly, "I must go," and he looked down at the fat hand, the fingers like caterpillars still clutching his elbow.

At once the fat man dropped his hand. "I'm sorry... I didn't realize... My enthusiasm carried me away, my obsession, my hobby horse. I can run off at the mouth all night." Suddenly his smile vanished, and he added more quietly, *"Take good care of yourself. The evil of Gehenna is loose tonight."* It sounded like a warning—or a threat.

Don Paolo hurried away. When he looked back, there was no sign of the fat American. Perhaps he had been harmless, just an eccentric. Too much Biblical study could affect a weak person's mind, especially reading the Old Testament. So bloodthirsty, so violent.

The mouth of the Tomb was ahead. It yawned open, but he couldn't yet see in through the gloom. His old eyes were slow to adapt, and he entered blindly, nervously imagining what he might find. It was a Jewish house of prayer cut out of the

rock, dedicated to David, the founder of Jerusalem, with a
display of silver vessels and sacred red cloths. Flickering
candles cast a dim light over the low, rock-walled chamber.
No one was there. The Tomb had an eerie loneliness.

There was a sudden scuffling sound near the entrance. The
old priest tensed, trying to see in the gloom. But no one
appeared. It was only the wind off the Jerusalem hills stirring
the ancient dust of the Tomb. Don Paolo slowly relaxed. The
next move was up to the other side.

"Shalom," said a deep voice.

Don Paolo turned, startled, and then he was ashamed of
having shown his fear. His weariness—and Gehenna—had
released the devils of his imagination.

"I was waiting for you under the trees," said the tall,
shadowy figure in front of him. "This isn't a place to linger."
One of the candles was held up, revealing the well-known
face of the vigorous young Israeli Prime Minister—Eli Abraham.

Don Paolo sighed with relief: The plan was working.

"Archaeology tells us these are really the remains of a
fourteenth-century inn and crusaders' chambers," the Prime
Minister said quietly, "but what does it matter as long as
people *believe* it's authentic, Father?"

This seemed too cynical to Don Paolo, but he didn't say
anything. He remembered the other man was a politician.
They often believed in nothing.

"You can't separate fact and fiction, reality and illusion,
anywhere in Jerusalem, Father. That's why it has always had
such a strong hold on men's imaginations." The Prime Minister brought the candle closer to Don Paolo's face. "I expected
the Pope's special messenger would be younger."

"The Holy Father and I were boys together in Sicily,
though he was a few years older."

"I know he wished to send his most trusted emissary. We
have both taken great care from the beginning to keep the
negotiations secret. That is why we meet here." Eli Abraham
put down the candle and the shadows sprang up again, hiding
his face. "How was the Pope when you left?"

"Sinking fast."

"Then he may not be alive when you return with the
document I have for you."

"If I arrive too late, he instructed me to keep it in my

possession until I can present it to his successor. No one else must be allowed to see it. He gave me very precise instructions. But I hope to return in time. It will make his death easier."

"When do you leave for Rome?"

"The ten o'clock flight from Amman. It was the only available flight tonight. The others were all fully booked. Everyone is heading for Rome. The Holy Father's death," he added with unusual bitterness, "will be a great social occasion for many people."

"Then you must leave immediately. It's a long ride to Amman, and even though we now have more normal relations, you'll be delayed crossing the border into Jordan."

Eli Abraham took out a long white envelope. "This is what you have come for," he said quietly. "Please deliver it to the Pope or his successor. No one except myself has seen it, in accordance with the Pope's wishes. For that reason, I even typed it myself, though I use only two fingers. It is in both Hebrew and Italian."

Don Paolo took the envelope and put it carefully away in a secret pocket inside his shirt. To come so far for so little, he thought, and yet its effect could shake the world.

"Now," said the Prime Minister, "I'll point you on your way."

They left the tomb, the dusty air of centuries past in the gloomy rock-walled chamber, and came out into the clear night air of the present. The stars seemed unusually bright and low in the sky, much closer than in Rome. But then Bethlehem, Don Paolo thought, was only a few miles away, and he remembered what the Bible said, ". . . and, lo, the star, which they saw in the East, went before them, till it came and stood over where the young child was . . ." And above them was the huge pillared room where the Last Supper had taken place, and Judas had learned Christ knew he was going to betray him. Don Paolo shivered slightly, as he had above Gehenna. Here, it all seemed too *real*.

"I must leave now," he said to the Prime Minister.

Eli Abraham glanced at his watch, which gave the time in both Jerusalem and Washington, D.C. "You're in good time, Father, but I wish you were flying directly from Jerusalem. There are more risks in going to Amman. I'd provide you with bodyguards, but it would arouse suspicion."

"I must travel alone," Don Paolo said. "That way I'll look unimportant. The Holy Father wanted it that way."

"Then be very careful. Many people would like to know what is in that envelope—Israel's enemies as well as the Vatican's."

Don Paolo patted his secret pocket. "It's safe. Nobody knows of its existence except you and I and the Holy Father."

I hope to God you're right, thought Eli Abraham. He described the quickest route down to the Zion Gate and the best place to get a taxi, and as Don Paolo walked quickly away, Marc Ram appeared out of the shadows of the tomb.

"We'll cover him as far as our side of the Allenby Bridge," he said. "Then one of our agents on the Jordanian side will take over. We'll have someone at the airport to travel in the same plane. Then others will follow him from the airport in Rome to the Vatican. He'll never be alone."

"Use only men you're absolutely sure of," said the Prime Minister, still staring down the hill, though Don Paolo was no longer in sight. "There must be no leaks. There'll be hell to pay if anything goes wrong."

"Nothing will go wrong, Eli," said the Colonel. But his black-gloved hand rubbed his lucky Star of David on the lapel of his jacket. This was carrying secrecy too far. It was too risky.

Going down through the darkness, Don Paolo shivered, but this time it was only from the night air. The Judean highlands rose here to 2,700 feet, and the city's ancient stones seemed to retain the chill of centuries. He no longer felt worried even in the darkness. He was buoyed up by the feeling he had accomplished his mission. The rest should be routine. He was anxious to hear the latest news of the Pope, to learn if he was still living. *Hold on, Alfredo . . .*

A young man coming up the hill passed him on the dusty path. That was the only person he saw until he reached the bottom. A yellow Toyota was parked there.

"Father! Fancy meeting you again!"

It was the fat American Biblical scholar—Cousins. He was sitting in the Toyota, looking enormous in the small car.

Don Paolo tensed watchfully, aware of the envelope pressing against his chest.

Cousins got out with a great effort. "Can I drive you

anywhere?" The American seemed nervous, unsure what to say. "When you think it took Moses forty years in the Sinai Desert to reach Israel from Egypt, what they could have accomplished with a few Toyotas!" He moved closer to Don Paolo. He seemed pathetically eager to please. "Let me chauffeur you somewhere. The distance doesn't matter—anywhere!"

His persistence worried Don Paolo. He had to get away from the fat American. He saw a taxi approaching from the Old City, but it already had a passenger—no escape there. He felt then how much alone he was in Jerusalem, in spite of all its Christian connections, and how vulnerable!

"Father!" The taxi had stopped, and a face at the window was calling him over—a youngish man with fair hair, sunglasses covering most of his face. The man was wearing a worn brown cassock, loose-fitting and open at the neck, and Don Paolo realized with surging relief he was a fellow priest. It was an act of providence. He hurried over to him.

"Can I give you a ride, Father?" the strange fair-haired priest asked in fluent Italian. "I'm going as far as the Allenby Bridge."

The border! "That's where I'm going," he said cautiously.

"Jump in then," the priest said, opening the taxi door.

Don Paolo hesitated. If the stranger hadn't been a fellow priest, he wouldn't even have considered it. It was the fat American who decided him. He saw him approaching. "Father, stop a moment!"

Don Paolo quickly got in the taxi. The driver, a thin-faced, middle-aged Arab in a grubby kafir, drove off immediately as if he had been delayed long enough. Don Paolo glanced back. The fat American seemed about to run after the taxi, but instead he stopped and watched it drive away, a strange worried expression on his sweating, fleshy face. The last Don Paolo saw of him was a glimpse of fat thighs glistening in the moonlight.

"You know him?" asked the priest casually.

"No," Don Paolo said. "He's an American, that's all I know."

"He seemed to know you."

Don Paolo looked at the tanned face, the little he could see round the large sunglasses. "You speak to me in Italian. How do you know that is my language?"

The priest leaned over and touched the small red Servus

Dei badge on Don Paolo's lapel. "I recognized this." While he was close, Don Paolo caught a whiff of scent or deodorant—a sweet, cloying odor that reminded him of something, somewhere, but he couldn't remember what.

"Let me introduce myself," the priest said, white teeth flashing beneath the sunglasses. "I'm Father Charles Harris of the Order of St. Francis."

Don Paolo remembered the Franciscans looked after the Catholic shrines in the Holy City. "You're a resident of Jerusalem?"

"No, I've finished my business here. I'm on my way to Rome."

"You're flying from Amman?"

"Yes, on the ten o'clock."

Don Paolo nodded. "I, too."

"What luck! We can travel together all the way."

"You're English?"

"How did you guess? From my accent?"

"Your name."

"I could be an American."

"You have an English manner." Don Paolo had lived with English soldiers at the end of World War II. English tourists sometimes came to Palermo. They were usually quiet, dignified people. Like Rome, they had once had a great empire and had lost it. He relaxed even more with the priest when he knew he was English.

"Have you heard any late news bulletin about the Holy Father?"

"The last I heard he was still alive," the Englishman said. "Let's see if we can get anything on the radio." He spoke rapidly to the driver in a language Don Paolo didn't understand. High-pitched, nerve-jangling Arab music suddenly filled the car, then a voice in Arabic cut in. The fair-haired Englishman listened carefully, grim-faced. "It's bad news. The Vatican says the Pope has gone into a coma."

Don Paolo touched the envelope against his chest. He didn't notice the Englishman look at him. All he could think of was that he might now arrive too late. Dear God . . .

"Here's the bridge," the Englishman said, his face at the window. "This is where we ditch the taxi. We have to get new transportation on the Jordan side. Don't worry. I've got it all arranged."

The Allenby Bridge—or the Hussein Bridge, as it was

called on the other side—was a plain, wartime crossing strung across the muddy Jordan River, which Don Paolo found as unimpressive as the Tiber in Rome. The moonlight shone on a landscape that resembled a battlefield. On the Israeli side, there were old, abandoned refugee camps in the bare, stony hills, along with barbed wire and hidden, ruined bunkers from past wars.

The Englishman led the way, obviously familiar with the border procedures at the bridge. Don Paolo behind him noted approvingly his tall, powerful, athletic body. Too many priests were overweight, and the Communists made propaganda out of it.

Israeli soldiers in khaki uniforms and green berets and police in dark blue interrogated and searched them, and made a careful study of their passports.

They were ushered into a plain, single-decker bus, and driven across the bridge for a second interrogation, this time by Jordanian frontier officials in Arab headdresses and plain uniforms. The Arabs, too, put them through a metal detector and asked them to take off their shoes. Probing Arab hands on Don Paolo located the hidden envelope, felt it, identified it, checked it contained only paper, and then passed on. It was a slow, tiring process, but at last they were free to continue their journey.

On the Jordanian side, the road to the bridge was lined with large, healthy-looking trees—a sign of how fertile and low-lying the Jordan Valley was there. Yet the desert started only a few miles away. There were military observation posts and pillboxes. But, in contrast to the Israeli side, there were no military wrecks to serve as memorials: Arab pride expressed itself differently. Arab police in blue uniforms controlled the traffic to the bridge. It wasn't busy tonight.

"This way," the Englishman said briskly.

Don Paolo was content to follow, relieved he didn't have to bother about the travel arrangements in this strange land. This Englishman was very kind and helpful; meeting him had truly been providential.

"Here we are." The Englishman unlocked the door of an old Ford parked by the side of the road.

"This is yours?" Don Paolo asked, surprised. The Englishman was well-organized.

"Borrowed. Come on, get in. We need to be on our way." The Englishman seemed to be a little nervous now among all the Arabs, and he concentrated on his driving. The old Ford sped quickly up the tree-lined road, past the Arab police. Sitting beside him in the small car, Don Paolo caught another whiff of that strange, sweet odor. He wished he could remember what it reminded him of—of whom or what.

The land was less fertile now, rocky and dry. There was a feel of the desert in the air, a lonesomeness unknown in Jerusalem. The only sign of life was a black Bedouin tent, with some horses standing near it.

"I don't know these Jordanian roads," said the Englishman as if apologizing for his silence, "and I have to remember the route." He glanced at Don Paolo and added casually, "Who do you think will be the next Pope? One of the Italians like Cardinal Garonne—or another foreigner?"

"With the Communists in power, it will be an Italian. We will need an Italian to deal with Italians." Don Paolo looked out of the window to hide his feelings. "But we talk as if the Holy Father were already dead."

Below them now was a desolate scene. The foothills were the color of cooled metal with banks of chemical slime stretching down to what looked like a vast cauldron of salt. There was no life anywhere—no trees, no water or plants, no weeds even.

"This is the Dead Sea," said the Englishman, his voice becoming cold and distant. "Here is the lowest point on the earth's surface—over a thousand feet below sea level. Everything here is dead. Sodom and Gomorrah are said to lie below the salt waters."

He stopped the car and looked at Don Paolo. The easy friendliness had gone, replaced by a strange remoteness.

"Why are you stopping?" asked Don Paolo, staring at the sunglasses, but seeing only the macabre scene outside reflected in them. He caught another whiff of the odor, and now he knew what it reminded him of—the smell that came up from Gehenna. But he had identified it too late.

The Englishman held out his hand.

"I want the envelope in your pocket."

The envelope! The old priest's heart began to pound. "How do you know about that?" he asked, too shocked to be more cautious.

"You've been followed from the Vatican," the Englishman told him, taking off his sunglasses to reveal chilling blue-green eyes, as dead-looking as the scene outside.

Then Don Paolo felt great fear. "You're not a priest," he whispered. "Who are you?"

The cold eyes glinted with amusement. "You may call me Judas," and his hand dipped under the seat and came up with a long-barreled black pistol. "Now give me what I want."

"It belongs to the Holy Father." Don Paolo braced himself to resist. "I must give it only to him."

The black pistol moved closer. "There's no time to argue. Turn around." When Don Paolo didn't move, a rough hand pushed his face to the window. "I haven't even time to let you say your prayers, old man."

Don Paolo felt the hard barrel touch the back of his white head, and his fear surged. "Why are you doing this? You will be damned! You will go to Gehe—"

Don Paolo's desperate cry ended abruptly as the pistol blasted. A bullet tore through his skull, splashing the window with streaks of blood and brain tissue. His tall, gaunt figure slumped lifelessly back against the seat. His mission was over. He had failed.

The man known as Judas calmly dropped the pistol into a pocket of his cassock, and then leaned over the body and pulled out what he wanted—the long white envelope. He quickly checked the contents. *So that's what they're up to!* It was even bigger than he had expected.

With a satisfied expression, he put the envelope away with the pistol, and then in the same businesslike manner, he began to undress the body. Suddenly his long fingers touched a sticky patch of blood on the dead priest's shirt. He recoiled instantly, holding up his hand to examine the dark smudges on his fingertips with a look of horror. The sight of blood on his own skin drove him into a frenzy. He rubbed his fingers frantically up and down on the floor of the car until the marks were erased. Only then did he slowly begin to relax . . .

7

Robert Miller arrived at the King David Hotel in a bad temper. He felt he had been outsmarted. He had tramped up Mount Zion in the darkness and the only person he had seen was an old, white-haired priest. No sign of the Prime Minister. It was possible "Zion" hadn't referred to Mount Zion, but he trusted his instinct was right. It usually was. Some of his best exclusives had come from following a lead even slighter than that. He'd simply arrived too late—thanks to the wily Colonel Ram.

The lobby of the famous hotel was crowded with men in black skullcaps, lightweight suits, and flowing robes, a mixture of Israelis, Europeans, and Arabs. As soon as he was shown to a room, Miller phoned Vaughan. It didn't matter if the call were tapped: Ram—and therefore Israeli intelligence—already knew what he was going to say. The delay didn't seem to worry Vaughan. "That's okay," was all the editor said about the agreement with Ram. "We haven't got enough on Judas yet. But keep pressuring Ram to level with you. If we scoop him on our own, we can always renegotiate —or publish and be damned. What's your next move?"

Miller said thoughtfully, "There's some connection between here and Rome. I can't put my finger on it yet. I want to talk to Tolloni's widow as soon as possible. There's a plane out of Amman late tonight."

"Watch your step in Rome. The situation's worsening there. Bellini's starting to crack down and—" Vaughan paused as someone spoke to him, then his voice rose with excitement. "The news has just come through that the Pope has died. Hell, that changes the whole ball game . . ."

The Amman plane was fully booked, but Miller was promised the first cancellation. He decided to chance it. Even a few hours might be important. The murder of the Il Duce informer haunted him. He didn't want Judas to get to Mama Tolloni before he did.

He left the Fiat at the Allenby Bridge and shared a Jordan taxi to Amman with a middle-aged American couple. The man didn't wish to go to Rome because of the Communist government, but the woman was keen to be there for the Pope's funeral. "People will come from all over the world," she said enthusiastically.

Robert Miller nodded politely and pretended to sleep, occasionally sneaking a look through the window. The dry, barren Jordan landscape passed quickly as the Arab taxi driver, steering with one hand and gesticulating wildly with the other, raced to get them to Amman on time.

Robert slowly sorted through his memory, searching for the fresh lead he sensed but couldn't yet see. There was some connection between Rome and Jerusalem, he was sure of it. He remembered the argument in The Knesset over the Pope . . . The Colonel's phone conversation . . . Seeing the Prime Minister drive away alone . . . Instinct took him from one to the other, but where was the connection? Why had Judas chosen Jerusalem next? Dublin, Munich, Rome . . . and Jerusalem. And was Judas *here?* There was no sign of him yet, and he was the kind of visitor who made his presence felt . . .

Suddenly the taxi braked. Robert tensed at once, eyes open. There was a roadblock ahead. Lights flashed, warning the driver to stop.

"Police!" There was fear in the taxi driver's voice, and he braked again so quickly that Miller and the two tourists were thrown forward. Miller cursed.

A long, narrow Jordanian face under a drab olive military cap appeared at the driver's window. Sharp black eyes examined the driver and then the three passengers.

"Get out," he ordered in English with an impeccable Oxford accent. "Line up at the roadside and have your passports ready for inspection."

Several Jordanian public security men in olive or light tan military uniforms stood behind the roadblock. One of them inspected the passports. The American couple tried to be friendly, they wanted to know what had happened, but they were ignored. When the man looked at Miller's passport, he passed it to an older officer, a broad-shouldered man with dark, tanned skin and a heavy black mustache. He came over to Miller.

"You are an American journalist?"

"Yes—for the *New York Mirror*."

"And your destination?"

"Rome via Amman. Can you tell me what has happened?"

"I can do better than that." Strong, tobacco-stained teeth gleamed in the dark face. "I'll show you. Come"—he glanced at the passport—"Mr. Miller."

The Jordanian officer led Miller off the road across the dry rock, lava, and sandy earth. Beneath the moonlight, it was like a bare lunar landscape. There was a smell of sulphur—of brimstone—in the air. The sky was so low it seemed to be closing in over the desert. Miller had an intense feeling of desolation.

"We are close to the Dead Sea," said the officer, as if he knew exactly how Miller felt.

Several more military figures were clustered round something on the ground. As Robert Miller drew nearer, he saw it was a body lying in a hollow. The officer pushed him forward.

"A European has been murdered. Perhaps you can identify him for us."

Robert Miller looked down. He had seen so many dead bodies he no longer had any personal feeling. It was the naked corpse of a thin old man with close-cropped white hair. He had been shot in the back of the head, and the bullet had come out through his right temple. No one had closed the bulging eyes, and they had a shocked, anguished expression. The only clue was a red mark on the neck. It looked like lipstick.

"It *is* lipstick," grunted the officer by his side. "We are already making a check at all the whorehouses." The strong teeth glinted. He looked down at the gaunt body, the disfigured head. "But he doesn't appear the kind to be robbed by a whore. And he isn't fat enough for a tourist. He looks more like a teacher a dedicated man. I suspect he was stripped of anything that would identify him, and the lipstick was daubed on him simply to mislead us. But certain things cannot be hidden. He is a European. He hasn't got that indefinable American look." He gave Miller a wicked grin. "You agree?"

Miller stared, fascinated, at the gaunt face. The dead body belonged in the lunar landscape. The skin had a strange pallor in the moonlight, and the white hair seemed to glow. He was reminded of the old priest he had passed on Mount

Zion, but he hadn't seen that man's face clearly. He decided to play safe. He couldn't risk a delay.

"No, I can't help you. I've never seen him before."

The officer shrugged. He walked Miller slowly back to the taxi. The middle-aged tourist couple were beginning to look very alarmed. Robert waved to reassure them. "We're trying to catch a plane in Amman," he told the officer. "We're late now."

"Don't worry, Mr. Miller. I'll let you proceed immediately. We wish to encourage American visitors to Jordan." He held out his hand. He had a strong, muscular grip. "My name is Major Falid." He saluted as the taxi started off again.

The American couple foolishly offered the taxi driver an extra tip if he made the airport on time. He finished the last few hilly miles in a nerve-wracking ride, still steering with one hand and taking blind corners in a wild sweep. Even Miller who enjoyed fast driving was relieved when they reached Amman and the driver slowed down to find the way to the small airport.

Robert discovered he had been lucky—someone had failed to arrive. "An Italian priest," said the Jordanian airport clerk, checking his list. "Ticket booked in Rome, but he has not come. Perhaps it is because of the Pope's death."

While Miller was waiting to board the plane, he examined a large, intricately designed Oriental rug on the wall of the reception hall, and then walked outside the small airport to enjoy the cool night air off the hills. The glint of a cigarette showed him where someone else was standing alone—a tall priest in a brown cassock, with big sunglasses. Had the missing Italian shown up after all?

Miller walked over to the priest, who was about as tall as he was, and powerfully built, youngish, with fair hair. "Father?"

The priest turned quickly as if taken by surprise, the sunglasses facing Miller. His eyes were hidden.

"Are you waiting for the Rome flight, Father?"

The priest slowly relaxed. "No," he grunted, turning his back on Miller again.

Miller walked slowly away, noting the priest hadn't said where he was going. His tone had been unfriendly. Miller sensed an aura of hostility, a powerful presence who wanted no more human contact that night.

When Miller glanced back, the priest had vanished into the shadows.

Strange . . .

In Rome, special editions of the newspapers were aleady on sale in the streets. Pages of photographs covered the Pope's life—from a week-old baby in his mother's arms to his last public appearance on the balcony of the Papal Palace.

Robert Miller bought copies of all the papers and read through them methodically over a drink at his favorite bar on the Via Veneto. His eyes passed quickly over one large picture, stopped, and then went back to it. Pope Alfredo was being welcomed in Palermo by a childhood friend, a tall, white-haired priest. The face was younger, the body wasn't as gaunt, but there was no mistaking who it was—the murdered man he had been shown on the road to Amman.

At his hotel, he put through a person-to-person call to Major Falid at police headquarters in Amman.

The telephone service between Rome and Jordan wasn't the world's fastest, and it took several hours to get through and then to locate Major Falid. At last the Major's deep voice came on. Miller identified himself and explained what he had discovered.

A heavy sigh came from the other end. "Yes, we have learned the same, Mr. Miller. Unfortunately, it is true. He came from Israel into Jordan. It greatly complicates the case. But thank you for telling us."

He came from Israel. Miller remembered the old priest he had passed on Mount Zion. Was this the connection he was looking for? Rome . . . Jerusalem . . . and the Vatican?

"What was he doing in Israel?"

"We're still working on that, Mr. Miller. We hope the Israeli authorities will cooperate with our investigation."

"And the killer?"

The Major hesitated. He was obviously deciding how much he could tell Miller. "We know he was accompanied by a priest who was last seen at Amman airport."

Miller froze. His mind flashed back to the priest he had spoken to. That must have been the man. Yes, he had sensed something wrong. A hostile presence in the darkness.

Quickly his memory jumped farther back—to the priest who was reported near the Tolloni villa just before the kidnapping.

It was the same priest.

The same man.

Judas.

Miller's big hands clenched angrily.

He had been face-to-face with Judas and had let him escape.

He tried to recall everything about the man at the airport. A big, powerful figure in a brown cassock. Eyes hidden behind sunglasses. Fair hair. Clean-shaven. Maybe early thirties. Only spoke one word, but no noticeable accent. Could be American or English.

Yes, there was enough to recognize him.

Judas wouldn't escape next time.

8

Major Falid, neat and formal in his best uniform, followed the Israeli security man down the long corridor in The Knesset. It was the first time the Jordanian had been in the Israeli parliament building, and he was as wary as a cat in a strange house. The Intelligence chiefs in Amman hadn't wanted him to come, even though relations between the two countries had much improved, but he had insisted it was the only way to pursue the Don Paolo investigation. You couldn't trust the Israelis, if they were involved.

At the end of the corridor was a small back office. The security man opened the door, then stepped aside for him to enter. Ever since crossing over into Israel, he had felt this way—like Daniel in the lions' den! The Major was proud of having read the Bible, which he considered the key to the western mind.

He entered the small office expecting to see a top Israeli police official behind the steel desk, instead he found himself looking into the face of Marc Ram. He didn't need to see the empty sleeve to recognize him. Marc Ram was well known in Jordan. All of the Major's doubts hardened. Something must be wrong if Ram was taking a personal interest in a murder case.

Marc Ram stood up to greet him, a big man with a friendly smile. Major Falid was impressed by the smile. All the Jordanian intelligence reports described Ram as very cold and ruthless. The black-gloved hand gripped his hand with almost human warmth.

"Sit down, Major." The two men faced each other warily across the desk. They were both dark-skinned, big, and hairy. They could have been related. But intensifying the automatic suspicion between Jew and Arab was the special situation they found themselves in: Marc Ram had something to hide and Major Falid sensed it.

The Colonel obviously felt he had to explain his involvement. "The Prime Minister has asked me to take a personal interest in the case since the Italian priest was a friend of the late Pope."

He picked up a typewritten report. "Let me tell you about the investigation on our side," he said blandly. "This report shows that the Italian priest, Don Paolo, landed in Jerusalem at 4:15 P.M. on a flight from Rome. The flight crew said the plane was too crowded for them to notice if he talked to anyone on the flight. We traced and interviewed every one of the 126 passengers on his flight who are still in Jerusalem. Nobody remembered seeing him in conversation with anyone. The American tourist who sat next to him—a woman from Nevada—said he seemed preoccupied, tense and nervous."

"That could mean he was expecting trouble," the Major said.

"As he was a foreigner, our security people noted his arrival—they said he wasn't met by anyone. A taxi took him to the Zion Gate. Roughly an hour later, another taxi picked him up in the same area. The taxi already had a passenger, a Franciscan priest named Harris. He had the taxi wait some distance away until Don Paolo appeared from Mount Zion and then he told the taxi driver to drive over to the old priest. They talked and then Don Paolo got in the taxi. The two priests crossed the Allenby Bridge—well, you know that from the checkpoint records logging their arrival on your side. We checked and found that nobody who was on the plane with him crossed the bridge at that time. So, if he was followed from Rome, someone else took over here."

"That missing hour—any clue as to what he was doing?"

The Colonel hesitated for a moment, then shook his head. "It's a blank in the record."

"That hour presumably covered whatever his purpose was in coming to Jerusalem," the Major persisted. "Have you learned anything from the taxi driver, anything he overheard perhaps?"

"They were speaking in a language the taxi driver couldn't understand, probably Italian. He said before Don Paolo got in the taxi, he was talking to a fat man in shorts."

"Have you traced this fat man?"

Again the Major noticed Marc Ram hesitate before he answered. "No, not so far."

"Is the taxi driver a Jew or an Arab?"

"An Arab."

"Can I talk to him?"

"That can be arranged, Major, but I doubt you'll learn anything we didn't. One of our Arab auxiliary officers questioned him."

"That missing hour is what I'm interested in—and that fat man in shorts."

Marc Ram said with ill-concealed impatience, "Now tell me what you've found out on your side."

"The body," the Major said reluctantly, "was discovered by a young couple who, we're satisfied, had nothing to do with the crime." He wanted to go on trying to trap the Colonel. But he had to be careful; he was in Israel. "Don Paolo was shot once from behind by a long-barreled, semiautomatic Beretta. It's a reliable weapon, as you probably know, a .22 caliber, unlikely to jam during rapid fire. It had been adjusted for close-up work, to make less noise. The bullet had less explosive force than normal. The range was so close, perhaps as little as two inches, that Don Paolo's head was scorched where the bullet entered. He must have died immediately. The bullet left the head through the forehead, but with so little force it was later found on the floor of the car."

"Who owned the car?"

"The Franciscan, Harris, had an old Ford waiting for him on our side of the bridge. This was later found to have been stolen in Amman. Two students own the car, but they only use it on weekends. They hadn't yet discovered it was missing. When we found it, there was some blood on the front seat. Don Paolo was obviously shot in the car, then the body was stripped and daubed with lipstick to make it hard to identify. Then it was dumped."

"There was nothing found on the body, of course." The

Colonel tried to hide his concern. "But was there anything on the ground nearby?"

"Nothing. We found nothing near the body."

"You searched over a wide area?"

"At least half a mile, Colonel."

"His clothes—"

"In the car. But nothing in them, nothing important."

"No secret pockets you might have missed?"

"We missed nothing, Colonel. There was a large pocket inside his shirt. Nothing was in it."

The Colonel's black-gloved hand tensed into a fist. "Where did you find the car?"

"On the outskirts of Amman. Harris took a taxi from there to the airport. He was taking no chances. Very thorough."

"How far did you trace him?"

"He took a flight that night to Beirut. He passed through the passport check and customs at Beirut, and then he disappeared."

"Into the arms of the Palestinian Liberation Organization!"

"We don't know that, Colonel," Major Falid said sharply. "But he is our prime suspect, whether or not he is a genuine priest. We don't yet know the motive. That will make everything much clearer. Was it Don Paolo personally, or his position, or the Vatican that was the cause of his murder? One thing we do know. It was carried out very smoothly. A very professional job. The killer took risks, but they were carefully calculated, not the work of an amateur."

Major Falid stood up, ready to leave. He had found out what he had come for. The Israelis had been interested in something Don Paolo had on him. Possibly something he was carrying in that inner pocket. He hadn't told Ram the pocket had been torn as if in a struggle. It was a problem for intelligence.

"Now," he said with a pleasant smile to match the Colonel's, "will you tell me where I can find that taxi driver? Perhaps he can lead me to that fat man in shorts . . ."

As soon as the Major had left with a security man to escort him out of The Knesset, Eli Abraham entered Ram's office. He read the news in Ram's face.

"It's missing?"

Ram nodded gravely.

"He's not trying to fool us?"

"He's a shrewd, professional cop, not Intelligence. He's no more an actor than I am."

"Falid? He's half-Palestinian, isn't he? Maybe the Jordanians at the top don't trust him completely."

"He'd know if they found it. He was at the scene soon after the body was discovered."

"Okay, Marc." The Prime Minister slumped into the chair the Major had sat in. He looked tired. "What does it mean?"

"Judas has it. He even used the same kind of gun he killed Tolloni with—an Italian-made Beretta."

"What went wrong on our side?"

"We were outsmarted. Kerak, one of our Jordanian agents, a good man, was to pick Don Paolo up at the bridge and follow him to Amman. Kerak's disappeared. All the Vatican restrictions got in the way. We should have been able to do a straight security job. The extreme secrecy helped Judas."

"The Pope wanted it that way. He was convinced the Communists had an undercover agent at the top level in the Vatican."

"Probably one of those left-wing Cardinals," Marc Ram said sourly.

"The Pope may have been right. Judas had to learn about Don Paolo's mission from someone."

"It means we better not trust the Vatican from now on."

"Our problem is to minimize the damage now that the secret's out. How long do you think we've got, Marc?"

"Judas will use it to strengthen his hand with the Arabs. He won't make it public until he's squeezed the maximum advantage out of it. That gives us a little time."

The phone buzzed. Marc Ram listened briefly. "Thanks, Major."

He looked grimly at the Prime Minister. "That was Falid. He's just learned from Amman that Kerak's body has been found about ten miles from the bridge. His throat was slit."

"Falid knew he was one of our agents?"

"Apparently. Judas must have known, too."

"Judas wasn't working alone, that's clear."

"Yeah, he's started to build his team here already. He couldn't have done the two, and throat-slitting's not his style. He's got some Arab help."

Eli Abraham said urgently, "I must go to Rome immediately, Marc. I'll attend the Pope's funeral as a cover. We must let the Vatican know before Judas can do any more harm with it."

"Even before the new Pope is elected?"

"We daren't wait. We'll have to inform the Camerlengo— the Cardinal who's in charge until the election. It's Garonne, the Vatican's Secretary of State."

"Can we trust him?"

"We'll have to. Judas has left us no choice. Damn that evil sonofabitch—wherever he is!"

9

Beirut ...

A run-down district in the Old Quarter.

In a labyrinth of narrow alleys, lamb carcasses hung in the doorways of butchers' shops, and donkey dung spotted the ground. Flies were everywhere, in control of the air. Late at night, when it was cooler, people without homes slept against the walls. No one came to this part of Beirut unless they were poor or they had to.

A tall, fair-haired man in sunglasses sat in a half-empty coffeehouse amid the flies and old men smoking water pipes. He was dressed in a white cotton, one-piece suit with a hood that made him look almost like an Arab. With him at an oilcloth-covered table was a handsome young Palestinian named Ayad, who wore a colorful, spotted shirt and faded blue jeans. Ayad had dusky, copper-colored skin that glowed like a furnace when he was excited. He had been loaned to the fair-haired man by Al Fatah, the main guerilla group within the Palestine Liberation Organization.

"Beirut is where St. George is supposed to have slain his dragon," the fair-haired man said, sipping Turkish coffee from a tiny, egg-shaped cup. "We always remember the dreams, never the reality. That's why we don't get anywhere on this bloody planet."

"You're a realist," Ayad said. He had been with the fair-haired man only a short time and was still treating him very carefully. But he had learned enough to realize this man could be very useful to the cause—the destruction of Israel.

"Being realistic," said the fair-haired man in a strange mocking tone, "means giving up your dreams. You Arabs will never beat the Jews until you give up your dreams and become as realistic as they are."

"The Jews have their dreams, too," Ayad said indignantly.

"Yes, but they have their dreams when they're asleep. You Arabs walk around with yours."

The hot-blooded Ayad suppressed a sharp retort, his skin glowing with anger. He had been told to stay friendly with the fair-haired man. It was not always so easy. All the other Europeans Ayad had known could be kept happy with liquor, drugs or sex—especially sex. The dusky Arab women always appealed to them as exotic, the way European women appealed to Ayad. But when he mentioned women to the fair-haired man, he wasn't interested. Then Ayad wondered if he wanted men. He always had a sweet smell, presumably from perfume or a deodorant. He also took long baths or showers like a woman. Ayad had once glimpsed him scrubbing his chest as if he wanted to rub off the skin. Maybe all that meant something. Ayad began to wonder if he himself might be expected to be available, and he stopped wearing his tight-fitting jeans for a time and tried to sleep as far from the man as possible. But the man had never showed any interest in him or in any of the street boys who solicited him. It was truly confusing. What kind of European was he? Ayad could understand his not drinking, not smoking, not taking drugs— he was a warrior. But no sex? A man needed sex unless he was a servant of Allah and even then . . . Perhaps the fair-haired man would tell him what satisfied his desires when he had settled the details of the next operation and could relax. Ayad hoped so. He could trust a man more when he knew what tempted him, where his weakness lay.

"They're late," the fair-haired man grunted. He took off his sunglasses and wiped them on his white suit. His eyes were as blank as the windows of a deserted house. Ayad wondered if they ever showed any feeling. "I don't like to be kept waiting."

"They'll have to walk from the main boulevard—"

"Hell, I took the trouble to get here on time."

Ayad noted his growing anger. He didn't know him well enough yet to be able to anticipate his moods and avoid trouble. He couldn't understand him until he learned more about his life. I wonder if he will ever trust me enough to tell me about himself, Ayad thought. It will probably depend on how long we are together and how much danger we share. We understood each other in Israel among the enemy.

"Here they are," the fair-haired man murmured.

But Ayad had already noticed.

A slim, erect European in a lightweight grey suit had just come inside the coffeehouse and was glancing round with obvious distaste. As soon as he saw them, he headed for their table.

"Judas," the man murmured in a low, guttural voice, his thin, sallow face bending over the table.

"You're not Sokolov," the fair-haired man told him. "He's a big fellow. I've seen his picture."

"I'm here in Comrade Sokolov's place," the man said. "My name is Vasil Hodic. I'm the military attaché at the Czechoslovakian Embassy. Can we go somewhere to talk more privately?"

"I'm only dealing with Sokolov," the fair-haired man said.

Ayad watched nervously. The fair-haired man was in a mean mood. It was going to be a bad meeting.

"Perhaps you don't understand how we work, Mr. . . ." The Czech waited to be told the real name. There was a hostile silence. The Czech tightened his thin lips with annoyance. "We usually represent the Russians as well as ourselves," he said. "They prefer to remain in the background until they're needed."

"They're needed now. Look, I only want to deal with them directly, Hodic. I've got something important to show them— nobody but them."

"You can show it to me. I'll pass it on."

"I told you—no middle man this time." The fair-haired man stood up impatiently. "Tell Sokolov to be here at the same time tomorrow or the deal's off."

He didn't wait for the Czech's answer, but strode out, watched by a waiter who was anxious about the bill. Ayad quickly paid and hurried out after him.

"You've made an enemy," Ayad said in the alley outside, brushing away the flies.

"A goulash Communist!" he snapped, walking past the carcasses in butchers' doorways with long angry strides. "They're nearly as unreliable as the spaghetti Communists in

Italy. If you want action, deal with the Russians directly. They respect you if you stand up to them. I owe them nothing. They owe me. After the Tolloni business, do they really expect me to deal with their puppets? No, they're testing me. Well, they've got my answer."

"You think Sokolov will show up tomorrow?"

"Of course." He smiled coldly. "I knew what I was doing back there. It was all carefully calculated. You can't afford to shoot from the hip with the Russians. Yes, Sokolov will come. He has to. They want what I've got."

When they walked into the coffeehouse next day exactly on time, the Russian was already there.

Sokolov was at a rear table with the Czech. At another table near the entrance was an obvious Soviet bodyguard. There was probably another one outside. Sokolov wasn't taking any chances.

The Russian stood up to greet them, waving jovially. Officially, Leonid Sokolov was the naval attaché at the Soviet Embassy, and he looked like the captain of an ocean liner—a tall, broad-shouldered man with wavy grey hair and a weather-beaten face. Shaking hands with a flabby grip, he said quietly, "What shall I call you, my friend? Judas seems . . . inappropriate."

"The name doesn't matter. We're here to do business."

Sokolov shrugged. "So be it. As Judas or whoever, you are our comrade. I've looked forward to meeting you because I admire your work tremendously."

Now you're taking the right approach, Ayad thought.

"The Tolloni affair was a classic," Sokolov said. "I hope we'll have a chance to work together."

"It's possible. That's part of my purpose in being here—to make you an offer."

"What have you brought back from Israel for us?"

"I wasn't working for *you*, Sokolov. Through your man in the Vatican, I learned about the priest. I said I would eliminate him. That was all."

"But what was he carrying?"

The man known as Judas glanced at Ayad and the Czech to make sure they were listening. He liked an audience. Ayad also sensed he was about to say something that was important to him.

"The time is ripe for a major strike in Jerusalem."

"The old priest—what was he carrying?" Sokolov asked again.

"The target will be an individual whose death will change the political situation. That's how I work, Sokolov. Armies—even yours—can't bring down democracies unless they're patsies on your border like Poland or Czechoslovakia, but one man with a gun pointed in the right direction can do the trick. I've already changed Italy's political picture far more than millions of voters could do. I intend to do the same in the Middle East, with or without your help. I am an agent of change, of *progress*—for hire by the right people."

"And how do you decide who are the *right* people?" Sokolov asked quietly.

"It's not a question of politics," Judas answered, "or even communism versus capitalism. I'm on the side of order, efficiency, and reason, in whatever form they come. The decadent vestiges of European imperialism, the absurd personality cults manufactured by Third World tyrants, the myopic arrogance and effete selfishness of the Americans—these are the enemies I fight. Corrupt authority in all its manifestations. And in my fight, I prove to these ego-stuffed vermin that an individual can still count. One man can still change the world!"

"A very interesting philosophy," said Sokolov with an ironic smile. "You have high ambitions."

"I'm not one of your fanatical amateurs, Sokolov." The sunglasses came off, and expressionless blue-green eyes, like chips of ice, stared at the Russian.

Ayad looked admiringly at Judas. People usually flattered the Russians, but the fair-haired man was acting with complete independence. He had also revealed a little more of himself, for wasn't this personal crusade, this fierce and ruthless hatred for the trappings of power, just as much a dream, an ideal, as those he scoffed at?

The sunglasses went back on, hiding the eyes. "This is my profession, Sokolov. It's how I earn my living, and I'm expensive. You have to pay for the best. You can back me or not over Jerusalem. It's merely a business decision. If you don't, someone else will. My kind of work is much in demand these days."

Sokolov realized he had been clumsy. He said seriously,

"There's obviously only one target in Jerusalem big enough for you."

"Who?"

"Eli Abraham."

"You think his death would really change so much? Wouldn't he merely be replaced by another Israeli politician?"

"Listen," the Russian said, "I've assessed this very carefully because Abraham's caused us a lot of trouble. If his assassination could be attributed to the Arabs, it would end the current peace movement in Israel. His successor would be a hawk, one of the older militants. The attempt to coexist with the Arab moderates would be finished. There would be no more of these international Camp David get-togethers with Egypt and the Saudis. The next war would be much nearer. The status quo would change to our advantage."

"If Abraham was my target," Judas said quietly, "would Moscow back me? I need money—a lot of it—weapons, passports, a team to work with. . ."

Sokolov stared at Judas, still unsure of him. "Tell me this first, my friend. What advantage is there in it for you personally?"

"I'm on the side of reality. That's why my next mission must be in Jerusalem. I intend to bring reality to the Holy City, the City of Dreams."

Sokolov tried to peer behind the dark glasses. There was some fanaticism in this man—it was understated, the way the English were fanatical, but it was there. A fanatic could be used, but you had to be careful he didn't get out of control. Moscow had had some unhappy experiences with fanatics, especially in the Middle East.

He said quietly, "It might be possible to get Moscow's approval and support, provided of course there's no public connection of any kind, no possible political embarrassment. We could use your services, but you'd have to work on your own, ensuring complete secrecy."

"Of course—as I did with Tolloni. I don't need to prove myself any more."

Sokolov said quickly, "Your Italian work was brilliant. That is why we are together now. The Middle East is full of amateur assassins, but there are very few professionals in the world capable of this kind of top-level work. We realize that.

As I've told you"—Sokolov glanced quickly round the coffee-house—"I'm personally convinced that the situation in Jerusalem merits the removal of Abraham. He's very dangerous. But I'm only the man in the front line. I only make recommendations. Moscow makes the decisions. I have to convince Moscow it's absolutely necessary."

Judas took out the long white envelope that had cost Don Paolo his life. It still had several faded spots of blood on it. He handed it silently to Sokolov.

The Russian read the contents quickly and then looked at Judas, grim-faced.

"Do you realize this would change the balance of power forever in the Middle East? The Israeli Prime Minister *must* be killed—and as soon as possible."

10

Gina waited until Inspector Scaglia had finished dictating. It didn't take long. The tough, efficient inspector rattled off his letters at a speed that strained even her express, award-winning shorthand. No wonder the Ministry's typing pool called him The Machine.

Gina was a tall, slim, dark-haired twenty-two-year-old with a very Roman face—round and olive-skinned, with high cheekbones and large brown eyes. She was used to being admired, but at the end of dictating, Inspector Scaglia didn't even look at her. "That's all," he murmured curtly as he picked up a top secret report that had arrived by special messenger that morning.

Gina closed her shorthand notebook indignantly. The Machine hadn't even given her a chance to speak! Well, she was determined to tell somebody about what she had seen on Ash Wednesday. It might be important.

"Inspector Scaglia," she said hesitantly, "there is something I wish to report."

He looked up, surprised she was still there.

"What is it, Signorina Altieri?" he asked impatiently.

"That old priest who was murdered in the Middle East— the friend of Pope Alfredo . . ."

She had his full attention then. His hard eyes searched her face, assessing her reliability.

"Yes, what about the dead priest?"

"Ash Wednesday, the day he was killed—that same day, I saw him driving into the Vatican. In a chauffeur-driven Vatican limousine."

"You are quite sure of this?" he asked quietly, still eyeing her, making her nervous.

"He was as near to me as you are. I spoke to him!"

"You knew him?" Now he sounded suspicious.

"No," Gina said quickly. "The limousine nearly knocked me over, and the old priest put his head out of the window to make sure I wasn't hurt. That was late Ash Wednesday morning, and the papers say he was killed that night—in Jordan. He certainly traveled fast." Her nervousness now was making her say too much.

"That is very interesting, Signorina," said the Inspector. "Now you have reported it, your responsibility is over. But tell me, what were you doing at the Vatican?"

Gina blushed. She had been afraid of that question. She opened her big brown eyes innocently, though that probably would have no effect on The Machine. "It was the anniversary of my mother's death. I went to St. Peter's in memory of her."

"Your mother was a practicing Catholic?"

"Yes, Inspector."

"And you?"

Gina shook her head. "No, not now."

"But you used to be?"

"When I was a child."

"And did you give this information on your employment record?"

"When I was first employed by the Ministry four years ago, you weren't asked about your religion."

"I see." The Inspector made a note on his desk pad. He was probably going to have everyone in the building cross-examined about his or her beliefs. "You've nothing more to tell me?"

"No."

"You can go then."

Gina went out, mad at him and mad at herself. She shouldn't have said anything. Not to him anyway. She sat at her typewriter, too angry to type his stupid letters. She decided to talk to her father. Vito Altieri should be able to help her! But he wasn't free to have lunch with her until next Monday—his voice sounded very formal on the phone. She said it was urgent. Finally he agreed she could come by his office at the Palace. A lifelong member of the Communist Party, Vito Altieri was now an assistant to President Moltani at the Quirinale. When Moltani the Socialist was chosen as a compromise candidate, part of the deal worked out in the Electoral Assembly was that the Christian Democrats and the Communists should each have a representative on the President's staff. Tolloni had arranged for his old friend, Vito Altieri, to be the Communist representative.

Vito Altieri's office was part of a former palatial reception room—an acre or two of marble and carpets, with Gina's father lost in the middle behind a huge oak desk. He was a small, pudgy man with thinning grey hair and a round, lined, ingratiating face. Gina had taken after her mother; she and her father were not at all alike. She didn't even respect him much. He was too scared of what people would say, of what the Party would think. But he was all she had left.

As soon as they had exchanged an automatic peck on the cheek, Gina began to pour out what was troubling her, but almost immediately her father interrupted her.

"Not here," he said, his eyes wide with concern, glancing round apprehensively at the high marble walls.

Without saying any more, he led her down the immense marble hallways and out into the ornate gardens. His short legs slowed then to a stroll, and he tried to act more casual. Anybody seeing them would have thought he was showing his daughter the palace grounds—he hoped.

"Papa, you've become paranoid," Gina told him in her forthright way.

"You don't understand the difficulty of my position," he said. "But first finish telling me what you began. I want to know how bad it is. I got you the job at the Ministry, so I'm directly involved. You're also my daughter."

His attitude cooled her down. She tried then to describe her conversation with Scaglia quickly and unemotionally. But he didn't let her finish.

"Why didn't you call me first?" he shouted, his face red

and angry. Then he stared round to be sure no one could hear. "Don't you know I have enemies who want to get something on me, to cut me down? And here you, my own daughter, have given them ammunition. Now Scaglia knows you were stupid enough to go on some sentimental pilgrimage to St. Peter's, he'll try to pin it on me. Just you watch. I know he will. I know the technique. Scaglia's a dangerous man . . ."

Looking at his angry, worried face, Gina was reminded of all the Sundays she and her mother had attended mass in St. Peter's, and afterward her father had met them, but always on the other side of the river. He was an organizer for the party in those days and didn't want his loyalty questioned. Now that he was in the government, he wouldn't be willing to risk even that. Yet it was very Italian, Gina thought, to want to have the best of both worlds. Alberto Tolloni had let his wife attend mass and had made no secret of meeting right outside the church afterward. Tolloni even sometimes exchanged jokes with the priest. No wonder he was so popular. He appealed to *everybody*—both the Communists and the Catholics, the two extremes of Italian life.

"Papa, Alberto Tolloni—"

"Gina, the Tolloni days are over, as dead as Alberto is. Now the party is in power, it has a great deal to lose. Discipline is much tighter, loyalty tests are far stricter. The party is far less tolerant. Gina, I've been meaning to have a talk with you for some time—in case anything happens to me. You should know what is going on." He sat down on a marble seat and patted the place beside him. Gina quickly joined him, staring anxiously at him. She felt a chill of fear as if the pale sunny day had suddenly changed back to winter. What did he mean *In case anything happens to me?* "When Alberto was alive, the party was divided. He was far too independent for Moscow. They wanted to oust him from the leadership and replace him with their own man—Bellini. But Alberto's popularity with the people saved him. The party members knew they couldn't afford to treat him badly. The Moscow group was voted down, but it was close. Moscow used everything to down Alberto—threats, patronage, bribes, blackmail, every political trick in the book. It didn't work in the party election that time. But then Alberto was taken out in a way that could be blamed on the Right Wing . . ." He put a fat hand to his mouth. "No, it's better that you know nothing about that."

"About what, Papa?"

"No, Gina, there are some things you shouldn't know. I wish I didn't know them. I have to keep quiet for the good of the party, you understand. Let me say only that with Alberto gone . . . May he rest in peace!" He paused emotionally, clutching her hand. "Alberto was a good man, Gina. He was my *amico*, always so *affabile* with people. But with Alberto gone, it has become a different game. If Alberto could be rubbed out so easily, then so could anyone. The chicken-hearted were even more scared and were easily persuaded that the party needed to be united behind one leader if the election was to be won. Sandro Bellini"—he almost spat out the name—"became the new Party leader, but only just—by only a few votes. But it was a big victory for Moscow. The great Italian Communist party had lost its independence. I am a Tolloni man still in their eyes, but I am also a party veteran. I know a lot—the skeletons, where bodies are buried—and they know I know. I have to be very careful. And now you have exposed me to possible danger."

"But, Papa, you have the protection of the President." She had never seen her father like this before, so emotional, so frightened.

"Moltani isn't safe himself, Gina. They want to get him out now they have a majority, and replace him with one of their own men."

"You make it sound like medieval intrigue—the Borgias, Machiavelli—it's just their style."

"It's human nature, Gina, when the prize is big enough. We forget our dreams then. You can bet even the cardinals in the Vatican will intrigue over who's going to be the next pope."

"What don't you retire and get out of it, Papa?"

"I know too much. They wouldn't let me retire. Besides, it is my life. I've been a member of the party since I was in my teens, and my father was before me. I regret only that we have let these Moscow-trained people take over." He held her hand. "You must tell me, Gina, if you hear any more from Scaglia. They're very nervous about their relations with the Vatican. Moscow hopes one of the left-wing cardinals will be made pope. The government here is unsure what the best strategy is—whether to appear friendly to the Vatican or openly hostile. Bellini's advisers are divided, and there's no clear line from Moscow. If the government acts friendly—so goes the argument—it might make the Conclave more in-

clined to choose a pope friendly to Communism. But then if
they're hostile—this is the opposing argument—it might persuade the Conclave that only a pope friendly to Communism
will be able to deal with the government. Moscow is very
keen to have a pope in the Vatican it can influence."

"I've heard rumors the government wants to drive the Pope
abroad, into exile, that Bellini boasts he'll hold a party rally in
the Piazza San Pietro and address it from the papal balcony."

"Bellini will do no more and no less than what Moscow
decides," her father snapped. "He's no more than a Soviet
puppet, a traitor to Italy."

"The old priest's murder—has it any connection? That day
I saw him, there was a government helicopter overhead. It
flew away as soon as the limousine disappeared into the
Vatican."

Her father was slow to answer, staring down at his polished
black shoes. "There is *some* connection. The government was
aware of his visit to the Vatican and his journey to the
Middle East. But I don't know what lies behind it. I shouldn't
even tell you that much. The less you know, Gina, the better.
Just be very careful. Don't make any more foolish moves—for
both our sakes."

Gina noticed then that someone was watching them from a
second-floor window of the palace. It was too far away to see
who. She decided not to tell her father. He was scared enough
already.

"Papa." She kissed him impulsively. "We *must* see more of
each other." They had lunch together about once a month.
Her father had married again and Gina didn't like his new
wife—a schoolteacher ten years younger than he—and so she
never visited him at home.

"Gina," he said, squeezing her hand, "I do my best. You
must realize that. I always tried to protect your mother and
you from knowing . . . too much."

"Oh, Papa."

She felt the way you shouldn't have to feel about your
father.

She felt sorry for him.

And afraid.

True Romans like to be a part of all the city's big public
events—Catholic, Communist, or whatever. Gina, born there,

a Roman for all her twenty-two years, had an intense feeling for the city. Sooner or later that week the crowds gathering at St. Peter's to see the body of Pope Alfredo would have drawn her there, too. But when she left her father, she immediately headed there for a different reason. She felt shaken, aware of dangers in the party she barely understood. At that moment, St. Peter's represented a refuge from all that was troubling her. It was as close as she could get to her mother, and to that sense of home and security and all's well with the world that had died with her. She wanted to escape for a short time from the reality her father represented.

Gina edged her way deeper into the crowd toward the fountains and the towering Egyptian obelisk. She remembered the old priest as she crossed where the near-accident had occurred. He had seemed a nice, gentle old man. But what had he been involved in? What did her father *know?*

"What's the fair hope of Communism doing at St. Peter's?"

Gina was shocked to hear someone recognize her. A man. She stared at the strong boyish face with a prominent broken nose.

"Remember me?" he asked. Unruly reddish hair fell over his broad forehead.

She looked blank for a moment, then suddenly she knew who he was—the American reporter who had come to see The Machine. The poor man had been kept waiting a long time. But he had been very determined, and at last The Machine had seen him. Reporters had to be like that, as dedicated in their way as religious or political people. She liked his direct manner.

"Come to see the circus?" he asked. "Nero couldn't have attracted a bigger crowd with one of his pagan shows."

"Pope Alfredo was a warm, human old man," she said, "and Romans respond to someone like that. I once saw him at a public audience in St. Peter's with my mother. He was carried above the crowd, and he was smiling at everybody as if to tell them not to take all the fuss too seriously because he didn't."

"Your mother's a Catholic?"

"She was. She's dead now."

"Mine, too. Mothers should live forever."

Something touched her in the way he said this, and she

observed him more closely. She hadn't had much contact with Americans aside from the hordes of tourists who deluged Rome every summer. The party took a sternly disapproving attitude toward anybody or anything American, and the loud, pushy, camera-bedecked tourists she had seen only reinforced her bias. But this American reporter was different. First of all she liked the way he was built. His hard, muscular body was nothing like the soft-looking big spenders who crowded the Via Veneto. And there was something fresh and appealing in his manner. He didn't leer at her like a Roman, he didn't have that I-know-you're-hot-for-my-body come-on that she was so tired of. She hadn't come across this kind of self-confidence devoid of arrogance in a man before, and she found it immediately attractive. But above all, the American was so different from her father. He gave her a feeling of security, of solid strength—there was no fear in him. She smiled, encouraging him.

"You want to see the Pope's body?" he asked.

"I can't," she said. "The line's too long. I'm only on my lunch break."

"I've got two press passes—one's for a photographer. I'll make a deal with you. You can use one of the passes if you'll have dinner with me tonight."

There it was, thought Gina, the slyest pass she had got in a long while. But she had no plans for the evening, she liked him—and she *did* want to see the body.

"Okay, it's a deal."

They went in a side entrance. A Swiss Guard in full ceremonial uniform inspected the two passes and then let them in past a side altar. St. Peter's was like a massive marketplace. People were everywhere.

The only peaceful place was the Altar of Confession, the main high altar, where the Pope's body lay in state in a simple casket of varnished cypress beneath Bernini's magnificent bronze canopy. The Pope's face looked much thinner than Gina remembered. The body was garbed in the vestments of his holy office—a red chasuble, red slippers and red gloves, and a tall gold and white miter on his head. Four Swiss Guards in their orange, yellow and blue medieval uniforms stood at attention on each side, holding their halberds, the traditional axlike weapons.

"They had to bring back the embalmers," he whispered.

"The jaw began to sag, the face became discolored, and the fingernails turned parchment grey. The body had to be injected with more formaldehyde."

"Please," Gina said, "I don't want to hear it. People shouldn't know such things about the Pope. Is *nothing* sacred to reporters?"

"That's a strange way for a Communist to react."

"I'm a human being!"

"I don't believe you're a one-hundred-percent genuine Red."

"And I don't believe you're a genuine Yankee!"

"From the Midwest . . . and Ireland."

Gina glanced at her watch. "I better be on my way. I've got a pile of letters to type."

Outside, he said, "I kept my side of the deal."

"And I'll keep mine. I'll meet you . . ." She was about to say outside her office, then she remembered her father's warning: *Be very careful.* What would The Machine think if he saw her talking to the American reporter? "I'll meet you here at six."

"Okay, that's fine."

She was grateful to him for not arguing. "I'm sorry, I forgot your name."

"Robert Miller," he said, sounding annoyed. "I didn't forget *your* name—Gina."

"I'm bad on names," she said.

As Gina walked away with Miller watching her, a man in a dark suit who had been following them was unsure which one to stay with. He chose Miller.

11

The large white villa was for sale. It had a vacant look as Robert Miller drove his rented Maserati up the wide, graveled drive. The lawn needed cutting, and none of the windows had curtains.

He parked in the courtyard under the canopy of eucalyptus

trees he remembered from Mama Tolloni's press conference. The furry leaves still gave the light a greenish hue.

Before going inside, he sneaked a look at the back of the villa. Below an overgrown, sloping lawn stretched orchards, greenhouses, rows of ancient Roman statuary, and a kidney-shaped swimming pool. Tolloni had certainly lived well. His widow ought to get a high price for the villa unless the present uncertainty in Italy had affected the real estate market.

"Signor Miller?" A young maid in uniform had come out and was watching him.

"That's right," Miller said very coolly.

"This way, please."

Packing cases were in the hallway. Furniture was neatly stacked in a corner, ready to be carried away.

"You must excuse the mess, Signor Miller," said a deeper voice. Mama Tolloni stood in the doorway of a small black room. She was still wearing black, a grim mourner's dress. She had lost a lot of weight and her face was much older. "I'm giving up the villa and moving back into Rome," she said politely. "It's too lonely here now. And there are too many reminders of the past." She pulled back the dust covers from two armchairs. "Sit here, Signor Miller. Now how can I help you? I thought the press had forgotten me—and my husband." Her red-rimmed eyes smouldered with bitterness.

Robert Miller leaned forward, hoping to persuade her to tell him what she knew. She didn't like American reporters. None of the Communists did.

"Signora Tolloni," he said quietly, "a member of the gang that kidnapped your husband contacted me. I understand he also contacted you."

Her hostess' polite manner vanished. "He phoned offering to sell information," she said in a harsh voice, her jaw tightening. "He said he'd phone again to arrange a meeting, but he never did."

"Because he was killed."

"So I understand." Her lips pressed tightly together. She was under considerable strain and it showed more now.

"Signora Tolloni, whoever killed him also killed your husband."

She didn't say anything, but stared at Miller with a hostile expression.

"Signora Tolloni, I'm trying to find the killer. Please help me. Does the code name *Judas* mean anything to you?"

She took a long time to answer.

"No," she said at last, not meeting his eyes.

He wondered if she was lying.

"Did you tell anyone he'd contacted you to sell information?"

She nodded. "Sì."

"Who was it?"

"The police."

"Anyone else?"

"He told me not to. But I felt I had to tell the police."

"Who did you tell?"

"The new investigating officer appointed by the government—Inspector Scaglia. But why are you asking me all these questions?"

"I want to find your husband's killer."

"That's the job of the police. What can you do they can't?"

"Find the truth."

She stiffened, and a hand went up to her mouth. She was very nervous.

"Signora Tolloni, I told no one—except my editor in New York. You told only the police. The man himself was excessively cautious. And yet he was killed. Who informed on him?"

She stared at him, without speaking. He couldn't read her mind.

"Signora Tolloni, have you ever thought your husband's murder wasn't as simple as it seemed?"

Her eyes were big now, full of feeling, but still she said nothing.

"Ask yourself who profited from it," he told her. "The right wing got the blame, but they certainly didn't get the profit. Were they really that dumb? I talked to the man who was killed. He told me the right-wing Il Duce group involved in your husband's kidnapping was used—and betrayed—by an outside organizer whose code name was Judas. But who was Judas working for? Who gained from your husband's murder? His own party! Tell me this, Signora Tolloni—who were your husband's enemies in the Party? Who were Moscow's men among the party leaders? And how many of them are now in the government? And if the government *was*

involved, that explains why the police—Inspector Scaglia—"

"Get out!" She stood up, her pale face flushed with anger,
"Get out of my house!" She rushed to the door. "Filomena!
Filomena, come here at once!" The maid hurried down the
hallway. "Show Signor Miller out."

Robert stood up. "Signora Tolloni, please think about what
I've said. I'm staying at the Cavalieri Hilton, you can
always reach me there—"

"Tell your vicious lies to those who will believe them!
Filomena, show Signor Miller out of my house!" She spat out
the words.

Robert gave up and followed the maid out. He wondered
if she was covering up. She was Tolloni's widow, but she was
also a member of the Party. The Communists could be very
loyal—and also very paranoid. It was possible she'd been told
to keep quiet, even threatened.

It was also possible she *was* as innocent as she sounded.

If so, perhaps he had sown some doubt.

As he walked across the courtyard to the Maserati, another
car came up the driveway. It was chauffeur driven. A small
pudgy man with thinning grey hair got out. Miller didn't
recognize him. It was Vito Altieri.

Robert Miller drove out to Fiumicino Airport for the
arrival of Cardinal Brady of New York. Brady was always
news for the *Mirror*. Miller also had in mind that Brady
might be a useful contact in the Vatican. The connection was
somewhere there, if he could only see it.

Cardinal Brady was the last of the cardinals to arrive for
the funeral of Pope Alfredo and the conclave to elect his
successor—the 266th Pope.

There were altogether 134 cardinals of the Roman Catholic
Church, and 122 of them had already reached Rome. Eleven
of the remaining twelve were too old or too sick, or were
politically detained in anti-Catholic, usually Communist
countries, and wouldn't be coming.

Of the fourteen American cardinals, twelve were in Rome.
One of the absentees was also the oldest. Cardinal Paul
LeFair of New Orleans was in a hospital recovering from a
heart attack, but he wouldn't be missed at the conclave
because being over eighty—four years over—he didn't have a
vote. The other absentee, however, was only forty-nine, which

made him the youngest of all the 134 cardinals. That was Cardinal Brady.

He was said to have delayed his arrival in Rome to attend the funeral of an altar boy in Brooklyn. Some of the American newspapers, short of an American angle, reported that his fellow cardinals were critical of him for letting a local funeral make him late. Groups of cardinals from different countries were already holding informal meetings to discuss the *papabili*, as the leading candidates for pope were called. The American group was hoping to have some influence in the election, not with any idea that one of them would be elected, but to persuade their fellow cardinals to choose a strong pope who would not compromise with the Communists —and, if possible, would not be an Italian. They missed Brady at these early exchanges because he was the most famous of their group and also the best linguist. But it was typical of him to act independently.

Robert Miller, like most journalists, was not a religious man and disliked having to do religious stories, but he had a strong respect for Cardinal Brady. When he had worked for the *Mirror* in New York, he had covered several stories involving Brady. Miller was sceptical of all people in public life, of leading religious figures just as much as prominent politicians. He had approached Brady with the same scepticism. Here, probably, was another man of power preaching what he didn't practice. But Brady he found was different. His special quality baffled Miller for a long time. He kept trying to fit Brady into a fat-cat stereotype, and Brady kept eluding him. He saw him among the poor in the worst slums of the South Bronx, and he saw him with the rich and powerful at the Waldorf Astoria, and finally he realized what it was about Brady that impressed him so much in spite of his own scepticism. Of all the powerful public figures he had seen in action, Cardinal Brady was the only one who treated all people as equals—whether they were rich or poor, old or young, handsome, ugly, or whatever. He didn't class people in any of the accepted ways. Miller had expected to find him most at home among the powerful. When he didn't find this, he then expected Brady to have some romantic attachment to the poor. He didn't. Nobody was special. Anybody he was with engaged his full attention. That was extraordinarily rare, Miller thought. It was the characteristic of a saint—or a con man.

A small group of reporters was already waiting at the airport when Robert arrived. Most of them were agency men. Also there was Mario Lepecci, looking more than ever like a veteran diplomat with his mane of silver hair, his fine Roman features, and his elegant grey suit. Robert hadn't seen him since they had discussed the Tolloni affair.

"Roberto," Lepecci greeted him, "you've just missed the Israeli delegation—Eli Abraham himself."

"Abraham has come?" Miller couldn't conceal his excitement, because it confirmed his idea of what was happening. Abraham wouldn't have come just for the funeral. It was a cover for something else—some link between Jerusalem and the Vatican.

"And you know that if Abraham came so did his shadow—Marc Ram," Lepecci said.

Good, Miller thought, he needed to talk to Ram.

"You, Roberto, must have come to welcome your Cardinal Brady. He's not only a fellow American, but a fellow Irishman. Aren't you half Irish, didn't you say? That explains why you are *simpatico*. But what a prima donna's trick for him to arrive last and so get all the attention!"

"That's not why Brady's done it."

"An altar boy's funeral in Brooklyn! Come now, Roberto, what could be a more obvious publicity gimmick?"

"You miss the whole point, Mario, in your eagerness to be cynical. The altar boy served at Brady's own church—St. Patrick's Cathedral. He was also an orphan, according to my New York office. Brady himself is an orphan."

"He's John O'Neill's son. Some orphan!"

"He grew up an orphan. O'Neill got a girl named Kathleen Brady pregnant in Ireland and then ran off to the States. You can guess what the girl went through with a child born out of wedlock in an Irish village fifty years ago. She died when Brady was ten. He grew up in an orphanage. Then he went to the States. In the meantime, his father had become a millionaire—a multi-millionaire through bootleg whisky during Prohibition, prostitution, real estate, oil, you name it, John O'Neill, the great entrepreneur, was probably in it. But father and son didn't meet until after Brady became a priest. Brady was said to be very bitter about the way his father had treated his mother. O'Neill wanted him to change his name to O'Neill and become his heir. He refused. They only really came together when John O'Neill had his stroke and was half-paralyzed. But Brady has always had a great sense of identification with orphans and orphanages. In New York, the one event he never turns down is anything to do with an orphanage. That altar boy who died was an orphan Brady had helped. He was killed in a fire in an overcrowded slum tenement. Brady went down there as soon as he heard. There's a picture of him with the boy's body in his arms. Look at that picture if you think his late arrival's just a gimmick."

"So you have a heart after all, Roberto. You are positively sentimental about your Cardinal Brady."

"He's one of the most interesting—and most enigmatic—people in American public life."

"Don't misunderstand me, Roberto. Before Brady became a cardinal, he worked for a year for the Secretary of State at the Vatican. We Italians had time to take a good look at him. He's an outstanding church leader. He's also unconventional. He may even be a good man, whatever that is." Lepecci smiled slyly. "If he was an Italian and was fifteen years older, I'd include him among the *papabili*. But he should have a strong influence on who is chosen. He's highly respected among his fellow cardinals, particularly those from Africa and the Third World. That is rare for an American."

"Who are you betting on, Mario?"

"I think Cardinal Garonne has a very good chance. He has all the traditional qualifications—he's an Italian, he's over sixty, he knows how the Vatican works. And as Secretary of State, he's experienced in dealing with the Communists. I'd say he must be the favorite to deal with the new Communist government. But you know what they say about the favorite. 'He who goes in the Conclave already picked out as the next pope will come out still a cardinal.' "

"Maybe they'll select someone from Eastern Europe again, someone who's already used to surviving in a communist country—what about Cardinal Bierek of Czechoslovakia?"

"He's a possible. He's over sixty, he's put in his time at the Vatican so he knows how the Curia bureaucracy works. But if they choose a non-Italian again, they're not likely to choose another European. They'd select someone from another continent, an African or an Asian. But I don't think it's the time for the Third World yet. No, they've had one non-Italian this century. That'll have to satisfy the internationalists for a while. This time, because Italy has a Communist government, they'll want an Italian pope. An Italian can best deal with Italians! That'll be the winning argument in the Conclave."

"Here he comes!" yelled one of the agency reporters ahead of them.

At the front of the Arrival Hall, a crowd was gathering around a small group of figures in black. Head and shoulders above everybody was a big, broad-shouldered priest with cauliflower ears. Miller recognized Father Joseph O'Malley, a former Golden Gloves champion and Olympic bronze medal winner, who had given up boxing to become a priest. O'Malley was Cardinal Brady's Man Friday. The two men had first met as boys in an Irish orphanage. O'Malley was now busy clearing a way for the Cardinal, using his great body like a battering ram with a huge, apologetic, gap-toothed grin that took all offense out of his aggression.

Behind him, Miller glimpsed the familiar slight figure. He was always surprised at how small Brady was—he couldn't have been more than five feet, seven inches tall. He looked smaller, of course, close to the massive O'Malley, and his body was only slight, though he was wiry and in good shape. He had a mop of unruly black hair, and a thin face with a strong nose and chin and intense black eyes. The man was not imposing physically, but he had some quality that drew all eyes. Even in that crowd, he looked lonely, detached, withdrawn into himself. He had the inner complexity and brooding melancholy of the "Black Irish." Yet there was no feeling of coldness. He was very vulnerable, and that was why the giant O'Malley was continually anxious about him. There was a tenderness that needed protecting. People felt it and immediately warmed toward him. They also understood they would never get close to him. There was a spiritual detachment. He conveyed an impression of solitary strength, and that gave him an imposing authority in any group. He was wearing a simple black suit with a small crimson band near the clerical collar; he seldom wore the full crimson outfit of a cardinal.

"Father O'Malley." Miller stood in the huge priest's way. He had once given O'Malley a free press ticket to a Muhammad Ali championship fight at Madison Square Garden, and he hoped O'Malley remembered. "Been to any big fights lately, Father?"

The huge priest looked as if he had been slapped, and then he slowly grinned with embarrassment. "Mr. . . . . Miller! You're a long way from home. Are you here for this solemn occasion, too? Of course this isn't the time to discuss boxing, especially as I've sworn off for Lent!" O'Malley was much subdued since Brady had become a cardinal. He felt he had to be more dignified.

Reporters now had cornered Cardinal Brady. O'Malley shouldered his way through to stand beside him, scowling round as if daring the reporters to give Brady a hard time. O'Malley was not the type of priest usually associated with a cardinal, but Miller respected Brady for breaking with convention there, too.

Someone asked the Cardinal about the dead Pope, and he spoke sombrely, with quiet intensity, about him. He and Pope Alfredo had been very close. It was the Pope who had consistently pushed Brady up the Catholic ladder and made him a cardinal at such a young age.

"Who do you think will be his successor?" Brady was asked.

Instead of giving a ready-made, diplomatic answer, Brady paused to think about it, his hands shaking a little. For all his experience in dealing with people, he was a shy man in public. His hands always shook when he made a public speech, though he tried to hide them.

"I can't say at this stage," he replied slowly. "There are several outstanding cardinals who would make great popes in my opinion. But," he added with a smile that revealed uneven white teeth, "when the doors close on the conclave, we'll hope for Divine guidance."

Robert Miller pushed forward. "Will Italy's new Communist government influence the conclave?"

Cardinal Brady stared directly at Miller as he thought about his reply. "Yes," he said. "All of us will have it in mind. We don't yet know the new government's attitude toward the Vatican as a state. The new pope may have to come to terms with an entirely new situation. In that case, he may have to be unusually strong physically to withstand the pressure."

O'Malley beamed, then grew grave as he remembered the occasion that had brought them to Rome. "The Cardinal's limousine has arrived. Now, gentlemen, if you'll just make way," and the great body began to push them back.

No one objected. The reporters were pleased. Brady hadn't ducked their questions like most of the other cardinals. They watched the slight figure walk away behind the massive

O'Malley, and many of them had a protective feeling about him. Miller noticed how Brady slouched as if minimizing his own importance. Yet he walked on the balls of his feet, poised almost like a cat. He was very keen on physical fitness. He was said to do fifty push-ups immediately after saying his prayers in the early morning.

A big hand gripped Miller's arm, squeezing the muscles, and a deep voice mumbled in his ear, "The Cardinal wants to see you, Mr. Miller."

It was O'Malley.

"Why me?"

"He just said to bring you."

O'Malley led him out to a long black Mercedes. Cardinal Brady was sitting alone in the back. "Can we give you a ride into Rome, Mr. Miller?"

"Thanks, sir, but I've got my own rented car."

"Sit with me for a few minutes then."

Miller got in the Vatican limousine, pleased to have been singled out by the Cardinal. O'Malley closed the door and stood outside like a guard.

"I read your reports on the Tolloni kidnapping," the Cardinal said. "I met Alberto Tolloni several times when I worked at the Vatican. The Holy Father used me as a go-between. So I was personally interested. But I was very puzzled by the behavior of the kidnappers. They played into the Communists' hands." The dark intense eyes studied Miller. "I wonder if you know what I mean and whether you have any further information."

Miller tried to hide his surprise. Brady was even more on the ball than he had expected. He felt certain he could trust the Cardinal with his own theories on the case. "I believe the kidnapping was planned deliberately to get rid of Tolloni as leader of the Communist party and also to help get the Party elected. It was a left-wing conspiracy backed by the Russians. The right-wing group was just used."

Cardinal Brady nodded. "I suspected as much."

"Little is known about the man who organized it—except that his code name was Judas."

"A strange sense of humor."

"He's fond of biblical references." Miller explained as much as he could about Judas without breaking his agreement with Ram. The Cardinal was quick. Miller could see that he'd pretty much pieced things together. "There's a good chance that the whole case will bust wide open within the next few weeks."

"Then be very careful, Mr. Miller. You're sticking your neck out in their territory. Very dangerous forces are involved."

"I believe the scandal could bring down the present government."

"Is the whole Italian Communist Party involved or just a few Moscow agents in the party?"

"I don't know yet," Miller said carefully. "There's a Vatican connection, I think." The Cardinal tensed. "The Don Paolo murder in Jordan. Judas was responsible. But why?"

The Cardinal said thoughtfully, "I'll find out if the Pope's staff has any answers." It was impossible to tell by his expression if he knew more. "Call on me, Mr. Miller, if I can help in any way. You can reach me through O'Malley day or night. I'll be staying at the Vatican for a few weeks after the election to help the new pope settle in. It's very important your investigation isn't stopped. You should make a tape immediately of what you've found out so far and put it safely away. *Take no chances.*"

The dark intense eyes looked into Robert Miller's. "The risks involved here are very great—there have been several deaths already. You're working on the side of truth and you must protect yourself. I'll pray for you."

The Cardinal's hand moved quickly in the air, and Robert Miller realized he was making the sign of the cross over him. The gesture moved him more than he cared to admit. Well, Robert told himself, I can certainly use all the help I can get.

He felt much better after talking to Brady. The Cardinal had picked up at once on the depth of his involvement in the story. Brady's reaction had also confirmed his feeling about the Cardinal's understanding of the contemporary world. It had proved to him that a man could hold strong religious beliefs and still view brutal political realities with open eyes. He felt strengthened in his determination to follow the Tolloni inquiries through to the end, whatever risks or dangers were involved.

Miller trailed the Vatican limousine all the way into the city as far as the Piazza San Pietro and then watched Brady and O'Malley vanish into the Vatican. Buses were double parked along the Via della Conciliazione. There was still a huge crowd waiting to see the body, and people recognized Brady and waved.

It was two minutes to six.

Miller found himself looking forward to his dinner with Gina. He had kidded himself she would be a useful contact. Maybe she'd be able to answer all his questions about Scaglia. He was trying to appease the workaholic/confirmed bachelor in himself. After his divorce he had sworn off women, or at least any serious involvements. No more Eves. But this Italian girl was not like Eve—much less sophisticated, much more basic and direct. There was something about her that grabbed him inside. He'd have to watch himself with her. She wasn't the kind of girl who'd settle for a one-night stand. And he didn't have the time for anything more. He'd soon be going back to Jerusalem.

Six o'clock came—and went.

No Gina.

Six-fifteen.

Six-thirty.

He waited until well after seven.

No Gina.

She had stood him up.

Or had she?

It worried him that she worked for Scaglia.

He hoped nothing had happened to her.

12

Pope Alfredo had left instructions cutting the traditional nine-day mourning period to four days. The Conclave was then to begin immediately. "The church cannot afford to be without a Pope a moment longer than necessary in these perilous times," the dying Pope had told his Camerlengo— Cardinal Garonne, the sixty-two-year-old Secretary of State, a tall, grey-haired, genial diplomat and scholar.

Government representatives from over one hundred countries were expected to attend the funeral, but because there

was so little time, Cardinal Garonne tried to avoid any
meetings with heads of state until the funeral was over. He
discovered, however, he couldn't postpone meeting the Israeli
Prime Minister.

"We can't afford even twenty-four hours' delay," Eli Abraham told him on the phone from the Israeli Embassy.

They met in the Pope's private library on the second floor
of the Palace. Marc Ram accompanied the Prime Minister.

Eli Abraham's solemn expression conveyed the seriousness
of what he had to say. It was an important milestone in the
development of a Catholic-Jewish alliance, he hoped. The
decisive meeting would come with the next pope, but it was
important now to make sure no great harm was done to their
progress so far.

"What I have to tell you," he said gravely, "concerns Don
Paolo, the priest who was murdered in Jordan recently."

Cardinal Garonne showed his surprise.

"Let us be completely frank," Abraham said. "Did you
know about his mission?"

The Cardinal shook his head. "I was here when Don Paolo
came to visit the Holy Father on that last day," he said
slowly. "The Pope's secretary, Signor Moravia, told me he
had been asked to arrange a brief visit to Jerusalem for Don
Paolo. But he didn't know the purpose of the visit."

"Don Paolo said the Pope had told him to report only to
him or to his successor. But his murder changes the situation
obviously. That is why we are here. I want to inform you of
what I know because you are the Camerlengo, the present
head of the Vatican. I cannot wait until the Conclave, even
though it is to meet much sooner this time. This is an urgent
and potentially dangerous matter. The Pope's messenger has
already been killed. What I have to tell you is of great
importance to both Israel and the Vatican—"

"Wait, gentlemen," Marc Ram said, staring round the
ancient library with a dissatisfied expression, his black-gloved
hand clenched tight. "Your Eminence, when was this room
last checked for electronic bugging devices?"

It was obviously the last question Cardinal Garonne expected. He said with a startled smile, "As far as I know,
Colonel Ram, it never has been. We have never found it to be
necessary—"

"But Pope Alfredo apparently was very worried about

Vatican security," Marc Ram said, trying to control his impatience.

"I knew of his concern," the Cardinal said, "and I shared it to some extent. There had been some recent leaks of important information. But of course in a large, open, international organization like ours—"

"Don Paolo's murder suggests the 'leaks' were well-organized and dangerous," said Eli Abraham gently. "Someone outside the Vatican learned about his most secret mission. Who? How? If you haven't the answers to those questions, then the danger still exists. We should therefore take what precautions we can with our meeting. Is there anywhere in the Vatican that has been checked out recently? Surely there is somewhere you are sure of."

The Camerlengo said quietly, "I appreciate your concern. There has been a preliminary check in the Sistine Chapel. There are very strict rules concerning security for the Conclave, and Pope Alfredo left additional instructions about electronic devices."

"Then I suggest we talk in the Sistine Chapel," Eli Abraham said.

"Very well," Cardinal Garonne replied.

Eli Abraham exchanged a quick, surprised look with Marc Ram. He had expected the Cardinal to object. Perhaps he knew more about the "leaks" than he was admitting and would be more frank in the secrecy of the Sistine Chapel.

The seats for the Conclave were already there in rows beneath Michelangelo's awe-inspiring ceiling frescoes of The Last Judgment. There wasn't enough space for the traditional thrones for the cardinals now that there were so many of them. Pope Alfredo had greatly increased the number of cardinals in Africa and Asia; two-thirds of the College of Cardinals were now non-European. This time 123 cardinals would have to be seated in the Sistine Chapel.

It was here in the celebrated canyon-shaped chapel that, twice in the morning and twice in the afternoon, the cardinals would drop their votes into the silver chalice until one candidate had at least two-thirds plus one. If no candidate achieved this after a reasonable time, a simple majority would be enough. But that seldom happened.

The effect of the chapel was so powerful that the Cardinal

and the two Israelis were momentarily silenced, their heads turning this way and that to admire the great ceiling.

"It's the ideal place to choose a Pope," the Cardinal said.

"It's all we lack in Jerusalem," replied Eli Abraham admiringly. "This—and St. Peter's." He turned slowly, following the scenes of Moses' life depicted above. "You're satisfied now, Marc, about security?"

"As much as I can be here," Ram said.

"Very well. Let's begin." Eli Abraham ended his inspection of the paintings and faced Cardinal Garonne. "I must preface what I am going to tell you by saying that it may well be the prelude to a historic event for both the State of Israel and the Vatican State." He paused gravely to make sure he had the Cardinal's full attention and then went on: "We have already overcome much of the old hostility that existed between us for centuries, thanks to a large extent to the efforts of the last four popes. On your side, we are no longer blamed for the Crucifixion, and on our side, Jesus, though not accepted as The Messiah, is being studied with increasing seriousness as a major prophet—which means that Christianity has become more important to us, too. This was an ancient barrier between us that affected even those of us who have no faith. But the barrier is down now. Gradually we have reached a much more understanding relationship—a friendship even, and a drawing together of what we have in common in our two faiths and in our shared histories in the Old Testament of the Bible. It is accurate to say we have come to recognize how much we have in common in a world in which faiths like ours are continually threatened. We have come to appreciate that we share many common enemies. This doesn't include the extremists of the Arab world, for we both recognize that our relationships there are quite different. Yet even there, we have made great progress in overcoming ancient hostilities on both sides and in drawing closer to some more positive, even friendly relationship. It is of course the last thing our enemies want—that the Catholics, the Jews and the Arabs should come together and coexist peacefully with mutual respect. My God, yes, they will do almost anything to keep us apart."

With a polite gesture, the Cardinal suggested they sit on two of the seats ready for the conclave, and Abraham immediately did so. They faced each other. But Marc Ram didn't join them. He prowled about the Chapel as if in search of bugging devices or other dangers.

"Now, you at the Vatican," Abraham continued briskly, "have recently had a special problem—your relations with the new Communist government. Your faith is the opposite of theirs. Some of you think it's possible to coexist—this was aimed directly at the Cardinal whose policy as Secretary of State had been to find a compromise between the opposing faiths—others, like Pope Alfredo, have been more apprehensive and therefore have been anxious to find another solution in case the Communist government became hostile to the Vatican State. I met secretly with Pope Alfredo during his visit to Spain earlier this year—it was easy to arrange as I was there on vacation and therefore an audience with the Pope seemed quite accidental and innocent. Pope Alfredo had decided that he must plan ahead in case the Vatican was forced to leave Rome. In his opinion, there was only one other place it could settle—Jerusalem." The Cardinal's bushy grey eyebrows went up, but he didn't interrupt. "Pope Alfredo wanted Israel's agreement and support to transfer the Vatican to the Holy City *if it became necessary*. I was immediately in favor of it. The advantages to Israel would be enormous. To have the center of the Catholic world in Jerusalem would greatly increase our security, bind us even closer to America, and help us in working out an agreement with the Arab moderates about the future of Jerusalem. Oh, I don't need to elaborate on why I was so strongly in favor of what Pope Alfredo proposed! After a lengthy discussion, Pope Alfredo and I reached a tentative agreement that can be summarized quite simply. In exchange for full recognition of Israel and Israel's right to have Jerusalem as its capital, but not including exclusive right to the holy places, we would do everything in our power to help the Vatican to transfer—if it so wished. The Pope hoped this wouldn't be necessary, that some kind of reasonable coexistence with the Communist government would be possible, but he felt he had to make preparations in case the situation deteriorated. We even discussed possible sites in Jerusalem close to the Old City that might be fitting and could possibly be made available."

The Cardinal's diplomatic poise was shaken. "I knew nothing about this!" he cried. "Why didn't he first discuss it with me?"

"Perhaps—"

"Perhaps he didn't even trust *me*."

"He was extremely worried that it would leak out. That

was why he insisted it should be just between the two of us. He wouldn't even let me tell the Cabinet or the President."

"Then it isn't binding," Cardinal Garonne said.

"I told the Cabinet in a secret session just before I left to come here," Abraham replied. "They were in favor of it. I also told the President in confidence and he approved. This means a majority in The Knesset would be assured. But I was confident of this when I first talked to Pope Alfredo. We have so much to gain from such an agreement—from the presence of the Vatican in Jerusalem."

"It would lose us much Arab support," said the Cardinal. "The Arabs would take it as approval of your exclusive ownership of all Jerusalem."

"The Pope said survival was his first consideration. He believed the Arabs would understand that, just as Europeans accepted it when the Pope went into exile in France in the fourteenth century. But Pope Alfredo also believed that with the Vatican in Jerusalem, it would help to bring Israel and the Arab moderates closer together. With the Vatican there, we might feel secure enough to work out some kind of Jewish, Christian, and Moslem alliance to run the Holy City."

"Pipe dreams!" said the Cardinal. "I wish he had first discussed it with me. I was supposed to be in charge of our foreign relations. Such an agreement meant a radical change in our Middle East policy. Surely I should have known about it! But the Holy Father was in a strange mood those last few days. I couldn't get near him. No one could, except his secretary—and Don Paolo. How does Don Paolo fit in?"

"Pope Alfredo wanted our agreement in writing with my signature. Don Paolo came to collect it. The Pope knew by then he was dying, and he wanted the agreement for his successor who would have to make the decision if trouble came."

"I see." The Cardinal was plainly very disturbed. "It says much for the Pope's fears that he had to summon someone from his boyhood days to find a messenger he could trust."

Marc Ram had been hovering in the background. Now he spoke up. "There must have been a great many serious security leaks for the Pope to be so worried," he said quietly.

The Cardinal looked embarrassed. "I assume, gentlemen, this whole meeting is on a confidential level. I haven't discussed this with anyone, though I shall have to tell my fellow cardinals before the Conclave. The truth is," he said gravely, "the Italian Communist leaders know about all our most important policy decisions. They seem to know as soon as we make them. There is an informer in the Vatican at a high level, but all our attempts to find out who it is have failed."

"Then the Pope was right not to trust anyone inside the Vatican," Marc Ram said.

Cardinal Garonne knew the Israeli was right, but he didn't see the point of discussing internal Vatican business further. He disliked the style of this arrogant colonel, and he fundamentally opposed the whole plan of moving the Holy See to Jerusalem.

"What happened to the agreement—the document?" he asked anxiously.

"I gave it to Don Paolo at a secret meeting on Mount Zion. I saw him depart with it. But it wasn't found with his body. We checked with the Jordan police and we're pretty sure they're not holding anything back. The document is missing. It can mean only one thing—that our enemies have it. Our *mutual* enemies. That's why we're here, to minimize the harm done. We felt we couldn't wait until there's a new Pope."

"I understand your urgency now, and I thank you for it," said the Cardinal. "What's the next step you recommend, Mr. Abraham?"

"It's now in the public domain. Undoubtedly it'll be used to hurt both of us with the Arabs. We must both decide on our policy for when it's made public. What are we going to say? Are we going to admit it's true—or deny it?"

"They could publish the signed document."

"Documents can be forged."

"I see you are ready to deny it."

"It's to our advantage to admit it's true, but I promised Pope Alfredo to do everything possible to keep it secret until the time was ready."

"I shall have to tell my fellow cardinals in case we have to make a decision before the election."

"We know the next move is going to be in Jerusalem." Eli Abraham explained the crucial involvement of Judas in this delicate affair.

"More wheels within wheels," the Cardinal murmured, looking very troubled. "The Tolloni case appeared too simple. I knew more must be involved, but I didn't see the connection . . ." Cardinal Garonne suddenly made a decision and walked over to the heavy wooden doors. "You have given me your sense of urgency. I cannot wait any longer to inform my fellow cardinals. We must meet at once." He looked gravely at both men. "This may have a great influence on the selection of the next pope."

Robert Miller phoned Gina's office.

"She no longer works here," a woman's deep voice told him.

"Where can I reach her?" he asked, suddenly anxious.

The phone went dead.

His anxiety greatly increased. She had worked for Scaglia, now she'd disappeared. Had she been seen talking to him?

In the late afternoon, he waited outside her office building. He had observed Gina chatting with several women in her office that time he went to see Scaglia. When one of them came out, he asked her about Gina. The woman didn't recognize him. She obviously thought he was one of Gina's men friends.

"She's been transferred—to Housing/Supply."

That was a dead-end administrative building on the far side of Rome.

He phoned there next morning.

A self-important man's voice asked, "Is it personal? Second-grade clerks aren't allowed personal calls."

"Put me through," Miller snapped. "This is the Ministry."

Gina eventually came on, sounding nervous. A rush of relief filled Miller and made him aware of his own high state of tension.

"Why didn't you show up?"

"I can't talk over the phone."

"Have dinner tonight then."

This time she did show up. They met at Miller's hotel, the Cavalieri Hilton, with its fine high view of the city. Gina came hurrying into the large luxurious lobby no more than five minutes late. She looked pale and much less sure of herself.

"I owe you an apology. I was transferred with no warning to Siberia—that's what we call Housing/Supply—and I got scared. I thought if they saw me meeting an American reporter, it would look bad. Being chicken must run in the family."

They had a quiet, leisurely dinner of filet mignon, fettucine Alfredo and insalata misto with two carafes of red wine. Gina called it a "capitalist" dinner, but she meant it as a joke. She was clearly enjoying herself. Her large sensual eyes were full of fun. He wondered if she knew the effect they had on a man. She couldn't be all that innocent.

It was his first chance to relax all day, and he enjoyed trying to learn more about her. He encouraged her to talk, wondering how the evening would end. He learned her father worked at the Quirinale Palace and that he was a Tolloni man. "When my mother died," she told him, "I saw more of my father than I had for years. He really made an effort to fill the gap. Everyone he introduced me to was Communist. That was a big change in my social life. My beliefs got turned upside down. My Mother was a devout Catholic, and the Vatican had seemed all good. Now it was the party that was the Savior of the People . . ."

Miller found his professional interest quickening. "I'd like to talk to your father. Could you arrange that for me?"

Gina shot him a wary glance. The suspicion that she was being used darted across her mind for the first time. "He wouldn't see you. Not an American journalist. He's much too nervous. He won't even talk to me, his own daughter."

"What's he so nervous about?"

Her expression changed. She became even more guarded. "He's a nervous man. Alberto Tolloni was his great friend—"

"And he's lost his protector?"

"Oh, don't let's talk about my father," she said quickly. "Sometimes, you know, I feel ashamed of his fear . . . and confused about what to do. It's as if I've inherited this disease, this timidity in the face of authority. I'm not explaining it well. You probably don't know what I mean."

Gina seemed upset and it touched Miller. He felt bad about pushing her too far on matters that were close to her heart. And he felt something in himself open up to the girl. Miller's customary style was to let the woman do the talking. He was a good listener and knew how to turn this trait to his own advantage. But suddenly none of these old games applied. He wanted to talk to Gina, wanted to make her understand.

"I think I do know what you're talking about," Robert Miller said slowly. "Inheriting hang-ups from your parents, living out *their* fears and anxieties in *your* life. I guess maybe

I'm guilty of it too. My father was a news photographer. He covered all the wars, revolutions, riots. Wherever there was danger, you'd know he'd be doing his damnedest to be there. He seemed to court danger, almost as if he doubted his own courage and continually had to be proving himself. Eventually his luck ran out and he was killed. Lately I keep thinking about him, wondering whether I've inherited the same need to—"

Gina touched his arm lightly. "You don't seem that way to me, Roberto. You seem very balanced and . . . and secure." She laughed shyly. "You must have a charming wife."

That brought Miller back to earth. His least favorite subject, and the one women always managed to bring up.

"Not any more," he said. "My charming wife Eve decided to get a divorce."

"Was it your fault?"

"Has it got to be anyone's 'fault'?"

"It usually is."

"My wife said it was my paper's fault. She said journalists shouldn't get married—like sailors. I guess I'm a loner at heart."

"Have you any children?"

The second big question. "No, I didn't want any. Neither of us did. My wife was a model. I guess she didn't want to spoil her figure. And I'm not like your Italian men who need a dozen bambinos to prove themselves. It's a hell of a thing to play macho games with kids' lives."

"You're annoyed. I'm sorry. I didn't mean to pry into your private business."

"I don't care." That was a lie. He *did* care. But he didn't want to admit it to her.

"Well," she said, "one good thing's come out of your not being married."

"And what's that?" he asked suspiciously.

"We wouldn't be sitting here talking like this if you were married. Good things can come out of bad." She smiled at him and gave him a look with those big sensual eyes. She was certainly a strange girl.

It was the smile and the look that probably caused him to make his first mistake with her. He blamed his loneliness and the peculiar frame of mind that the Tolloni business, and Brady, and that talk about fathers had put him in.

After dinner, when they were standing awkwardly in the

lobby—it seemed to him she was waiting to be asked—he invited her up to his room. He did it on a sudden impulse, half surprised at himself, the man who didn't want any involvements.

"No, thanks," she said. "I didn't come for that." She had an awkward honesty that appealed to him. Maybe she wasn't aware of the effect of those big eyes of hers. He tried to smooth over the tension between them by walking her out to a taxi and offering to escort her home.

"It would be a waste of your time," she told him. "I wouldn't invite you in—not the first time." But she said it kindly, smiling again, obviously intending no wound. And she hesitated, as if she didn't want to leave him this way.

She said casually, "You know why I got in trouble with The Machine at the office?" She was trying to show she trusted him and wanted to see him again. "You know that old priest who was murdered in Jordan? Earlier the same day, I saw him going into the Vatican. The Machine didn't like that—me being at the Vatican."

She opened the taxi door.

"Wait," Robert said. "You saw Don Paolo going into the Vatican the day he was killed—"

"*Ciao,*" she said to him, and closed the taxi door in his face.

Miller watched her ride away. So Don Paolo *must* have been on a mission for the Pope—to Israel. A mission Judas was against. The Vatican didn't yet recognize Israel, but maybe . . . The pieces began to fit together.

But as he went back into the hotel, it wasn't Don Paolo's mission that was on his mind. It was Gina. He couldn't imagine now what had come over him when he had opened his heart to her earlier in the evening. Involvements with women were only a distraction at a time like this. He knew that from hard experience, didn't he? Gina was just a contact, a small link to some powerful people in the party. But it was not her words, not her function in the party, not her usefulness that kept coming back to him. It was the image of those eyes that he couldn't shake, and her lovely olive skin under the long, dark hair.

He went to the big new Israeli Embassy on the Via Garibaldi to meet Marc Ram. After passing through the tight security check at the Embassy, he was shown into a small conference room where Ram was studying a large wall map of the Mediterranean area.

"There." Ram pointed to Beirut. "We know Judas is there, but we can't nail him. Our agents don't have the run of the city like the Palestinians. The whole PLO network protects him. He met the Russians recently in the Old Quarter—their top man, Sokolov. As far as we can piece it together, the target is . . . Eli Abraham."

Marc Ram looked as grave as if he had predicted an attempt on the life of his own son. His black-gloved hand clenched tightly with suppressed emotion. "We have one big public event coming up in Jerusalem soon and the Prime Minister will have to attend it. That's our International Bible Quiz, one of the most popular events of the year. My bet is that Judas will make his attempt then. It would appeal to his sick imagination. We know already of his fondness for biblical references. What better gimmick than to stage his latest operation at a biblical quiz?"

"Operation Abraham."

"Exactly," said Ram sombrely.

"He'll fall right into your trap."

"He better."

"Any idea where he is now in Beirut? I could probably take a day off from here and fly there. I'd recognize him again."

"Our men have a sketch made from the descriptions by the taxi driver who took him to the bridge, and our border officials. They'd know him. But he's vanished underground. He could be anywhere."

The door opened, and a burly man in his mid-thirties, dressed in a dark suit, came in. Ram introduced him as Lieutenant Kahn of the Mossad Aliyah Beth.

"Out paths have already crossed," Lieutenant Kahn told Miller. "We observed you meet Gina Altieri, go to the Tolloni villa, and then drive to the airport to meet Cardinal Brady. We had you under surveillance the whole time until we identified you and knew what you were up to. Government agents are watching you, too, so be very careful."

"Lieutenant Kahn is trying to fit the jigsaw puzzle together here before it's too late," Ram said. "The CIA are working with him. As soon as the Bellini group consolidate, they're in power for ever, we think. They'll also then probably seize all foreign investments. But at present they're vulnerable. That's why they're so eager to get a new Pope they can manage, one

who won't cause trouble and will help to keep the Catholic
opposition docile. We're keen of course to have a pope who
will further Vatican-Israeli relations along the lines Pope
Alfredo began. But we're not doing anything to influence the
conclave, unlike Bellini and the Russians."

"What did Pope Alfredo begin?" Miller asked carefully.
"What was Don Paolo's mission?"

"You better ask the Vatican that," Ram said quickly.

"I have. No comment."

"I can't help you, Miller."

Robert decided this wasn't the time to press him.

Lieutenant Kahn took a small photograph from an inside
pocket.

"Know him?"

Miller looked at a thin, round-shouldered, unsmiling man
in his fifties.

"No, who is he?"

"The Grey Eminence of the Italian government—Niki
Rostov, the First Secretary at the Soviet Embassy. Judas
contacted him when he came to Italy, and then Rostov sold
the Tolloni plot to Bellini."

"Where is Rostov now?"

"He left this morning for Beirut."

"And Judas is already there," Miller said, glancing at
Ram.

The black-gloved hand clenched. "It must mean only one
thing—they're finalizing their plans for Operation Abraham."

13

It was an immense public occasion. The faithful and the
curious took over the huge basilica, packing St. Peter's as
tightly as sardines, and they overflowed into the Piazza San
Pietro and filled that, too. Over half a million people came
for the funeral of Pope Alfredo, and an estimated billion
around the world watched it on television.

When the time came for the traditional eulogy, a slight pale
figure ascended to the high pulpit. Many people had obvious-

ly expected one of the old Italian cardinals who had known
the Pope as a young priest. There were exclamations of
astonishment and excitement when they saw who it was.

Pope Alfredo had left instructions in his will that the
eulogy should be "very short and not too personal, looking to
the future, not the past." And he had chosen Cardinal Brady
to deliver it.

The old Pope's respect for the young American Cardinal
was well known, so his choice was not surprising to the other
cardinals. It was also felt to be the old Pope's way of giving
Cardinal Brady some prominence at the funeral because his
age and nationality gave him no chance in the Conclave.

Cardinal Brady looked strained and nervous as he stood
above the vast congregation under the great dome. His hands
trembled violently as he began to speak in a high, intense
voice that had intonations of Dublin and New York. There
was no sound, not even an occasional cough, from the
thousands below as they listened to him. Yet it was not what
he said that held them spellbound so much as the deep
emotion his slight, solitary figure conveyed. People felt as if
they were listening to him alone, in private, and not in a vast
basilica among thousands of others.

"Pope Alfredo need not be idealized in death more than he
was in life," the Cardinal began, his voice sounding harsh and
strained, like that of a man controlling high emotion. "He
should be remembered for what he was—a good and decent
human being who became a great pope. He died at a time
when the materialistic forces that seek to collectivize and
degrade human beings appeared to have won a big victory.
This did not scare him. He knew it was a hollow victory,
based essentially on *deception* . . ."

A ripple of surprise pased through the crowd below, and
some people nodded and smiled in agreement. It seemed to
Robert Miller, crammed in the seats for the media, that as the
Cardinal said this, he leaned over the pulpit and stared down
at Prime Minister Bellini among the VIPs. Miller saw Bellini
flush angrily and his big jaw rear up. He must be wondering
how much Brady knows, Miller thought.

" . . . We fail only when we are weak, when we try to
compromise our beliefs. If we lose all this"—the Cardinal's
right hand gestured nervously round the huge ornate basilica
—"we have lost nothing vital to our Faith . . . and perhaps if
we did lose it, our spiritual life might be easier . . ."

Marc Ram nudged Eli Abraham among the VIPs. "Garonne must have told him about your agreement with Alfredo, and he's urging whoever will be the next pope to leave the door open." The Israeli Prime Minister didn't reply; he seemed totally absorbed in what Brady was saying. Ram went back to examining the crowd. The lack of tight security worried him. Judas might spring a surprise and strike here in St. Peter's.

" . . . We live in a very materialistic time and yet people cry out for something more in their lives. The materialists condemn our dreams as mere escapism, as empty illusions. Face reality, they say, and by reality, they mean the materialistic life. But our dreams are what ennoble us, are what inspire us to go on and do better. Our faith essentially is a belief in the value of the individual life. Anything that destroys or degrades life is wrong. For that reason alone, the materialistic forces are always doomed to failure, no matter what fashionable face they come up with . . ."

Mario Lepecci whispered to Miller, "Your boy's talking to his fellow cardinals on the eve of the Conclave. Don't forget the older ones, particularly, may have been demoralized by recent events. He's giving them a pep talk—and judging by the looks on their faces, he's having some effect."

The slight pale figure above them was nearing the end. " . . . The church in its long history has survived more crises than its enemies thought possible. We will survive the crises of today in the same way. But we mustn't be afraid of change. Remember, we are not materialists. The materialistic side of the church is not important. If we realize that, then we cannot commit the sin of fear, for we have nothing to lose—except our Faith. Pope Alfredo liked to say, 'I believe a dog should not be afraid to bark.' We should all do more barking. If we did, there might be no more hollow victories for our enemies, no more fooling of people, but only true victories of the spirit—of love . . ."

He was disappearing from the high pulpit almost before the thousands below realized. There was spontaneous applause from some people, an unusual act in St. Peter's and a rare demonstration of affection for a foreigner from a crowd essentially Roman.

But suddenly all eyes were on the VIP section. Prime Minister Bellini and other representatives of the Italian government had risen together and were walking out as publicly as possible, looking highly indignant to show they were leaving in protest.

"Now the fat's really in the fire," Lepecci whispered to Miller. "The chicken-hearted among the Cardinals will be scared to death. Brady's shown very clearly what's involved— and he's told them they better choose a pope with real guts, a dog that barks!"

"It not only puts the Conclave under pressure," Miller said. "It pressures Bellini and his government." With one speech, Brady had accomplished what Miller had been trying to do—to show Bellini he hadn't got away with it . . . yet.

The battle had entered another, more dangerous phase.

When Miller reached the *Mirror* office, Russell Hammond, the Rome bureau chief, was still there. Hammond had the same powerful build as Miller, but he was about twenty years older and very age conscious. He dyed his hair a dark brown, a noticeable deception since he had the complexion of a fair-haired man.

Hammond was sitting at a desk facing the window that Miller had used on his last visit. Probably going through my notes, Miller thought. There was an antagonism between the two men that they managed to keep just below the surface. Hammond resented anyone from the New York office, and he found Miller's aloofness and brusque manner particularly threatening. Miller, on his side, wished nothing more than to be left alone by the older journalist. He doubted that Hammond had much to contribute to the story, and he was too absorbed in it to worry about muscling in on someone else's territory.

"Vaughan tells me you've got something on the Tolloni case," Hammond growled without looking at him.

Miller sat down at Hammond's desk and, pushing a pile of letters to one side, put his feet up. Hammond didn't like it.

"It looks like some of the Bellini government were involved," Miller said casually, not keen to share anything with Hammond. "It was a Communist plot in a right-wing disguise."

"Why didn't you report to me? It's my territory."

"I'm still digging," Miller said. He had to prevent Hammond from taking over and blowing the whole thing. Hammond was a political correspondent, a goddamn Princeton man and an Italian expert, not an investigative reporter. His idea of journalism was to ask difficult questions at press conferences, not to risk his neck.

"Was Bellini involved himself?"

"It looks like it," Miller said unwillingly.

Hammond whistled softly and looked for his Cuban cigars. A box was on his desk.

"Here." Miller threw the box at him.

Hammond lit one and sat back. "The Russians made a bad choice with Sandro Bellini. He's not big enough for the top job." Hammond blew a cloud of smoke up at the ceiling. He should let his hair grow out a distinguished grey, Miller thought sourly, and go back to Princeton as a professor. Of journalism.

Hammond said thoughtfully, "What's happened in the States has happened here, too. The best brains don't go into politics any more. Professor Luigi Valeri is the most respected member of the Communist party, but he's withdrawn, he's put himself above the battle. He refused a cabinet job, but he hasn't opposed Bellini—at least not openly. It's not a matter of guts, it's party loyalty. Now that the party's in power at last, none of the members wants to hurt its chances with an internal fight."

"So Bellini gets away with it! If we faced Professor Valeri with the facts, with the prospect of a big international scandal," Miller said, "would he be willing to act then?" Miller didn't want to include Hammond in any aspect of the story, but he had to give the guy credit for telling him about Valeri. It was just the kind of inside information that he needed.

"Yes, I think Valeri could be persuaded to act," Hammond said slowly. "Valeri's a man with a conscience—a Marxist conscience. There's nothing spiritual in his thinking. He's accepted too completely a materialistic conception of the world. But I think he does believe a certain practical morality is essential to social order and even to the survival of our civilization." Hammond stubbed out his cigar in an ash tray. "Have you got enough facts to convince him?"

"I'm short of a witness, but I'm hoping to get one soon—a leading party veteran."

Hammond stood up, smoothing down his hair. "I've got to get home now, but we better have a session sometime tomorrow so you can give me everything you've got." He looked coldly at Miller. "The Reds are my beat."

Miller didn't reply. It wasn't the time to argue. But he'd make sure he was out of the office during the times Hammond was there. The bureau chief never stayed late. He wasn't married, but he always left in the early evening as though he had to get home to somebody. Maybe a boyfriend, Miller thought savagely.

He sent over the end of his funeral story to New York and then went back to the hotel. After his exchange with Hammond, he was tense, in need of some release. But he didn't feel like going on the town. This is the time when I should be married, he told himself, and have someone to come home to.

Someone was waiting for him in the lobby.

"I missed you at the funeral," Gina said. She looked upset about something and unsure of her reception. She was in a brown woolen dress that clung to her wide shoulders and her narrow waist. She looked very pretty. Be careful, Miller told himself. Don't spoil anything this time.

"I must change my shirt," he told her. "Wait for me here and then have dinner with me."

"I can wait upstairs just as well."

It surprised him, but he immediately led her to the elevator. His room was on the eighteenth floor. The elevator purred up at a great speed. Neither of them spoke until they were in his room.

"Let me order drinks," he said.

"From downstairs?" She was suddenly nervous.

"I've got a bottle of vodka in my bag. If you can take it straight or with water . . ."

They both had it straight. He gave her a big one. It helped her.

"I was outside in the piazza for the funeral," she said quietly. "Cardinal Brady's eulogy had an unsettling effect on me. He's like no other preacher I've ever heard. I had a sense of raw emotion without any of the usual phony rhetoric. His kind of Catholicism could be a big challenge to the party. At least it shook me up. I wandered around by myself for a long time thinking. Then suddenly I couldn't stand being alone any longer. I came here because you're not with the party or the church. You don't make me think. You know what I mean?"

He wasn't sure he did. She had the frank, innocent, direct approach of a child. Her words left him a little confused, but he found her manner more attractive than ever. One thing he was sure of, though—this woman was feeling as confused, upset and lonely as he was. Both of them were caught up in events and feelings they only dimly understood.

Gina sat down on the edge of the bed. Miller sat next to her. He decided to make a move—after all it was her suggestion to come up to the room. He wouldn't be committing himself, he thought, he wouldn't be getting involved. Hell, no involvements didn't mean no sex.

He put his glass on the floor and began to stroke her thick dark hair. She touched his broken nose. "It is Roman," she said.

"I got it from a hard right. Maybe the surgeon who repaired it was Italian."

She lay back on the bed with a half-smile he couldn't read, those big sensual eyes staring at him.

"Seduction by vodka," she murmured. "The party'd condemn me for associating with a capitalist journalist. The church'd condemn me for being with a man in his bedroom when we're not married—"

"Forget the party and the church," he said, assuming her teasing was a come-on. He leaned down and kissed her. But it was like kissing a statue, her lips didn't move. *Damn,* he'd misread her again, he'd pushed it too fast. But as he drew back, her hands suddenly gripped his head, and she kissed him hard, her lips open.

Then it all happened very fast. His fingers felt instinctively for the buttons of her woolen dress and she helped him. She was no virgin, and that relieved him. Soon their clothes were scattered on the floor. He was rapidly losing all self-control. He had to have her now, whatever the consequences. He entered her very carefully, and they began to move slowly at first.

"When . . . you're ready," she murmured in his ear, "move out. *Per favore.*"

"*Sì,*" he said, approving her caution.

But when the time came to do it, she held him so he couldn't move out. He struggled, but she wouldn't release him, and then it was too late.

I hope she's into birth control, he thought, a bambino would be the last thing I need. But there was no reason to get worried. Abortion was legal now in Italy. Hell, Miller, he railed silently at himself, the times you pick to get uptight about such things! Just relax and enjoy it. She's a rare find, this funny Roman girl.

"Gina," he murmured, and for a while he forgot about the outside world and its dangers.

14

A young Arab soldier stopped them close to the Sabra district. When Ayad showed him their army passes, the soldier became more friendly and offered Ayad a cup of thick Turkish coffee he was heating in a can in a nearby alleyway. He had a coffeepot and several egg-sized cups in an old shoe box. Ayad thanked him, feeling an Arab brotherhood.

"Wait for coffee until we get there," Judas grunted.

His face was hidden by the sunglasses and the hood of his white, one-piece suit, but the soldier recognized the foreign accent.

"Christian?" he asked Ayad suspiciously.

"European," Ayad replied quickly.

The soldier lost interest.

The dusk-to-dawn curfew certainly kept the streets quiet at night. Even in the Sabra district, crowded with many of the refugees from Palestine, whole blocks were deserted. There had been trouble between the Christians and the Moslems, and the city government wasn't taking any chances. Beirut was equally divided between Christians and Moslems, and an elaborate system for sharing power and living peacefully had been worked out, but it kept breaking down. Playing host to extremist guerilla groups was a constant source of trouble.

They remained silent until they reached the Rue Jeb el-Nakhel. Ayad led him down an alleyway into a small courtyard that was in darkness.

"Be ready for their security," Ayad whispered.

They walked close together, their arms touching.

Suddenly pistols prodded their backs and flashlights were thrust into their faces, blinding them. A harsh male voice asked them in Arabic to identify themselves. Ayad recognized the accent as Syrian. He quickly gave both their names.

"Let the other one speak for himself," the harsh voice commanded.

Ayad wondered if Judas would give his real name now—at gun-point.

"I'm Judas" was all he said. Then, in an angry tone, he added: "Turn that damn light off."

Flashlights and guns were immediately withdrawn.

"Walk on," said the voice.

Sokolov was waiting for them in a quiet upstairs room. Sokolov had wanted the meeting to be held at a Soviet villa outside Beirut, but Judas had insisted on meeting here—at an Al Fatah hideout in the city. Another man was with Sokolov, and Ayad assumed he was the Russian from Rome Judas had mentioned. Ayad wondered if the two Russians had been held up at gunpoint in the courtyard. He liked to see Arabs humiliating Russians.

Judas and the stranger shook hands. If they had been Arabs, Ayad thought, they would have embraced. But Europeans were always so businesslike. Judas introduced the stranger to him as Niki Rostov. "We worked together in Rome," he told Ayad. "The Tolloni job."

"We shouldn't talk so openly," the Russian said. He was a thin, middle-aged man with a pale, indoor complexion and hard eyes. Ayad divided Russians into two types—the shrewd, genial, social kind like Sokolov, and austere, dedicated, humorless ones like this man, Rostov. The Rostovs were much the more dangerous.

"We can talk openly in front of Ayad," Judas said. "We have already done a job together. I trust him completely."

Judas' commendation pleased Ayad, but he understood what Judas was telling the Russian. When two men did a job together involving murder, they had something on each other. They *had* to trust each other. But he and Judas had become closer than that.

"You must take extra precautions now," the Russian said coldly, ignoring Ayad. "Beirut is riddled with Israeli spies and informers. You can't trust any of the Christians. But there is more than that to watch, Judas. Inquiries are being made in Rome. That American journalist talked to Signora Tolloni—"

"She knows nothing."

"She's been in touch with some of her husband's old supporters. She has learned how Bellini tried to oust her husband before the kidnapping. That may make her dig a little deeper and change her attitude—"

"Get rid of her then."

"Too risky at present. Bellini isn't strong enough yet. The last thing he needs is anything that might reopen the Tolloni affair. He's already panicking over what the American Cardinal, Brady, said at the funeral. I hope Bellini doesn't do any damn fool things that will stir up the Vatican. He badly needs a friendly pope for a few months until the whole of Italy is firmly under control. Italians aren't the easiest people to manage . . ."

As the Russian talked about Bellini, Ayad remembered what Judas had told him. *Rostov's future is bound up with Bellini's. Rostov is the golden boy of the secret Soviet KGB since the success of the Tolloni affair, but if the Bellini government fails, he'll go down with it. He'll do anything to prevent . that.* Ayad had remarked that the KGB people he had met talked more like gangsters than diplomats. *All intelligence agents are like that, Ayad,* Judas has told him. *They'd kill their grandmother if they had to. The KGB are less brutal and more sophisticated than they were in Stalin's day, but like the CIA in the sixties and the early seventies, the organization is a law unto itself. Never trust their agents, Ayad, even when you work with them. They'll dispose of you in a flash if the situation changes and your being alive no longer serves Moscow's best interests. Even though I gave Niki Rostov his biggest triumph and got him his promotion, I'm very expendable if it suits him. Never trust the bastards. Ayad . . .*

Rostov told Judas, "Of course a close watch is being kept on Signora Tolloni and the other Tolloni people as well as the American journalist, Miller. If a dangerous situation develops, then something will have to be done. But you, too, must be extra careful yourself now, Judas." Rostov stressed the importance of what he said next with choppy gestures. "Someone must have talked. The Israelis have learned that you intend to do something in Jerusalem before Easter. They will be waiting for you."

Judas abruptly took off his sunglasses and wiped them. He was covering up his concern, Ayad thought.

"It was my mortar man," Judas said at last. "He was the one who talked. He was my one error. I offered him another job—in Jerusalem—before I was sure of him personally. I've never seen anyone with a better sense of timing, a shrewder judgment of distance and wind interference. Someone as good as that is very hard to find. I wanted him professionally so I trusted him personally before I should have—a classic error."

Judas put his sunglasses back on, hiding the glint of concern in his eyes. It wasn't like him to admit errors, especially to the Russians, Ayad told himself. He must be feeling very bad about it.

"Maybe you should cancel your plans or switch to somewhere else," Rostov said, watching Judas very carefully.

"There's only one setting for what I want to do, and that's Jerusalem," Judas said sharply. "It simply means I'll have to be more careful . . . if that's possible. A professional always takes care. What do the Israelis know? That I'm going to carry out an operation in the Holy City sometime between now and Easter. They don't know what or where or when. They don't even know me except for the descriptions they'll have got from people who saw me with Don Paolo. As long as I look different and use another passport, what do they know that'll help them—*nothing!*" Judas had his confidence back; now he wanted to regain his authority over the Russian.

"They will set a trap for you," Rostov said.

"Let them. They won't even know where to set it. I never do the obvious, Rostov. You know that."

"Let us proceed then, Judas. We have an aim—to break up the Arab, Jewish, Christian get-together symbolized by Jerusalem. And we have a target—the glamorous and dangerous Israeli prime minister. Knock him off and the Arabs get blamed, the Jews change from doves into hawks, and the Christians, the Catholics, are scared off from their idea that Jerusalem might be safer than communist Rome. End of get-together."

"But will the Vatican really be scared off simply because an Israeli Prime Minister gets killed?"

Ayad suddenly understood Judas' game. He was maneuvering the Russian into having to persuade him to take the Abraham job.

"Abraham isn't just another Israeli prime minister," Rostov said. "He symbolizes a whole peace movement. What are you getting at, Judas?"

"Ideally what is needed in the Holy City is a religious target. With that, we'd make the maximum impact, get the maximum worldwide publicity. The dramatic symbols would be right for television. That's how TV people think, Rostov, and that's the kind of exposure we need to have the huge effect we want. Do you remember, Rostov, the last big assassination in Jerusalem that got world attention—the shooting of King Abdullah of Jordan in 1951?"

"I remember it well," the Russian said. "At the time, I was a young man on the Middle East desk in Moscow."

"Then you'll understand how much more meaningful it was because it was a religious event. King Abdullah was a religious leader. He traced his descent directly from the prophet Mohammed. When he was killed, he was making his weekly visit to the Dome of the Rock, the great shrine so closely associated with Mohammed. That's the kind of event I would like to stage in Jerusalem. Then we'd have no doubt of its effect on the world. Our plan lacks the ultimate dimension. I realize I will have to settle for Abraham. There are no religious leaders in Jerusalem who are big enough. But perhaps I can choose the right background. I wonder if there's any possibility of getting Abraham at the Wailing Wall before Easter. That setting would be right. I shall have to study his schedule for the next few weeks."

"Don't worry, Judas," Rostov said soothingly. "The assassination of the Israeli Prime Minister will be a *big* event, and I mean BIG! Eli Abraham's another Kennedy to a great many people. Have you and Sokolov discussed terms?"

"Not in detail," Sokolov put in quickly, speaking for the first time. He had been content to stay in the background and listen until then. Rostov was the top man in the Mediterranean area since his Italian success. Sokolov had only had a string of defeats over the past year. Moscow blamed him for the success of Eli Abraham's recent meetings with Arab moderates, and Judas' discovery of the agreement with Pope Alfredo portended an even bigger blow to his prestige. If he didn't reverse the situation soon, he'd be recalled to Moscow. That explained his obsession with getting rid of Eli Abraham.

"How much do you want, Judas?"

"It'll be costly, Rostov. I'll need to recruit a back-up team. Afterward, I'll have to retire for a while and go into hiding. The world network of Israeli agents will be looking for me."

"And that will cost—how much?"

Enjoy the Best
of the World's Bestselling
Frontier Storyteller in...

THE
LOUIS L'AMOUR
COLLECTION

Savor <u>Silver Canyon</u> in this new hardcover collector's edition free for 10 days.

At last, a top-quality, hardcover edition of the best frontier fiction of Louis L'Amour. Beautifully produced books with hand-tooled covers, gold-leaf stamping, and double-sewn bindings.

Reading and rereading these books will give you hours of satisfaction. These are works of lasting pleasure. Books you'll be proud to pass on to your children.

MEMO FROM LOUIS L'AMOUR

Dear Reader:

Over the years, many people have asked me when a first-rate hardcover collection of my books would become available. Now the people at Bantam Books have made that hope a reality. They've put together a collection of which I am very proud. Fine bindings, handsome design, and a price which I'm pleased to say makes these books an affordable addition to almost everyone's permanent library.

Bantam Books has so much faith in this series that they're making what seems to me is an extraordinary offer. They'll send you <u>Silver Canyon</u>, on a 10-day, free examination basis. Plus they'll send you a free copy of my new Calendar.

Even if you decide for any reason whatever to return <u>Silver Canyon</u>, you may keep the Calendar free of charge and without obligation. Personally, I think you'll be delighted with <u>Silver Canyon</u> and the other volumes in this series.

Sincerely,

Louis L'Amour

Louis L'Amour

P.S. They tell me supplies of the Calendar are limited, so you should order now.

Take Advantage Today of This No-Risk, No-Obligation Offer

You'll enjoy these features:

- An heirloom-quality edition

- An affordable price

- Gripping stories of action and adventure

- A $6.95 calendar yours free while supplies last just for examining <u>Silver Canyon</u>

- No minimum purchase; no obligation to purchase even one volume.

Pre-Publication Reservation

( ) YES! Please send me the new collector's edition of <u>Silver Canyon</u> for a 10-day free examination upon publication, along with my free Louis L'Amour Calendar, and enter my subscription to <u>The Louis L'Amour Collection</u>. If I decide to keep <u>Silver Canyon</u>, I will pay $7.95 plus shipping and handling. I will then receive additional volumes in the Collection at the rate of one volume per month on a fully return-able, 10-day, free-examination basis. There is no minimum number of books I must buy, and I may cancel my subscription at any time.

05066

If I decide to return <u>Silver Canyon</u>, I will return the book within 10 days, my subscription to <u>The Louis L'Amour Collection</u> will expire, and I will have no additional obliga-tion. The Calendar is mine to keep in any case.

( ) **I would prefer the deluxe edition, bound in genuine leather, to be billed at only $24.95 plus shipping and handling.**

05074

Name_____

Address_____

City_____ State _____ Zip _____

This offer is good for a limited time only. Supplies of calendar are limited.

E 01

Detach and Mail Today.

NO POSTAGE
NECESSARY
IF MAILED
IN THE
UNITED STATES

BUSINESS REPLY MAIL
FIRST CLASS   PERMIT NO. **2154**   HICKSVILLE, N.Y.

POSTAGE WILL BE PAID BY

THE LOUIS L'AMOUR COLLECTION
BANTAM BOOKS
P.O. BOX 956
HICKSVILLE, NEW YORK 11801

Judas looked at Rostov and then at Sokolov. "Half a million plus expenses."

"Is that in lire?" Rostov asked quickly.

Judas shook his head.

"Lebanese pounds?"

"No, Rostov, American dollars. Don't look so shocked. The Middle East is cheap at the price . . ."

15

"Extra Omnes!"

Everybody out!

The shout of the Swiss Guards echoed through the two hundred high-ceilinged rooms and tapestried corridors of the Papal Palace.

It was the formal dismissal of everyone not allowed in the Conclave.

The election of the 266th Pope was about to begin.

For the last time, two electronics specialists swept every Renaissance nook and cranny of the canyon-shaped Sistine Chapel for recording and bugging devices. They covered every inch of the Michelangelo frescoes, ceiling and walls, but found nothing. A Bible was then laid out ready for the cardinals to swear not to disclose the secrets of the Conclave. The punishment for doing so was excommunication from the church.

Dressed in scarlet robes over white surplices, with red birettas on their heads, the cardinals began to enter the Sistine Chapel two by two in order of seniority—123 men of varying races, nationalities and ages, ranging from Bracca of Turin, aged seventy-nine, to Brady of New York, aged forty-nine. They were accompanied by a small army of confessors, doctors, cooks, pharmacists, barbers and other maintenance men, in case the Conclave lasted a long time. Usually it was over quickly, in a day or two, but a few in the distant past had dragged on for weeks. The first ballot was generally a formality with votes for friends, heroes and favorite sons, and then the voting got down to business, concentrating on the

top candidates representing the main influential groups. But
sometimes a compromise candidate or an unexpected dark
horse no one had thought of gathered strength in the later
ballots. It had been that way with some of the most beloved
popes, such as John XXIII and Alfredo I.

Selecting a pope was an onerous task, but these princes of
the church were used to great responsibilities. They were
grim because they had just heard Cardinal Garonne's chilling
news. He had told them what he had learned from the Israeli
Prime Minister. Then he had read to them a report of a speech
made the night before at Togliatti Stadium by Prime Minister
Bellini before a huge audience of the party faithful. It was
Bellini's answer to the vast Catholic show of strength at the
funeral. Bellini had made a very aggressive reference to the
Vatican, telling his enthusiastic audience that it was time to
negotiate a new treaty restricting the Vatican state's power
"much more." With his prominent chin thrust out, Bellini
roared: "They better choose a pope who talks our language."
The party faithful rocked with laughter, interpreting his
remark as a crack that the Conclave should elect both an
Italian and a procommunist.

"You must ask yourselves," the tall, grey-haired Cardinal
Garonne had told his fellow cardinals, "which among you has
the character to resist this new paganism of state that
threatens the church so openly. You must search your hearts
to discover which of your noble fellowship has the toughness
of mind and spirit, and is best fitted by experience, knowledge
and God's grace, to bring the church—and our civilization—
through the very perilous times ahead."

This was chilling enough, but even more so to the assembled cardinals was the change in Cardinal Garonne. As
Secretary of State, he had been known as a conservative
compromiser who believed the church had to make concessions to coexist with the communist nations. Live and let live,
and everything would be all right had been his attitude.
Normally a genial, smiling man, he was grave-faced now and
spoke like a messenger of doom.

So the cardinals assembled—chilled, frightened, grim—to
make their choice. Never had a conclave seemed so fateful,
so important to the future of the church and of the world.
Cardinal Bierek of Czechoslovakia remarked that it reminded
him of the fourteenth century when the Vatican had been
driven into exile in Avignon. Nobody disagreed with him.

The next year—the next few months—would be vital.
Who was the right choice for this crucial time?
Who?
The question weighed heavily on them all as the meticulous medieval rite of sealing off the Conclave was carried out. With lighted torches, a committee of three cardinals led by the Camerlengo searched the Sistine Chapel for the presence of unauthorized persons. None was found. Then the heavy bronze doors at the foot of the Pius IX stairway were closed and locked on both sides—three locks were turned on the outside by Vatican officials, and the key was placed in an embroidered purse to be guarded by the marshal of the Conclave. Then on the inside, in the presence of two senior Cardinals, Varga of Spain and Broch of Germany, the Camerlengo turned the key controlling the three inner locks.

The outside world was shut out.

The election could begin.

But the question still remained.

Who should be the next Pope?

Outside, in the Piazza San Pietro, a crowd of Romans and foreign visitors gathered to watch the tall, narrow steel stack above the roof of the Sistine Chapel. The stack was connected to a gray cast-iron stove that stood in a corner of the chapel. After each round of voting, ballots were to be burned in the stove mixed with a chemical stick that produced black or white smoke. Black smoke curling into the sky meant no decision, white smoke indicated that a pope had been elected.

Robert Miller stood on the far side of the piazza facing the Papal Palace with Mario Lepecci and a group of other journalists, including several writers for Catholic newspapers in Italy and France. The Catholic journalists were the experts on the ritual, historical background, and the inside gossip.

A temporary media headquarters for over five hundred journalists and TV and radio teams from six continents had been opened in a Vatican-owned office building only a few hundred yards away. Draped in the Vatican's white and yellow colors, it had fifty telephones and a continual supply of espressos and tall beers. But most of the journalists preferred to gossip together in the piazza, watching the stack with the crowd.

Although the deliberations of the cardinals even before the formal start of the Conclave were supposed to be private, some of the journalists talked as if they knew exactly what had gone on. An ex-Jesuit priest who was writing for a French magazine said the two favorites were Garonne and Bierek—Garonne because he was an Italian, a skilled diplomat used to dealing with the Communists, and was backed by the Vatican's powerful Curia bureaucracy; and Bierek because he was non-Italian, had experience in dealing with the Communists in Czechoslovakia, and was a liberal committed to social justice. Garonne, according to the ex-Jesuit, was the choice of the Italians and the conservative bloc; Bierek was the favorite of the liberal bloc and the Third World cardinals, who didn't want an Italian and favored a champion of social justice to attract the poor. The ex-Jesuit expected Garonne to be elected after two or three ballots.

The knowing gossip of the other journalists more or less agreed, though a few other names were mentioned as compromise choices if a long deadlock developed between the supporters of Garonne and Bierek—Van Dek of Holland, Ramirez of Argentina, Abu of Tanzania. Mario Lepecci said a reliable source inside the Vatican had also mentioned the possibility of Bracca of Turin. "He comes from a communist-run city—Turin—and his age—seventy-nine—means he wouldn't be with us for long. That's one reason the Conclave's not in favor of anyone in their early fifties—they'd be pope for *too* long. If the conclave elected someone who was only in his early fifties now, he could be pope well into the next century! The Vatican stagnates under a long Pontificate. That of Pius XII was a good example. It lasted almost twenty years, and a lot of problems went unsolved until Pope John replaced him."

As he spoke, smoke was starting to curl upwards, but at first its color wasn't clear against the cloudy sky. The growing crowd in the Piazza waited expectantly.

"It's black," said Lepecci, peering through a small pair of binoculars. The crowd groaned with disappointment. "That's to be expected. The first ballot gets rid of all the tributes. Next time will be more indicative of how the conclave's going. If any candidate has a big majority, he could be elected next time."

But next time the smoke was still black.

And the next time.

The ex-Jesuit was sure the Conclave was deadlocked over Garonne and Bierek—the conservatives and the liberals, those who wanted an Italian and those who didn't. "Some of the Third World cardinals," he said in his slight French accent, "are convinced the time calls for a non-Italian again. They think this is an important gesture of independence at this time. A non-Italian pope asserts the universality of the church, and he'd be stronger in dealing with the Italian government than an Italian would be. It looks like Bierek, but it may take him some time to get enough votes. If Garonne was going to be elected, he would have got it early. But the Italians won't give up so easily. It'll seem like a revolution to the older ones if there is another non-Italian."

After two days of black smoke, there was a day's break for prayer and meditation—"and lobbying," said Lepecci.

But the day's break had no discernible effect.

Two more days of black smoke followed.

"There must be a very big disagreement," Lepecci said. "Usually they're keen to make a reasonably quick choice so it will seem as unanimous as possible. Some of the cardinals wanted an especially fast Conclave this time to show the Communists there was a very united front, that the new pope had the strongest possible backing. The disagreement must go very deep."

Maybe Brady has told his fellow cardinals what he knows, Miller thought, and they realized how scary the situation is. Maybe they all know what is behind Don Paolo's murder . . .

Two more days of black smoke.

The crowd grew bigger in the Piazza San Pietro as the tension mounted. Hour after hour, thousands of eyes concentrated on the shuttered windows of the Sistine Chapel as if trying to follow the drama that was going on inside. Then there would be sudden cries of excitement as the tall, grey stack began to belch smoke again, only to change into a roar of disappointment when the smoke once more turned black.

It was going to be a long Conclave . . .

The phone rang in the middle of their lovemaking. They ignored it. They had reached a stage when they were totally into each other, hardly aware even of the hotel room. But the phone's harsh ringing went on and on, insisting on an answer.

"It *must* be urgent," Miller murmured at last.

"They'll call back," Gina whispered, holding him so he couldn't move.

The phone rang on and on.

"Maybe it's New York," Miller said. "I better answer it."

Gina gave an exasperated cry as he moved away from her and reached for the phone. She turned her back on him. He remembered going through the same kind of scene with Eve. Women didn't understand how a journalist felt about the phone. Many big stories started with a phone call, and not answering might mean missing something important.

"Signor Miller?"

It was a woman's voice, one he didn't recognize.

"Yes, this is Robert Miller." He felt Gina move away from him. She must be really angry.

"Thank God. I am Signora Tolloni." Miller immediately sat up in bed, much more alert. "I'm sorry for my rudeness. I was wrong, Signor Miller. You told me if I ever wanted to talk again, to call you." Her voice was low and urgent. "I want to talk *now*—tonight. Can you come out to the villa to see me now? It won't wait until tomorrow. I have something I must tell you. You were right, Signor Miller. I know that now. There are things I want to tell you that I have found out. My husband's death must be revenged. Can you come now . . . to the villa? That will be more private—safer. The new people don't move in until next week. No one is there now. My apartment in the city is watched. Can you come to the villa *now? . . .*"

It was late, but he had to go.

"Very well. I'll leave immediately."

"Please . . . hurry. I'll be waiting for you."

The phone went dead.

"You're leaving me?" Gina said, sitting up.

"I've got to, Gina. That was Signora Tolloni, Alberto Tolloni's widow. She wants to see me."

"At this time of night?"

"She said it's urgent." Miller was more worried than he wanted Gina to know. Mama Tolloni had sounded under great pressure. Maybe even *scared*. Her voice was so low it was hard to tell. But something big had obviously happened to change her mind. Or was it a trap? "Look, Gina, she seemed in distress. I don't know what it's about. But powerful forces could be involved." This wasn't the time to tell her any more. "If you haven't heard from me by, say, dawn at the latest, call . . ." He thought of what Brady had said about getting in touch with him if he needed help, but the Cardinal was shut up in the endless Conclave. "Call Hammond, the paper's Rome bureau chief." They didn't like each other, but Hammond would help out in an emergency. "Here"—he scribbled on a pad by the side of the telephone—"this is his home number."

"What are you afraid of?" Gina's eyes were wide with concern, and she pressed against him.

"Don't look so worried, Gina. It's just a precaution."

"Why does Signora Tolloni want to see you so late?"

"I'll tell you when I get back." He felt like a heel, leaving her so abruptly. "Gina, I'm sorry. It won't be for long." He tried to take the .44 out of his bag without her noticing, but he wasn't quick enough.

"Roberto, you *are* expecting trouble."

"It's part of my job, Gina, to take risks."

Miller ran his fingers through his unruly reddish hair in exasperation. Damn, he thought, why am I explaining myself to this girl? Suddenly the old traps seemed to be closing in on him again. And the old feelings of resentment—the same feelings he had harbored silently against Eve—were welling up. I *like* my independence, Miller thought, I like being free—no wife, no family, no responsibility. No one to account to, living on the edge, the danger, the private satisfactions. Do I have to lose all this just because I'm sleeping with Gina? My life—my death—are my own affair. What's it to her anyway?

Yet all at once Miller found himself feeling very vulnerable.

As if sensing his feelings, Gina put her arms around his neck. "Roberto, you *must* be careful—for my sake."

Suddenly his resentment vanished. Maybe, just maybe, Miller was thinking, this feels *more* right.

"Wait for me," he said softly.

He left her sitting on the edge of the bed, looking very pretty—and very anxious. The thought that she would be there when he returned reassured him as he went out into the dark Rome night to face . . . he didn't know what.

He still had the rented Maserati, and he shot down the Autostrada wondering about Signora Tolloni's strange phone call. *What did she want to tell him?* The anxiety was beginning to get to him as he turned off at Valmontane. A few cars whizzed by—peaceful-looking couples returning home from a film or the theatre or a late dinner. Even at this perilous time in Italy's history, ordinary family life went on.

The route was familiar even in the dark. He knew immediately when he was approaching the scene of the kidnapping, even though there was no sign now of what had happened. The gap in the hedgerow had been filled in. But it was eerie in the moonlight because it looked so lonely and deserted. *Had Mama Tolloni learned the truth of what had happened here and was that why she sounded scared?* What had she said? "My husband's death must be revenged."

The large white villa was no longer for sale. A large SOLD sticker had been slapped across the real estate agent's printed notice at the gate. But the new owners couldn't have moved in yet or Mama Tolloni wouldn't have arranged to meet him here . . . unless it was a trap. He touched the .44 in his pocket for comfort as the Maserati sped up the wide, graveled drive. The lawn had been trimmed since his last visit, but the windows were still without curtains. The moonlight was reflected in the black glass, making the white walls of the villa seem to glow ghostlike in the night. There were no lights on in the villa. It was all in heavy, ominous darkness, the interior one immense shadow. The only sign that someone might be there was a black Alfa Romeo parked in the courtyard under the canopy of eucalyptus trees. The doors were locked; he couldn't see inside. Maybe the car was hers.

Miller's shoes crunched on the gravel as he walked over to the villa. His fingers felt for the bell, and the heavy oak front door slowly wheezed open. He took out his small pencil-shaped flashlight and looked for a light switch, but couldn't find one. Probably the electricity had been cut off. The flashlight's narrow beam revealed the bare hallway. The stacked furniture was gone. The hall was empty. He walked slowly, carefully, down the hallway to the small back room where he had talked to her before. Maybe she was waiting for him there. His small flashlight explored ahead of him. It made only a narrow pathway of light in the darkness. It crossed the open doorway and streaked up a blank wall where the empty bookshelves had been. The boxes of books were gone. So, too, were the armchairs under dustcovers. The room seemed to be empty except for something on the floor under the heavy, stained-glass windows that let in only a faint glow of moonlight. Miller moved the narrow beam of light across the floor . . . and suddenly a face showed in the darkness.

A face as white as the walls of the villa outside.

He shone the narrow beam down on it.

The face of Mama Tolloni stared up at him.

"Good God!" he murmured aloud.

For a moment he thought she was still alive. The flashlight played tricks with her eyes. When Miller knelt beside her, he noticed the neat bullet wound at the back of her head—she had been shot exactly the same way as her husband. He searched for the exit wound and found it toward the front of her scalp where her grey hair was matted and stained a darker color—blood-red. Death had caught her worn, lined face in an expression of great terror. She was wearing her topcoat, which suggested she had been surprised soon after entering the dark, empty villa. He had arrived too late to hear what she had to tell him. She had been silenced forever. He felt almost as if he had had some responsibility for her death . . . as if he had helped to cause it . . .

There was a sound of footsteps rushing across the floor above.

Immediately he tensed, listening, hardly daring to breathe, his hand on his gun.

There was a heavy silence, and then he thought he heard voices in the garden outside.

He felt cornered.

His fear of a trap returned. Whoever had killed Mama Tolloni might be waiting now to get him.

The only sound was his breathing—quick nervous panting in the darkness.

He switched off his flashlight and moved on tiptoe across the room and into the hallway. It was hard to move silently on the bare floorboards. Someone listening intently would be able to follow his progress. The hall was even darker than the room. He felt his way along the wall, holding a hand out in front of him, the fingers rigid, ready to strike.

Suddenly he touched someone's jacket, and immediately he struck out and felt his jabbing fingers cut into a man's face. There was a cry of pain and angry cursing in Italian.

And then he was running for the front door, .44 in hand, his feet sounding like explosions down the bare hallway, not caring who heard him in his eagerness to escape.

He made the front door and then was running out into the garden, aware that he made an easy target in the moonlight.

He expected to be shot in the back at any moment, but nothing happened.

"This way," a voice called from the courtyard. As he hesitated, suspecting a trap, Lieutenant Kahn, gun in hand, appeared in the moonlight. He was dressed in an old, faded leather jacket with a bulge marking his shoulder holster.

"I'll hold them," he told Miller. "Get your car started."

No one had come out of the villa yet. But as Miller ran for his car, he heard a series of shots, very close together. Was it the Israeli lieutenant—or someone shooting at him? He kept as low as he could, running through the darkness.

As the Maserati roared to life, sounding impossibly loud in the stillness, he stared at the villa, but couldn't see anything— or anybody. He waited anxiously for the Lieutenant to come. Perhaps he'd been hit. Miller wondered how long he should wait.

There were more shots.

Then he saw a shadowy figure racing through the court-yard toward him.

It was Kahn.

He opened the door for him.

"Wait," the Lieutenant shouted, and he turned back and shot out the front tires of the Alfa Romeo on the far side of the courtyard. "We don't want anyone following us." he said, out of breath, as he got in the Maserati. "All right, Miller, drive like hell!"

Two men waving guns were running across the courtyard. The Maserati roared away from them down the wide drive-way and out onto the narrow country road. They were halfway to Rome before Lieutenant Kahn relaxed.

"We're probably safe now," he said, looking back along the deserted road. "They won't try to intercept us now. Too much publicity."

"You saved my life," said Miller.

Kahn shrugged. "You were supposed to go the way of Mama Tolloni in the darkness, and then the two murders would be blamed on the Christian Democrats. Scaglia had it all set up back there. My arrival threw them off. They didn't know who I was. Scaglia got rattled—it spoiled his little trap for you."

Kahn looked back again, but nobody was following them. He put his gun in his lap. "We were watching Signora Tolloni for days. She was ready to talk. Who would have thought they'd take such crude action? Of course if you've got the government on your side, you can get away with it. But we should have been able to do something. She would have made a valuable witness."

By the time they reached the outskirts of Rome, Miller felt drained. He had gone through what a soldier or a cop was trained for, not a journalist. Feeling safer in the city streets, he thought of Gina and pulled up at the first public phone.

"I've got to call my hotel," he said apologetically.

Gina answered at once, as if she'd been sitting beside the phone, waiting for it to ring.

"Thank God," she said, and her voice trembled. "Are you all right, Roberto?"

"I'm on my way," he said. He had almost said *home*.

He hurried back to the Maserati, eager to get to the hotel.

Lieutenant Kahn was no longer in the car.

The Israeli had vanished as easily as he'd appeared.

Miller's grim experience affected his attitude toward the Conclave when he returned to the Piazza San Pietro next day. He no longer shared the other journalists' impatience with the long, drawn-out election. He had much more sympathy for the cardinals arguing and agonizing over their decision in the Sistine Chapel. The important thing was not how long they took but whom they chose. Let them take weeks, as long as they chose the right one and not someone Bellini could scare. The new pope would have to be a great spiritual leader, capable of inspiring millions, but he would also have to be a bulwark against the Bellini forces, who had become as ruthless as Judas.

Was Garonne strong enough for that?

Was Bierek?

Was Bracca?

Did the cardinals doubt the strength of the leading candidates? Was that why they were so undecided?

Large, expectant crowds still gathered in the vast Piazza and roared with disappointment when the smoke curled up into the sky and turned black yet again.

Rumors circulating through Rome claimed the cardinals were still so divided that they had decided to settle for a simple majority rather than the usual two-thirds plus one. The rules allowed them to do this when the Conclave dragged on and showed no sign of reaching a decision. But what truth could there be in the rumors when the Conclave was sealed off from everybody?

Or was there an informer in the Conclave getting information out?

The Conclave began its fourth week with still more black smoke...

16

Mama Tolloni's funeral was almost as big as her husband's. Unlike Papa Tolloni, she had never totally given up the church; she occasionally went to mass even when he was alive, and her will called for a Catholic burial. But to accommodate all her old friends in the party and to prevent trouble, a nonreligious funeral service was first held in the Alberto Tolloni Workers' Auditorium. It was packed.

Prime Minister Bellini and members of his cabinet attended. Robert Miller saw Bellini take an aisle seat near the front and sit solemn-faced with his arms folded, his prominent jaw thrust out. Guards wearing black suits like uniforms sat in front and behind. Sandro Bellini was taking no chances. Row after row of the party faithful made the service look like a party rally. Old Communist friends from the early days in Sicily who had come to Papa Tolloni's funeral had returned for this one. Most of Mama Tolloni's Catholic friends stayed away, planning to go to the burial service. Some of the Italian cardinals would have been there but for the Conclave. At least the absence of a strong Catholic presence prevented any clash similar to the one at Pope Alfredo's funeral.

All eyes watched sympathetically as the Tollonis' eighteen-year-old daughter, Carmela, her face hidden by a black veil, walked up the aisle behind the coffin, followed by a long line of Tolloni relatives in black. As Carmela Tolloni took her seat in the front row, her short, powerful figure reminded people of her father—reminded them, too, with a sense of outrage, that this was the second funeral in the Tolloni family. Carmela Tolloni had now lost both her parents—both *murdered*. It was enough to shatter anybody. She was studying to be an opera singer in Milan, and after the party eulogies, she tried to sing extracts from her mother's favorite Verdi operas, but she broke down in the middle, tears streaming down her face. A murmur of sympathy sounded through the whole auditorium as Carmela was slowly led back to her seat.

Miller saw Gina and her father sitting near the front. Gina hadn't told him she would be there. He waited for them to come out at the end. Gina blushed when she saw him. She whispered to her father and then came over to him.

"Why didn't you tell me you were coming?" Miller demanded.

"I never thought about it." She was obviously lying.

"Introduce me to your father."

"Not now, Roberto. Some other time. He's too upset."

"I want to talk to him."

"Not here."

He was annoyed with her and, impulsively, he pushed forward through the crowd of mourners still coming out of the auditorium. The government party was just leaving in a line of black Fiat limousines. Bellini, grim-faced, went first with his bodyguards.

"Mr. Altieri."

The grey-haired, pudgy little man turned round, startled. He was ashen-faced, as if still suffering from the great shock of Mama Tolloni's murder.

"My name's Miller. I'm a correspondent for the *New York Mirror*—"

Vito Altieri put up his hands as if to push Miller away. "No, no, I have nothing to say," and he began to elbow his way through the crowd toward the cars.

"Roberto!" Gina cried angrily. "Why did you frighten my father?"

"I only introduced myself."

"Can't you see he's very shocked by the murder?"

"But I must talk to him, Gina. It could be very important."

"He's in no state to talk to anybody. He thinks whoever killed Signora Tolloni may attempt to kill him."

"He may be right. That's why I want to talk to him."

Vito Altieri, looking very nervous, had joined a tall, imposing-looking man with a grey beard.

"Who's that with your father?"

"That's Professor Valeri." Gina's tone was respectful.

So that was the Professor Luigi Valeri Hammond had mentioned. Robert stared at the strong, well-chiseled face and the sharp eyes. It was possible hope lay there . . .

A black Fiat limousine drew up to Vito Altieri. He said goodbye to Professor Valeri and gestured to Gina to join him.

"We can talk tonight," Robert told her.

"No," she said. "I won't be able to see you tonight. I'll be with my father. He *needs* me now."

She left him quickly, and Miller watched her join her father and get in the black limousine. She had acted almost like a stranger, almost as if it were dangerous to acknowledge that she knew him.

And perhaps she was right.

He'd been careless.

For watching on the edge of the crowd was Inspector Scaglia. As the black limousine drove away in the direction of the Quirinale Palace, the Inspector's hard eyes followed it until it disappeared.

Vito Altieri had reason to be afraid.

The twenty-sixth day of the Conclave began like all the others—with black smoke curling up into the sky over Rome.

Few journalists bothered to show up now, and the crowd was much smaller. People were getting tired of waiting. They could watch the result on television or hear it on the radio— when there was a result. An Italian cartoonist pictured the cardinals emerging in a year's time with long grey beards. Yet it didn't satisfy true Romans to sit at home before a television set or a radio. It hurt their sense of occasion. They wanted the feeling of being there when the new pope made his first appearance. So people drifted in and out of the Piazza San Pietro, trying to be patient.

The only reason Miller showed up that day was to meet Gina. A typical Roman, she had suggested meeting there so she could also be with the crowd. They had met only once since Mama Tolloni's funeral. Miller had introduced her to Mario Lepecci over cocktails. Lepecci had been charming but distant, and Miller had realized Lepecci was still hoping he and Eve would get back together again. "He thinks I'm leading you astray," Gina said. Since then, they'd only talked a few times on the phone. Miller had been surprised how much he'd missed her. He found himself sitting in the hotel bar at night to avoid the loneliness of his room without her.

He was anxious to know if their separation was having the same effect on her, and he examined her face tenderly for any clues as to how she felt. She looked pale, he thought—pale and worried.

"Papa's in a bad way," she told him. "He's *really* scared now. He won't go to the Palace, he doesn't even want to see anybody. He's sure whoever killed Signora Tolloni will try to get him. He's suspicious of everybody. He's not even sure of his own wife. She's been given a job in the government in the Ministry of Education. She used his position at the Palace to further her own career. Now he suspects her of informing on him. He overheard her talking to someone—giving them an account of his movements. She's a career bitch. Such people are capable of anything. I could never stand her."

"Gina, I must talk to him before anything else bad happens—"

"Look, Roberto!"

With a squeal of excitement, Gina pointed across the Piazza. Smoke was beginning to appear again from the tall, grey stack above the Sistine Chapel.

Miller didn't bother to look.

"Gina, if you'd watch as many of those smoke signals as I have—"

"Roberto, look—I think it's white! *Bella bianca!*"

Then he looked.

At first it was difficult to be sure. The smoke seemed to be a grey color—it could have been turning black again. But then a stronger cloud billowed out of the tall stack, and the smoke lightened steadily until it was white beyond any doubt.

A great roar of delight went up from the crowd in the piazza.

A new pope had been elected!

"Oh, Roberto, we're here to see him make his first appearance!" Gina threw her arms around Miller's neck and kissed him.

It was as if a long-awaited signal had flashed through the whole city. Romans began to pour into the Piazza from all directions. Every street west of the Tiber was soon overrun with people ignoring traffic lights as they headed for the Vatican. A monumental traffic jam ensued. Drivers abandoned their cars and joined the crowd streaming across the broad stretch of the Via della Conciliazione. Everyone was anxious to get there in time to see him appear. Whoever he was. The long delay had generated a tremendous excitement. This was undoubtedly a historic moment, a moment to tell children and grandchildren about. *I was there to see him at his first appearance . . .*

But who was he?

The whole city, the whole country, the whole world waited to learn who had been elected after such a long time.

Who?

Gina and Robert had a bet of 10,000 lire.

"It sounds like a fortune in lire, but it's only about ten dollars," Robert said, grinning at her excited face.

Gina bet on Bracca of Turin. The Roman in her wanted if not a Roman, then at least an Italian. She was positive they wouldn't elect another non-Italian.

Miller chose Bierek. He was equally positive the pressure of the time would lead to a radical choice. The long conclave seemed to prove it . . .

They didn't have to wait long.

By then, the huge Piazza was packed. It was a greater turnout than even for Pope Alfredo's funeral, and this was a happy, festive occasion. Priests were cheerfully praying aloud; nuns were singing hymns of thanksgiving; families were holding hands and staring up at where a floodlight picked the central balcony of St. Peter's Basilica out of the darkening stone. It was almost dusk. Windows in the palace that had been closed and covered over were now opening onto the piazza. There was a flurry of movement behind the large windows in the Hall of Benedictions. A portable radio in the crowd near the ancient Egyptian obelisk reported that the doors of the Sistine Chapel had been unlocked. The Conclave had been unsealed! A troop of the Swiss Guards in full ceremonial uniforms had entered the Sistine Chapel to pay tribute to the church's new leader as soon as he was proclaimed. There was a great feeling of celebration. The Eternal City was about to greet the new pope! For this day he was *their* pope—he belonged to Rome. After that, he belonged to the world.

A group of nuns on the steps of St. Peter's began to sing in Latin, "Christ triumphs, Christ reigns."

The triple-barred golden papal cross was carried out to the illuminated balcony, now filling with monsignors and canons who were careful to leave an open space in the center.

Just over an hour after the first wisp of white smoke was

seen, in an electric hush heightened by the hugely amplified
whisperings of the microphones, seventy-four-year-old Cardinal Nicola Parone of Genoa, senior Cardinal Deacon, suddenly appeared at the stone railing overlooking the piazza
and the crowd. He cleared his throat, and it sounded like a
cannon firing over the microphones. He was a small man,
barely visible above the stone railing, but the vast crowd fell
instantly silent. Speaking in Latin, in a voice so charged with
emotion that it broke in the midst of the historic pronounce-
ment, he cried, *"Annuntio vobis gaudium magnum. Habemus
Papam!*—I announce to you a great joy. We have a pope!"

There were cheers and hand-clapping, but the response was
polite, almost automatic, as people waited to learn the name.

A huge tapestry was unfurled over the edge of the balcony.
It was the coat of arms of Alfredo I, a dove bearing an olive
branch. Windows were now thrown open on either side of the
balcony, and groups of cardinals, looking weary having just
come from the Sistine Chapel, were standing and watching,
too. The only difference was that they already knew who had
been elected.

The vast crowd grew increasingly quiet as it waited patiently to learn who was the new pope—who was the new
Vicar of Jesus Christ, Successor of St. Peter, Supreme Pontiff
of the Universal Church with over 700 million members,
Patriarch of the West . . . the new Holy Father.

Cardinal Parone cleared his throat again. "He is . . ."

The old Cardinal's voice failed him in the wave of excitement that swept over the vast crowd below.

"He is . . . the Most Eminent and Most Reverend Lord
. . . Cardinal . . . David . . . BRADY . . ."

"Good God!" said Miller.

" . . . who has taken the name of David the First."

For a moment, the crowd seemed to be shocked . into
silence, stunned by the extraordinary, tradition-breaking
choice. It was clearly totally unexpected.

One moment there was silence; the next moment, a thun-
derous roar broke loose from the thousands below and swept
up to the balcony with almost volcanic force.

"Brady . . . Brady . . . BRAD-Y . . . *Il Papa* . . ."

It went on and on and on. The monsignors and canons on
the balcony shuffled uncomfortably among themselves, then
fell back. There were cries throughout the Piazza of "Is he
coming? . . . Do you see him yet?"

Almost unexpectedly he was there, a slight, intense figure in white. He was unsmiling, looking almost embarrassed. Other popes had been borne to the balcony on portable thrones amid the full splendor of the Vatican court. He came alone and on foot, and he stood there so still and unassuming that seconds passed before most of those below were aware of his presence.

Then a tremendous shout arose.

"Viva il Papa!" people cried out, and the cry was taken up and directed in a joyous, roaring wave up to the lighted balcony and the solitary figure. The whole Piazza seemed to fill with shouts and applause that rose up in successive waves, and people held up their hats or scarves or handkerchiefs, so that from the balcony it looked as if a great army of the faithful was showing flags of allegiance and demonstrating their approval of this *Papa Americano*—this American Pope.

He came then to the edge of the balcony and smiled with unmistakable pleasure as he raised both arms in greeting and benediction. To those below, he seemed a tiny, almost defenseless figure in white, but when someone whispered to him, suggesting what he should do, the microphones caught a vigorous, resonant voice. "I know, I know," he said briskly, and began to intone the traditional *Urbi et Orbi* blessing—to the city and the world.

But he realized that his first public appearance as the *Papa Americano* called for something more. He stepped forward and, gripping the balustrade, arms outstretched, he made a brief speech in Italian.

"I speak to you in your—*our*—Italian language," he said in a quiet but firm tone. "If I make a mistake, correct me." There was a roar of appreciation from the crowd below. His lightly-accented Italian was so polished that his remark was more a gesture than an apology. "You will forgive me if I do not feel like *un papa americano.*" The huge crowd laughed. "In fact," he added with a smile, "I do not even feel like *un papa straniero*—a foreign pope." The huge crowd liked that. "I was born in Ireland, I became an American citizen, but as your Pope, I know no boundaries." The crowd roared its agreement.

As he raised his arms again, thousands crossed themselves and dropped to their knees, and mothers held up their babies to receive a blessing from the new Pope—David I.

17

The bells of St. Peter's Basilica and the five hundred other Catholic churches in the Eternal City rang out all evening. A big crowd remained in the Piazza San Pietro, even though there was a light shower of rain. After repeated cries for "Il Papa," David went out onto the balcony again. A portly Monsignor was seen to offer him the protection of a large black umbrella, but he waved it aside as if to say he would share the rain with the faithful below. This gesture was much appreciated as the rain began to darken his white cassock. Wave after wave of applause came up from the piazza as he blessed the crowd again in a strangely intimate ceremony.

Then, suddenly, the shower was over. He gestured happily up at the sky and waved with a wide, yet almost shy smile. He wasn't taking for granted his relationship with the Romans. When he went back inside, the applause was so insistent that he had to come out again. The cardinals, crowded together on the loggias flanking the central balcony, smiled with relief at the response of the crowd. Some of them had worried about how the Romans would react, but they were left in no doubt all that evening. David I was recalled yet again. He lifted his hands slowly in the traditional papal gesture and smiled, this time more radiantly, less shyly.

"He's a *very* popular choice," Gina cried above the cheers, staring round at the smiling, happy faces.

"He's the right man at the right time," Miller said. Brady as pope brought real hope.

Behind them, a television reporter with a small microphone in his hand could be heard sending over his story: *Pope David is the first American to be elected pope. He is the first pope of the New World. The Irish will also claim him because he was born there. He is only the second non-Italian to be elected in over four centuries. The other was John Paul II in 1978. Before him, the last pope selected from beyond the Alps was the hapless Hollander, Adrian VI, who served twenty months in 1522–23 while Martin Luther's rebellion*

137

raged. Pope David is the youngest pope elected this century . . .

Not only in this century, Miller thought. The youngest for many centuries. Brady's age was as much against him as his nationality. That was why the Conclave lasted so long. As far as he could find out from Vatican sources close to those old cardinals who talked too much now it was all over, the Third World cardinals had started the Brady movement. They entered his name on the very first ballot. There was a general feeling among them that Brady had both the physical and spiritual strength needed in the crisis of the present. They were convinced the man had a strange, rare ability to make people listen, whether in his own country or in the rest of the world. They had found a visit from him not only created an unusual excitement among people in African and Asian countries, but left a lasting effect. Other cardinals obviously felt the same way, for Brady collected more votes in the next few ballots, although he remained far from the two-thirds-plus-one that was needed. A large group, led by the Italians, was firmly against him—and the radical change he represented. After an unbreakable deadlock lasting for two weeks, it was decided a simple majority would have to be enough for election, but Brady was short of that until the twenty-sixth day when Cardinal Bracca, the ancient and powerful Archbishop of Turin, unaccountably changed his mind and voted for Brady. Miller hadn't been able to discover Bracca's reason for changing. But it took only three more ballots after that for the opposition to cave in. Brady's election, Miller thought, meant the cardinals must be very scared—scared enough to break with tradition . . .

The slight, intense figure in white looked almost frail as he came back in from the balcony and stood among the cardinals and monsignors assembled in the great high-ceilinged room. Father O'Malley, a very subdued Father O'Malley, towered protectively over him, and Cardinal Garonne, who was standing near them, noted the change in their relationship. The two men had known each other since they were boys in an Irish orphanage, but O'Malley was addressing the new Pope with awe, as if he were a stranger of supreme importance.

What Cardinal Garonne thought of as The Papal Transformation had already taken place. He had seen the same change in six other cardinals who had become popes—from

Alfredo back to Pius XII. Overnight the man who became pope seemed to shed much of his common humanity, and became instead a mystical being.

This change already showed in O'Malley's subdued face and manner. Yet there was nothing in David Brady's own behavior that had changed. Cardinal Garonne, who had been against his election, had to concede that. He watched Pope David walk over to speak to old Cardinal Bracca, whose sudden change had helped him to be elected. A different kind of pope would have expected Bracca to come to him now— into The Presence. Cardinal Garonne watched him listening intently as Bracca talked. He certainly didn't expect to be the center of attention all the time. He was a genuinely modest man, Cardinal Garonne had to admit. But he was an American and young at a time when an experienced Italian pope was needed!

Pope David moved over to speak to the tall black Cardinal Abu from Tanzania. Abu had been behind the first votes for Brady. The Third World had asserted itself in this Conclave, Cardinal Garonne thought. The domination of the European Cardinals was over.

"May I speak with you briefly, Cardinal Garonne?"

The new Pope was at his side.

"I am at your service, Your Holiness. In fact, I wish to speak to you, but I assume this time of celebration isn't the right occasion to raise a business matter. Perhaps tomorrow—"

"Cardinal Garonne, you and I haven't much time for celebration at present. We have perhaps a month, maybe even less, to save the situation here. The Bellini government will accept only a servile Vatican, and we have to make sure in any conflict that the church is protected. We have to present the issue in a way that is clear to the Italian people. They must be free to make their choice. In the last election, they were not. They were conned, to use a blunt American expression. It's not a question of our attitude toward communism so much as not condoning Bellini's route to power." He spoke quickly and firmly, with intense conviction.

"Your Holiness," Cardinal Garonne replied carefully, "this is precisely why I wish to talk to you. As you may know, I didn't vote for you in the Conclave. I felt our ideas about how to deal with the present crisis were not in agreement. I also believed that electing a non-Italian, especially an American, would be too provocative, a red rag to the Bellini bull—and to the Russians. I wish therefore to tender my resignation as Secretary of State."

Pope David gave a wry smile. "Please, Cardinal Garonne, don't spoil my first day. I have already had to reject Father O'Malley's resignation. He thought 'a common priest,' as he called himself, wasn't up to being a Pope's assistant. So I made him a monsignor and told him now he *was* up to it. As for the Conclave, I have no idea who voted for me and who didn't. It doesn't much matter now. In your place, Cardinal Garonne, I'm sure I wouldn't have voted for me. You must realize I had no wish to be elected. I thought Bierek would be the best choice in the present crisis. He's had to weather similar crises in his own country. As the Conclave remained undecided for so long, I hoped my own chances would diminish. When, at the end, Cardinal Parone as Dean asked me if I accepted my election, all my being wanted to say no, believe me, but it isn't possible to refuse. But, Cardinal Garonne, I will need people close to me who will disagree with me, people who won't be afraid to express disagreement with the Pope. I will need *you* and therefore I hope you will reconsider your resignation.

Cardinal Garonne bowed his head. "Then I, too, cannot refuse."

"Now that's settled," the Pope said more briskly, "let me tell you why I came over to you. I believe Pope Alfredo served us well in those last days. He was on the right lines in providing for an alternative in case it is needed. But now that our enemies know about his agreement with Israel, perhaps we can use it to our advantage in the war of nerves here. We are close now to Holy Week. I have plans I wish to discuss with you concerning Good Friday and Easter Sunday. But first of all I have asked the Israeli Ambassador to come here immediately—tonight. I wish to waste no time in getting a message to Eli Abraham. That is the first step."

"Don't forget the Arabs, Your Holiness. Pope Alfredo's agreement with Israel will greatly upset them."

"I haven't forgotten them, Cardinal Garonne. I have already asked the Jordanian Ambassador to see me tonight, too. We have very little time, but good will come out of our meetings tonight, you will see . . ."

Guns flashed in the sky over the Christian quarter as Ayad dished out the food in the kitchen of the Al Fatah house in the Sabra district. More trouble, thought the young Palestinian, wondering if his people were involved.

He took Judas a plate of *kibbeh,* the national dish of crushed lamb and wheat. Ayad was proud of his cooking and he waited for Judas' reaction. There wasn't any. Judas was sitting in front of a television set. He accepted the heaped plate of steaming food without taking his eyes off the screen, his fingers feeling for it as he watched.

Ayad moved round to see what was holding Judas' attention so completely. It was a news program about the new young American Pope. Ayad watched the slight figure in white walking through a crowd in a big Italian square. Judas was of course very interested in Italy.

The camera showed a close-up of David I as he spoke briefly to the hushed crowd in the Piazza. The intense voice might have been addressing one person rather than a vast congregation, so intimate was the tone without any rhetorical flourishes: "The danger for modern man and woman is that the earth may be reduced to a desert, the individual to an automaton, brotherly love to planned collectivization. The church, rejecting such so-called achievements, intends to safeguard the life of love—the human life—from these dangers that attack it. Never forget that people are still being jailed for their Christian beliefs, are still suffering torture and humiliation for Christ. You should always make clear which side you are on—the side of Christ. There is no middle road. The materialistic way is not Christ's, though both the so-called capitalistic and the Marxist liberation ideologies are very seductive. But, remember, there is much more to life and to personal salvation than political, economic, and social liberation. Don't ever be misled into thinking that *Ubi Lenin, ibi Jerusalem*—where Lenin is, there also is Jerusalem . . ."

Ayad had begun to listen because Judas was so interested, but then he became genuinely interested himself. The man didn't talk like an American or a European. He had the intensity of an Arab.

"He's an unusual Christian," Ayad said aloud.

"He's a very dangerous man," Judas replied.

The intense voice was nearing the end. The slight figure in white bent over, closer to the crowd, as if he had something especially personal to impart.

" . . . For my first Holy Week as Pope, I intend to link the two great cities of our faith—Rome and . . . Jerusalem . . ."

Ayad saw Judas tense.

"On Holy Thursday," the Pope continued, "I will cross the Tiber into Rome for the commemoration of the Last Supper, on which by tradition the Pope washes the feet of twelve young seminarians or deacons at San Giovanni in Laterano, the Cathedral of Rome. I will then fly to Jordan, landing at Amman, to pay my respects to the Arab Nation—the Nation of Islam—and then I will proceed by road to Jerusalem, where the Crucifixion took place, to be there in time for Good Friday. I will pay my respects to Israel and then I will carry a cross along the Via Dolorosa where Jesus carried His cross. I will stop at each of the fourteen Stations of the Cross for prayers, ending at the memorial site of the Crucifixion in the Church of the Holy Sepulchre. After Jesus has risen from the dead, I will fly back to Rome to be here with you on Easter Sunday to celebrate the Resurrection . . ."

Judas had slowly leaned forward toward the television screen so that his nose was almost touching the image of the Pope. He watched the figure in white slowly walk through the applauding crowd. He reminded Ayad of a spider watching a fly. There was real venom in his eyes. Ayad wondered why. He still didn't know this man.

The Russian, Rostov, came into the room. Judas didn't look around or speak. The screen still held his full attention. Ayad noticed how carefully Rostov looked at Judas, as if trying to read his mood. Even this Russian who had worked with him in Italy was uneasy with him.

"Judas," Rostov said quietly, "the camp near Baalbek will supply all your needs. I must return to Rome before the new American Pope drives our friend Bellini into doing something desperate."

"Tell your stooge Bellini to be patient," Judas replied. He glanced at Ayad. "Remind him of the old Arab saying, 'If your enemy insults you, go and sit outside your door; you will see his corpse pass by.' "

Judas stood up and faced the Russian with a look of triumph. "Scratch Abraham, Rostov. We've found our real target." He gestured at the screen. "You see how the world has received his election—it's a seven-day bloody wonder. Well, what we're going to do, Rostov, will be the biggest media event since Kennedy in '63. And what better day for him to die than . . . Good Friday."

PART TWO

GOOD FRIDAY

18

The taxi turned off the busy Jericho Road and began the gentle ascent up the Mount of Olives. The famous biblical hillside was golden and olive green in the pale spring sunlight that covered Jerusalem.

Et Tur, thought Major Falid, peering through the taxi window at the familiar landscape. *The Mountain.* The Jordanian police officer was teaching himself to think in English as well as Arabic.

"It's on the left," he told the young taxi driver, who seemed unsure of the way. Major Falid hadn't been to the Mount of Olives since the 1967 war, but he still remembered the layout. The ageless olive trees of the Garden of Gethsemane were close by—there Jesus had suffered his agony as he imagined his forthcoming crucifixion.

The Major paid the taxi driver, giving him a smaller tip because he hadn't known the route. At the side of the large, handsome hillside house, the home of the Apostolic Delegate, a young chauffeur was hosing down a black Mercedes limousine. He was small and muscular with a swarthy Arab face.

"Police," the Major grunted.

The young chauffeur swung round, very tense and suspicious.

His reaction surprised the Major. He had expected a friendly greeting, for they were fellow Arabs in Israel. But people often responded strangely to the police. The young chauffeur's manner didn't necessarily express guilt. The Major took out a close-up photograph of Don Paolo's dead face, retouched so that the bullet's exit hole didn't show. "Ever seen him?"

The young chauffeur gave the photograph a long look. "No," he said. "I've never seen him."

Major Falid stared at him. He was telling the truth. No doubt about it. An Arab couldn't fool him. There was an unusual tension in the young chauffeur, but perhaps it was no more than the wariness of an Arab among the Israelis. It certainly made sense for the Apostolic Delegate to employ an Arab chauffeur. The Jews seldom converted to Catholicism; most of his work was among the Arabs. And he was not only the Pope's representative here in Jerusalem, but in Jordan and Lebanon, too, and often visited those countries by car. But the chauffeur no doubt felt a natural tension living among the Israelis. The Major felt it himself as soon as he crossed the Allenby Bridge.

He left the young chauffeur to continue washing the Mercedes and walked on to the house. A severe-looking nun, one of the Sisters of Calvary, showed him into a cool, pleasant study where the Apostolic Delegate was sitting behind a neat, tidy rolltop desk, reading his way through a pile of letters. He was Monsignor Le Clair, a small, quick, middle-aged French intellectual whom the Major had met several times in Amman and didn't like. Monsignor Le Clair was one of those Europeans who thought he was an authority on the Arab world, and the Major found him patronizing. He might know all about the Koran, but he didn't *feel* it. Like me with the Bible, the Major thought. It is an alien world.

The Monsignor's soft, scrubbed hand grasped the Major's larger, harder one as if they were old friends.

"Good to see you again, Major Falid. How can I help you?" The Monsignor's face and hands looked very white against his black clerical suit. He had a scholarly pallor, the complexion of a man who seldom let the sun touch him, unlike the tanned, athletic Major. "I'm a little out of touch with what's been happening in Jerusalem. I've been away ever since the Pope died. I'm trying to catch up now with my correspondence." He gestured at the pile on the desk. "Some people think I can work miracles."

"I've waited patiently for your return," said the Major. He pushed the photograph of Don Paolo across the desk. "I'm investigating Don Paolo's murder, Monsignor. I hope that, as the Pope's representative here, you may be able to tell me what Don Paolo was doing in Jerusalem."

Monsignor Le Clair stared at the photograph. Major Falid sensed that he was unsure what to say.

"I never met him, Major. I was away in Beirut at the time. When I heard of the Pope's death, I flew directly to Rome. I understand he was doing something for the Holy Father, but I can't tell you what."

"You can't tell me, Monsignor—or you *won't?*"

Monsignor Le Clair's cheeks reddened slightly. He wasn't used to being spoken to like that. He didn't reply.

"Isn't it unusual, Monsignor," Major Falid persisted, "that you, the Pope's special representative here, should know nothing about Don Paolo's visit?"

"I was away, as I've told you," Monsignor Le Clair replied sharply, "and of course it would depend on the purpose of the visit, whether it was official Vatican business or a private, personal matter—"

Major Falid said bluntly, "There's a report our intelligence people picked up in Beirut that the Vatican and Israel have negotiated a treaty and that Don Paolo was the messenger— the go-between."

"Ah, rumors, Major!" The Monsignor gave a very Gallic shrug. "The Middle East is like a rumor factory in full production. There are rumors everywhere, but are *any* of them true? All I can tell you, Major, is that Pope David on his visit here in Holy Week will be talking with both your King and the Israeli Prime Minister. Until then at least, the Vatican's position remains the same. We have no treaty with Israel. It's a very difficult situation, Major. But the official Vatican position is now in the hands of the new Pope, and undoubtedly his visit here will decide future policy. I cannot anticipate him."

"But where does Don Paolo fit in, Monsignor? A man has been murdered. Someone must be punished for it. If he was a go-between for governments, then there was a political motive—"

"Major, I've told you all I can. I'll pass on a report about your inquiries to the Secretary of State, Cardinal Garonne, at the Vatican. If he has any answers to your questions, I'll relay them to you in Amman immediately."

"Perhaps I will talk to the Cardinal directly by phone . . ."

Monsignor Le Clair walked with the Major to the front door. He was trying to give the meeting a friendly ending. The young chauffeur was still working on the Mercedes. It had a shiny look now.

"Nayef is getting the car ready for another trip," said the Monsignor. "The trouble has broken out again in Beirut. Christians and Moslems have been killed. It's becoming as bad there as in Ireland. I must go back and see what I can do to help. But I can't be away more than about three days. I must get back here to prepare for the Holy Father's visit . . ."

The young chauffeur was watching intently from behind the hood. He worried the Major. There *was* something in his attitude that went deeper than just being an Arab in Israel.

The Major left, very dissatisfied. Monsignor Le Clair *must* know more than he said. The Major remembered his equally unsatisfactory meeting with Marc Ram. He was convinced now that there was some kind of cover-up by the Jews and Catholics. Jordanian Intelligence thought Palestinian terrorists were behind Don Paolo's murder. But that was too easy. The Palestinians were always the whipping boys.

Major Falid decided to walk until he found a taxi. It was a way of checking whether the Israelis were following him. Several cars passed him, but none lingered. Yet he could have been observed through binoculars from the Mount of Olives or any of the other hills along the way. In a city of hills like this one, someone could always be kept under surveillance from a distance. According to the Bible, he remembered, the Mount of Olives was "distant from Jerusalem a Sabbath day's journey." Jerusalem presumably meant the Old City, and a Sabbath day's journey was the walk a Jew could take without infringing upon the Law of the Sabbath rest, said by Rabbis to be 1,392 meters. The Major had almost completed a Sabbath day's journey before he found a taxi.

"Mount Zion," he told the old Jewish driver.

"That's not far to walk," grumbled the driver, seeing little profit in the Major.

"I've walked enough," grunted Major Falid, wondering if

the Jewish driver didn't want an Arab passenger, too sensitive to realize it was just a matter of money. To hell with him, he thought. He felt too exposed walking in the center of Israel, an easy target for any crazy person who wanted to express his hatred. Israel has its crazies just like we do, he thought. Intelligence had told him to be very careful. There had been some bomb scares in Jerusalem recently, and the Israelis might want to take their revenge out on someone. A half-Palestinian Jordanian policeman might seem like a good target! He sat back in the taxi, feeling paranoid.

He paid the driver at the foot of Mount Zion, giving him an extra large tip to compensate for the small fare, but the old Jew didn't thank him or even smile. It was about here that Don Paolo had set off for the last fateful journey with the fair-haired "priest."

The Major had been told exactly where to find the fat man. Ideally, one of the Jordanian agents should have accompanied him as a witness, but that would have blown the man's cover, though the Israelis probably knew about most of the Jordanian agents as he had known about their agent, Kerak, long before he was killed. That murder was probably connected to Don Paolo's. Was the fat man involved in that, too?

The fat man was said to be at work halfway down the hillside leading into the Valley of Hinnom—Gehenna! It was a stony wilderness with a forest of thistles, the slopes bleached white by the thousands of old gravestones of Jews and Moslems. Gehenna was a hateful place to the Major because of its history of cruelty to children. He had three children of his own, was a great family man, and although he had become accustomed to great cruelty between adults, he could never tolerate cruelty toward children. It was here that, in the seventh century before Christ, children were sacrificed by fire inside the brazen belly of the god Moloch while priests beat drums to drown out their screams.

Then he saw the fat man. He was *very* fat, almost grotesque in blue shorts that showed off great bulging thighs. He was watching another, younger man who was digging a trench —or a grave—through the thistles.

"Mr. Francis Cousins?" the Major asked in his formal police voice.

The fat man smiled pleasantly. "At your service."

Major Falid introduced himself. The fat man seemed interested, but not at all worried—perhaps he was a little *too* casual, the Major thought. He took out his photograph of Don Paolo. "Have you ever seen him, Mr. Cousins?"

The fat man glanced at the photograph.

"He's dead, isn't he?"

"Why do you say that?"

"The muscles of the face are too relaxed."

"Yes, he is dead. That's quite correct. But did you know him when he was alive?"

"No, I didn't know him. Why?"

The Major stared at the fat man the way a boxer measures an opponent before delivering a knockout punch.

"Because, Mr. Cousins," he said very carefully, "we have a witness, a taxi driver, who has identified you as the man who was seen talking to the dead man on ... it was on the Christian Ash Wednesday if that means anything to you."

"Let me see the photograph again, Major."

"Certainly, Mr. Cousins."

He had known the fat man would do that. Cornered, he had to play for time and try to talk his way out of it.

The fat man stared at the photograph for a long time. "I recognize him now," he said slowly. "It's an old priest I bumped into on Mount Zion up there. He had rather a lost look so I spoke to him to see if I could help."

"And could you?"

"No ... he seemed to want to be ... alone."

The Major gave him an interrogator's hard look. "The taxi driver said you and he seemed to be arguing."

"Your taxi driver is mistaken. Is he a dependable witness, Major?"

"Certainly."

The Major waited for the fat man to ask if the taxi driver was a Jew or an Arab, but he merely smiled blandly and said, "Everyone can make mistakes, Major, even dependable witnesses. It was after dusk, the light was poor. Here, if you've got time, I'll show you."

"Very well," the Major said. Give the fat man enough rope and he might hang himself. "The man was murdered. Didn't you read about it in the papers?"

"I've been too busy to read the papers, Major. Who murdered him?"

"That's what I'm trying to find out."

"Oh, I see." He didn't seem concerned. He said to the younger man, who was still digging, "I won't be long, Isaac."

He explained to Major Falid as they walked up the hillside: "I'm an archaeologist and biblical scholar. I'm interested in a thorough examination of Gehenna. If we could find, say, the remains of Judas, we would have hard evidence."

"How would you recognize his bones among so many?" asked the Major, watching the fat man closely.

"I think there would be a sign. Something indicating who he was. But Gehenna must be able to yield many invaluable secrets. Prove the evil side of Christianity exists and the good side is proved conclusively, too. I'm a great believer in that approach."

"I, too, Mr. Cousins, am interested in uncovering secrets. But not that far back. Now show me where you were that night."

They were moving down the wide path leading to the foot of Mount Zion. The Old City stretched out in front of them. Sweating slightly, Cousins said, "It was about here, Major, that I first spoke to him . . ."

Now for the lies, the Major thought, his hand resting lightly on the butt of his gun. But I will find out the truth.

19

A long line of people waited at the new Jerusalem airport to have their passports examined. Since runways had been built to accommodate big international jets, the airport was always a busy part of the Israeli frontier. But the new Pope's forthcoming visit had greatly increased the flood of new arrivals.

An old French nun . . . a German priest . . . a Japanese manufacturer of neon crosses . . . a Dutch family of four, all wearing Sacred Heart badges . . .

The line seemed endless and nearly all Christian.

When a young, ex-army official examining non-Israeli passports saw a tall figure all in black towering over him, his first reaction was that the man had strayed into the wrong line— he belonged among the Israelis. Orthodox Hasidic Jews like this man in the flat, wide-brimmed black hat and the long black coat came in the hundreds every year from the ghettoes of eastern Europe.

The man held out his passport with a nervous smile.

"I am here," he said shyly, "to fulfill my lifetime dream—to see the Wall."

The passport official nodded sympathetically. He had heard that plenty of times before, and he understood why people felt so deeply about the Wall. He remembered his own visit after the '67 war. To him, then, it was just a wall. Probably part of the original temple, probably built by Herod, but still just a wall. But the feeling generated by people praying there had affected him. People needed a holy place, a visual representation of their dreams. Every Jew should visit the Wall and have the same emotional experience.

"I also intend to visit King David's Tomb and the eternal flame at Yad Vashem commemorating the Holocaust, which we experienced in my own country . . ."

Examining this man's passport was hardly necessary, the young official thought, but he was conscientious. He looked quickly through it. The man was a rabbi in Warsaw—poor devil. Communist Poland was not as bad as the Soviet Union, but still it wasn't an easy place for a Jew to live in. *I'd stay here with us if I were you,* the official thought. But being a rabbi, the man probably had a great sense of duty. The official glanced briefly at the photograph in the passport and then handed it back.

"Enjoy your visit," he said respectfully, already looking to the next person in the long line, a handsome elegant woman with a silver crucifix around her neck—she looked American . . ."

The tall rabbi bowed politely and then hurried quickly to the nearest exit to find a taxi.

Only when he was sitting back out of sight, en route toward the Damascus Gate, did he relax. The nervous, humble manner vanished, and his blue eyes became cold and calculating.

Judas had come to Jerusalem—on a passport provided by Sokolov through the KGB in Poland—to check out the Pope's route on Good Friday and make his plans.

He first went into the Old City to make a quick inspection of the long, winding, busy Via Dolorosa. The Street of Sorrows! he thought with an ironic smile. Now, two thousand years later, it looked more like the Via of Commerce. Shops, wide open in the oriental way, lined the narrow street like traps for tourists—anything from Bedouin jewelry to holy rosaries on sale. The three major faiths of the city were a big business of hybrid Moslem, pseudo-Jewish, and commercial Christian. Smells of charcoal, leather, pastries, hides, spices, excrement, and rotting meat filled the air. The only transport was by donkey or hand-wheeled cart, and the street, partly covered like a tunnel, was often too narrow even for them. Judas joined a packed, rushing crowd of Arab porters hunched under heavy loads, United Nations soldiers, clerics of all kinds, Israeli policemen, tourists from everywhere . . . and some stray sheep. A tall rabbi in black didn't stand out.

Judas had a small camera around his neck. It was a tourist touch probably out of character for a rabbi of the kind he was impersonating and an attraction for countless beggars who offered to be his guide, but it was also another good cover. Tourists were harmless and could go anywhere.

Via Dolorosa. The street sign was in three languages—Latin, Hebrew, and Arabic. The traditional Way of the Cross began up a ramp in the courtyard of the El Omariyeh College, on the site marking the Palace of the Roman Governor at the time of the Crucifixion, Pontius Pilate. Jesus had been sentenced in the Palace courtyard paved with flagstones, but custom placed the First Station ("Jesus is condemned to death") up some steps on a rocky platform where Pilate supposedly presided. The Second Station ("Jesus receives the cross") was commemorated at the foot of the steps on the other side of the street opposite the Chapel of the Condemnation.

Judas took one look at this cramped scene where Pope David would first stop for prayers, he rejected it, and walked quickly on under the Ecce Homo Arch to the Third Station ("Jesus falls the first time"), where a Polish Chapel had been built. That was no better for Judas' purpose. Nor were the next six Stations along the Via Dolorosa. The street seemed to become narrower and more enclosed as it grew busier in the commercial clutter of the crowded bazaar area. It dipped downhill and then rose steeply on tiers of steps, where little vaulted shops hung out their wares on the walls. Above the Via Dolorosa were buttresses covered with shrubs and latticed windows jutting out. There was a feeling of being shut in, of being trapped between the Stations of the Cross and the merchants chanting their offerings.

Judas imagined the packed scene with the Pope safely in the middle of a tight Israeli security guard. The Israelis were efficient at security—they had had plenty of practice. No, Judas told himself, my original thinking was sound. A close-range attack is too chancy in these conditions, too much could go wrong. It *has* to be long range.

He noted that from the First Station to the Ninth ("Jesus falls the third time"), which was indicated by a Roman pillar outside the Abyssinian Monastery, had taken him just under twenty minutes without hurrying. But there was no way to estimate how long it would take on a crowded street with nine stops for prayers. Yet the timing was all important in a long-range attack. That was one problem he would have to solve between now and Good Friday.

The Via Dolorosa vanished under a low arch into the courtyard of the holiest shrine in Christendom: the Church of the Holy Sepulchre. The last five Stations were all inside the church, which was built on two main sites, the hill of Golgotha, or Calvary, where the Crucifixion took place, and the garden tomb of St. Joseph of Arimathea "in the place where he was crucified," where the body was laid.

Judas hesitated at the entrance to the courtyard. A rabbi in such a Christian setting would be very conspicuous; years ago he might have been barred or even assaulted. Judas had only a superficial knowledge of Jewish customs, just enough to play his role for a brief time. He had no idea if entering the church, even as a camera-carrying tourist, was strictly against the rules for someone as orthodox as the rabbi he was impersonating. He didn't want to draw any unnecessary attention to himself, yet he needed to see the interior, especially the area of the sepulchre where the Pope would spend the longest time. He had a professional interest in the strength of the walls and the ceiling, and he wished to check whether the Pope would be directly under the main dome. He balanced caution against his needs, and decided he had to risk going in the church.

He took off his flat, wide-brimmed hat and his long black coat, unbuttoned his shirt at the neck, and made the camera more prominent. But these precautions seemed unnecessary when he joined the crowd waiting in the open, sunlit courtyard. Nobody seemed even mildly interested in him.

The sunlight was suddenly shut out in the gloom of the interior. The church was a dark labyrinth of faith in many different styles, a combination of chapels and often conflicting ways of worship rather than one harmonious whole. On every side were vaulted passageways, crossed by gangways and overhung by chapels. Walls were covered with icons, lamps, and fire extinguishers. The dirt of centuries, mixed with the smell of incense and candles, seemed to be everywhere. Banners dripped dust, and in musty side-chapels, great triptychs and neo-Renaissance paintings of glorious spiritual events had a grimy, decaying look. In places where the bare rock was left exposed under the glow of silver lamps, the surface was worn smooth by the hands of the faithful.

Judas shut out the people round him from his thoughts, and concentrated on his inspection of the building. He had no emotional commitment to this ancient church. but merely studied it coldly from the viewpoint of his developing plan.

The center of the church was a crusader nave, but lesser shrines had been dug beneath it, and even perched on its roof. It was essentially a round church with the sepulchre—the tomb—in the middle. There was a series of chapels clustered round the sepulchre, and on the far side, at a slightly higher level, two separate chapels, one belonging to the Latins and the other to the Greeks, marked the Hill of Golgotha. Around them was a chaos of architecture, with Byzantine and medieval styles, pillars of the time of Charlemagne, leering with stone demons, Syrian doorways, Armenian mosaics, all jumbled together.

The shrines themselves held little interest for Judas. He glanced into the sepulchre, a small cell lined with marble, but only to note that it had room for no more than three people. The Pope would only pray briefly in that confined space. With a grave, respectful expression, he asked a tall, impassive Greek monk, who was giving out candles to light in the sepulchre, where the Good Friday service would take place.

"A special mobile altar will be placed outside the sepulchre," said the monk, gesturing to a clear space in the central rotunda area beneath the dome.

"How long will the service last?" Judas asked quietly.

"Probably about twenty minutes," the monk replied. "There are many services on that day."

That was long enough, Judas thought, gazing up at the main dome directly above. Ugly steel beams supported the dome. A flaking skin of paint dropped on his face. The Dome looked quite frail—like the rest of the church. It would offer the Pope little protection, he thought with satisfaction.

He noted the abundance of scaffolding that showed the weakness of the main structure. The divided ownership had made even essential repairs difficult over the centuries. Much had been left undone. He touched the surface of the walls and felt the deep cracks and fissures in the stone and marble, the signs of decay in the wood and iron. Good, he thought, it can have little strength left to resist.

He went back for a final look at the Sepulchre and the inside of the great dome above. It was the last time he would see them from here.

"It is very beautiful, yes?" said the monk, looking curiously at him.

No, Judas thought, it isn't beautiful. He associated beauty with strength and cleanliness. It's decaying and dirty and . . . *weak*.

But he was drawing attention to himself.

He nodded respectfully to the monk.

"Very impressive," he said and went slowly down through the church to the courtyard, where the sunlight blinded him for a moment after the gloom of the interior.

On his way out of the Old City, he bought a large, detailed map of Jerusalem and studied the hills with a clear view of the Church of the Holy Sepulchre. The Mount of Olives attracted him as the scene of the Ascension, but it was too far away. He decided to inspect the closer Mount Zion. He walked up the wide, gently ascending path until there was a clear view of the Old City. The onion-colored main dome of the Church of the Holy Sepulchre protruded above the surrounding roofs. It couldn't be missed. The pale sunlight makes it shine like silver—like a *target*, Judas thought.

There were several possible hiding places. He examined a clump of cypress trees and high bushes that had a clear view of the onion dome, and he inspected a small cave, possibly an old burial site, halfway down the stony hillside toward Gehenna.

Yes, Mount Zion was the place he was looking for.

His work was finished in Jerusalem . . . until Good Friday.

20

The Curia was uneasy. The 3,200 officials of the Vatican's civil service waited anxiously in the honeycomb of offices around the Piazza San Pietro to learn what changes the new Pope intended to make. Every Pope tried to reform the cumbersome administration, its powerful congregations, secretariats, councils, commissions, and tribunals, and then generally gave up. "Popes come and go," was an old Vatican saying, "but the Curia remains."

But this young American Pope made the conservative bureaucracy uneasy. The cardinals in the Curia had vigorously opposed his election in the Conclave. His tireless energy and unconventional methods were still remembered from the time he spent at the Vatican working for Alfredo I. As Pope, he had not immediately reappointed the Curia's major officials as was customary, but said he wanted to check them out first. Already he had made sudden, unannounced appearances in key places in the 110 acres of the Vatican, a slight unassuming figure shyly introducing himself as if no one knew who he was, but then asking tough, pertinent questions.

In the Vatican's broadcasting station where he appeared at lunchtime, an announcer stammered, "N-no one is here, Your Holiness."

"Nonsense, *you* are here," David I replied affably. "Come, show me how everything works."

In the carpentry shop, where he showed he knew how to use many of the tools, he ordered wine for the startled workmen, and they toasted his health. Wherever he went, he always asked about wages and seemed shocked at how low they were. "You can't bring up a family on that," he told one clerk. "There will be changes."

He also made his first visit to Rome as Pope—alone and unannounced.

Nobody at the Vatican knew where he'd gone until calls started to come in from the media, wanting more details.

He had left very early that morning dressed in the black

cassock and wide-brimmed black hat of a simple Roman priest. Hiding his face behind a handkerchief, he walked past the guards at the Angelic Gate. They were so used to seeing priests come and go that they barely glanced at him. He then vanished alone into the city.

The children, nurses, and attendants at St. Joseph's Orphanage in the working-class area around the Via Colloni were just sitting down to breakfast when their cracked front-door bell rang. The old doorman came rushing in to the matron. "The Pope has come," he stammered. Nobody seemed to know what to do in the face of their distinguished visitor. But the children were far less inhibited. *"Papa! Papa!"* they were soon shouting excitedly as he went round talking to them. "I am one of you," he told them repeatedly. "I was brought up in a home very like this one of yours, though not as nice." But there was one child, a boy of six, who wouldn't talk to him or to anyone else. It was his birthday, and there was no one to come to visit him; his mother was dead and his father was in prison. The Pope was enormously patient in persuading the boy to talk, and their long discussion ended with their walking hand in hand to the Regina Coeli Prison a mile away. The prison guards, caught by surprise, let them in. The boy's father, a convicted murderer, was in a section of the prison sealed off from the rest. The Pope asked that the gate be opened. "Do not bar this boy from seeing his father on his birthday," he said. "They are both children of the Lord." He told the boy's father: "You could not come to see your son so he came to see you. One sin cannot spoil a whole life. Begin again. You must be a good man to have a son who loves you so much . . ."

The news had spread through the surrounding streets, and by the time David emerged from the prison, a crowd had gathered. He was loudly cheered. He looked faintly embarrassed and waved shyly. "Aren't you going to bless us?" called out an old woman. He smiled and impulsively grasped the old woman's hand. It was a strongly communist area, but everyone gathered round as he blessed the old woman.

He reappeared at the Vatican in the late morning, saying only that he had been for a walk and had had "such a good time."

By early afternoon, the calls from reporters started.

Then there came a formal protest from the Ministry of the Interior.

Cardinal Garonne decided to see the Pope at once. He had taken over Alfredo I's plain, simple apartment, including the old parrot. The Cardinal found him in the frugal little room where he had his meals. He was talking to Orlando Moravia, Alfredo I's former secretary, with the big colorful parrot perched on his shoulder, nibbling his ear.

"Come in and join us, Cardinal," he said.

"I have an important matter to discuss, Your Holiness," Cardinal Garonne said stiffly.

Moravia, plump and elegant in a fine grey suit, moved toward the door.

"I have asked Signor Moravia to stay on as my liaison with the Curia and the various department heads," David I told Cardinal Garonne.

"Good," said the Cardinal. Although Moravia had been of little help during Alfredo I's last illness, he respected his loyalty to the dead Pope. Moravia was also a useful go-between with the Christian Democrats, and he understood how the Curia worked. He'd be a good restraining influence on the new Pope.

"I'm worried about the Vatican's finances," said David I. "Alfredo got most of our investments out of Italy as soon as he knew the Communists were certain to be elected. We still have some real estate holdings we can hold in case we need them to negotiate with. What I want to make sure of is that our investments have been transferred to undertakings worthy of us. Alfredo was worried that some of our money might be used for the wrong causes in other countries. Money can get channeled in strange ways. So I'm going to bring in a team of outside accountants to examine our whole financial situation."

"You will upset the Curia's financial advisers," Cardinal Garonne said. "Don't you agree, Moravia?"

"They certainly won't like it," the plump secretary agreed.

"They're men of zeal, I'm sure, Cardinal," David I said firmly. "But they're not running the church. I'm in charge and I won't have anyone else trying to stop the momentum of change. Let's take the Bellini government as a warning to clean up our own house." He looked at Moravia. "I needn't keep you any longer. But arrange a meeting for me tomorrow with the Secretariat for Promoting Christian Unity. I want to discuss my visit to Jerusalem with them."

"Very well, Your Holiness."

Moravia waited, as if reluctant to leave. "The mail response to the Jerusalem visit is overwhelmingly favorable," he said.

"I'd go even if there wasn't one letter in favor," said the Pope. "But don't linger. Get home to your family."

Moravia went out then. The Pope looked at Cardinal Garonne. The Cardinal was obviously upset about something and he was now free to talk openly about it.

"I have come to report an official protest from the government," Cardinal Garonne said stiffly.

"So soon?" David I replied with a smile.

"The Ministry of the Interior points out that although the Lateran Treaty of 1929 between the church and the Italian government freed the Pope from self-imposed confinement inside the Vatican, the Holy Father has to announce his intention of visiting Rome at least two hours in advance so that the *Carabinieri* can be informed and provide protection—"

"Against whom?"

"The church's enemies."

"What if those providing the protection are among our enemies?"

"The Ministry claims that, without any warning, early this morning you visited St. Joseph's Orphanage and the Regina Coeli Prison."

"Correct. The Bishop of Rome visited his flock."

"The Ministry says this mustn't happen again or the Italian government cannot be held responsible for what happens."

The Pope stroked the parrot thoughtfully.

"I do urge you, Holiness, to observe the ground rules, to give them no excuse to stage an incident—"

"At that rate," David I said, "they might as well set up a frontier post and stamp my passport every time I cross the Tiber."

"It may come to that."

"Stage one in harassment. Then what would follow? No, Cardinal Garonne, we have to anticipate them, outwit them. It's a chess contest between Bellini and us. Why do you think I'm going to Jerusalem?"

"To complete Pope Alfredo's work."

"Partly. I also want to put pressure on Bellini." His white teeth glinted. "I also, believe it or not, want to see the fabulous Jerusalem. The prospect has me as excited as a kid.

I think the Pope should know the actual places where it all began."

Cardinal Garonne studied the new Pope's face. What a complex man he was! It was difficult to tell whether his actions arose from the simplicity of a saint or the shrewdness of a Machiavelli. His visit to Rome that morning had been a good example. He had put pressure on the Bellini government in the same way as he had on the Curia. He was an activist Pope. But such men made a great many enemies. In this century, they often didn't have a long life. He suddenly had a feeling of great concern for this man.

"One thing more, Cardinal Garonne." The thin, intense face was sombre. "I want to find the informer in the Vatican. Until then, it's impossible to be sure we can keep any secrets from Bellini. That's an impossible position to be in at the present time. The informer *must* be found before I go to Jerusalem. I'm also under pressure about it from friends of Don Paolo in Sicily. Representatives of the Mafia and Servus Dei came to see me. They both made the same point—that he was betrayed by someone within the Vatican. Being Sicilians, they want revenge. I promised them quick action—"

"The head of security, Mazzoni, has had no luck in his investigations."

"I have talked with Mazzoni. I asked him if you, Cardinal Garonne, were a suspect. He was almost as shocked as you look now, Cardinal. And that is my point. A successful detective excludes no one. But Mazzoni has worked at the Vatican for twenty years. He is too respectful for a successful detective. For that reason, I have asked Monsignor O'Malley to carry out his own investigation."

"O'Malley—"

"—will get results." The Pope smiled reassuringly. "Don't be misled by O'Malley's bluff Irish manner, Cardinal. He kissed the Blarney Stone when he was a kid. But he's the opposite of Mazzoni. The Vatican is new to him. He's under obligation to nobody here. He can be open-minded in a way Mazzoni can't. We were once troubled by a persistent thief at St. Patrick's in New York, and I wanted to avoid police involvement. O'Malley found the unfortunate person for me—"

"A Communist informer is far cleverer than a common thief."

"Oh, this thief wasn't so common. He was a bishop."

* * *

Late that afternoon, the call came that the Pope had been dreading. The past once more thrust itself into his life.

"Mr. John O'Neill is here to see His Holiness. He has an appointment."

His father!

His first thought was still one of revulsion. The mere name brought back all those years his mother had been humiliated in the little Irish village where the old parish priest, as all-powerful as a feudal lord, had treated her as a great sinner because she was pregnant without having received the Sacrament of Matrimony. When he went to the local church school, the other children called him "bastard." And when he asked his mother what that meant, she said a bastard was a child without a father. Where was his father? he asked her. Somewhere in America, she told him. His father had left when he knew she was pregnant. She spoke of him with cold indifference, which made a lasting impression on her son. He remembered the day of her death with great vividness—the crowded tuberculosis ward in the local hospital, the spots of blood on her greying lips, and her last thoughts worrying about leaving him. It was nearly forty years ago now, but he could still feel her fingers slowly loosen their grip on his hand as the life left her. A panic had seized him then at the realization he was completely alone in the huge, pitiless world. And when in later years he met his father in America, he couldn't feel any more for him than the cold indifference his mother had expressed. *Dear God,* he thought, *how could you allow a man to be elected pope who can't even love his own father?*

There was a knock at the door.

He stilled his thoughts and stood up, his hands beginning to tremble. "Come in."

A male nurse opened the door and wheeled in the wizened figure. Washed-out brown eyes looking impossibly large in a wasted face stared at David I. How did a father greet a son who had become the Pope?

"I have . . . stayed away . . . until now," John O'Neill murmured in a husky, strangled voice. His stroke had paralyzed his left side and affected his vocal chords. Countless operations costing a fortune had not got him out of the wheelchair.

"I invited you to my inaugural mass in the Piazza San Pietro," David said gently, struggling to suppress his feelings.

"The crowd would have been too much, Davie . . . Your Holiness," his father panted. Even now, in John O'Neill's days of physical ruin, there was a distinct resemblance between the two men. David had his father's strong bones—his nose, high cheekbones, and chin—but the gentle, yet shrewd eyes were his mother's. "What can I do for you?" his father asked. "Anything I have is yours. You are my only child. There will be no one to carry on the family name."

"Why don't you adopt someone?" David said, trying to suppress his impatience. "Give an orphan child a good start in life. Make somebody happy. That will also give you great pleasure, believe me."

"I will build an orphanage," the old man panted, "if that is what you want."

"I want nothing," David I said brusquely. The old man was still trying to buy him. He had learned *nothing!*

The shrunken, fleshless face scowled in an agony of frustration. "You still try to punish me. Here . . ." His hand sought his pocket and then fell back into his lap. "I have my checkbook. You can have anything you want. You are my son of whom I'm very proud. You have become one of the most powerful men in the world. Let me make out a check now."

"I have no need of money," the Pope said, trying not to let his irritation show. "Money means nothing to me. It never has . . . not since I was very young."

"There you go again . . . rubbing it in, punishing me." The old man stared at his son's eyes, which reminded him of the girl he had once known and left—Kathleen Brady. "If I could buy back the past, I would."

John O'Neill's look in the impotent body pleaded for forgiveness, but David couldn't bring himself to pretend with this man. There was an uneasy silence between them, and then his father said: "You will never forget or forgive. But one thing I ask you—do not go to Jerusalem. It is too dangerous for you."

The Pope's slight body tensed. "I must go. The future of the church demands it."

"You risk . . . too much. I will bequeath the church my entire fortune if you cancel your visit."

"The church has great need of your money," the Pope said quietly. "But this is not a matter of money. It is beyond money," he added, no longer concealing his impatience. "I

must go to Jerusalem to ensure the survival of the Church. I
must!"

21

The sun was setting over Rome when Robert Miller left his
rented Maserati outside the *Mirror*'s office and went inside to
collect his mail. There was a message from Hammond on his
typewriter: "Two Italian police types came by to see you.
Didn't say what they wanted."

Was Scaglia about to follow up on their meeting at Mama
Tolloni's ?

He better keep Hammond up to date in case anything
happened.

It was dark by the time he came out.

Lieutenant Kahn was sitting in the car.

"Ram asked me to stop by to tell you Judas may have been
identified in Dublin . . ."

According to Lieutenant Kahn, there was a crumbling old
Catholic church waiting to be torn down on the outskirts of
Dublin. Large sections of the grey slate roof were missing and
all the stained glass windows were broken. The inside of the
church had been stripped bare and was rotting with the
damp.

But when the demolition men arrived with the keys to the
cellars, they discovered one room underground was dry and
intact. Someone had lived there within the last few months.
There was an old army surplus sleeping bag, a small radio, a
hot plate . . . and a hunting rifle with a telescopic sight. They
called the police.

The rifle was checked against the bullet that had killed the
British Home Secretary. It was the gun all right.

The cellar was where Operation Delilah had been planned.

A team of fingerprint experts covered every inch of the
cellar's peeling whitewash and the passageway leading to it.
"Not a bloody sausage," summed up Superintendent Milligan
of Scotland Yard, whom Miller remembered meeting in
Dublin. The Superintendent reported directly to the Home

Office in London: "There are marks that show whoever lived in the room always used gloves. No flies on Judas—he's a real bloody pro."

That was where it might have ended if Superintendent Milligan hadn't had an upset stomach. Miller remembered the bloated, beery face—he probably had a hangover. He had to get up in the middle of the night and go to the toilet. His Dublin lodging house had only one toilet at the end of the landing, and the toilet seat was freezing cold when he sat down on it. How defenseless a person was in this situation, the Superintendent thought gloomily. His mind suddenly flew to the old church. Where had Judas gone to the toilet? Was there one in the old church?

As soon as it was daylight, Superintendent Milligan drove back there. At that time, the secret underground life in the church was not ready for a disturbance. As he unlocked the doors, a scared rat raced across his foot. He searched the cellars for a toilet. There wasn't one inside, but there was a small outside toilet in the back yard. It was locked. He brought back the fingerprint team. There was a chance that even someone as professionally careful as Judas might make a slip in the confines of the toilet and not use his gloves. The fingerprint team checked the whole of the outside toilet and found nothing . . . until they examined the toilet roll that had been left there. As a sheet had been torn off in the dark—the toilet had no light—a fairly clear print of a thumb and an index finger had been left on the side of the metal holder.

"Did the prints belong to Judas?" Miller asked.

"Scotland Yard have identified them as those of an Englishman named Paul Brett."

"Who's Paul Brett?"

"At one time he worked for British Intelligence. Ram's waiting for a full report from the Yard."

"Where is he now?"

"He disappeared in 1973. There's been no trace since until these fingerprints showed up in Dublin."

Paul Brett.

It seemed strange to give Judas a real name.

Three thousand people were headed for the huge modern convention center for the final day of the International Youth Bible Contest.

The Bible contest was one of the most popular events of

the year in Jerusalem. It was sold out weeks before it started, and Israelis who couldn't obtain tickets followed it on television and radio the way people in other countries followed big sports events. Streets were often half-deserted during the live broadcasts, and newspapers came out with special editions.

Robert Miller's taxi couldn't get through the lively, festive crowd, and finally he paid off the driver and joined the great mass moving toward the convention center. It reminded him of a homecoming game in his home town in Illinois—except for the army of security men guarding all the approaches.

Big as the Bible contest crowd was, everyone had to be searched before being allowed inside. Police and soldiers were on duty at all the entrances, guns ready.

The men searching Miller froze when they found his .44. An Uzzi submachine gun prodded his stomach. They ignored his explanation and the *Press* card he wanted to show them. "Walk," said one of the soldiers, covering him with the submachine gun. They marched him through the lobby to the manager's office, which had been turned into security headquarters for the day.

"We found this on him," the soldier said, showing the .44. All the hard-eyed security faces examined him.

"Name?"

"Judas."

Nobody smiled. The atmosphere was as tense as in an operating room.

"In trouble again?" growled a voice behind Miller.

It was Marc Ram.

"Okay, I'll vouch for him," he told the soldiers. They looked disappointed. "Give him back his gun. He may need it." Ram's black-gloved hand clapped Miller's back. It was meant to be a friendly gesture in front of the others, but the steel fingers felt like claws. "So you've come for the showdown, Mr. Miller."

"Maybe your army will scare him off."

"He doesn't scare that easily. Remember the risks he took in the Tolloni affair, in the Don Paolo murder, in Ireland and Germany. With his fondness for biblical allusions, he'll probably show up among the contestants here—on stage!"

"Do you know any more about . . . *Paul Brett?*"

Ram took a typewritten sheet from an inside pocket. "Here's his *curriculum vitae* from the Yard."

Miller glanced quickly through it:

PAUL BRETT

Born:	Jan. 11, 1942, in St. Margaret's Hospital, London.
Parents:	The late Col. Wm. Ewart Brett and the late Helga Brett, née Manheim. The Bretts are an Anglo-Irish Catholic family associated with the British Army for generations. Col. Brett won the V.C. at El Alamein in World War II. Mrs. Brett was born Helga Manheim in Hamburg, Germany, and came to Britain as a governess in 1936. She committed suicide, 1944. Col. Brett was shot by persons or persons unknown on his Surrey estate in 1970.
Education:	Cambridge University, Modern Languages—B.A., M.A., special studies in Russian, Polish, German, Italian, Arabic, Hebrew, 1960–65.
Other Activities:	Soccer, cricket, swimming, Rifle Club, Drama Society.
Employment:	Brief career as an actor with Liverpool Repertory and BBC radio, 1965–66.

(That's why he's so clever at disguises, Miller thought.)

	British Army Intelligence (special A-7 Group)—service in Northern Ireland, Europe, Middle East, 1967–73. Reason for discharge: Disappeared. (Ram had circled this last item)
Identifying Marks:	Tattoo of a Christian crucifix on the chest acquired as a teenager before he gave up the family Catholicism.
Indentifying Characteristics:	Panic at the touch of blood.

Miller handed back the report.

"Being affected by blood like that must be a big handicap for someone in Intelligence. He'd be useless if he was wounded. What's the A-7 Group?"

"A disposal team," Ram said. "All nations have them. Of course, nobody admits to them. But they are necessary. Many foreign spies can't be brought to trial because it would reveal too much. And they're too dangerous to let escape. So you arrange for them to . . . oh, slip under a train, fall from a high building, take an overdose. The trouble is it destroys your own people, too. Only those with no moral sense at all can do the job for long."

"Judas sounds like a natural for it."

"Nobody's a natural," said Ram harshly. "I'd like to know more about his early years. Both his parents died violently. I'd like to know more about *that* certainly. But this could be our man. He's had the right kind of experience."

A plainclothes security man talking into a phone called over to Ram: "It's just leaving."

"Okay, tell Eli to get ready." Ram explained to Miller, "People will expect Eli to come in the official limousine from The Knesset, but we're going to sneak him in the back way while someone else comes in the limousine. Then we'll keep him in a strongroom behind the scenes, and just rush him on stage for the presentation to the winner. Eli won't like it, but we can't take any unnecessary risks. Not with Judas." The black-gloved hand touched Miller lightly on the chest. "Don't forget our agreement works both ways. There are about three hundred media people covering the Bible contest. We told them all the extra security is a precaution because of the recent bomb scares. Not a word to any of your friends, Miller. We don't want anyone getting in the way."

The security man on the phone called over: "The Prime Minister's just leaving."

Ram glanced at his watch. "He'll be here in ten minutes— at the same time as the limousine. That's the only chance Judas has got. Eli will be exposed for about three minutes when he steps out of his Pontiac. But we're hoping Judas will have his eyes on the limousine." Ram loosened his shoulder holster. "I'm going to check him in personally. Want to come along, Miller?"

"That's why I'm here, Colonel."

*　*　*

Major Falid watched the fat man talking to one of the guards in the lobby. It was too much of a coincidence that he should show up where Don Paolo's killer was expected. He was wearing a dark suit much too small for his bulging figure. To the Major, with his military correctness, the fat man's sloppiness seemed like further proof of his guilt.

"Major!" He came squeezing past the clusters of security men, waving cheerfully. "Are you a contestant?"

"They don't have questions relating to the Koran, Mr. Cousins," the Major replied warily. What was the fat man's game? Was he distracting him while something was happening elsewhere?

"There are contestants from twenty-two countries," Cousins said. "My money's on the Israelis. It's local history to them. If they don't win, they'll consider it a national disgrace!"

The vast auditorium was in semidarkness except for the huge lighted stage. The audience listened in complete silence as a question was asked.

"Who in the Bible employed an absorbent hygroscopic substance to collect dew?"

The audience gave a chuckle of appreciation.

"Was it . . . Moses?" whispered the fat man.

The Major shrugged. It was beyond his biblical knowledge.

One of the contestants on stage, a slim self-confident young man, promptly recalled a passage in the Old Testament: "And Gideon said . . . I will put a fleece of wool in the floor . . . he rose up early on the morrow . . . and wringed the dew out of the fleece, a bowl full of water."

The audience applauded admiringly.

"Gideon!" said Cousins, tapping his large brow. "I should have known that."

The fat man began to edge away down the side aisle. The Major followed him.

"Look, Major." The fat man sounded exasperated now. "Don't you think we better circulate on our own?"

The Major said obstinately, "I follow."

Cousins seemed to realize then the intensity of the Major's suspicions. He came back, and, with a fat hand on the Major's shoulder, whispered, "You're letting Israel affect your judgment, Major. I'll break the rules and level with you, because this is getting to be a pain in the ass for both of us.

I'm after Judas just like you are. I'm with Central Intelligence. You know, CIA."

Ram stood among the security men in the manager's office, grim-faced.

"Eli is safely backstage and Judas still hasn't made a move. It can mean only one thing—Judas is here, *inside,* somewhere among us. I want every inch of the auditorium covered when Eli walks out on that damn stage."

A plump, dark-haired woman stood near Miller, watching Ram give his orders. It was Ram's secretary, Sonia Petrovich. She was about forty and looked as though she had slept badly. Ram probably worked her too hard.

"You're in the front line today," Miller said.

"I'm here to hold Marc's hand," she replied with a faint smile. "He's very jumpy because Mr. Abraham's involved."

Miller smiled. "Were you born here?"

He was only making conversation, but he had obviously asked the wrong question. "No," she replied flatly. "I'm an immigrant," and she walked out of the office.

"What did I say?" Robert asked one of the security men standing nearby.

"You touched a nerve," Marc Ram's voice boomed up from behind him. Ram's eyes narrowed as he watched Sonia disappear into the corridor. Miller couldn't read the Colonel's expression. "Her parents died in a Soviet camp. She escaped only because she was traveling with a ballet company in Germany. She still can't talk about it and she's been here a couple of years."

"She seems very attached to you," Miller said carefully.

"She is sorry for me," Ram said with a hard laugh. Miller had never heard him use that tone of voice before—the tone of a man deliberately disguising deep feelings. Ram usually maintained a stoic control over his emotions, an enforced professional calm. But for a moment he had slipped and Miller caught a glimpse of the human being underneath. Ram was in love with the woman, Miller guessed, yet he regarded it as impossible. Miller marveled inwardly at the suffering this tough military man had been forced to endure.

A roar came from the auditorium. There was prolonged loud applause and cheers.

The winner!

Ram immediately hurried away. Even the hardened, cynical security men wanted to know who the winner was—from which country. There were broad smiles when someone brought the news that a young Israeli clerk had won the first prize—a two thousand-year-old glass vase like those used in Solomon's Temple.

Ram had all the lights on in the auditorium when Eli Abraham came on the stage to make the presentation. Robert Miller searched the audience yet again for a tall, powerful figure with fair hair.

The young Israeli Prime Minister beamed and looked completely relaxed. Nobody would have guessed his life might be in danger. Marc Ram, standing behind him, his hand on his lapel near his shoulder holster, never taking his eyes off the auditorium, was the one who looked nervous. The walls were lined with security men. Even the audience caught the atmosphere of anxiety—of waiting. Several people hurriedly left, fearing a bomb might go off.

But nothing happened.

Eli Abraham, looking very calm and confident, congratulated the young winner, made a brief speech, and then departed. Ram insisted on accompanying him in his Pontiac to The Knesset.

Robert Miller saw the black-gloved hand clenching and unclenching.

Ram had been wrong.

The Prime Minister wasn't the target.

Ram had misread Judas' mind—the mind of Paul Brett.

Miller decided he had to learn more about Paul Brett.

22

The meeting place was Baalbek.

It was like arranging to meet in a ghost town.

Baalbek was the most famous ruin in Lebanon.

Two thousand years ago, the Romans had begun to build a whole city there. Earthquakes had demolished most of their work. Now little remained but marble columns, the fragments of temples, and crumbling walls.

As Judas and Ayad came up the hard rocky ground, six massive, weather-beaten marble columns towered above them. This was all that was left of the fifty-four columns of the Temple of Jupiter. Yet the very size of the columns was imposing. The Romans had never built such giants until then. Judas stared up at them as a cool wind stirred the ancient sandy dust like a breath of life and moaned through the nearby colonnade of the Temple of Bacchus. This second temple was smaller, but more remained of it—enough for the imagination to build the rest.

"God, it's sinister," Judas said with a shiver, "all this—this sacred rubble."

Ayad looked curiously at him, not knowing what he meant. The ruins of Baalbek were noble and sad to the young Palestinian. Here had once been a great, shining city with massive temples in which people hoped and prayed and loved together. He felt a strong link with the beauties and mysteries of his past. But Judas seemed somehow threatened by the monuments. He had been in a strange mood ever since he had returned from Jerusalem. It was as though their new mission had begun already, even though Good Friday was a week away.

"Can't you feel it, Ayad?" Judas asked, gesturing around at the crumbling temple ruins, the stark broken walls, the rubble of what once had been a huge sanctuary. Ayad listened attentively, anxious to understand the demons that motivated this man. "Can't you feel the corruption, the evil lurking here? The Romans certainly sensed it. Why else would they erect their stoutest marble columns, their most soaring temples here? Even the smaller temple was bigger than the Parthenon. But they were wasting their time! Trapped by their own self-deceit. Evil is not something man can harness and control . . ."

In his white cotton, one-piece suit, Judas looked like a priest seeing some kind of vision. Ayad felt almost frightened at the intensity of his emotion. His words had some logical sense, but was this man sane? The young Arab pondered, his eyes sweeping the horizon. Suddenly he noticed something.

"Look." He touched Judas' arm quickly.

Two hawklike faces had appeared between the columns of the Temple of Bacchus.

The spell of Baalbek was broken.

"They have come for us," Ayad murmured.

He waved to the two young Arabs, who wore black and white *kafiyehs* on their heads, rough olive green uniforms, and heavy army boots.

Ayad was a fellow Arab, a brother Palestinian, yet because he was with Judas, he was a stranger to them. He had broken the old Arab rule, "My brother and I against our cousin; my cousin and I against the alien."

Without any sign of friendliness, they gestured for him and Judas to follow.

As agile as mountain goats, they quickly left the ruins and hurried down the paved modern road, with the green depths of the Bekaa Valley in the distance. Parked near a clump of ancient cedar trees was a battered Ford station wagon.

The two Arabs each took out a long piece of black cloth. "Your eyes must be covered now," one of them said in a hostile tone. Before Judas was blindfolded, he checked the time on his watch. He wanted to estimate how far the camp was.

It was a long, fast, bumpy ride. The changes in the air suggested they traveled through a mountainous region and then a stretch of desert. Nobody spoke the whole way. Judas in the back could feel Ayad beside him, sitting tense and alert. He was a dependable lieutenant. He would be very useful in Jerusalem.

The station wagon had been traveling at about 50 miles an hour, now it slowed, and soon the noise and smells of some kind of shantytown came through the open windows. It had the bazaar excitement of a *suq*. Next the station wagon dipped and went down a smooth roadway, and the noise faded behind them. Then they were on hard level ground and the station wagon stopped. The air had the sultry heat of underground.

"Get out," one of the Arabs said.

They obeyed and stood by the station wagon, still unable to see.

"This way."

Rough hands gripped their arms and guided them foward through a doorway and along some kind of passageway.

"Sit."

Hands pushed them roughly down into straight-backed wooden chairs.

"Take their blindfolds off," ordered an older, deeper voice.

The same rough hands pulled off their blindfolds. For a

few moments, even the dim lighting by oil lamp blinded them. They were in a plain army-style office with bare rock walls, facing a man behind a steel desk. They both recognized the man—he was the one they had come to see.

He was tall and powerfully built with a lined, tanned face that had many Bedouin features—a broad low forehead, a high sharp hooked nose, brown-green eyes slanting outward, and a large mouth that was half-hidden by a black mustache tinged with white. He was wearing a black checkered *kafiyeh*, an olive green battle dress, and a gun belt round his waist with two pistols in holsters. The pistols had silver handles and were famous among Palestinians. This was Hamed, who was regarded by many as the leader of the more extreme wing of the *jihad*, the holy war, against Israel. But now he was not only at war against Israel, but against the more moderate elements in the Palestine Liberation Movement. The Russians had tried to bring all the warring Palestinians together, but without success.

Ayad had warned Judas that the success of his visit to the camp depended on how well he got on with Hamed. The Palestinian leader was not an easy man to deal with. He was essentially an independent of the desert.

"I know *him*," Hamed said, pointing to Ayad. "You, I have only heard of," he told Judas. "Where do you come from?"

Ayad was afraid Judas would respond in the same way he had to the Russians. Hamed wouldn't trust him if he was evasive. But Judas was shrewder than that.

"I was born in England," he said quietly.

"I don't like the English," Hamed told him. "They were once dependable. My father rode into Damascus with the great Lawrence. But now they are too friendly with the Zionists."

"You can't accuse me of that," Judas said calmly. "What I plan will ruin Israel's future. But you don't need to like me for us to do business."

"I need to trust you," Hamed said, his brown-green slanted eyes staring at Judas without friendliness.

Ayad watched the two men. He was worried by Hamed's attitude. It was probably not good that Judas had come recommended by the Russians. Perhaps, to assert his independence, Hamed would refuse to give them what they wanted.

"Test me," Judas said.

Hamed continued to stare at him, hard-eyed.

"We have a situation," he said at last, "you can perhaps help us with. There has been a killing in the camp over a woman—a European woman. The details are complex. All you need to know is that the dead man's family demand her life—blood for blood. But who is to carry out the execution? If someone here does it, then his life will be threatened, a feud will develop. It must be a formal execution by a stranger, an outsider. She must clearly die as punishment. An outsider would not be counted qualified for a feud—for revenge." Hamed took out one of his silver-handled pistols and laid it on the desk, the handle pointing towards Judas. "You are a stranger. I want you to execute her. Of course, if you prefer not to kill a fellow European, I will understand."

Judas didn't speak. He stared at Hamed with an unreadable expression. Then he picked up the pistol. "Where is she?"

"Come," Hamed said.

He led Judas down a passageway cut through the rock to an open space about fifty yards square, with high rock walls and far above a view of the blue-white sky. A young woman —she couldn't have been thirty years old—was sitting on the hard rocky ground with her hands tied behind her back. She raised her face to see who was coming, her eyes wide and sky blue and unafraid.

Judas stood still, shocked, when he saw her. Small, lithe, almost boyish looking, the woman had the same strong features and short, fair hair . . . *as his mother*. She was wearing a rough open-necked blue shirt that revealed the curve of her breasts—just like the photograph of *her*.

The resemblance was uncanny, Judas thought. As his eyes met the woman's—blue like *hers*—images went flashing through his brain. There was his mother, sitting on the edge of a bed, her face raised in the same attitude as this woman's, meeting his father's hostile gaze with a look of cold indifference—the same expression this woman had now.

Hamed noticed his hesitation, the slackening in his determination. "So," Hamed commented drily, "perhaps you spoke too soon."

No, this woman had to be sacrificed.

"I am ready," Judas said, controlling himself. "Leave us now. Some tasks are best done without an audience."

Hamed smiled bleakly and left. The woman got up awk-

wardly and approached Judas. The relief shone in her eyes.
She thought he had come to help her.

"What's your name?" he asked her in a cold voice.

"Thank God you're here," she said in a harsh, lilting
Belfast accent. "My name's Sheila Larkin. I'm Irish—Provisional Army, getting weapons training here. This is all a
mistake. I don't understand it myself. I was sleeping with an
Arab boy. So what? An older man makes a pass at me. I tell
him to get stuffed. Happens all the time, right? But the boy
doesn't take it that way. Stabbed him in the throat, can you
believe it? What's it to me anyway, though? What do they
intend to do with me? . . ."

The rush of words suddenly ceased as Judas took the pistol
out of his jacket pocket. She's better off dead, he was
thinking. She was just a fool, a common slut. The resemblance
was merely physical, a trick of nature—of memory. Killing
her was nothing, just business. He watched the horror and
fear flooding her face as she realized what was about to
happen. And he felt nothing. It had been just a momentary
weakness.

"Say your prayers," he said softly.

"Look, man," she began to plead, "you can't do this. I'm a
woman. I'm not an Arab, I'm like you. Help me escape and
I'm yours. Anything you want . . ."

Judas shut his eyes for an instant. His mother's face burned
behind his eyelids. His hands trembled. He shut out her
memory and extended his arm, taking careful aim from just
the right distance so there would be a minimum of blood.

"You're nothing to me," he said coldly, steadying his hand.
And as her voice rose hysterically, he shot her neatly in the
center of the forehead.

The woman pitched backwards, dead before she even hit
the hard rocky ground.

He didn't bother to examine her, but walked out of the
open space, slowly, calmly, as if what he had done was
merely routine. He felt a small glow of satisfaction inside. It
was as if he had put the memory of his mother forever to rest.

Hamed was waiting for him. He took back the pistol and
dropped it into his holster.

"Now let us do business," he said with obvious respect.

They returned to his office. Ayad, who had been waiting
anxiously, saw at once their changed relationship, and smiled
with relief.

"Now what do you want from me?" Hamed asked briskly. "I agree with your mission. If the Latins and the Zionists form an alliance in Jerusalem, it will be very harmful to our cause."

"I will stop them," Judas said. "But I need the means to do so from you."

"Tell me."

"I need your best mortar man—someone capable of pinpoint accuracy over a distance of about one thousand to fifteen hundred yards. He must provide the weapon and the explosives."

"You need a back-up man, too?"

"No, I'll be his back-up man."

Hamed looked thoughtfully at Judas. "I will show you my best three. You can choose among them. Two men and a woman."

"I don't want a woman," Judas said.

"She is brilliant, hard, tough—as ruthless as you are yourself, my friend."

"A woman introduces the sex element. I don't want that. I want to keep it as simple as I can."

"Frustrated males often complicate things more than a woman."

"We won't be there long enough to be frustrated," Judas said. "A woman is out."

Hamed shrugged. "Then it is between the two men—a German and a Palestinian."

"Are they both equally accurate?"

"Over that distance, yes."

"What is their track record?"

"The German has been a mercenary in Africa. He fought in the '73 war against the Zionists. The Palestinian has been with me since the '67 war."

"How old are they?"

"The Palestinian is thirty-five. He began young. The German is three years older."

"Has either of them any problems? Any personal hangups?"

"They are warriors, not city neurotics fit only for psychiatrists."

"Good. The Russians tell me they have a Jewish informer who can provide accommodation. A German will be less noticeable in a Jewish area. I would like to watch him perform."

* * *

They were taken to a training area in the desert. Great mounds of sand fell away to an arid valley. It would be hard to see from passing aircraft. The target—a large wooden disk—was set at twelve hundred yards.

The German had the appearance and mannerisms of a professional soldier—short clipped black hair, a tanned keen-eyed face, and a hard-muscled body. He acted quickly and confidently, with no attempt to please. Judas didn't speak to him, but watched his every move.

His weapon, which he had designed and made himself, was a sophisticated mortar with a four-foot-long barrel, a complicated set of cross leveling, elevating and traversing gear, the latest sighting device, a bipod supporting the barrel, and a heavy metal circular baseplate to pass the downward force of the explosion directly into the ground.

The German began by holding up a small black box that resembled a tape recorder. Connected to it was an eyepiece shaped like a monocle, through which he stared at the target.

"Good," Judas said. "That's the latest kind of laser range finder," he told Ayad. "You can find out the exact distance by measuring the round-trip time of a pulsed laser emission to the target and back. It takes no more than a second after he presses the button marked *Fire*. It's a little more complicated when the target's hidden."

Next the German held a small case in the palm of his hand.

"He's evaluating the effects of the meteorological data," Judas said. "The temperature's important, so is the wind velocity. Cross winds particularly can affect the accuracy. The upwind thrust has to be greater than the downwind drag."

With quick, sure movements, the German made adjustments to the mortar. Almost before Ayad could follow what he was doing, the small, grenade-shaped bomb was placed down the barrel. There was a noise like a loud hand-clap, a rush of air, and then Ayad saw the target collapse in a cloud of smoke.

"Excellent," Judas told the German, clapping him on the back. "What did the bomb weigh?"

"That was only a light one for exhibition purposes." The German laughed. "No use wasting a good bomb on target practice."

"What would you need to collapse an old building with a big dome?"

"A four-pounder in the center of the dome should do it easily."

"Over what distance could you be sure of that kind of accuracy?"

"Up to thirty-five hundred yards. The bomb has a terminal guidance device using the latest form of infrared homing."

Judas studied the German. "What's your name?"

"Karl Mundt."

"Well, Karl, I'm going to borrow you from Hamed for a couple of days. We leave on Wednesday. I'll tell you then what it's all about."

"Who will be my back-up man?"

"I will be."

"You are familiar with mortars?" the German asked doubtfully.

"I was in charge of the Tolloni kidnapping. We hit three armored cars traveling at 60 miles per hour. I learned the rudiments with the British Army. I'll practice for a few hours with you before we leave."

The German seemed satisfied. He asked no more questions but began to dismantle the mortar. It was just another job to him.

Before leaving, Judas talked with Hamed again. They discussed the problem of transportation.

"Someone is leaving for Israel at the start of the week," Hamed said. "He can transport the bombs for you."

"He won't be searched at the border?"

Hamed shook his head and winked. "Very important personage. But the mortar would be too big for him—too risky."

Hamed would only do so much.

"Don't worry about the mortar," Judas said. "I'll work on that."

"You have an idea?"

"Even mortars can be disguised."

Hamed clapped Judas on the shoulder as if he were a comrade in battle.

"May Allah be with you on your mission," he said. "The Koran tells us, 'When ye encounter the infidels, strike off their heads until ye have made a great slaughter of them.' May you bring death to . . . the great Latin Father."

"You can count on it," Judas told him.

Going back in the station wagon—blindfolded again—

Judas murmured jubilantly to Ayad, "A very successful visit. Now I've only got to check with Zurich that Rostov has deposited the first payment in my numbered bank account, and we're ready."

23

Robert Miller flew to London—there and back the same day.

He *had* to learn more about Judas.

By noon, Miller was sitting in a London office facing a tall, thin, balding man in a dark blue blazer. William Barkley was a top investigator for British Military Intelligence. The meeting had been arranged through Vaughan's CIA contacts in Washington, D.C.

Barkley was one of those quiet, poised Englishmen it was easy to misread. His elaborate, languid politeness and his clipped, precise way of speaking seemed to fit a university professor rather than a professional killer, and yet he was a seasoned member of the A-7 disposal squad—as Judas had been.

He was also extremely cagey.

At first Miller thought he understood why. Intelligence services never liked to discuss their mistakes. But Barkley's attitude went beyond that. He was extremely careful, as if he were under orders to reveal only so much—as if there were something the British wanted to hide.

"I'd like to know more about the death of Brett's parents," Miller said. "They both died violently."

The pale brown eyes opposite him stared out of the window as if he had only a boring list of facts to relate. "His father came from a distinguished military family. His ancestors fought at Waterloo. Probably at Agincourt, too, if you go that far back. His father was mentioned in dispatches at Dunkirk and was tipped for a top army position, a future general."

"But he never passed colonel. Why?"

Barkley said reluctantly, "I suppose because of his marriage."

"Because she was German?"

"No . . ." The Englishman didn't volunteer any more.

"Because she was a Nazi?" Miller pressed.

"No . . ."

"Why then?"

The pale brown eyes met his across the desk. "Because she was spying for the Germans."

That admission seemed to make it easier for the Englishman to talk. "Colonel Brett was in his forties when he married, she was in her twenties. She'd come to Britain as a refugee in the early thirties, ostensibly to work as a governess, one of those people the Nazis placed abroad throughout that period. All the European countries were riddled with them. She learned a lot about British army activities by marrying the Colonel. And he, a dumb army officer of the gentleman class, inexperienced where women were concerned, never realized why she was pumping him. He thought it was a loving wife's devotion to her husband and his career. She even bore him a son and heir. Someone to continue the family line! What more could a husband ask for? When British intelligence finally found out what she was doing and informed him, he wouldn't believe it at first. He was so completely infatuated. But the evidence against her was overwhelming. He was finally convinced. Then, of course, he went to the opposite extreme. He wanted to kill her. Apparently he gave her a choice—suicide or handing her over to the authorities. She shot herself and it was hushed up—it was still wartime. But it ruined his chances of promotion in the army."

"And when did the son learn about his mother?"

"I don't know. She was never mentioned by the father unless someone else brought up her name, and then he abused her memory. He reared his son very severely, as if trying to erase the mother's influence. The boy's childhood must have been rather like an unending army basic training. He also brought him up as an extremely devout Roman Catholic. When the boy was in his early teens, he had a crucifix tattooed on his chest. Of course the son rebelled as he grew up, and then he rejected everything associated with his father, including Catholicism. He even tried—unsuccessfully—to have the tattoo removed. Father and son developed an extremely hostile relationship."

"The father was killed," Miller said, "but no one was ever charged with the murder. Was anyone suspected?"

The pale brown eyes refused to meet Miller's.

"It was an unsolved crime. The old man became a local magistrate after he retired from the army. It could have been some psycho he sent away to prison getting his revenge. At least that was one theory at the time."

"Or some Nazi revenging the wife's suicide?" Miller said to see what the response would be.

"Extremely unlikely, I should think."

"Did the son ever talk about his father's murder?"

"Not to me, and I saw quite a lot of him for several years. We were at Cambridge together. Later we . . . er . . . worked together. We used to go to cricket matches. And soccer games. He never talked about his family, not to me. I thought I knew him quite well, but when he disappeared, I realized I didn't know the real man at all."

"Was he ever married?"

The Englishman shook his head. "No, he never seemed to bother much with women. To tell you the truth, he always seemed to me to have certain qualities I associate with . . . er . . . a priest. But I realize now I was wrong. One sometimes makes that mistake with a loner like him. I see him now as more like an antipriest." The Englishman's hands began to play with the papers on his desk, as if signaling he'd said all he intended to. "The key to him, I suppose, lies in his childhood —in his relationship to his parents."

"How old was he when his mother killed herself?"

"Six, I believe—the impressionable age, according to the . . . er . . . Jesuits."

That was as much as Miller could get out of him. The father's murder was the sensitive subject. Miller raised it again before he left, and there was the same veiled response, the same refusal to meet his eyes. He would have to find out what he wanted to know from someone else.

Robert checked on the whereabouts of the Brett estate, and when he discovered it was no more than an hour's train journey from London, he decided to go there.

He also discovered he was being followed. By a short, youngish man in an anonymous dark suit.

British intelligence must really be worried about *something* —unless the man worked for Judas.

He spent an hour taking buses and taxis, crisscrossing London. He was satisfied he was no longer being followed by the time he got on the train. He sat and watched the English countryside pass by, grey and wintry compared to Rome. Spring was still a few weeks away here.

He took a taxi from the local station. The driver was a fat, middle-aged woman who had lived in the area all her life, and she remembered Colonel Brett well.

"He broke his heart over that German wife of his," she said over her shoulder, driving as slowly as if her taxi were a stagecoach. "He couldn't even face the child—he reminded him too much of her. The boy looked *very* like her. He even had her German, Nordic fair hair. She was supposed to have killed herself because of an incurable disease, but I never believed it. We all thought she was a Nazi in the village. She had that high-necked, arrogant attitude."

"Who inherited the estate?"

"A cousin who lived in Scotland. An artist. Colonel Brett didn't leave his son *anything.*"

"They didn't get on?"

"They hated each other. The old man couldn't stand the sight of him."

"And what about the murder?"

She said over her shoulder, "You're asking a lot of questions."

Miller had an explanation ready: "I once met Colonel Brett's son." He remembered Judas at Amman airport—a short time after the vicious murder of Don Paolo.

"Poor boy," the woman said. "I remember him at the time his mother died—a darling little fellow with beautiful blond curls. One of the maids told me he used to sleep with her photograph under his pillow every night until his father found out and took it away. Colonel Brett couldn't stand any reminder of her. He was broken-hearted, poor man."

The estate had a high iron gate, high walls, and a big "trespassers will be prosecuted" notice.

"Imagine the Colonel and the little boy in this vast place alone together. The Colonel never had any visitors after she died." The woman was suddenly more friendly. "One of the detectives who worked on the murder is retired now and lives in the village."

"I'd like to talk to him."

"I can take you to meet him after we leave here."

"I've seen all I want to." Judas wasn't here in this vast English estate, merely the ghost of a little boy.

A village street of thatched cottages and red-bricked

houses stretched ahead. The taxi stopped outside a small ivy-covered cottage where a heavily built, grey-haired man was weeding a flower bed.

"Mr. Hargreaves, this is Mr. Miller. He's interested in the Brett murder."

"Come in, Mr. Miller," Hargreaves said jovially. "I'll help you if I can."

Miller paid the taxi driver and gave her a handsome tip. She offered to come back to take him to the station.

"Give me an hour," Miller told her. He couldn't spare any longer if he was going to get back to Rome that night.

"Come for him at *The Lion's Head*," said the ex-detective. "I'm thirsty after gardening."

There were only two other drinkers in the local pub, and they were playing darts in a corner. Miller asked Hargreaves if he would have something stronger than beer.

"Thank you. I like scotch—Johnny Walker—but I can't afford it on my pension."

Miller insisted on buying him a double.

They sat by themselves at a table on the far side of the bar, away from the dart board. Robert wanted to question the ex-detective in a relaxed, confidential atmosphere. He bought him another double. He worked up slowly to what he wanted to know. Hargreaves seemed pleased to reminisce about his police work. His neighbors had probably heard it all many times and he had no ready audience left. He had become very talkative by the time Robert asked casually, "Did you have a suspect in the Brett murder?"

The ex-detective stared knowingly at Miller.

"We're talking between ourselves, Mr. Miller?"

"Certainly."

"Well, I don't mind telling you it was a strange business, the most frustrating in all my years as a policeman. I thought we had a good case against the son, Paul Brett—good enough to take him in for questioning. But they wouldn't let me. He was doing some kind of hush-hush government work involving Military Intelligence. The Official Secrets Act was invoked. A trial would have revealed too much, I suppose. A stop was put to our inquiries at a high level. We were told Military Intelligence would question him, and if anything came of it, we would be informed. That was the last I heard of it. He disappeared, you know."

That explained Barkley's reticence, Miller thought. A-7

had protected a murderer to save its own secrets. Perhaps Judas had disappeared because he was afraid A-7 would dispose of him. Justice within the family. Or perhaps he was ready to form his own one-man international A-7.

"What was his motive?"

"Father and son hated each other ... with a passion," the old ex-detective said slowly. "The child was the one who discovered his mother's body. He was only about six at the time, but it's amazing what a child of that age can take in. He got some of her blood on his hands and, you know, ever afterwards apparently he has had a pathological fear of touching blood. It was reported in his army file. Of course Military Intelligence shouldn't have taken him, but he had a good academic record at Cambridge, and his family background appealed to all the right British snobberies. That might have blinded the investigators. He's 'one of us,' they'd think—all that nonsense."

"Some people might have hated their mother for being a Nazi, not their father."

"That's too logical, Mr. Miller. The human mind, especially a brilliant but unbalanced one, doesn't work that way. Hating the old man, he automatically idolized the memory of his mother, I suppose. When he found out the truth about her, it was too late—he simply rationalized and blamed it all on his father. Discovering her body probably had such a traumatic effect on him that it's ruined his relations with women ever since. We also don't know what she said to him, how she poisoned his childish mind, before she did it. Perhaps she made him something of a Nazi at heart, too. You have to be a bit weird to join Military Intelligence. They lose all moral sense, these intelligence chaps, all conscience. Like Paul Brett. I don't care what anyone else will tell you in the village here. They only remember the sweet little child—he seldom came home after he went away to school. But I'm convinced he killed his own father by cold-bloodedly shooting him with a hunting rifle with a telescopic sight from several hundred yards away—killed him as though the old man was no more than a deer he was gunning down ..."

Patricide, Miller thought. That was what he had come to find out. Patricide ... and a Nazi mother. That—and A-7—explained Judas. He killed the hated father figure in his life. And were the others all father figures, too? The British Home Secretary, Jeremy P. Sampson. The German Foreign Minister, Herman Abel. The leader of the Italian Communist party, Alberto Tolloni. And if Eli Abraham wasn't the next father figure, then who was?

Who?

24

Uniformed police on motorcycles closed the Via Barbo to all traffic in mid-afternoon. Angry motorists, who were diverted along a roundabout route, were told that the picturesque old street leading to the Tiber was being repaired. They were not allowed to see the real reason for the roadblock—the two black, official-looking limousines that were parked side by side near an abandoned warehouse on the river bank.

How Italian it was to hold a secret meeting with so much public drama! Niki Rostov thought patronizingly as he walked from his limousine to the other. All we lack is some opera singing!

"Niki!" Sandro Bellini's smooth, jutting jaw relaxed into a welcoming smile. He opened a well-stocked, portable liquor cabinet in front of him. "What will you drink?"

"Vodka of course," said the Russian, sinking back into one of the government limousine's plush leather armchairs. The police, the roadblock, this luxurious limousine were all meant to impress him with the Italian's power.

"Wait outside," Bellini told his uniformed chauffeur, who promptly left them alone. "I arranged our meeting here, Niki, to show you where I plan to build the party's museum. The Via Barbo will be renamed the Via Bellini!"

The man's vanity was incredible, Rostov thought. It made Bellini easy to manipulate—but also vulnerable to his enemies. He had to be closely watched. Failure would be fatal to both their careers.

"You look good, Niki," Bellini told him. "How was your trip?"

"I saw Judas." They exchanged quick, knowing glances. "He gave me a message for you—*be patient.*"

Bellini scowled. "Patience will get me nowhere against the

Papa Americano. He is already putting pressure on us—on the orders of the American CIA, no doubt! He slipped out again early this morning and showed up in a predominantly Communist district to visit a hospital. Big crowds *cheered* him."

"I know," Rostov said. "I saw him on television."

"He must be barred from television!" Bellini said angrily. "He must be kept inside the Vatican until we're ready to deal with the church! We need a wall around it like the one in Berlin!"

"Sandro," Rostov said gently, "you're letting him upset you too much." Italians were obsessed with the Vatican, even members of the Communist party. They should remember what Josef Stalin once said, 'How many divisions has the Pope?' *None!* His power was based only on illusions.

"Niki, you don't understand Italy where *Il Papa* is concerned. It is a family matter. And he is taking advantage of his unique position to challenge us. The Catholics have stiffened their position already, because of him. It has had an effect even inside the party. We must act quickly against him."

"No, Sandro, that's not the right way to deal with him. Judas is right—you must be patient. You will understand what he means when I tell you that . . . Judas is going to Jerusalem. He will be there on . . . *Friday*."

Bellini's great jaw rose in the way that made his enemies compare him to Mussolini.

"You mean . . . he intends to . . ."

"Exactly. Judas will take care of your *Papa Americano*—personally. All you have to do is wait and stay calm. Do nothing, especially no hostile act against the Vatican. Be neutral until Friday. Then there will be no suspicion of you. It will be a Middle-East affair. The Arab extremists will be blamed! And once he is out of the way, you can move as ruthlessly as you wish. The Catholics will be scared. They will have lost their champion—their David. The Vatican will no longer consider a refuge in Jerusalem. Instead, they will elect an Italian Pope to appease you. The Christian Democrats will be thrown into a panic. *Then* is the perfect time for your show trial."

Bellini nodded thoughtfully. "That makes sense." He held up his glass. "Let me propose a toast—to Judas' success!"

"Yes," Rostov agreed, holding up his glass, "I'll drink to that—to Judas!"

* * *

Driving away from his meeting with the Russian, Bellini wondered if he could afford to wait until Friday before taking any action.

Pressures were growing that he hadn't mentioned to Niki Rostov.

Vito Altieri was close to breaking point. If he talked, it could be very dangerous.

The American journalist was a growing threat. If the truth about the Tolloni Affair came out before Friday, a link might be discovered between that and what happened in Jerusalem. He wasn't yet strong enough to withstand that.

Be *patient*, Niki had said.

But how long could he afford to wait?

Friday was four days away.

It depended on what happened in the meantime . . .

There had already been one important development at the Vatican.

Monsignor O'Malley had discovered the identity of the Communist informer—with the help of one of his cousins, Lieutenant Thomas Hague of the Boston Police. The promise of a private audience with Pope David had persuaded the burly, grey-haired Lieutenant to visit Rome for a few days. The Monsignor put his suspicions to him and asked him to check them out.

It took only two days for Hague to discover the truth.

O'Malley immediately took the bad news to the Pope. Signor Moravia was there with some letters to sign. O'Malley waited for him to leave, pretending to play with the Pope's parrot. But as soon as the door closed, he turned serious.

"I have found the informer as you requested," he said unhappily, "though the credit for proving it belongs to my cousin."

The thin, intense face looked up quickly. "Who is it?"

O'Malley looked at the door. He seemed unwilling to convey the bad news, but it couldn't wait any longer.

"Tell me the worst, Joe."

"You won't like it."

"Tell me anyway. I need to know."

A giant fist gestured toward the door. "That jerk who just went out."

"Orlando Moravia?" The Pope sat forward. "You're sure, Joe?"

"Apart from Pope Alfredo, he was the only one who knew about Don Paolo's flight to Jerusalem. He arranged it."

"Others could have learned about it."

"For the past two days, my cousin, Lieutenant Hague of the Boston Police Department, has followed him. He made contact with the Communists twice, meeting at the Trevi Fountain one time and at the Pantheon the other. Just for a second to pass on something. My cousin said it was very slickly done—obviously from long practice."

The Pope instinctively touched the plain black crucifix around his neck. "What was Moravia's reason?" he asked sadly. "Is he a committed Communist or are they black-mailing him into doing it? Moravia's married, but he has certain mannerisms that suggest he could be bisexual."

O'Malley gave David I a quick, admiring look. He didn't miss anything.

"My cousin says he keeps a boy in an apartment on the other side of Rome. But whether the Communists have threatened to divulge it, tell his wife, we don't know."

"I prefer that explanation," said the Pope, "to his being a hardened, committed informer."

"What do you want me to do, Holiness? Confront him with the truth?"

The Pope was silent for a long time. His fingers touched in the act of silent prayer.

"I think we better wait until after Jerusalem," he said at last. "Moravia has connections with the Christian Democrats, and we don't want to demoralize them any further until Bellini is dealt with."

"But Moravia is supposed to accompany you to Jerusalem."

"Then let him." David smiled sadly. "If he accompanies us, Joe, he can't do any more harm here in the Vatican. And—who knows?—perhaps a visit to Jerusalem will even do him some good, poor man."

25

Israeli agents had penetrated the refugee camp that was the cover for Hamed's operations, but they hadn't infiltrated the top level of his organization, where intense family and tribal loyalty had to be proved beyond question. Thus Marc Ram didn't learn of Judas' visit to Hamed, but he did hear about the shipment of the grenades.

They were taken into Beirut by truck on Palm Sunday—the Sunday before Good Friday. When the truck reached the outskirts, smoke was pouring out of the Christian quarter from a Moslem rocket attack. There was a military curfew in the center of the city. To avoid a search of the truck, the transfer was switched to a suburban area close to the beach. Even with Beirut in a state verging on civil war, people were sunning themselves on the white sand as if it were a normal Sunday.

They'll still be doing that when the Apocalypse arrives, thought the truck driver, a tanned, hard-looking man of thirty-eight in worn jeans and a blue sweatshirt. In his mirror, he could see one of Hamed's top men sitting in the back with the big, reinforced suitcase. Hamed's man was in his forties with sharp Bedouin features. He also wore the jeans and sweatshirt that looked anonymous in the city. The big suitcase he was guarding was marked *Handle with Care*. The truck driver hadn't been told what was in it, but he could guess. Guns or explosives or both. All he knew was that the suitcase was going to Jerusalem—to cause more trouble for his people.

The truck driver was an Israeli agent, whose cover was that he had been born in the old Palestine. And it was true. Even though the Palestinians had been dispersed, it was not something you dared make up. In the refugee camps, you might meet someone from the same area. The truck driver was Palestinian, but he was also born of a Jewish father. He identified, like most Palestinians, with his father's side—with the wandering Jewish people who had found their home after two thousand years, not with the thousands of recent Arab refugees now seeking somewhere they could call their own again. But because he was Palestinian, his Jewish roots unknown, he had slowly won the trust of Hamed's men— enough to serve them, labor for them, drive their trucks.

"Here he comes," murmured Hamed's man behind him.

A black Mercedes limousine passed the truck and parked along a side road. A small, muscular young man with a swarthy Arab face got out. He was dressed in a white open-necked shirt and dark pants, neutral clothes in the divided city. Only Arab clothes made you seem to take sides. He looked at the truck, but didn't move toward it.

Hamed's man tapped the truck driver on the shoulder. "Bring this over," he grunted.

The truck driver jumped out, flexed his arm muscles, and lifted the suitcase to the ground. It was very heavy.

"Be careful with it," Hamed's man said nervously. He made no attempt to help with it, but walked ahead. He treated the truck driver like a servant.

The small, muscular young man opened the trunk. "Put it in there," he said. He ran the Arabic words together in the accent of northern Lebanon.

"It will be safe?" asked Hamed's man.

"It'll be with the luggage. No one will examine that."

"You are honored!"

They both laughed.

Hamed's man told the truck driver, "Wait for me in the truck," and then he began to talk privately with the young man.

The truck driver sat in the truck smoking a cigarette, watching them. When they were both turned away from him, talking intently, he took out a small pocket camera and quickly photographed the young man. It would help to identify him.

As Sunday changed into Monday, the truck driver's report and film reached Jerusalem. They were passed up the security ladder until they arrived on the desk of Inspector-General Reuven Feinberg of the Israeli Police. He at once took them over to Marc Ram. Feinberg, a short, mild-tempered man in his forties, was one of the most experienced detectives in Israel, and Ram had borrowed him for this last week. Judas had only until Sunday—Easter Sunday.

Ram read the report. "What do you think?" he asked Feinberg thoughtfully.

"It could be more bullshit bombs for indiscriminate terrorist scares like we've been having for the past couple of months. Or it could be what you're looking for."

"Hamed's training camp has international terrorist personnel and the latest weapons through Czechoslovakia. Judas' Russian friends would probably take him there for whatever he needed. The question is how the hell did they hope to get the suitcase past our security checks?"

Feinberg picked up the report. "Listen to this, Marc. 'It will be among the luggage. No one will examine that.' . . . 'You are honored.' That can mean only one thing—the car didn't need to undergo a security check."

"But then it would have to belong to one of us at a fairly high level—"

"Or some non-Israeli on the privileged list! Some bastard has taken advantage of his privileged status to smuggle in terrorist supplies!"

Ram's black-gloved hand thumped his desk. "Get a complete list from the checkpoints of all the privileged travelers who came over in the last twenty-four hours. The suitcase probably came by road and crossed the border at Rosh el-Nikra, but in case they played cute and came through Jordan or by air, cover all checkpoints." He stared at the photograph. "Anybody recognize it yet?"

"No," Feinberg said, "the face isn't clear."

"He's an Arab, young, short, with a well-developed body. It narrows the list. Who among the privileged fits that description?"

"He could be one of their employees."

"True, but someone should recognize him anyway. We've got to find him as fast as we can. Time's running out. It's already Monday . . ."

By midday, Feinberg had a list of five people with privileged status, who had arrived in Israel during the last twenty-four hours:

The United States Ambassador.

A United Nations representative for refugee relief.

An Israeli cabinet minister.

Major Falid.

The Roman Catholic Apostolic Delegate.

By early afternoon, the photograph was identified.

The young man photographed by the truck driver was the chauffeur of the Roman Catholic Apostolic Delegate, Monsignor Le Clair.

"*Shit!*" Ram said. "That upsets our Catholic apple cart. The last thing Eli wants is trouble with the Latins during the present delicate negotiations with the new Pope."

"We don't know that the Apostolic Delegate himself is involved," Feinberg said.

"It's his car. He's the boss. He's an Arab lover—one of those French intellectuals who revere de Foucauld and Sharbel." Ram's black-gloved hand clenched with tension, and then slowly relaxed, the fingers spread out like claws on the steel desk top. "But you're right, Reuven. We don't know *for sure*. We better play it very cool. Just bring the chauffeur in for now. Leave the Monsignor to stew a while."

"The chauffeur's driven the Apostolic Delegate over to Bethany."

"What's happening there?" Ram asked suspiciously.

"Today, the Monday of Holy Week, they celebrate Christ's visit to the house of Lazarus, whom He raised from the dead. 'Jesus therefore, six days before the Passover, came to Bethany.' I checked it wasn't a trick."

"Okay, let the chauffeur drive the Monsignor back home, but keep him under strict surveillance the whole time. When the Monsignor's safely inside the Apostolic Delegate's residence, grab the chauffeur and get out of him everything he knows. *Everything.* As fast as you can. Hell, Monday's half gone already."

"Gloves off?"

"Yeah, gloves off. This is an emergency. That guy's an accessory to Judas' next operation. He's the only clue we've got."

Major Falid had just reached his home outside Amman and was saying good night to his young children before they went up to bed. His wife had kept them up so they could see him.

The phone rang. He let his wife answer it, and he heard her voice suddenly tense.

"Who is it?"

"Jerusalem."

He gently disengaged himself from his children and went into the study to find out what the Israelis wanted.

"Falid here."

"This is Marc Ram, Major." The Israeli sounded worried. "We've got a suspect we believe is a link with Judas, but we're having trouble with him. Could you help us with our interrogation?"

Major Falid said suspiciously, "He is an Arab?"

"Yes—from Lebanon originally."

"And you want me to question him?"

"He knows something."

"I will come to Jerusalem tomorrow morning."

"Can you possibly come now, Major? We have so little time."

The Major sighed. He saw the resigned look on his wife's face. "Very well. I'll be there as soon as I can, Colonel."

Top-secret security interrogations took place in a large house behind a tall stone wall in the village of Ein Kerem, the birthplace of John the Baptist. Major Falid was driven there from the Allenby Bridge in an Israeli limousine that was waiting for him. The Major was shown into a large lounge at the back of the house. Several sallow, Israeli-looking men were sitting in armchairs. Nobody was talking. Everybody seemed drained and depressed. There were half-empty cups of coffee and an empty bottle of scotch on a small table. The atmosphere was grim, almost like a wake, the Major thought, but worse because there was no purging grief, only profound frustration and guilt. The Major knew the scene from his own experience. It was when you had an important suspect and you couldn't make him talk. You knew you had to break him.

A grim-faced Marc Ram came into the lounge. "Major, this is very good of you." The black-gloved hand gripped the Major's. "Let me take you down immediately so we don't waste any time."

The interrogation room was in a soundproofed section of the basement. As they approached the steel door, a high-pitched scream, muffled but audible, came from beyond it.

"Wait here a minute, Major."

Ram disappeared into the room.

They're cleaning him up for the visitor, Major Falid thought.

He was kept waiting nearly ten minutes.

Then three hard-eyed, tired-looking men, their white shirt

sleeves rolled up and dark with sweat under the armpits, came out and went upstairs. They would be the interrogators taking a break.

"This way, Major."

Marc Ram led the way into the interrogation room. It was in darkness except for an intensely strong table lamp shining directly on the prisoner, whose legs and arms were strapped to a steel chair that was bolted to the floor. The only other person in the room was an armed guard with a shoulder holster, also in his shirt sleeves. There was a strong, almost overpowering odor in the room—the odor of stale smoke, sweat, vomit, blood, the reek of pain and the sourness of fear and frustration. It was an odor the Major knew well. He looked at the face of the young man under the strong light.

Ram said, "He's—"

"I know who he is," the Major said. He remembered the young man's strange tension that day he had spoken to him outside the Apostolic Delegate's residence. It was explained now.

Ram told the Major what he knew, but not how he had obtained the information. He still didn't know how far he could trust the Jordanian.

"What do you want me to tell him, Colonel?" Major Falid said.

"Tell him we'll make him talk eventually. Tell him he should save himself any more unnecessary pain. Everybody talks eventually. We can't afford to wait too long. We'll have to put more pressure on him." Ram pointed to the electrical equipment Major Falid had already noticed—the control box on a table, the small electrical transformer lying on the floor, the little copper connections ready to be fitted to the nipples, and the larger one with serrated teeth that would be clipped to each side of the head of the young man's penis. "Tell him he's a brave man. We respect him. *But* we, too, must do our duty. We *have* to learn what he knows. Tell him to save his body any more suffering . . ." The black-gloved hand clenched and unclenched. Only someone who had lost a whole limb could respect the human body the way Ram did, and this young man kept his in good shape. It seemed profoundly inhuman to harm it in anyway, and yet he would have no choice if the young man didn't talk.

"Leave us alone together, please," said Major Falid.

Ram nodded. "Very well."

Major Falid had expected him to refuse. The Israeli must have a concealed microphone in the room, he thought. We shall be overheard.

Ram gestured for the guard to follow him out. The door closed behind them.

Major Falid moved close to the chair so the young man could see him. There were ugly bruises on the young man's face, and one eye was swollen shut. The wide, boyish mouth was drawn tight with pain. The Major remembered how he had looked cleaning the Mercedes. He was a handsome young Arab with a proud bearing. He should have been out walking with his girl, enjoying the spring weather, full of peaceful dreams. He reminded the Major of himself twenty years ago when he had first met his wife. He, too, had had the same fiery pride in being an Arab and in his strong body—the young man obviously lifted weights regularly.

"I am Major Falid from Amman," he said formally with respect. "I am here to help you if I can. You are one of my people . . ." He remembered the name Monsignor Le Clair had used—a boyhood friend of his had had the same name. "Nayef . . ." The one good eye opened wider with surprise. "You are my brother. We struggle for justice together." The eye looked at him with close attention. "But if we murder for justice, then it is not justice. We must be true to our dreams, to the spirit of our homeland. Tell them what you know—to stop this unnecessary killing . . ."

Immediately, the eye's expression changed and darkened with hatred.

"You are . . . one of *them*," the young man hissed.

"They have all the modern technical devices, Nayef. They can force you to talk. Nobody can resist forever. Already you have demonstrated your courage. But you are fighting the wrong war . . . at the wrong time. This secret terrorism is not the way we Arabs should fight. It is against our pride."

"You are . . . a traitor . . . to the cause!" the voice cried. The tight, cracked lips opened wider, and he tried to spit in the Major's face, but the spittle fell instead on his own bare, brown chest.

"Listen to me, Nayef . . ."

But it was useless. The eye burned with hatred and the head turned away.

At last the Major said, "I go now. But I can always return if you need me. Ask for me . . ."

The eye looked contemptuous.

As he came out, the interrogators went back in.

Marc Ram said, "I'm sorry, Major, to have wasted your time. But it seemed worth trying. I hoped to prevent what we now must do."

A muffled scream came from the other side of the door. It seemed to lacerate the Major's nerves.

Marc Ram said quickly, "It's always a nasty business. But what alternative is there? We must know."

"Perhaps he knows nothing," Major Falid said.

"No," Ram said, "He knows something. You can tell it by his resistance. He hasn't got the suitcase any longer. It's been delivered. To whom? . . . And for what purpose?"

The Major said bleakly, "I must leave here." He walked out in silence. Ram drove him to his car at the Allenby Bridge. They said very little. Both men's thoughts were back in the interrogation room they had just left. They parted with a silent handshake. I've lost whatever progress I had made with him, Ram thought. I'm once more one of *them*—a Zionist, a Jew.

Feeling unable to return immediately to the interrogation, he went for a ride in the moonlight—the ride he always took in similar circumstances, especially when he had had to kill somebody. He got out of the car when he could see the ridge called *Har Hazikaron* or the Hill of the Remembrance. There was the long Avenue of the Righteous Gentiles, lined with trees, leading to Yad Vashem—the memorial dedicated to the six million Jews murdered by the Nazis. The lower walls were formed out of mammoth, uncut boulders; the massive structure had a stark, primitive quality that was entirely appropriate.

This is what we must remember, Ram told himself. Always. This justifies our efforts, all our efforts, to survive . . .

He drove slowly back to the interrogation. It did not make it any easier, but it gave him renewed determination to see it through.

The young chauffeur broke just after dawn on Tuesday morning, and the tape recorder was switched on. He rambled, often incoherently, for several minutes, and then collapsed into deep unconsciousness. He couldn't be revived. He was rushed to the private wing of a hospital used for security cases and put on the critical list. He wasn't going to die, the doctors decided, but he would take a long time to recover consciousness. There was no hope of talking with him any more for at least a week, and by then, it would all be over.

Within two hours, a complete transcript of what he had said was on Marc Ram's desk, with the relevant sections underlined in red by Inspector-General Feinberg.

> Q: How did you deliver the suitcase?
> A: I . . . was told . . . to leave it . . . under a pine tree . . . near the . . . Russian Church . . . of . . . St. Mary Magdalene . . . on the . . . edge of . . . Gethsemane.
> Q: Who collected it?
> A: I wasn't told . . . but I . . . checked . . . It was gone . . an hour later.
> Q: Was any code name used?
> A: In Beirut . . . when I got it . . . yes.
> Q: What was it?
> A: Op'ration . . . Go . . . l'th.
> Q: Repeat that last word.
> A: Go . . . l'th.

Ram couldn't make sense of this answer, nor could Feinberg. At first Ram thought it might be an Arabic word, but none fitted. He asked for the tape and played it back several times.

Go . . . l'th . . . Gol'th . . . Gol-th . . .

Ram stared out at the distant glimpse of the Old City in the early morning sunlight—the City of David—and he suddenly realized what the word was.

Goliath.

He recalled his biblical training as a youth. "And there went out a champion out of the camp of the Philistines, named Goliath of Gath, whose height was six cubits and a span . . ."

And who was associated with Goliath in people's minds?

"And when the Philistine looked about, and saw David, he disdained him: for he was *but* a youth . . ."

David.

Ram grabbed the phone to alert Eli Abraham.

They hadn't long.

Pope David was due in Jerusalem in just three days.

26

The Israeli Ambassador to Italy, a career diplomat named Arthur Blomberg, brought the news to the Vatican.

He met with David I in the Pope's private library on the second floor of the Palace. He was a big, heavily built man who towered over the slight figure in white.

The Pope listened in silence, his expression serious and intent, as Ambassador Blomberg told him of the forthcoming attempt to assassinate him.

"The Prime Minister respectfully suggests, Your Holiness, that you cancel your visit to Jerusalem," the Ambassador concluded. "This man is too dangerous to take lightly. The Tolloni case showed what he is capable of doing."

The Pope nodded. "I understand what we are up against, Mr. Blomberg. Please convey my thanks to the Prime Minister for his message, and I am grateful to you for bringing it to me. But," he added gently, "we can't let assassins dictate our schedule, because that would mean giving in to them. It would be especially harmful for the church at this time to seem to be afraid. If we cancel our visit to Jerusalem just because of this threat, we will seem weak, indeed, and our enemies will take advantage of it."

"Wouldn't it be worse, Your Holiness, if the assassination attempt was successful?"

The Pope regarded the Israeli Ambassador with a wry, almost wistful look. "My bags are always packed, Mr. Blomberg. Leaders don't have a long life in the modern world. One may not even have to wait for an assassin. I could die in bed at any time, like Pope John Paul I. In 1978, he was pope for a mere thirty-four days. A good man, he promised to be a great pope. His death was entirely unexpected, yet it was not a disaster for the church. Another pope can always be found. Popes are not all that important, Mr. Blomberg. The church is full of potential popes. But at this time, faced with a hostile government here in Italy, it is *very* important for the church not to appear weak. If I cancel my visit, our enemies will take

it as a sign that the church is very open to pressure, is very
vulnerable. Please convey this answer to the Prime Minister.
My plans are unchanged. I shall be in Jerusalem on Good
Friday." The tension in him relaxed a little. "Now tell me,
Mr. Blomberg, what is going to happen to the Apostolic
Delegate?"

"We cannot prove a case against him personally, Your
Holiness. The young chauffeur insists that Monsignor Le
Clair was not involved, that he knew nothing about the
suitcase or its contents. Of course he shares some responsibility because his privileges were abused and the young man
worked for him. But we won't arrest him if you agree to
withdraw him from Israel. We cannot accord him the privileges of the Apostolic Delegate any longer. He must leave
Jerusalem immediately."

David nodded. "That seems advisable. Monsignor Le Clair
would probably benefit from a return to his native France,
which he probably understands far better than the Middle
East. The church needs a less innocent representative there in
the years ahead if we are to be more closely involved—and
we may well be if the forces of darkness win in Italy . . ."

Both men were sombre and thoughtful as they walked to
the door of the private library. But as they were parting, the
Pope suddenly called the Ambassador back.

"Mr. Blomberg," he said softly, "would you convey a
request to the Prime Minister for me? When I arrive in
Jerusalem on Friday, I don't want my visit stifled by excessive
security. Good Friday is the most solemn time of the year for
the church. When I follow the route taken by Jesus with His
Cross along the Via Dolorosa on Good Friday, it will be
comparable to the solemnity in one of your synagogues on
Yom Kippur. The faithful must be undisturbed and free to
pray. The meaning of the occasion must not be spoilt by the
demands of security, the atmosphere of fear. That will merely
play into the hands of our enemies."

"I will pass on your request, Your Holiness," said Ambassador Blomberg unhappily. He knew what Marc Ram's reaction would be.

"They're planning to get Pope David," Robert Miller told
Vaughan. Lieutenant Kahn had come to the hotel to tell him,
and he had immediately gone to Colonel Crane at the U.S.
Embassy. This conversation had to be secret. "One thing I

can't understand. In the other operation codes, Judas—Brett
—used the names of winners. Delilah, Cain. But Goliath was
a loser."

"You don't understand Brett's psychology," Vaughan said.
"The truly evil dream of reversing the trend of history. In the
rematch, Goliath wins. What name did Paul Brett choose for
himself? Not Sir Galahad. Judas! Was Judas a winner? And if
you follow Delilah or Cain to their just ends, were they
winners? But that's irrelevant. When it comes to identification, everything is reversed for a man like Paul Brett. Christ,
Mohammed, David . . . these are the enemy, and he is convinced he will beat them. So for him, Goliath will win the
rematch. And maybe he's on to something. What student
of our recent history will claim Good is winning all over?
Hasn't Goliath won victories in many parts of the world? So
far isn't Judas—Goliath—winning in Italy?"

"So far," Miller said grimly. "But the tide's turning."

"I hope to God you're right," Vaughan said.

Miller next went to the *Mirror*'s bureau office to tell
Hammond. They were now on much better terms. Miller had
lost a lot of his combative edge since Gina's arrival in his life.
In case anything happened to him, Miller had leveled completely with the bureau chief. He had found him much more
cooperative than he expected, willing to play a supporting
role. Maybe he's a bit scared of what I've got into, Miller
thought. Well, no more than I am.

"Now you've got a double reason for going back to
Jerusalem," Hammond said.

Miller had already decided to cover the Pope's visit, but
this made it a much bigger story and promised what he had
been waiting for . . . another confrontation with Judas . . .
Paul Brett.

The plan to assassinate David I was closely related to what
was happening in Italy, he thought. The whole business was
interconnected, like a Borgia intrigue. Bellini and the Russians behind him had decided David I was too dangerous to
live. With him out of the way, the opposition would crumble.
God, Miller thought, Bellini will win if David is killed. Judas
must be stopped.

Hammond lit one of his strong cigars. "Any progress with
Vito Altieri?" he asked between expansive puffs.

"No, Gina's still working on him. He's left his wife and is
staying with her. He's still scared shitless. Mama Tolloni's

murder certainly had the desired effect. It was meant as a warning, a threat, and it successfully silenced him—so far."

"Soon it won't matter," Hammond said. "Once Bellini is firmly established, Vito Altieri's testimony won't make any difference. Now's the time to sock it to Professor Valeri with evidence he can't ignore. His prestige could still sway the party. The President could dissolve Parliament if he had enough support. Bellini isn't completely in control yet, but time's running out. Something's needed to bring Valeri down from his ivory tower. Vito Altieri could do it."

"I know," Miller said, "but how do you give a man the balls to risk his life?"

Robert hadn't seen Gina for over a week. Her father was too scared to be alone. He was surprised then to find her waiting for him when he returned to the hotel. He had given her a key to his room, and she was lying on the bed watching a soap opera on TV. She had been there some time; the cigarette butts in an ashtray showed how nervous she was.

He leaned over and kissed her. "It's been a whole week."

"Eight days to be exact," she said. "I just had to come. I thought you'd never get here. You reporters never stay home."

"Can you stay all night?"

"All night? You must be kidding, Roberto. Papa would go out of his mind with fright. I must leave as soon as I've told you the news. I didn't trust the phone here at your hotel. Not with this. *Papa has decided to see Professor Valeri!* He's made an appointment to see him at his home tomorrow morning."

"What made him change his mind?"

"Carmela Tolloni came to have dinner with us. She has been very depressed. She thinks her parents died for nothing. Their murderers are getting away with it. She moved Papa to tears. She pleaded with him as an old friend of her parents to do something. *Something!* She became very emotional and so did my father. He couldn't very well turn her down. He promised her he would do what he could. He phoned Professor Valeri for an appointment while she was there. She made sure of that. She knows him."

"He used the phone? Wasn't that risky?"

"Yes," she said slowly. "I suppose it was. We had all had too much wine. We weren't thinking very clearly." She began to get up. "I better go back to him."

He pushed her gently down again. "You can't run away so soon. You've had me crawling up the wall with frustration."

"I've got to go, Roberto. I can't leave him alone too long."

He grinned down at her. "You've got time for a quickie. *Please*. Then I'll drive you back."

"No," she said. "I must go."

But she stayed. And it was even better than he had remembered. She fulfilled once more all the promise of those big sensual brown eyes. She was more fun to be with than any woman he had ever known. Their bodies blended easily together, but afterward, just lying there, doing nothing but touching and talking, it was still a great sensual experience. He felt relaxed and renewed as always with her.

"Roberto," she said softly.

"What is it?"

"I have been thinking lately of returning to the church. I'd like to try it again. Pope David has given me a new perspective on some things."

"Don't go back because of one individual's charisma, Gina. It's got to be for a better reason than that."

"You don't have much faith in my intelligence, Roberto. I have my reasons. But somebody can help you to see more clearly what you want. Pope David is right from my point of view. A materialistic philosophy doesn't satisfy. It puts us on the level of animals—or machines."

Miller said quietly, "They've uncovered a plot to assassinate the Pope when he goes to Jerusalem."

"Oh, no!" she cried in a shocked tone. "Why do they always kill off the people who really want to do something—who really stand for something good in this lousy world? No wonder Papa is so scared of standing up."

"Easy now," he said. "They haven't killed the Pope yet."

"They will," she said. "Give them time. They never let up." She was suddenly anxious. "What's the time?" She sat up.

He glanced at his watch. "Ten to nine."

"Oh, no." She scrambled over him, stood up, and began to put on her clothes. "I've been away nearly three hours. I've never left him alone for so long before. He's very nervous about tomorrow. I shouldn't have come out. I should have stayed with him."

"Gina, he's not a child."

"He is in many ways. All men are, but Papa especially. Are you going to drive me back like you promised?"

"Sure."

"Then get dressed, Roberto! I must hurry."

Her hand shook as she lit a cigarette. He realized how worked up she was, and quickly put on his clothes.

It was a twenty-minute drive across Rome. Gina worried all the way. "Can't you go any faster?" she kept saying.

"Gina," he protested, "if I drive any faster in this crazy Roman traffic, we'll have an accident."

"I've got a strange feeling, Roberto. My father and I have become very close, and we often feel the same things. I am sure something is wrong. Please hurry. Please. It's my fault. I shouldn't have stayed out so long."

She was working herself up into a very nervous state. She sat forward, her eyes looking straight ahead as if straining to see as far as she could in the hope of seeing her father.

"Gina, relax. Everything's all right. You're just nervous. Your father's all right. He's probably fast asleep by now."

"Roberto, there *is* something wrong. I know. I feel it. I stayed out too long."

She was so insistent that gradually he caught her mood and felt the same urgency she did. Perhaps they had tapped her phone or Valeri's, and knew about the meeting tomorrow morning. He began to race the traffic, cutting corners, jumping traffic lights, taking risks, with angry Italian voices and car horns sounding behind him. At last the car came roaring down the tree-lined street to Gina's home. As soon as it squealed to a stop, she was out and rushing up the high steps to the old marble building that, like so many in Rome, had the fine, high proportions of a palace—but a very rundown, decaying palace.

Miller followed her down the dimly lit, high-ceilinged hallway to the ancient creaky elevator. They were jerked upwards past huge dark floors, Gina grimly desperate, more sure than ever that something was wrong. The whole building was silent—so still and peaceful, a haven of people getting their rest or watching television, that Robert's natural scepticism began to return. Gina was being hysterical. It was understandable after all the strain she'd been through with her father. She had caught some of his fear, some of his dread, but she would cool down once she was home, once she saw him.

When the old elevator finally reached the fifth floor, Gina ran ahead down the dim passageway, past the row of large ornate doorways. Her apartment was at the far end. Even from where he was, following her more slowly, Miller could see her door was already wide open. Suddenly he knew something *was* wrong, and he raced after her.

Gina had already disappeared inside, and her scream started just as he reached the open door. It was a small, two-room apartment. Gina was on her knees at the bedroom door. Miller started walking towards her. There was someone lying on the floor. He could see short fat legs in dark trousers. Gina was cradling a grey head. He went down on his knees so he could see the face.

The eyes were wide open, staring upwards with a look of great terror.

The pudgy little man had been shot twice in the chest.

Vito Altieri had been dead for some time. Miller could tell that by the skin.

"Oh, Papa," Gina was moaning, "I'm sorry."

Robert spoke her name, but she didn't respond.

He touched her shoulder to try to comfort her, but she shook his hand away. Then slowly she stood up. This was a Gina he had never seen before. Her face was drained of all color. The eyes that usually looked so warm were cold and full of hatred.

"They are not going to get away with *this!*" she cried. "I will keep Papa's appointment with Professor Valeri."

Then she wept.

27

Wednesday.

This was the day Judas, Ayad and the German, Karl Mundt, arrived in Jerusalem. Judas wanted them to be there for the whole of Thursday to have time to solve any last-minute problems.

They traveled separately to the Holy City.

Judas, with the same beard, wide-brimmed black hat, and long black coat, used his Polish Rabbi's passport, but went this time across the Allenby Bridge. He gave the same ingratiating performance before the Israeli officials as he had the first time at the airport, even mentioning his longing to see the Wall, which gained the same sympathetic response. His interest in Old Testament remains was readily accepted as his reason for coming through Arab Jordan. His passport was given only a quick, cursory examination before he was waved on to make way for the next person in the long line of arrivals.

Ayad crossed over from Lebanon at Rosh el-Nikra at about the same time. The young Palestinian entered Israel as a Lebanese Christian, part of the flood starting to arrive for the Pope's visit. He had a picture of an Arab-looking Jesus stitched on the back of his white shirt, and he carried a heavy four-foot black crucifix with a very oriental, contorted, dying Christ figure carved in ebony and crudely tied on with wire, complete with a metal base to stand on. Israel was sympathetic to Lebanese Christians, taking their side in the civil war in Beirut, and Ayad crossed over in the middle of a long line of them, but the border guards still searched him for weapons, passed him through a metal detector, and thoroughly checked his passport. They didn't show much interest in his big crucifix, but it was doubtful if even a close examination would have spotted its other function.

Karl Mundt went the easy way by air on a German passport obtained six months earlier. Before leaving Beirut, he asked Judas about the mortar and the grenades, but Judas said only that both would be in Jerusalem "in plenty of time." Judas gave him the name and address of a Soviet informer who would give him lodging and arranged to meet him on Mount Zion outside the entrance to David's Tomb at eleven A.M. the following day.

"You're not staying at the same place?" Mundt asked.

"No," Judas said. "We're split up." He didn't explain why. Someone had to stay with the informer to satisfy the Russians. It was the Russians' way of keeping in touch with the operation. But Judas didn't trust the Russians enough for them all to stay there. The German was the most expendable. He told him: "She'll give you a suitcase to bring to me. It'll be pretty heavy. Better come by cab."

The woman lived in an apartment block in the New City. Mundt had memorized her name—Sonia Petrovich—and when he pressed the bell marked *Petrovich*, a voice asked him who he was.

"Karl Mundt."

She must have been expecting him because the door immediately buzzed, and he pressed it open. Her apartment was on
the nineteenth floor. The elevator going up was full of
European Jews. They looked at him as if sensing his hostility.

She was a Jew, too—a plump, dark-haired woman about
forty with a pale, washed-out face. He hadn't expected a
Soviet informer to be Jewish. He thought the Russian Communists and the Jews hated each other. Of course, informers
could be anything. They had no real identity of their own.

She looked over his shoulder, surprised to see him alone.

"I thought there were three of you."

"The other two are staying somewhere else," he said.

"Oh." She seemed disappointed. She held the door open for
him to enter. He sensed she wasn't an altogether willing
hostess. There wasn't much of an attempt to make him feel
welcome.

"This is where you'll sleep." She opened a bedroom door.
"That's the kitchen. There's food in the refrigerator. Help
yourself." She led him down a hallway. "This is the lounge.
There's a TV. Beyond it is a balcony with a view of the city."
She looked at him. "Any questions?"

"Won't the neighbors wonder who I am?"

"I've already told them I was expecting some cousins from
Europe."

"There is a suitcase for me—"

"Yes, I have already collected it as arranged. I left it for
you in the bedroom."

He smiled at her, his hard, mercenary's brothel smile. She
had an efficient, spinsterish manner. She probably needed
waking up with some heavy sex. "Maybe the neighbors will
think we're lovers," he said, putting one of his powerful
hands on her shoulder.

She stepped back and said coldly, "I have been told to
accommodate you. I have no choice. But we don't need to
pretend it is anything more. Now if you will excuse me, I will
go to my room."

Mundt washed up and changed his shirt. The suitcase was
in the bedroom as she had said. It was very heavy, marked
Handle With Care. That will be the bombs, he thought.

He went looking for her. There was one room with the
door shut. He knocked.

"Yes?" her voice called. "What do you want?"

He opened the door. It was a large woman's bedroom, decorated in blue, with a sweet scent. She was lying on the bed reading a letter in Russian. She didn't look pleased to see him.

"Why are you doing this?" he said. "For money?"

His directness surprised her.

"I've got a job. I don't need money."

There was only one other explanation. "You've got relatives still in Russia?"

"If you must know—yes! My father and mother." For a moment, their faces flashed through her mind—the gentle, aging faces she would do anything to protect, *anything*, even help this man. They were all she had left in the world. She knew she would never see them again, but it was enough to know they were alive and well. Many Soviet Jewish families were divided that way . . .

"They threaten if you don't do what they say, your parents . . ." Mundt knew the way they worked.

She was suddenly aware of the German standing over her. Her lips tightened. This man was one of *them*. "Look, Mr. Mundt, this is my personal business. I don't want to talk about it to a stranger."

He sat on the edge of the bed. "You seem like a nice woman."

His hand caressed her leg. It was a long time since he'd had a European woman who wasn't a whore.

She got up abruptly. "I said I'd let you stay here and that's all."

"You've got a lot of spirit. I like that."

"I don't care what you like. I want to be left alone."

"You've got some of that Jewish arrogance, but I could soon cure you of that."

"And you've got some of that German superiority complex," she said, suddenly angry. "That day is over, Mr. Mundt. I don't know why you're here, but if we're going to get along, we better not see much of each other."

His temper rose, but he controlled himself. Better not hurry it, he told himself. There's all night and all tomorrow night. You'll give me some ass, bitch, before I leave. I'll tame that Jewish temper of yours.

He cooled off on her balcony, staring out over the city, golden in the early afternoon sunlight. He wondered what the target was. Judas had promised to tell him tomorrow.

* * *

Gina woke up Carmela Tolloni, who was living at her mother's old apartment, and together, like a delegation, the two of them, escorted by Miller, went immediately to Professor Valeri's home on the outskirts of Rome.

It was nearly dawn when Miller's Maserati drew up in front of the small, compact, modern house. Valeri didn't live as well as the Tollonis had in their white villa; this was only the modest home of a university professor.

Gina pressed the bell and kept her finger on it. "I'm going to keep ringing until he wakes up," she said. She acted as if she were high on something, her red-rimmed eyes appearing almost feverish in the first streaks of early morning light across Professor Valeri's neat little garden. She's still in a state of shock, Miller thought. She'll come out of it and then break down. Let's hope she keeps going long enough to see Valeri.

At last footsteps could be heard on a hard polished floor, and the door opened slightly on a chain.

"Who is it?" a deep voice asked.

"Professor Valeri? This is Gina Altieri." Her voice broke and then recovered. "My father, Vito Altieri, has been murdered."

They heard the chain rattle. Then the door opened wide.

"Come in, my dear," a tall, bearded figure greeted Gina. "Your friends, too." With his arm around Gina's shoulders, Professor Valeri led them to a big, warm-looking lounge with high yellow walls, huge modern paintings and crammed bookshelves.

"Signorina Tolloni," he said gently with a slight bow, and he shook hands with Miller, whose name obviously meant nothing to him.

"You must first have a strong drink," he said and, without asking them, poured out a small brandy for each of them. "This is a very good friend in any emergency," he told Gina gently. "Drink it straight down." She obeyed, for he wasn't a man to argue with, and her eyes at once seemed to clear and become less feverish. "Now tell me what has happened."

Gina told him everything. He listened quietly with rocklike self-assurance. His strong, dominating personality made itself felt even when he was silent. But it was obvious that, beneath his great poise, Vito Altieri's murder had shocked him profoundly. The Tollonis, now Altieri . . . it was the last straw, something he had to deal with.

He held Gina's hand. "Your father was a loyal member of the party and a loyal Italian—the two do not always go together these days. Above all, he was a decent man. You can be proud of him . . ."

But Gina wanted more from him than that. "I want to revenge him," she said.

"I, too!" said Carmela Tolloni. "I lost both my parents. They cry out for vengeance now. We *must* hear them!"

Valeri looked impressed. He said thoughtfully to Gina, "Do you know what your father intended to tell me?"

"Yes," she said. "He told us—Carmela and me. We insisted that he tell you. But they got to him first. Shortly before Signor Tolloni was kidnapped, he confided to my father that he was afraid of being killed. That was why he got the armored cars. But it was not the fascists he was afraid of. It was people in his own party—and the Russians. He specifically named Bellini and the First Secretary at the Soviet Embassy."

"Rostov?"

"Yes, the KGB chief here. Signor Tolloni was too independent for the KGB. Bellini was their man. My father said that after the kidnapping Bellini would do nothing to pressure the Government to agree to the kidnappers' demands. He didn't want Signor Tolloni released! My father heard him say as much to Rostov." She smiled without humor. "My father was sitting on a toilet at party headquarters, and he overheard Bellini and Rostov talking as they urinated. They thought they were quite alone."

"Signor Altieri told my mother about it," Carmela Tolloni said, "she pressed him to make it public. She thought it had to come directly from him to the Italian people. When he wouldn't, she approached some of the older members of the national executive of the party, men who had worked with my father. But they were too scared to do anything. She wanted to talk to you, Professor Valeri, but you were away lecturing in Milan. She was going to get all the evidence she could and present it to foreign reporters like Signor Miller here who wouldn't be afraid to publish it. When she was murdered, I didn't think my word would carry much weight. Signor Altieri had to do something—or you. And now he has been murdered. Is there to be no end to this murderous intrigue? Professor Valeri, has Italy lost its courage?"

Carmela Tolloni's impassioned words obviously affected

Valeri. He stood up as if she had challenged him personally, and towered over them with great dignity, his penetrating black eyes looking at each of them in turn.

"I know the message that you three young people have brought to me," he said gravely. *"The time has come to act.* I agree with you. Perhaps if I had acted sooner, my friend Vito Altieri would still be alive. Party loyalty can be as blinding as religious faith. The church has survived even its poor popes. The party will survive its Bellinis—but only if it takes action to cut out what is rotten. Greed is like a fever with men as with nations. We must be careful not to succumb." He stared sympathetically at Gina and at Carmela Tolloni, who looked so much like her father. "I can't tell you how sorry I am for you both. You have lost parents and I have lost dear friends. Is there anything more you want to tell me?"

Gina looked at Miller.

"Signor Miller?" Valeri asked expectantly.

Miller said quietly, "There's a plot to kill the Pope during his visit to Jerusalem. The assassin is the same man who killed Alberto Tolloni." He quickly told what he knew about Judas. "If the Pope is killed, Bellini's—and Moscow's—hold on Italian politics will be unbreakable. You are the natural leader of the opposition within the party, Professor Valeri." Miller looked directly at him to make it as strong as possible. "They can't let you stay alive. Your murder will be next."

For the first time, the whole situation really struck home. Valeri looked startled. He absentmindedly smoothed back his hair as he thought about what they had told him, and then his whole body seemed to tense as he reached a decision.

"We must act at once," he said. "Only the President has the authority to move against Bellini. I will go to see President Moltani this morning. The army and the *Carabinieri* are not yet completely under Bellini's control. When Bellini's power has been broken, we can confront the Russians. Perhaps they can stop Judas . . ."

28

Robert Miller now had a sense of the curtain going up on the final act. What had begun for him that day in Dublin was now nearing its end, but it was too early yet to see which side was going to win—Judas, Bellini, the Russians, or David, Ram, Abraham, Falid, himself. Or as Vaughan had put it: Was Goliath going to win the rematch? The final battles would be fought in both Rome and Jerusalem . . . which was fitting, he thought. But he knew that he had to be in Jerusalem for the confrontation with the man he now tried to think of as Paul Brett, for he seemed less formidable that way than as Judas.

Leaving the two women with Professor Valeri, he went to the U.S. Embassy to give Colonel Crane a message for Vaughan, and then he went on to the *Mirror* office to bring Russell Hammond up to date. Anything might happen over the next few days. Vito Altieri's murder marked the point of no return. Bellini and Valeri were now on a collision course.

By now, it was siesta time and the building was quiet. Miller hurried along the corridor to the *Mirror* office. Hammond was the only one there. The bureau chief was sitting at Miller's desk, facing the window, his back to the door.

"Hi," Miller said when he didn't turn round.

No reply. Hammond was having a quick nap. Maybe he had a hangover.

When Miller touched Hammond's shoulder to wake him up, the bureau chief slipped sideways and fell heavily to the floor. He just lay there without moving, face down. Robert quickly knelt and turned him over. There was a neat bullet hole in the center of Hammond's forehead. He had been shot through the open window, probably from one of the nearby buildings. And Miller suddenly knew what had happened. *Hammond had been mistaken for him.* They were really getting desperate now. As he looked down at the body, he felt a rush of guilt. Russell Hammond and he had got on so badly in the past, and now he had cost Hammond his life. But, as his father would have said, that was "the luck of the game."

He decided it was too dangerous to call the police. Scaglia might use it to detain him. He went back to Colonel Crane and phoned Vaughan.

"I'm coming over on the next plane," Vaughan told him. The old man had great nostalgia for his World War II days with army intelligence; this was his chance to be in on the final act. "I'll hold down the Rome end while you cover Goliath."

The old man could always be counted on in an emergency.

Miller began to feel better.

Cardinal Bracca insisted on meeting Pope David before he left for Jerusalem. The Lion of Turin—as he was often called because of his amazing vitality at seventy-nine—was usually a loud, forceful, cheerful presence, but on this visit he arrived looking grim and sombre, not willing to talk to anybody except David. He went straight up to the simple little papal apartment on the top floor of the palace, ignored Monsignor O'Malley and Orlando Moravia, who were having a strained conversation in the modest reception room, and went in to confront the Pope over his solitary lunch—a dish of fresh fruit and a glass of milk.

"Holiness," the white-haired old man said gravely, "I'm sure you know that at first I was opposed to your election. It was not your American—foreign—nationality so much as your age. I thought you were far too young to be Pope. You would be with us for too long! I will tell you what changed my mind. Do not laugh when I say it was a dream. On the twenty-fifth night of the Conclave, I awoke at dawn from a dream that I remembered in great detail. I had dreamt that you were made pope, but a short time later I was walking down a long narrow street and I met a woman who was weeping. I asked her what was wrong. 'The Pope is dead,' she said. I took this as a sign from the Lord that He wanted you elected, but I needn't worry because your pontificate would not be a long one. So the next morning, in the Conclave, I voted for you."

David said lightly, "Perhaps, Cardinal Bracca, you took your dream too literally."

"No," the Cardinal replied firmly. "It was definitely telling me something. To remember a dream at all is extraordinary for me, but to remember one in such detail is unique in my seventy-nine years. It was an altogether remarkable occur-

rence in my life. I believe my dream was given to me as a
warning—a warning to *you*, Holiness."

"In what way was it a warning to me, Cardinal? Death is
waiting for the pope as much as for anyone else."

"But death before one's time is a waste—a foolishness!"
The old Cardinal leaned forward with the intensity of his
words. "I remember the street in my dream, the long narrow
street where I met the weeping woman. I saw the street sign.
It was in Latin, Hebrew, and Arabic. The street was the *Via
Dolorosa!*" David frowned, but didn't speak. "My dream was
a warning to you, Holiness, not to go to Jerusalem." The old
Cardinal gripped the young Pope's hand. "I implore you *not*
to go! Something terrible may happen if you do."

"The Lion of Turin would have the church show fear?"

"Not fear, Holiness—caution."

"Our enemies would interpret it as fear, Cardinal."

"Then may I accompany you, Holiness? I would like to be
at your side throughout your visit to Jerusalem to share the
dangers."

David made the sign of the cross over the vital old man.

"You would certainly be a great comfort to me. But I need
you in Italy while I'm gone. Momentous changes are going to
take place here over the next few days. The Italian people
will need reassurance from leaders they respect. Whatever
happens in Jerusalem, you need to be in Turin, Cardinal.
That is one of the biggest Communist centers in the country
and the shock will be great there. Each of us has his duty in
this perilous time . . ."

Eli Abraham met with his chief intelligence and security
advisers in the subterranean cabinet room of The Knesset. He
informed them of the Pope's request to play down security
during his visit.

"Pope David spoke to our Ambassador, Arthur Blomberg,"
said the young Prime Minister, "and he also phoned me
personally. He made the same point to us both—that Good
Friday is their most solemn day, comparable to our Yom
Kippur. He was very serious about not letting our efforts
against Operation Goliath upset the religious services along
the Via Dolorosa and in the Church of the Holy Sepulchre."
The Prime Minister stared round gravely at his advisers. "Of
course we shall have to disregard the Pope's wishes. His visit
is too important to the future of Israel to take any chances.

His assassination would play right into the hands of our enemies. Good Friday commemorates Christ's death; it mustn't also commemorate Pope David's. But we must be as discreet as possible, gentlemen. If that means dressing up our men along the Via Dolorosa as priests, then do it. Only make sure the Pope has maximum protection at all times. Security had its hands tied in the case of Don Paolo and we all know what happened—Judas won. He mustn't be allowed to win this time. The stakes are too great. Gentlemen, I'm giving you an order. *Stop Goliath.* Don't fail me—even if it means upsetting the Vatican."

Eli Abraham strode out, leaving Marc Ram in charge.

"So begins Operation Stop Goliath," Ram told them with a grim smile. "Our plans must be kept secret. I'll therefore ask my secretary to take notes to keep it in the family." He walked to the door. "Sonia, join us, please."

Sonia came in, quick and efficient as ever, yet with an indefinable air of loneliness and helplessness about her. Ram found himself studying her and wondering once more why this obviously troubled woman had insisted on turning down all his invitations. She was alone—according to her security clearance, she didn't have a lover, and she seldom left her apartment in the evenings. She was always pleasant, but she never let him get close to her. He had learned more about her from her security report than he had from her personally in all the time she had worked for him. Perhaps, he thought as he waited for her to sit down, she would never recover from the tragic death of her parents. She had been very close to her father, who was a violinist. Her mother had been a promising ballet dancer when she was young, but had given up her career to get married. Maybe her parents' death explained Sonia's loneliness and detachment; some women made better daughters than wives. He smiled encouragingly at her as she took her seat beside him at the conference table and opened her shorthand notebook.

"Take a note, Sonia, of all that we shall need in terms of extra manpower and equipment." He faced the others. "We've got a crash schedule from now on until Sunday. No Passover for us. David will be here in less than forty-eight hours."

Karl Mundt was bored. Sonia had been out all afternoon and evening, and he had had the apartment to himself for hours. The balcony, television, food from the refrigerator, exploring the apartment—it had all helped to pass the time, but now he had done everything, and he was thoroughly restless. He was essentially a man of action, and the apartment began to seem like a prison to him. He waited eagerly for her return.

It was late when he heard her key in the lock, and she went straight into her bedroom and closed the door.

Friendly bitch, he thought.

He waited for her to come out to get some food from the refrigerator, but she didn't appear.

She must have eaten outside, he thought. She didn't intend to fraternize at all. Well, we'll see about that, he told himself.

He had a bath and put on his white cotton shorts and then knocked at her door.

There was no answer.

He knocked again.

No answer.

He turned the door handle.

The door was locked.

"Sonia," he shouted, "I want to talk to you."

She didn't reply.

Cursing her, he went back in the other bedroom and lay down.

But the frustration continued to build up inside him.

He would have to find a release for it before Friday or it might affect his judgment.

He'd have her tomorrow.

29

"Let these three—faith, hope and charity—abide in you, but the greatest of these is charity," chanted a priest in a side chapel of St. Peter's huge basilica. Shafts of pale sunlight fell like gentle spotlights on the large congregation as the Gospel according to St. John was read out: "Before the feast of the Passover, Jesus knew that his hour had come to pass out of this world . . ."

Holy Thursday had begun.

As Gina came out of St. Peter's, crossed the Piazza San Pietro, and headed for the river, she saw *Carabinieri* on motorcycles waiting on the far side of the Tiber to escort Pope David to San Giovani in Laterano, the Cathedral of Rome, for the traditional washing of the feet of twelve young seminarians. There was no way Pope David could avoid the government escort. He would be taken and brought back as closely guarded as a prisoner. Later he would be escorted the same way to Fiumicino Airport for his flight to Jerusalem. Prime Minister Bellini intended to show the government's power over the Pope as soon as he stepped out of the Vatican.

Gina shivered. The atmosphere in the city seemed so ominous to her, so charged with foreboding. There was an eerie sense of some great drama going on behind the scenes.

Who was going to win: Bellini or Valeri?

The National Executive Committee, the Politburo, of the Italian Communist party (*Partito Comunista Italiano*) held its private, top-secret meetings in a large, converted movie house near the Via Caetani.

After Tolloni's murder, Sandro Bellini, as the party's new General Secretary, had dominated the Executive, but since becoming Prime Minister, he rarely attended its meetings. When he received a special request to attend an emergency meeting that day, he assumed it concerned the murder of Vito Altieri, who was a longtime member of the Executive, and decided he ought to go. Although he was contemptuous of most of the Executive, he wanted to stay on friendly terms until he felt strong enough to replace them with a rubber-stamp committee of his own. It was also wise to join in the Executive's official lamentations over Altieri's death. It didn't matter what any of them suspected as long as the Executive backed him in public. The meeting would give him a chance to tell them that the special government investigator, Scaglia, had found evidence involving the Christian Democrats—as in the case of the Tollonis. The way would soon be clear for a big public trial.

He deliberately arrived an hour late. The Prime Minister, with the country to run, couldn't be expected to be on time. They were lucky he could spare them *any* time from the seat of power—the Room of the Push Buttons, as the Italian jokes called it.

Police on motorcycles accompanied his government limousine. Four armed bodyguards went inside with him. They waited outside the upstairs committee room. As he entered the large, smoke-filled room, the murmur of voices suddenly stopped and he was greeted by complete silence. He took this as a mark of respect. Most of the members of the Executive were there, sitting at the round table waiting patiently for him. They were dressed very formally in dark suits, as if it were a very special occasion. He noticed even Valeri, who seldom attended meetings, was present, but then he remembered that Valeri had been a good friend of Altieri's. Valeri's phone was already tapped, but perhaps he better be put on round-the-clock surveillance now. He might react badly to Altieri's death.

Bellini sat a little apart from the others to assert his independence, the power of his position. His vanity didn't allow him to recognize the cold, stony way he was watched. He identified their attitude as fear—the same fear they had shown when Tolloni died. Let Altieri also be a lesson to them.

When Professor Valeri stood up, Bellini assumed he was going to give a tribute to Vito Altieri. Bellini's expression became attentive and sympathetic. Valeri certainly had an impressive presence, and he was widely respected, even by the Catholics. He had offered Valeri a cabinet position, his prestige would have been useful, but, like all professional intellectuals, he was unreliable.

Bellini was astonished to hear Valeri begin to read a long list of charges against him—*him!* Sandro Bellini! The Prime Minister of Italy! The man must have read too many books and gone out of his mind! Bellini looked quickly at the other members of the Executive and was equally astonished by their reactions. They were all staring at him with accusing, merciless expressions. He knew them all, though some of his closest supporters were missing, and they were regarding him with cuconcealed hatred. They were all on Valeri's side!

"You are accused," Valeri was saying, "of complicity in the murder of our comrade, Alberto Tolloni, a fellow member of this Executive . . ."

Bellini's prominent jaw rose in defiance; he decided to end the meeting immediately. If it was confrontation they wanted, he would give it to them. He rose swiftly before anyone could stop him and hurried over to the door to call in his bodyguards. The door opened wide to reveal a line of armed soldiers. There was no sign of his bodyguards.

"Arrest these men," he ordered the soldiers, pointing back into the room.

The soldiers stared at him with blank expressions.

"I am your Prime Minister. I am commanding you—"

One of the soldiers leaned forward and slammed the door in his face. Bellini heard the lock turn. He was being shut in with the hostile Executive.

He rushed over to the window to summon the police waiting with his limousine. There was no sign in the street below of limousine or police, but there were several army trucks.

He began to realize what he was up against, how he had been outsmarted. The Executive must be working with the President against him. It was the only way they could command the loyalty of the army. If only he could get out of this room ... Niki Rostov would save him ... but he was cornered. His jaw defiantly thrust forward, he faced his accusers.

"You have betrayed your comrades," Valeri told him coldly. "You have endangered the future of the party in what should have been its hour of triumph. The party cannot afford the scandal and deep divisions that a public trial would cause." Valeri slowly took a pistol out of his pocket. "We, the Executive, have therefore decided that you must be judged within the family, as it were, in the privacy of these four walls ..."

Bellini understood then what they intended to do.

The German was coming up the hill now. The way he walked up the easy slope showed how heavy the suitcase was. He was about to pass Judas without recognizing him, when Judas said, "Shalom." Judas realized the German hadn't seen him in his rabbi clothes before.

"You look pretty convincing," the German said, smiling with a mouthful of gold teeth. Long-serving mercenaries always had a lot of gold teeth. It was something to spend their money on apart from women.

"You came by cab?" Judas asked casually, checking up on him.

"No, the bitch brought me." To Mundt's surprise, she'd suggested it. Probably on the instructions of the Russians. "I should have gotten her to carry it up the hill for me."

Judas scowled with disgust. The man had the usual mercenary's hang-up about women. He wouldn't have been a good
choice for a long job.

"She said the Israelis know about something called Goliath.
They captured the delivery boy."

Judas stiffened. He thought quickly about how much the
young chauffeur could tell them. He could alert them to
Goliath, that was all. He knew nothing about the people
involved—or the contents of the suitcase.

"She also got this." The German took a yellow sheet of
paper out of his pocket and gave it to Judas. It was the Pope's
itinerary in Jerusalem. Rostov had said they had an informer
in the Vatican. "What is Goliath?" asked the German.

"Here." Judas led him farther up Mount Zion until the Old
City was clearly visible. He pointed to the onion-colored
dome protruding above the surrounding rooftops. "That's
your target."

"What is it?"

"The Church of the Holy Sepulchre."

The German didn't react. The name probably meant nothing to him.

Judas, trying to suppress his excitement, explained, "It's the
center of the Christian myth, the scene of the Crucifixion and
the Resurrection. Your mortar will destroy it . . . and when
you hit the dome, standing beneath it will be the Pope!"

That did impress the German.

"The Pope . . . Christ, the whole city will be looking for us.
What are your escape plans?"

Typical, thought Judas. He's got the bourgeois mercenary's
mentality. He's worrying about his own neck, not the job. I'd
probably have done better to take Hamed's Arab mortar man.
He's probably a fanatic who thinks nothing of his own life.

"We get off Mount Zion as fast as we can—that's the
escape plan. There'll be a brief time when they're working out
what hit them from where. As long as we're not caught
red-handed, what proof is there? Our passports will stand up.
You can arrange to have the Russians' woman waiting to
drive you away if you like. It's just a matter of timing."

He didn't tell the German he planned to leave Mount Zion
ahead of him, just before he fired. The few minutes might
make all the difference. The German, anyway, was expendable.

"And where's our firing position?"

Judas walked him over to the clump of cypress trees and high bushes he had inspected on his last visit.

"We can clear some of the brush here. There's a clear view and it's protected from observers. Nobody will be able to see us."

The German stood beneath the trees, surveying the distant target.

"It'll have to be fast," he said. "One quick shot. As soon as the mortar is set up, it might show on their radar. That doesn't give us much time. According to the weather forecast, conditions tomorrow will be as mild as today. That's good. There's very little wind resistance."

Judas clapped him on the shoulder. "We better not be seen together. I'll meet you here tomorrow at one o'clock. That'll give us plenty of time. The Pope's due at the church at three, but the crowds along the Via Dolorosa will probably delay him." His cold blue eyes surveyed the German. "Don't get too close with that woman. Remember, she works for the Russians. Jack off if you get hot pants. I don't want your horniness to interfere with this one, understand. It's too important."

The German looked angry, but said nothing.

Judas watched until he'd disappeared down the hill. There was no one else in sight. It would probably be deserted tomorrow with everybody making for the Old City. He picked up the suitcase and went down into Gehenna in search of the small cave he'd inspected on his last visit. It was a black hole in the side of the stony hillside. He thrust the suitcase deep into the blackness—it was like entering a womb. The grenades would be safe there overnight. As he stood, bent-backed, in the cave, there was a weird echo, like people whispering in the dark. Perhaps it was the murmur of an underground stream—Jerusalem was riddled with tunnels and subterranean streams—or maybe it was the cries of souls roasting in the fires of Gehenna, Judas thought with a cold smile.

A mist was rising from the valley like smoke as he climbed back up Mount Zion. A group of Franciscan monks was walking toward the stairway leading to the upper room commemorating the Last Supper. Public acts of cult were usually forbidden there, but the Franciscans were allowed a pilgrimage to pray and sing hymns late on Holy Thursday.

Holy Thursday would soon change into Good Friday . . .

and then it's my turn, Judas thought eagerly. He could already see the onion-colored dome exploding . . .

Marc Ram stood at the beginning of the Via Dolorosa, surveying the busy, narrow, enclosed street with a grim expression. It was even worse than he had realized. It was like trying to protect someone in the middle of a marketplace. And it would be a hundred times worse tomorrow—not only was the Pope arriving, but the Christian Easter coincided with the Jewish Passover and the Moslem Feast of Nebi Musa this year. The followers of the city's three faiths would all be crowding Jerusalem.

He said to Feinberg, "We need men there at the Franciscan oratory. Which Station of the Cross is this?" Some of the Stations were badly marked—an unobtrusive sign on a door, sometimes hidden by a movie poster.

"This is the Fifth," Feinberg said. He had done his homework on the Via Dolorosa before meeting Ram. "Simon of Cyrene helps Jesus carry His Cross."

"We'll need men above the street, too," Ram said. "We'll have to put at least an extra thousand men in the Old City. He could try to do it any number of ways."

Ram gazed moodily up the crowded bazaarlike street as it rose on the traditional way to Calvary—and the Church of the Holy Sepulchre. "I've gone over the record of his past three assassinations and the *curriculum vitae* of this Paul Brett again and again, looking for a pattern."

"It's four assassinations if you count Don Paolo," Feinberg said.

"That was more just the disposal of a messenger—like the murder of the Italian kidnapper. They were just postscripts. They weren't his big shows. He always plans in detail and usually at long range. We'll have to cover the whole city with men and radar and helicopters. I want soldiers on all the hills. You know the usual drill. But if I had to bet, I think, with his biblical hang-ups, it will appeal to him to do it on the site of Calvary—in the church itself if he can find a way to get in . . . and out. We're not dealing with a normal criminal or terrorist mind with normal impulses and desires. An assassination must give him the same kind of ecstatic feeling saints or great artists are supposed to get. There are a thousand opportunities for him from the moment the Pope steps off the plane in Amman. Let's face it, we can't cover every inch of his route. An assassin always has the advantage of surprise unless you can reach him beforehand. Finding out about Goliath gave us a chance." Ram stared up at the rooftops of the Old City. "He must be here already ... somewhere in Jerusalem, and we've got twenty-four hours to find him."

A formal announcement was made from the Quirinale Palace. Signed by the President of the Italian Republic, Giuseppe Moltani, it stated that the Prime Minister, Sandro Bellini, had resigned and then shot himself. The President had dissolved Parliament so that a new government could be elected. Luigi Valeri would be the interim Prime Minister until the election. No further explanation was given, but it was stated that a full inquiry was in process. President Moltani and Prime Minister Valeri would speak to the nation on television.

The Soviet Ambassador, Leonid Dobrinsky, was summoned to the Quirinale Palace. A sleek, grey-haired career diplomat, Dobrinsky denied any knowledge of his first Secretary's involvement with Bellini in the Tolloni affair.

With President Moltani at his side, Prime Minister Valeri told the Soviet Ambassador: "We appreciate the fact that Niki Rostov's position as First Secretary was merely a cover for his KGB activities. We also realize that the KGB, like all intelligence services, is a law unto itself, and the local ambassador doesn't necessarily know about all its activities. Senior agents like Rostov sometimes take part in illegal actions without informing anyone in order to protect their security or to save official interference or embarrassment. We are willing to accept what you have told us about your own personal noninvolvement, Mr. Ambassador. But your First Secretary, Niki Rostov, is now persona non grata in this country. We cannot tolerate such interference in our internal affairs. It is a throwback to Stalinist days. He must leave immediately."

"Very well," Ambassador Dobrinsky replied bleakly. "I give you my personal assurance that Rostov will be on a plane to Moscow within twenty-four hours."

"We have one other demand," Prime Minister Valeri said. "Do you know what Operation Goliath is?"

Again the Soviet Ambassador claimed complete ignorance.

Valeri told him what he knew. He concluded: *"Goliath must be stopped."*

"I will make immediate inquiries," Ambassador Dobrinsky said, "and I'll get back to you within an hour."

"If you find you can't stop the assassins personally from Rome," Valeri told him, "then the Israelis *must* be informed where to find them . . ."

Gina sensed a difference in the Eternal City already—a gradual relaxing of the enormous tension and uncertainty of the last few days. The change was reflected in the fine spring weather. Not even the news of the attempt on Roberto's life could spoil it. Roberto had escaped, that was all that mattered. He was a survivor—like her. Yet the thought of his going to Jerusalem worried her greatly. *There* the real battle would be fought—if Judas won there, Valeri's victory wouldn't count for much. David was needed now more than ever—and Judas would be desperate for success after the news from Rome. Roberto would be in the middle of it, in the firing line. Her Roberto, perhaps the father of her child . . .

Sonia Petrovich didn't come home until the middle of the evening. Mundt was waiting for her and met her in the hallway. She was wearing a grey wool sweater that showed off her plump breasts. Her look of dislike made him want her even more.

"You leave me too much alone," he told her. "I'm going to complain to the Russians. It won't go well for your mommy and daddy."

Ignoring his threat, she walked past him to the refrigerator and poured herself a glass of milk.

"They're covering the city with security forces," she said. "Two army units have come in from Tel Aviv. You haven't got a chance."

Her pleased tone annoyed him. "You like that, don't you? Whose side are you on?"

"Not yours, Mr. Master Race," she said and tried to pass him. He barred her way.

"Do you always insult your guests?" he teased her.

"Not all my guests are so arrogant," she said.

He put a hand on her plump breast and squeezed. "Show me your primitive side, bitch."

They stood face to face, and he could smell her sweet heavy scent. Her eyes were wide with hatred, and it amused him now that he felt she was in his power. He was about to kiss her when she suddenly kicked his ankle. The sharp, unexpected pain made him fall back against the wall, and then she was past him, running to her room. He was furious at his own carelessness and pursued her, shouldering her door open as she was trying to lock it. Her hand went in her bag and came out with a small, snub-nosed automatic.

"Stop bothering me," she hissed. "Go and watch television. Do you think I want to have you here after the way this country has helped me? I'm only doing it because I *have* to, but there's a limit to what I'll take from a pig like you."

He smiled broadly, showing all his gold teeth. He was going to have her now whatever the cost.

"Put that toy away. If you shoot me, you'll ruin Goliath and then what will the Russians do to your beloved parents?"

The automatic wavered, and he grabbed it and slipped it into his pocket.

"Now we're equal." As he moved toward her, she edged backward against the bed. Her look of hatred was mixed now with fear.

"I'll scream," she said. "The neighbors will hear me."

"Go ahead. Cause trouble, and your mother and father are *kaput*. You're trapped. You and me are going to get together at last and have a nice time." He grinned at her, his fourteen-karat Clark Gable grin. "You'll love what I've got. You'll be sorry I'm not staying longer."

He pushed her down on the bed. She struggled desperately, but had no chance against his strength and cunning. He knew how to punish a woman. He'd had plenty of practice in the whorehouses. He ripped her skirt off with a great tearing sound. She began to scream, but he put a hand over her mouth.

"You bring anybody here, and you're an orphan. Understand that, Jew bitch!"

His big hand relaxed over her face, but she didn't try to scream again. Her eyes were wide with loathing. It worked him up more. He rolled up her sweater and tore off her bra. Her plump breasts hung free. He unzipped his trousers and lay on top of her, forcing her legs open. She still tried to struggle, but he had her pinned so she couldn't move.

"I'll make you so you can't get enough of it. Feel it. Now you're going to hurt."

Suddenly the doorbell rang.

He froze on top of her.

"Who's that?"

"I don't know," she said, watching him.

"Go and find out. Don't let anybody in unless you have to."

She put on a blue robe, went to the door, and peered through the peephole.

"It's my boss," she said, wide-eyed. "Colonel Ram."

"What the hell does he want so late?"

"I've no idea."

The doorbell rang again—longer, more impatiently.

"Let it ring."

"He'll know I'm here."

"Tell him you can't let him in. You're with your lover. Tell him, bitch."

"Who's that?" she called.

"It's me—Marc Ram," replied the familiar deep voice from the other side of the door. "Let me in, Sonia."

"I've got somebody here, Marc."

"Open the door, Sonia. I must talk to you."

Mundt stared desperately up the hallway at the balcony. Was there any escape there if he needed one—to the roof? As he was searching, a rope snaked down to the balcony and the heavy army boots of a soldier came into view.

"It's a trap," Mundt snarled. He drew her automatic and shot the soldier just as he stood up on the balcony, holding a submachine gun. The young, tanned face under the army helmet looked astonished as the bullet went through his neck. He fell backwards over the balcony rail into space, nineteen floors above the ground.

"Is there another way out of the apartment?" Mundt asked desperately.

Sonia didn't reply. She was staring at the balcony with a shocked expression.

He shook her. "Is there another exit?"

"No, there's no way out. You're trapped."

"Stand clear, Sonia!" a voice shouted, and the lock on her door was riddled with bullets, splintering the woodwork.

Mundt grabbed her and held her as a shield as Marc Ram recklessly pushed his way in, a pistol in his black-gloved hand, soldiers behind him.

The German fired and hit Ram's hand. He was astonished when it had no effect. Ram didn't feel a thing, didn't even drop his pistol from the steel grip.

"Keep back," Mundt cried, his back against a wall, "or I'll blow her head off."

Ram stood still, covering them with his pistol. Soldiers with submachine guns pressed behind him. There was a noise from the balcony. Two more men were arriving that way.

"You haven't got a chance," Ram said. "Hand your gun over."

Sonia struggled. Mundt prodded her with the gun, but he couldn't hold her. She pulled to the side exposing his chest, and Ram shot him fast, but not before Mundt had pulled the trigger on her. Mundt's gun made a muffled sound against her back. She gave a sharp cry and fell forward, with him on top of her.

Ram quickly stepped over them and checked the bedrooms, though he had no hope of finding anyone else in the apartment. This had been his big chance to get Judas, and he'd missed him.

He returned to Sonia. Inspector General Feinberg was bent over her, waiting for a doctor. He shook his head at Ram. Sonia's eyes were open, but the life was already beginning to fade from them. She stared at Ram with an expression he couldn't read. She struggled to say something. Ram hesitated. When the message had come from Rome, he hadn't wanted to believe it, and yet it explained so many things about her, even her detachment and solitary way of life. He had felt very bitter toward her, the way she had deceived him, betrayed him . . . and, even more, Israel. He stood above her, hesitating, struggling with his feelings. He still felt bitter, but he couldn't let her die this way. With nothing. He went down on his knees and gently touched her cheek, already losing the warmth of life, though Ram couldn't feel the change. He wanted to take her in his arms, to kiss her, but he hadn't the right. She had always shut him out.

She struggled to say something to him. The effort was terrible to witness as blood frothed from her lips and her whole body strained to get it out.

"Forgive . . . me . . ."

She wanted to say more, but the effort was too great. Her eyes turned glassy, and her head was suddenly heavy against his glove. She was gone. Whatever she had done, she had paid for it now. Suddenly Ram gave a muffled cry and, pulling her head close to his, kissed her on the lips. Then he gently laid her head back on the carpet and stood up, grey-faced, struggling for self-control.

"Search the apartment with a fine-toothed comb," he said thickly. "There may be some clue to where Judas is hiding."

But all they found of more than routine interest was a pile of letters in Russian, held together with a rubber band. Ram had taken Russian lessons, and he read a few of the letters, thinking they might reveal secrets of her relationship with the Russians. But all the letters were from her mother and father, and were mainly about conditions in the prison camp they were in. The tone of the letters was fearful and pathetic, almost childlike. Ram suddenly realized the anguish Sonia had been going through all these months. He was relieved then that he'd overcome his bitterness before she died. He understood better what she had gone through. She had been blackmailed into helping the Russians. She felt she *had* to. But how had the security report missed it? That had stated both her parents were dead. She must have lied to the investigators, and they had believed her, maybe she'd even produced some forged proof provided by the Russians. And what would happen to her parents now? Sympathetic as Ram was, the idea of putting an individual, even one's family, before the security of Israel was something he found hard to accept. Maybe that's why I'm alone, he thought. But I wish she had been able to trust me enough to talk to me about it. She might still be alive—and we might have Judas. He looked at the dead man and regretted killing him. The man might have talked . . .

After the two bodies had been taken away, Marc Ram went out on the balcony where the rope still dangled from the roof. He stared down at the dark, sleeping city, trying to forget about Sonia. Don't stumble now, he warned himself, not when you're so close. He wondered if Judas knew the bad news yet—that his Russian and Italian backers had disowned him and that he had lost part of his team. Unless he had Arab help, he was now on his own. But Ram felt he knew enough about Judas—Paul Brett—to be sure that wouldn't change his plan. He had come too far to turn back. He would try to complete what he had come to do—at any cost. Judas was somewhere down there now in the Holy City . . . waiting patiently for the arrival of the Pope.

30

A heavy bank of fog, swirled by howling desert winds, shrouded the small Amman airport in the Jordanian hills. Planes were grounded, and even cars had to crawl cautiously up the approach roads.

Flight 180 from Rome was still somewhere over the Mediterranean, but unless the foggy weather cleared very quickly, the jet airliner bringing Pope David would have to be diverted to Beirut. The waiting crowd was informed through loudspeakers that the Pope had asked his pilot to put off making a decision until the last moment and to land at Amman "if at all possible."

The short, sturdy King of Jordan, dressed in full military uniform with a chest full of medals, waited in the airport building with a group of other moderate Arab rulers from neighboring countries. An experienced pilot himself, the King planned to assist personally at the radar landing controls. Outside, in the cutting desert winds, a big crowd was gathering along the edge of the tarmac. A long line of nuns, shivering in the cold, could be heard praying for the weather to clear.

The airport meteorologist, watched by the King, anxiously huddled over his isotherms and bravely forecast the fog would clear in time. Up in the airport tower, the airport manager followed the checkpoint messages from Flight 180. The fallback plan to divert to Beirut might still be needed. The Pope's plane was now descending from 29,000 feet to 10,000 over Damascus, and the Holy Land wasn't yet visible. The airport manager told the pilot the latest ground conditions: " . . . wind twenty knots and gusty . . . visibility still poor . . . " Flight 180 passed the Jerusalem beacon, came down to 4,000 feet, and then waited, like the crowd on the ground.

Marc Ram, standing with Major Falid at a window overlooking the tarmac, waited as anxiously as anyone. A diversion would upset his security plans, especially his last-minute

decision to be with the Pope from the start, even though it
meant crossing into Jordan. Standing there in full view of the
predominantly Arab crowd, in this Arab country with so
many Palestinians, Ram felt very exposed, aware that he was
hated by so many Arab extremists and that the families of
men whose death he was responsible for had sworn revenge.
He understood better now how Major Falid felt when he
came to Israel—the sense of dangerous uncertainty, of not
knowing who were friends or enemies. Eli Abraham had told
him not to risk it, but he wanted to be in at the beginning, in
case Judas planned an early surprise. Major Falid had been
cooperative but reserved, probably feeling that Ram's presence meant he didn't trust Jordanian security arrangements.
To try to offset this bad feeling, Ram had suggested that
Major Falid should accompany the Pope to Jerusalem—his
Arab experience would be useful in protecting him there. The
Major seemed pleased and became more friendly, describing
to Ram all the security arrangements in and around Amman
airport and along the Pope's route to the Israeli border. They
were adequate, Ram thought grudgingly, but the Israeli arrangements were far more thorough. No loopholes had been
left for Judas in Jerusalem. No one would even get into the
Church of the Holy Sepulchre without a pass, and the passes
were only just being printed so duplicates couldn't be made.
The various Christian groups were angry, but Ram ignored
them. Although he had tried to prepare for any kind of
attack, he had a gut feeling Judas would try to stage it in the
Church—on the site of Calvary.

The weather was changing rapidly now, as sometimes
happened in the Jordanian hills. The fog was beginning to
clear at last, and the howling winds quietened. Soon the
biscuit-colored airport was golden under a clear blue sky. The
airport meteorologist was vindicated. The praying nuns
looked up, triumphant, as Flight 180 became visible, a shining silver streak fast approaching them.

A puff of smoke burst from the tires as Flight 180 touched
down. While the braking jet roared in reverse, a howitzer's
salute echoed off the rocky hills, the first of twenty-one guns.
The silver plane's main door opened, and there was the
familiar slight, shy figure, all in black—black, flat-topped,
wide-brimmed hat, long black topcoat, black shoes—the color
of mourning, of Good Friday. On the Pope's chest lay the

ancient Cross of St. Gregory, given to Pope Gregory in the year 603 by the great Queen Theodolinde.

Pope David stood at the top of the plane's steps, waving shyly with one hand while he held on to his hat against the wind with the other. The Vatican's protocol experts had advised him not to give a public blessing with the sign of the cross in this Arab, essentially Moslem country, but now, spontaneously, he did so with a quick, nervous gesture, as if he wished to give some personal sign of his pleasure at being there, in the Holy Land.

The Jordanian King stood on a small wooden platform and said into a microphone: "We welcome you to Jordan, to the Holy Land, on behalf of all Arabs, as well as on behalf of all men who believe in God and goodwill." The Pope, much slighter than the King, his voice barely audible above the desert wind, replied: "This visit is essentially a spiritual one, a humble pilgrimage . . ."

Behind him gathered the Vatican group accompanying him, including Cardinal Garonne, Monsignor O'Malley, and Orlando Moravia. A special plane chartered by the media had landed immediately behind the Pope's, and the tarmac was now crowded with TV cameras, microphones, and gesticulating reporters. Robert Miller went over to talk with Marc Ram.

"I've come as we arranged, Colonel, to be in at the finish. There's a rumor you've got somebody already."

"Just a German mercenary, Mr. Miller. He flew in from Beirut. I'm running a check on him there in case it can lead us to Judas. We've nothing on Judas yet. He could make his move anywhere along the route."

Miller watched the Arab rulers in their colorful, resplendent robes crowd round the somberly dressed Pope David. "The Arabs wanted an official conference," he said to Ram, "but David turned them down because he said his visit was purely religious in character."

"It looks as though he hasn't much choice," Ram grunted. "They've cornered him into an impromptu conference now."

"They're worried about what concessions he's going to make to you wily Israelis, Colonel."

Major Falid joined them. "My people are concerned about the rumors that the Vatican intends to move to Jerusalem. Does that mean the Pope recognizes Israel's right to the whole of Jerusalem? People have been killed for less in the Middle East."

"That's true, Major," Ram said gravely, "and that's Judas' rationalization for Goliath. The assassination of this man would make a public statement that would divide us more deeply than ever before and put us back thirty years. That's why we must prevent it."

The Pope and the Arab rulers seemed to be parting in a mood of great friendliness. There were smiles and warm handshakes. The Arabs treated the Pope very courteously as a religious leader, though not *their* leader. He acted as if he didn't expect any special consideration from them.

The Pope and the Jordanian King walked toward the King's helicopter. Miller asked Monsignor O'Malley what was happening. The schedule called for the Pope to leave Amman by limousine.

"The King offered to fly His Holiness to the River Jordan to the place where John the Baptist baptized Jesus," said the big man. "His Holiness can change to a limousine there."

"Damn," Ram said. "Why can't he keep to his schedule? It's an added risk."

"He's never been very good at keeping to schedules," O'Malley said.

"At least Judas is as unprepared as we are," Major Falid told Ram as the King's helicopter rose above them. "The King is well covered by security forces wherever he goes."

"I don't like it," Ram said. "They're going near where Don Paolo was killed. We better get over there fast . . ."

". . . The papal party approached the Jordan River just before it flows into the Dead Sea, the lowest point of the earth's surface. Pope David walked to the river bank where John, precursor of Christ, is said to have baptized Jesus. As the Pope blessed the crowd gathered round him, many must have thought of the Evangelist's words in the Gospel: 'Jesus came from Galilee and stood before John at the Jordan to be baptized by him . . . And as he came straight up out of the water suddenly heaven was opened, and he saw the Spirit of God coming down like a dove and resting upon him . . . And a voice came from heaven: 'This is my beloved Son, in whom I am well pleased . . .' "

Judas, far back in the dark cave above Gehenna, put down the pocket radio he had bought to follow the Pope's progress and crawled to the entrance to check his watch in daylight. It was 12:55. The German would arrive in five minutes.

"... The Pope said goodbye to the Jordanian King and completed his journey across the border into Israel by limousine. He is to meet the President and the Prime Minister of Israel at the ancient historic site of Megiddo, the city that Solomon built. The formal Israeli greeting ceremony is being held at Megiddo partly out of respect for Pope David's predecessor, Paul VI, who met Israeli government representatives there during his Holy Land tour in 1964, and partly to give Pope David a chance on his very short visit to see Nazareth, the town twelve miles away where Jesus spent his youth."

The German was late. Judas checked his watch as he waited under the tall cypress trees overlooking the onion-colored dome. The German was nearly fifteen minutes late. Battles could be lost by such carelessness. The man was probably chasing some cheap skirt. He was crude, no class, a moron except for his skill with a mortar.

At 1:20 he decided to phone to check on him.

The phone rang four times, then was picked up.

"Hello," said a man's voice in Hebrew. It wasn't the German. "Who do you want to speak to?"

Judas hung up. Something had gone wrong. *Damn* that German to hell everlasting. He walked quickly down Mount Zion, and took a taxi to a spot near the woman's address, and then cautiously approached her building on foot. There was no sign of trouble outside, but of course there wouldn't be. They would wait inside, hoping he would come.

An elderly woman with a shopping bag came out of the building. He let her walk down the street and then he stopped her.

"Shalom," he said gently. "Someone told me there has been trouble. I came to see if I could help."

"It's all over, Rabbi," the woman said excitedly. "The army and the police were here. They killed somebody. They say an Arab terrorist."

He thanked her politely and walked away. If they killed the German, he couldn't have talked. And if he had talked, they would have kept his appointment on Mount Zion. *Damn.* Goliath had come close to disaster because of the German's stupidity. But there must be more to it than that. Either the woman had ratted or the Russians had double-crossed him.

He took a taxi back to be in time for Ayad. There was a news broadcast on the taxi's radio. The big news now wasn't from Megiddo but from Italy—Bellini was dead, and there was to be a new election. Ah, that explained everything, Judas thought. If Sandro Bellini had lost, so had Niki Rostov. To try to save his neck, Rostov had told them all about Goliath. They thought they could stop him. But he didn't depend on the Russians or on anybody else. He worked alone. He'd show them all now. How right he'd been not to trust the Russians!

He could kiss the money goodbye. But he wasn't in this only for the half million, he told himself. This was something he *had* to do. It was the culmination of a lifetime's work—his *Armageddon,* he thought sombrely. Bring this off successfully and he could ask his own price anywhere in the world. The international terrorist network would be his. But better than that, the whole religious dream would be brought down like a house of cards—the world of his father! This time Goliath would win!

He carefully reviewed his plan, revising it now that the German wasn't available. The main change was that he would have to fire the mortar himself. But that didn't worry him. He'd spent several hours at Hamed's camp practicing with the German. He'd got used to the German's specially constructed mortar. Its accuracy was amazing. He was confident he could hit the dome the first time. He'd only been a fraction out once in ten times at practice. The real difficulty was that escaping would be harder on his own. He would have less time to get away. But surprise and speed were still on his side ...

"... At Megiddo, a Guard of Honor of the Israeli Army presented arms. The blue and white flag with the Star of David was dipped. Pope David walked across a red carpet to meet the President and Prime Minister of Israel. Also in the official Israeli reception group was the Chief Rabbi. This was a marked change from the visit of Pope Paul VI in 1964, when the Chief Rabbi of the time showed little interest. It reflects the much closer relationship between the Vatican and Israel, between Catholics and Jews ... The Prime Minister, Eli Abraham, elegant in a top hat, greeted his distinguished guest in biblical language: 'Blessed be thou in thy coming.' Pope David replied: 'May God deign to bestow upon today's

tormented world this incomparable gift, *Shalom, Shalom* ...
Peace, Peace. On this humble pilgrimage to the sacred places
made holy by the passion and death of Jesus Christ and by
His glorious Resurrection, I shall pray for that peace which
Jesus left to His disciples' ..."

Marc Ram watched the two men, roughly the same age,
both young for world leaders, as they talked together in the
back of the Israeli Prime Minister's bullet-proof limousine
which was parked facing the road to Afula. Eli Abraham
towered over Pope David, but both men talked easily as
contemporaries, as if they understood each other. This would
probably be their only opportunity for a private discussion.
The Pope had a very tight schedule on his brief visit. But
exclusively religious as his visit was supposed to be, political
discussions kept intruding, as was inevitable in the divided
Middle East. Ram wished this meeting could have been in a
safer setting. They were just below the narrow, steep path
leading to Megiddo. Armageddon was the kind of symbolic
site that would appeal to Judas. Ram checked the security
ring yet again—nobody could get near. But still he felt uneasy.

"You've done everything possible," Major Falid assured
him, knowing how Ram felt.

Their situation had been reversed again. Ram was safely
back in Israel on his own ground, Major Falid was the
apprehensive outsider. But at least they were now more
relaxed with each other.

"He could strike any time," Ram said gloomily. "He could
show up in any disguise. All we know for sure is that Paul
Brett has a crucifix tattooed on his chest. But we can't strip
every stranger to take a look."

Major Falid watched the two men in the limousine. They
were still deep in conversation. The Pope had taken off his
wide-brimmed black hat, and his unruly dark hair made him
look even younger. He was not a man who bothered much
about his personal appearance, the Major decided. Nor about
his personal safety. He had given no sign since his arrival in
Amman that he knew his life was in danger.

"He remains very cool, very serene," the Major said
admiringly.

"David's the coolest person here," Ram grunted. "It probably seems nothing compared to a crucifixion."

* * *

Fingering prayer beads, Ayad approached the Dome of the Rock—*El-Harem esh-Sherif*, the holy treasure—under the ancient arcades where, it was said, the scales would hang on Judgment Day.

The young Palestinian stared with awe across the paved platform at the great, eight-sided shrine topped by a huge golden dome. This was the third-ranking of Islam's holy places, after Mecca and Medina, the place where Mohammed ascended to heaven on his horse, where Abraham offered to sacrifice his son Isaac, and where Jesus cast out the money-changers.

Ayad took off his shoes and then, feeling like a warrior before going into battle, he went inside to pray to Allah for their success. *Allah akbar*—Allah is great—he chanted, and pressed his head to the floor. He recited his favorite prayers from the Koran, his dark skin seeming to burn with the strength of his conviction. When he arose, he had a mark on his forehead from the floor.

He quickly left the Dome of the Rock, put his shoes back on, and returned to the small, simple room in the Old City that Hamed's men had provided for him. He changed into his Christian clothes, took the heavy "crucifix" from under the high camp bed, and set off immediately to meet Judas.

Ayad felt ready now.

Eli Abraham spoke privately to Marc Ram before he left Megiddo to return to The Knesset. "He confirmed that the Vatican will formally recognize Israel, Marc. But he's not taking sides over Jerusalem. As for coming here, he's waiting to see what happens now in Italy. The agreement worked out with Pope Alfredo will remain open."

"I hope formal recognition of us won't be announced while he's here," Ram said. "The atmosphere's tense enough already."

"He insisted we should announce it together to the media. He feels it's long overdue."

"He must want to get killed," Ram said grimly.

". . . Pope David went next to the official residence of the Vatican's Apostolic Delegate here at the foot of the Mount of Olives. The Apostolic Delegate, Monsignor Le Clair, had to leave unexpectedly for his native France a few days ago, but members of his staff were there to receive the Pope. A short

meeting was held with representatives of the Eastern Orthodox Church, who regard the Pope as the Patriarch of the
West but not as the supreme head of the church. At the end
of the meeting, they all said the *Our Father* together and
prayed that Christians all over the world would be reunited.
'Our differences seem small beside our common Christian
belief,' said Pope David. 'We believers need to be united in a
world of such deep divisions. Let us seek unity not only
among Christians but among all those who believe in God,
including our Arab and Jewish brothers. Let the Holy City be
a symbol of the unity we seek.' Pope David then visited the
Garden of Gethsemane, where Jesus anguished over his
coming Crucifixion. '. . . he fell on his face and prayed. 'My
Father,' he said, 'if it is possible, let this cup pass me by.
Nevertheless, let it be as you, not I, would have it.' Gethsemane comes from the Hebrew *Gat Shemanin*, meaning 'oil-
press.' Eight old olive trees still stand in the Garden, and
some botanists claim they may be three thousand years old
and therefore were there during Jesus' agony in the Garden.
The Basilica of the Agony or, as it is more often called, The
Church of All Nations is built around the rock where Jesus is
said to have suffered his agony. It has the same primitive
effect as the rock in the Dome of the Rock. The Pope went
on his knees and kissed the rock and meditated there for a
long time in private. He was accompanied by only one of his
staff, Signor Orlando Moravia . . ."

Elegant in a perfectly cut Italian black suit, Orlando
Moravia was admiring the historic view from outside the
Garden of Gethsemane. He felt a hand touch his arm. It was
Pope David looking very pale and tired in the clear Judean
air. "Come with me to see the garden," the Pope said
gently.

Moravia was pleased by this special attention. He had felt
rather isolated so far on the visit. He hadn't been asked to
take part in any of the events. He had been shut out of the
conferences with the Arab rulers in Amman and with the
Israeli government leaders in Megiddo. Monsignor O'Malley
seemed to have taken a dislike to him. It was almost as if the
huge American priest suspected something, but that was
impossible. He had surely covered his tracks too well after all
this time, though he had to be more careful with this new
Pope than with old Pope Alfredo.

Moravia hurriedly followed the slight figure into the tiny
olive grove beneath the melancholy darkness of cypress trees.
Here, surrounded by the scent of lavender and by drifting
butterflies, were the eight ancient olive trees, their wood like
ageless stone, of a dark, incorruptible beauty. Yet leaves still
sprouted from them, and their branches thickened with olives, their stones strung into holy rosary beads by the Franciscan priests who looked after the garden. No one else was
there. The Pope closed his eyes for a few moments, obviously
deeply moved. Moravia wished he could feel something
himself; but all he saw was a tiny olive grove.

The Pope led the way into the dim, deserted Church of All
Nations. Its twilight spaces, with columns rising to ceilings
pricked with gold, suggested the closeness of a grove at night.
Through the alabaster windows, almost no light came. David
prayed before the bared Rock of Agony in the gloom. In this
setting, it was possible to imagine the lanterns of the crowd
that came to seize Jesus. Moravia was suddenly eager to
return to the daylight outside, but he had to wait until the
Pope was ready.

David suddenly clutched his arm. "Can't you feel it *now*,
Moravia? The Agony—and the betrayal. How does the Gospel put it? 'And he that betrayed him had given them a token,
saying, Whomsoever I shall kiss, that same is he; take him,
and lead him away safely. And as soon as he was come, he
goeth straightway to him, and saith, Master, master; and
kissed him' . . ."

Moravia began to tremble. He couldn't control himself. He
looked at the Pope. Surely the Holy Father did know something. Had guessed. But the Pope's eyes were intent on the
Rock of Agony, deep in thought, and Moravia gradually
relaxed. He was letting the atmosphere affect him. Nothing
had *happened*. It was all in his imagination.

An estimated three thousand reporters, camera men, and
technicians were in the Holy City to cover the Pope's visit.
This strained Jerusalem's hotel accommodation and communication facilities. Israeli security plans were trying to restrict
most journalists to covering events in the city through closed-
circuit TV. Passes to the Old City, especially the area of the
Via Dolorosa, were restricted to a select few. Robert Miller
went directly to Marc Ram to get one. The pass was colored
blue. "Shouldn't it at least have black edges?" Miller asked

when he finally found Ram on the Mount of Olives waiting for the Pope to finish his private visit to the Garden of Gethsemane. Ram didn't smile. The strain was beginning to get to him.

Miller had to share a hotel room with a Spanish TV reporter. The man was forever on the phone to Madrid, saying things like "Athens is the city of the Mind, Rome of the Heart, and Jerusalem of the Spirit." Miller waited impatiently to phone Gina only to be told when at last the phone was free that there was a delay of at least two hours for calls to Italy. All the world must be calling Italy to find out what was happening there.

Miller went downstairs to the hotel bar on his way to the Damascus Gate. The Pope was about to follow the Way of the Cross along the Via Dolorosa—the real start of his Good Friday pilgrimage.

"Salaam," Ayad said at the mouth of the cave. He wore his white shirt with the Arab-looking Jesus stitched on the back.

"Shalom," came a low answer from far back in the dark cave.

Ayad, bent-backed, went in to find Judas. Finally he had to crawl on his knees. Judas was lying on a bed of hard rock, perfectly relaxed.

"You left the crucifix among the cypress trees?"

"Of course." Ayad grinned, his teeth flashing in the gloom of the cave. "Coming through the Old City, I received a lot of respect. People wanted to touch or kiss the crucifix."

Judas clapped the young Palestinian on the shoulder, suddenly pleased. His plan was beginning to work.

"Where's the German?"

Judas thought of lying. He didn't want to discourage the young Palestinian at this time. But neither did he want to baby him. He was a *fedayeen,* a warrior to the death. So he quickly told him the truth, as much as he knew of it.

"How does it change our plans?" was all Ayad said.

"For you, Ayad, not at all. For me, it means I do his work."

"You can manage?"

"I am experienced with a mortar. His is a very good one—very accurate, unusually so, and easy to use. There is no problem." He didn't mention the problem of getting away or dealing with any opposition. He had no one to watch his back. Ayad couldn't help there. He was needed elsewhere. "You can get close enough to the church, Ayad?"

"Hamed's men have arranged it. There are many tunnels in the Old City. They know them all. One from the time of Solomon leads to within yards of the church."

"Israeli security don't know about it?"

"No, it's quite safe."

"Good. You know the rest. Relax for a few minutes. You have enough time."

"There were soldiers at the foot of Mount Zion when I came up."

"They were coming up the hill?"

"Not yet."

"Don't worry. I'll manage. They'll have only routine guards on each of the hills overlooking the old walled city. That's all. The Old City will be like a magnet for everyone for the next couple of hours. I bet there wasn't anyone on Mount Zion when you dumped the crucifix."

"No, they're all massed at the Damascus Gate. There's a tremendous crowd there."

"All the dummies. Relax for a few minutes, Ayad, and then be on your way." But now Judas couldn't relax. He felt the sudden camaraderie that soldiers experience just before a battle. "You have never told me much about yourself, Ayad. Are your parents still alive?"

"I never knew my parents. They were killed soon after I was born—fighting the Zionists."

"There are worse fates than not knowing your parents. I wish to hell I'd never known *anything* about mine."

"Why?" Ayad sounded shocked.

Judas hesitated. He had never spoken about his past to anyone. But some force, some foreboding inside him compelled him to talk now.

"My parents had too great an influence on what I am, Ayad. I was absorbed into their petty private tragedy before I had a chance to think or grow or decide for myself."

Ayad looked very puzzled.

"I killed my father, Ayad. You are shocked. You have the Arab's respect for the patriarch. But what I did was necessary. The man was a monster, brutal beyond belief. When I was six, he ordered my mother to execute herself and then he forced me to discover the body. It is nearly forty years ago, and yet I still remember the touch of her blood on my hands.

Oh, yes, my father deserved to die. I would do it with great pleasure again today—I would do it every day of my life!"

Judas gazed toward the mouth of the cave as if seeing much farther—back into the past. "Yet killing him wasn't enough, Ayad, the death of his body alone wasn't the point. It took me years to realize that. One becomes so trapped by personal passion that it is difficult to see to the truth beyond. His death alone meant nothing. What I seek is much grander —the death of his world! The world of besotted tyrants setting themselves up as gods on earth, enslaving us with their dark dreams of religion, idealism, faith. Look, Ayad, power is here for those who know how to seize it. *This*"—Judas gestured to the mortar—"is power. Our fathers would convince us that they alone hold the secrets of power—in their primitive, putrifying religions, in the claptrap of their politics, in the greedy brotherhood of their business conspiracies. But they are wrong. This man we kill today is my father's ideal—the closest to God on earth in my father's eyes. But we shall dispose of him as easily as I disposed of my father. And when we do, the whole stinking structure will come tumbling down around him!"

Ayad listened without any expression. He *was* shocked; this was clearly madness. He fought for a cause—the cause of his people. But Judas, he saw now, was guided by insanity alone. But it was too late to back out now. Until the job was done, he had to depend on this Englishman. And the job, Ayad knew, would be done right. He had no doubts about Judas' tactical brilliance. He tried to calm Judas. Intense personal emotion was bad for a warrior on the eve of battle.

"What about women," he asked casually, "you have never been married?"

"Good God, no! My father put my mother to death because he felt betrayed by her. I would never place myself in that position. I intend to destroy my past, *not* repeat it. My mother's end haunted me for years. But no longer! I have paid my dues to her memory."

"And you're not interested in women at all?"

"Priests have the right idea. When you're trying to get something done, be celibate. Conserve your energy."

He picked up a rock and watched the insects underneath run for cover.

"That is the way a warrior should see women—and human beings in general. If you deny they have souls, they have no more importance than those insects. Then they are easy to kill, Ayad. Remember that today."

"But then nothing is important," said the young Palestinian, "not even what we do now."

"Ah, yes," Judas said softly, "that *is* important. Very important, Ayad. Don't doubt it. What we do today will bring about great changes."

Ayad said quietly, "One day, when we Palestinians have a homeland of our own, I want to marry and settle down and have children."

Judas scowled. "If that's what you want, good luck to you. But it's not for me."

"You don't trust *anybody?*"

Judas thought about it.

"No, I don't think I do." He checked himself. He was beginning to talk too much.

"Not even me?" Ayad persisted.

"Oh, you, of course. My success today depends on you. Of course I trust you, Ayad. We're comrades." He moved abruptly toward the entrance. "Come, it's time you started on your way. The crowd will be hard to get through."

"I'll go by way of the Armenian Quarter and miss most of the people."

They half-stood up at the entrance. Judas clapped the young Palestinian on the shoulder.

"May Allah be with you, my friend!"

"And may your God be with you, Judas."

Judas laughed.

"No, my friend, I travel alone."

Ayad hesitated, wanting to say something, but not sure what. They might never meet again in this world.

"Come on," Judas said brusquely. "Get going!"

The young Palestinian smiled and nodded. He stepped out of the cave and was gone.

". . . The size of the crowd awaiting Pope David at the Damascus Gate, particularly the number of Arabs who have turned out, has taken the Israeli security men by surprise. When the Pope's limousine at last appeared, part of the crowd managed to break through the roadblocks. 'Long live the Pope' was shouted in a score of languages as people surrounded the limousine. Vatican plainclothes bodyguards and private guards employed by Anti-Terrorist International became very nervous and openly cursed the excited, unruly crowd, but the Pope himself was an island of serenity, smiling and blessing his way to the Damascus Gate where his cross was awaiting him. Usually high churchmen carry token light-weight crosses, but Pope David has a heavy wooden cross similar to the one Jesus must have carried along the Via Dolorosa two thousand years ago. He looks a very slight figure and yet seems to lift the heavy cross with ease as he moves toward the Damascus Gate, a fine example of six-teenth-century architecture and the most important gate in the Old City. Pope David is obviously stronger than he looks ..."

"Here it comes," Marc Ram said to Major Falid. "The Pope is entering the real danger zone. I'm certain Judas will strike while he's in the Old City. The next hour will decide everything ..."

31

Judas moved closer to the mouth of the cave so he could see his watch. It was 2:40 P.M. He switched on his pocket radio.

"... The crowd along the Via Dolorosa is making it very difficult for the Pope to stop at each of the Stations of the Cross. The Israeli security forces have tried to limit access to this honeycomb of alleys, stairs, arches, and passageways, but a vast marketplace, an oriental bazaar, mingles with the Stations of the Cross, and the people who run the shops with all their relatives pour out to watch the Pope go by. Cries of joy and applause precede the Pope along the jammed street. He is just leaving the Sixth Station, 'Veronica wipes the face of Jesus.' The Via Dolorosa ascends rapidly past a delicates-sen to the Seventh Station, 'Jesus falls the second time.' No wonder Jesus fell having to carry his heavy cross up this hill! Pope David looks weary with the weight of his ..."

He was only at the Seventh Station. There were still two more Stations to stop at before he entered the church. He was

going to be very late. When he reaches the Ninth Station at
the Roman pillar at the entrance to the Abyssinian monastery, then I'll leave here, Judas told himself. Catholic proces-
sions aren't allowed to go directly through the Abyssinian
monastery into the church, so he'll have to go the long way
round to reach the courtyard. That'll give me plenty of time.

His only worry was that the radio reports might not be
accurate and up to the minute, but delayed by Israeli security
to fool him. He had had Ayad, however, as a check, and the
young Palestinian had so far proved reliable.

". . . Jesus must have passed through the Judgment Gate.
Along the way from the Gate to Calvary, where the Crucifixion took place, there was an avenue of young trees at the
time of Jesus. According to legend, the little trees bent over
to give Jesus more shade. Only an aspen remained upright,
but under Jesus' sad look the tree began to tremble, as aspens
do to this day. The Via Dolorosa now passes butchers',
bakers', and greengrocers' shops, and a tattoo and casket
store. Security men stand in each of the doorways, and shy
Arab women peer expectantly from the grilled crescent windows above as the Pope slowly passes by with his cross
toward the Ninth Station, 'Jesus falls the third time' . . ."

Judas stepped out of the cave into the mild, clear air.
There was hardly any wind. That pleased him. It meant there
would be little wind resistance to calculate. He stretched his
tall muscular body, straightened his long black topcoat, and
touched his beard and sidelocks to check that all was in place.
He then reached back into the cave and lifted out the suitcase
with the grenades. It was heavy, a substantial load of destruction. One of these dropped on the dome will do it, he thought.
That weak, crumbling structure will collapse on top of David.

He made his way up the hill, leaving Gehenna behind him.
The final stage had begun.

". . . Pope David has reached the greatest Christian shrine
in Jerusalem—the Church of the Holy Sepulchre, sometimes
known as the Church of the Resurrection. The only comparable visit to the church in recent times was that of the
Egyptian President Anwar Sadat in 1977, and then the
church was closed for all except the official group. Not even
media photographers were allowed in then. But for his visit,
the Pope has insisted that the church be open for Good
Friday observances as usual. This hasn't quite worked out in

practice, however, for the security men have insisted on admission by pass and have restricted the crowd as much as possible. But they are obviously still very nervous about the situation . . ."

As Pope David entered the crowded courtyard, an old Arab in a black and white kafiyeh stepped toward him. Immediately Marc Ram blocked the way with his black-gloved hand and gestured for two security men to take the old Arab away to be searched and questioned.

"I want only to help him," protested the old Arab.

Ram brusquely pushed him away. A hand touched Ram's shoulder.

"Let me speak to him," said Pope David sternly. He smiled at the old Arab.

"You look very weary," murmured the old man, now thoroughly frightened. "I wished only to offer you a drink," and he held out a can of Coca-Cola.

"Thank you," said the Pope. "I appreciate it, but I am fasting until the end of the service. There's not far to go now. Would you like to accompany me?" He turned back to Ram. "Colonel, I expressly requested that there be no excessive security measures. You are already grossly interfering with our most solemn service."

Ram looked grim, but didn't reply. The Pope lifted up the heavy wooden cross and approached the twin doors of the church with the old Arab beside him.

"What does he want," Ram growled to Major Falid, "to be a martyr?"

". . . The crowd in the fine open courtyard with its rich Crusader-style beauty surged after the slight figure of the Pope, bent under the weight of the cross, and tried to follow him into the ancient church. Grey-haired Cardinal Garonne was pushed aside and had to be given first aid. Monsignor O'Malley, a former boxer, was spared only by his great size and strength. A line of Israeli security men formed across the entrance to the church and eventually the crowd was brought under control. The Pope is now standing at the foot of Calvary inside the church. The next four Stations are on Calvary. He is now ascending the fourteen steps to the holy hill on which were enacted the last scenes of the Passion. The site of the Crucifixion was a rocky knoll, the summit of which

was bare and rounded in shape, which earned for it the Latin
name of Calvary (bald) or the Hebrew name of Golgotha (a
skull). Calvary is divided into two chapels, Latin and Greek.
Never have Greek and Roman Catholic been more deeply
opposed than here, in their faith's heart. The tiny open
sanctuary is divided between them. The Tenth Station, 'Jesus
is stripped of his garments,' is on the Latin side . . ."

Judas saw Ayad's Arab firecracker, confirming the Pope
had entered the church, rise above the Old City just as he
reached the clump of cypress trees. It shot into the clear sky
above the onion-colored dome and then spent itself in a
sudden flash of crimson light. As usual Ayad had done his
work well. It confirmed the radio reports were reliable. Judas
wondered what the Israeli security people would make of it.
Maybe they'd attribute it to an excess of Christian enthusiasm
—Good Friday was a day of mourning, but surely the Pope's
visit was an occasion for firecrackers. According to the radio,
the famous Colonel Ram was inside the church with the
Pope. The world would be well rid of him, too.

Judas put the suitcase down, well back under the cypress
trees, found the key, and opened the suitcase. The grenade-
shaped bombs were neatly strapped in place. Packed there,
too, were the laser range finder and some of the other gear
for the mortar. He took out a bomb to feel the rounded solid
shape and the weight. It gave him a great feeling of satisfaction. It wouldn't be long now before it was homing in on its
target. The gaunt-looking crucifix was leaning between two
cypress trees, well concealed. He untied the Christ figure and
tossed it away in the grass beneath the trees. Then he
unscrewed the heavy tube-shaped sections and the heavy
metal circular baseplate. The four-foot-long barrel, the complicated set of cross levelling, elevating, and traversing gear,
the latest sighting device, the bipod supporting the barrel
—all were soon fitted together again to make a mortar,
the long barrel pointing upwards. Judas put the mortar
back between the two cypress trees so it wasn't visible from
a distance. The gloomy shade of the trees provided a perfect
cover, and when he was ready, he would only have to lift
out the mortar a few feet, still covered by the outer trees,
for a clear shot.

He stared then at the dome in the far distance, imagining
the busy scene inside the church. The Pope had four more

Stations to go. Judas was impatient now to begin. This was
the time when he was most vulnerable. But he had to wait a
few more minutes until the Pope reached the last station, the
fourteenth, at the sepulchre . . . directly under the dome.

". . . The Eleventh Station, 'Jesus is nailed to the Cross,' is
marked by the Latin altar in the right chapel. The Pope
kneels at the silver-plated bronze altar, erected in 1558.
Today, for Good Friday, it is entirely bare, without cross,
candlesticks, or linens. There is a crude mosaic of Christ in
agony; above him, a picture of Mary, his mother, her face
grief-stricken. There is a sense of sadness and of restrained
horror . . ."

Marc Ram, keeping a short distance from the Pope, followed him to the Greek chapel, marking the Twelfth Station, "Jesus dies on the Cross." Between the columns, which
supported the altar, was a socket, said to have held the cross.
On the right was a metal slab which covered a great rent in
the naked grey rock of Calvary, believed to have been caused
by the earthquake at the time of Jesus' death. A perpetual
flame illuminated the cleft floor. In spite of the costly marble
covering, much of Calvary, the cleft earth, even the dripping
dust, conveyed an overwhelming sense of the past, a primitive
feeling of truth.

The Pope knelt with his head in his hands, shutting out the
noise and the crowd behind him. Robed priests and privileged
pilgrims from the divided chapels, plainclothes Israeli security men, people who looked as if they belonged more in the
oriental bazaars outside, pressed about the slight, silent,
kneeling figure in black.

Marc Ram watched with a feeling of helplessness. Israeli
jurisdiction covered the whole of the city, but in practice his
authority today stopped at the entrance to the church. He felt
as if everybody there, all the divided Christian sects and their
worshippers, Latin, Greek, Armenian, Syrian, Ethiopian, Cop-
tic, all of them, were handicapping the smooth working of the
Israeli security team. Few of the priests had been willing to
cooperate with his men, no doubt taking their lead from the
Pope's indifference to his own safety. Maybe David had some
complex Christian desire to die in the same place as Jesus,
Ram thought impatiently, uneasy in the atmosphere of darkness and decay. His idea of religion was a clean, bright, and

orderly modern synagogue, not this ancient decaying laby- rinth, full of foreign Christian sights and smells.

At first the uncontrollable crowd, the continual mounting pressure of people around the Pope, had alarmed Ram. Judas might be any one of these strange faces edging toward David. A gun could poke out under some of these heavy robes, in these shadowy corners, and might easily be missed until the fatal explosion—and even that might be drowned in the continual buzz of whispers and chants. Yet the crowd was pressed so close together that there was no way Judas could make a fast escape. He might shoot the Pope, but then he would be hemmed in. A *fedayeen* or a Japanese suicide pilot might risk it, but Judas' record indicated much greater caution, the attitude of a mercenary who intended to survive, however personally obsessed he was. There was something here Ram felt he didn't understand. Had he fallen into a trap himself? Had Judas outfoxed him? Perhaps Judas had guessed he'd think the site of Calvary would be the perfect setting for him, and he planned instead to attack somewhere else later in some quite unexpected way. Ram didn't relax his vigilance, continually examining the faces massed in the tiny chapel, but he wasn't quite as sure as he had been that he had read Judas' mind correctly. His concern grew. Anticipation was the key to successful security. Perhaps Judas still had the advantage of complete surprise.

His miniature radio crackled—he was linked on an ultra-high frequency that could neither be interfered with nor intercepted. Beside him, a Greek priest with a heavy black beard glared at the sudden noise.

"Yes?" Ram whispered.

"Marc?" Feinberg's voice sounded like an explosion. Other priests and pilgrims stared at Ram indignantly. "We've got a report on the German—Karl Mundt. He *was* a mercenary. He was on the Egyptian side in the '73 war. He was working for Hamed . . ."

Why the hell was Feinberg telling him this now? Ram wondered, acutely aware of the sensation he was creating in the tiny chapel. What did he care about the German's record at this time? File it.

"There's one interesting point, Marc. That's why I'm telling you now instead of later. He was a mortar expert, one of their best. Boasted he could hit a tank from four thousand yards . . ."

But Ram was no longer listening. If Judas had brought a mortar expert with him, then he didn't plan on a close-up killing in the Church.

"What's the latest from Radar Control?"

There was a pause.

"A false alarm in the Arab Quarter, Marc. Another on the Mount of Olives—".

"That's too far away. Anything closer?"

"Something keeps showing up on Mount Zion. We've asked one of the soldiers on duty there to investigate . . ."

Mount Zion—that was within mortar range.

He made a quick decision.

"Tell the helicopter to come and get me." He turned to one of the Israeli security men behind him. "You take over here. Stay with the Pope all the way."

"Remember this is a holy place," snapped the bearded Greek priest next to him.

He ignored the priest, pushing his way through the crowd, using his black-gloved hand like a battering ram in his impatience to get outside. He was leaving the Pope well protected, but he was convinced now Judas wasn't here. There was no clever way out of this confined space—as he was discovering for himself, and he had the law on his side, he wasn't on the run. No, Judas wouldn't allow himself to be trapped here. Much as Ram wanted to stay by the Pope's side, he now had to look at this from long distance.

At last, pushing, shoving, elbowing through the crowd, his heavy hand cutting a way through, Ram reached the bottom of the fourteen steps from Calvary and forced himself past the people blocking the entrance into the still-crowded courtyard. The helicopter was stationed above the Via Dolorosa, and already he could hear it dropping down toward the church, the familiar whirring sound like a giant insect's approach. There was nowhere clear for it to land. It soon hovered into view above the ancient walls of the courtyard, like a vision of the future appearing in the far distant past. The helicopter dropped with a rush and then simply hung in the air above the crowd. Police and soldiers pushed people roughly aside to give Ram room to grasp the steel ladder that dropped from the underbelly of the helicopter.

Suddenly a big hand held him back.

"Forgetting me?" It was Robert Miller.

"There's no room," Ram said angrily.

"Remember our agreement, Ram. I want to be in at the death."

"Okay, I'll have another chopper pick you up."

Ram grasped the bottom rung and pulled himself up. He rapidly began to ascend the gently swinging ladder, remarkably agile for a man with only one arm.

"Get me Feinberg," he panted as soon as he clambered into the small cabin.

"Marc . . ." Feinberg's voice was much stronger, seemed much closer, than in the confines of the church.

"What's happening on Mount Zion *now?*"

A pause.

"We've momentarily lost contact, Marc."

Hell, something *had* happened.

"We're trying her again now."

"Her?"

"It's a woman soldier."

"Hell! Remember who we're dealing with. Killing means nothing to Judas. Any response from her yet?"

A brief pause. Ram stared at the upturned faces in the courtyard below. What the hell was keeping Feinberg?

"No, she's not responding, Marc." Feinberg's voice was suddenly anxious. "You think Judas is on Mount Zion?"

"We'll soon find out," Ram told the helicopter pilot, "get to Mount Zion as fast as you can."

The helicopter trembled in a numbing downwash of air and noise, and rose with a rush, soaring upward above the Old City.

I hope we're in time, Ram thought, loosening his shoulder holster.

Aliza had been on guard duty at the Wailing Wall, the last remnant of the Second Temple and Judaism's holiest prayer site, when she was transferred to patroling the lower slopes of Mount Zion.

The change had pleased the twenty-year-old Israeli woman because, at the Wall, she had run into trouble with one of the Orthodox and she anticipated more.

She had been stationed with a male soldier named Daniel at the pathway leading to the huge honey-colored Wall, situated below the Arabs' golden Dome of the Rock. Suddenly a young, aggressive, Orthodox rabbi had accosted her, quoting Deuteronomy: "A woman shall not wear anything that pertains to a man . . . for whoever does these things is an abomination to the Lord your God." A woman soldier was "an abomination," cried the Rabbi. He was unpleasant and persistent, but Aliza didn't argue with him. It was her own business, she told herself. Her young husband had been killed in a bomb explosion on a Jerusalem bus a few months before, and her army service wtih the Israeli Defense Forces helped her to cope with her grief and her loneliness.

But she was pleased to be switched to Mount Zion that day. It was busy at the Wall—the Sabbath began at sundown and it was also the week of Passover—and she anticipated more trouble. Many of the people praying in the men's and women's sections, putting written prayers and requests in the crevices between the Wall's massive stones, stared disapprovingly at her. It would only be a matter of time before she was accosted again by someone with enough *chutzpah*.

Mount Zion was a nice relief. It was deserted except for the other soldiers at the foot of the hill and on the higher slopes. Everyone was away in the Old City for the Pope's visit. She was content to be by herself on Mount Zion. It was very peaceful. She remembered coming here once with her husband to visit King David's Tomb. That wasn't far away from here. She felt a stab of grief at the memory.

Her thoughts were interrupted by the crackle of her radio. There were new orders for her. Radar had located something farther up Mount Zion. It might be another false alarm, but please investigate and report back as soon as possible.

She was glad of the diversion. She moved briskly up the hill, the past temporarily forgotten.

There was a movement among some cypress trees. A dark figure showed against the green and then ducked back out of sight. Gripping her Uzzi submachine gun, she went forward across the hard rocky ground to investigate. As she drew near, a tall man in black suddenly stepped out from under the cypress trees. He was a bearded rabbi in a wide-brimmed black hat and a long black coat. He had sidelocks. He looked *very* Orthodox. Aliza groaned to herself and stopped, not wanting to have to talk to him and perhaps receive another lecture. He had probably gone under the trees to urinate. But what had radar found?

The rabbi waved and gestured for her to join him. Reluctantly, her submachine gun casually held by her side, Aliza walked over to find out what he wanted.

* * *

Judas had just finished his preparations. He had checked the range with the laser and allowed for the weather conditions. There was hardly any wind. Then he switched on his pocket radio to check the Pope's position.

". . . The Pope is just leaving the Thirteenth Station, 'The body of Jesus is taken down from the Cross,' marked by the Latin altar of the Stabat Mater with the famous bejewelled wood statue of Jesus' mother Mary. The Pope is now approaching this tomb, the site of the fourteenth and final station, 'Jesus is laid in the sepulchre.' The Pope enters the rotunda under the dome and proceeds to the sepulchre . . ."

Good, Judas thought. Now he's directly underneath.

". . . First, the Pope enters a small vestibule, the Chapel of the Angel, so named because it was here that the angel, sitting on a stone, announced the Resurrection. An arched doorway leads into the sepulchre itself. A marble slab marks the burial place of Jesus. The original rock, which from Friday sunset to Sunday sunrise served as the funeral couch for the body of the Redeemer, is hidden beneath the marble covering . . ."

Judas took out one of the grenade-shaped bombs and laid it gently on the grass. Then he lifted up the heavy mortar and began to carry it to the edge of the trees.

It was then that he saw the soldier.

He quickly put the mortar out of sight again. He had to deal with the soldier before he could fire the mortar. He hoped to hell there were no more soldiers close by. He watched the soldier approaching. He was relieved to see it was a woman. The Israelis couldn't have expected any trouble on Mount Zion to put a woman on guard there. They probably had another guard somewhere up on top. It would have been better to play a waiting game, but he couldn't afford the time. The Pope would be only a few minutes in the sepulchre, then he would hold a short service on a portable altar outside, and then he would leave the area of the dome, and go down to the entrance and out into the courtyard . . . and be safely out of range. There was no time for waiting.

It was then Judas decided to show himself and wave to her to come over. She responded immediately. The relaxed angle of her Uzzi submachine gun showed she suspected nothing. Her attitude boosted Judas' confidence that he would get away. The rabbi disguise was very effective with the Israelis.

She approached with a friendly, respectful look. She was

young, an attractive dark-haired woman with healthy olive skin and a well-developed body. Her breasts pointed upwards through her uniform, and her strong, bold thighs stretched the khaki tight. It seemed a pity to kill someone so sexually attractive.

"Yes, Rabbi," she said, "what do you want?"

"Back here," he mumbled fussily, as if he were confused by something. He mustn't do anything in the open in case there were others nearby.

She followed him under the cypress tree, her Uzzi submachine gun still held slackly, not at all suspicious of him.

"Look," he said, pointing to the mortar in the grass. As she came forward to look, he slipped his long-barreled Beretta out of the deep pocket of his topcoat, stuck it against her body between her breasts to muffle the sound, and fired before she had a chance to resist. The bullet must have passed through her heart because she died instantly, as quietly and naturally as an animal. He caught her as she fell and lowered her body to the ground back among the trees.

He glanced around, but could see no other soldiers. He switched on his radio to check on the Pope.

". . . The Pope has just finished praying in the small sepulchre. He laid an olive branch of gold he brought from Rome on the marble slab. Even though he is only slightly built, he had to bend to pass under the low entrance. He is now kneeling at the small portable altar that has been set up outside the sepulchre . . ."

Good timing, Judas thought, imagining for the last time the scene he was about to make real: The Pope kneeling in solemn prayer as the big onion-colored dome exploded and collapsed on top of him, burying him in a tomb of rubble.

So little remained to be done to make it come true!

He quickly carried the mortar out to the firing position. The barrel pointed upwards in the direction of the dome. He carefully brought over the grenade-shaped bomb. He laid the dead soldier's Uzzi submachine gun in the grass nearby just in case he needed it. He then made a last-minute check of the mortar. All was ready. *Now,* he thought . . .

It was then that he heard the helicopter.

From the air, Mount Zion looked green and stony and deserted. Marc Ram peered down through binoculars. The hard, sloping ground was as clear and sharply focused as if he

had it under a microscope. The helicopter was flying so low
that it cast a shadow like a giant grasshopper.

This was the location on Mount Zion that radar had
pinpointed. This was where the woman soldier had disappeared. There were soldiers coming up the broad path looking for her, their Uzzi submachine guns ready. But where was
the trouble spot?

The massive towers of the Church of the Dormition,
looking more than ever like a medieval fortress, lay on one
side, the room of the Last Supper and David's tomb on
the other. There were dense bushes and clumps of trees
dotting the gentle slope. Ram slowly turned the binoculars
from side to side, examining every change in the landscape
below.

A flash of sunlight in a clump of trees straight ahead
caught his attention—the kind of bright glint on metal that
sometimes betrayed a sniper. Ram concentrated the binoculars on the trees and saw very clearly the protruding barrel of
a mortar and a man in black behind it.

A big man.

Dressed as a rabbi.

Ram knew at once who it was.

"There," he cried to the pilot, pointing down, and the
helicopter dropped toward the trees.

Judas was already loading the mortar.

It was aimed toward the Old City—at the Church of the
Holy Sepulchre.

There wasn't much time left to stop him.

Minutes . . . seconds . . .

"Drop as low as you can," Ram told the pilot.

He watched with horrified fascination the man he had
hunted for so long. Although Judas was aware the helicopter
was rushing toward him, he went on working over the
mortar. He obviously had no intention of giving up.

If only this was a military helicopter equipped with a
cannon or rockets! Ram thought desperately.

As the helicopter brushed the tops of the trees, Ram leaned
out and aimed his pistol at Judas, fired—and missed. He
cursed his black-gloved hand for letting him down, aimed
again and fired. And missed again. There was no time for
another shot. Judas had leaned down and come up with an
Uzzi submachine gun. He raked the helicopter with bullets as
it rose sharply to climb out of range. Then he put down the

submachine gun and calmly, nervelessly, went back to the mortar.

"Go down again," Ram snapped, never taking his eyes off Judas. He knew he was asking the pilot to risk his life, but Judas *had* to be stopped.

The helicopter turned with a great shudder and dropped toward Judas again. Ram rested his pistol on his knee, aimed, prayed, fired . . . and this time he scored. Judas stumbled forward as if he'd been punched on the shoulder. But he didn't fall. He steadied himself and turned back to the mortar. The man was determined to finish. But he wasn't an iron man, impervious to bullets; this was a battle of wills between them. Who could endure the longer?

Judas picked up the submachine gun and fired a quick burst upwards at the helicopter window. Bullets cut through the cabin, hitting the pilot in the chest and thrusting him backwards out of his seat. The helicopter shuddered violently, tilted dangerously to one side, and then plunged forward out of control. But Ram had no time to struggle with it. He had to stop Judas, who was bent over the mortar again, ready to fire.

As the helicopter dropped into the trees, the branches tearing at its sides like giant fingernails, Ram leaned farther out, near enough almost to touch Judas, and shot the big man in the back, a solid hit through bone.

But he was too late. The bullet struck Judas at the same moment as he fired the mortar. There was a great whooshing sound as the bomb burst out of the barrel in a lightning-fast trajectory toward the Old City. It shot upwards in a great arc and disappeared over the horizon of the hill. And moments later there was a loud explosion in the far distance. *The church.* Ram thought with a bitter sense of failure, *Judas got the church—and the Pope!*

He had no time to worry any more. The helicopter crumpled up among the trees and overturned with a tremendous wrenching of metal. Ram was thrown through the shattered window and momentarily lost consciousness. He recovered to find himself lying in a clump of bushes, his pistol still clutched in his gloved hand—a human hand would have dropped it. Badly bruised, blood trickling down his chin from where a branch had torn his cheek, he stood up with only one thought—he *had* to find Judas. He had seen him pitch forward into the undergrowth. He had definitely been hit. But

Judas was still dangerous until he was found, even though the mortar was no longer a threat. It lay in broken pieces now, wrecked by the helicopter as it overturned.

Ram pushed through the trees, searching the bushes and the tall grass. No Judas. But he stumbled across the body of the woman soldier. Her dead, unmarked face looked very young, but he had no time to examine her. He came rushing out of the trees to face several submachine guns. Soldiers had arrived. But where was Judas? . . .

Then he remembered with a bitter feeling that Judas had blown up the church. And the Pope? . . . Ram ran forward desperately until he had a view of the Old City. He stopped in amazement, his spirits rising. The onion-colored dome was still there, as solid as ever. Judas had *failed!*

Just outside the walls of the Old City, a great column of smoke was rising from a half-completed skyscraper. Judas had hit that instead. Ram suddenly felt much better. But where was Judas now?

The only way clear had been down into Gehenna. Bleeding heavily from the bullet wounds in his shoulder and in his back close to the spine, frantic at the feel of his own blood, Judas staggered like a drunken man down the hillside, searching for the cave. He felt that if he could reach it, he would somehow survive. A mist seemed to be coming up from the valley. He wasn't sure if it was real or was inside his head, the result of losing so much blood. He kept falling and then dragging himself up again, leaving big spots of blood behind him that the sun soon dried out.

At last he made it. He stumbled into the darkness of the cave and crawled like a wounded animal as far back as he could. His back burned with the pain. Soon it would stiffen up. He hoped it wouldn't get infected. He didn't want to examine it for fear of getting more blood on his hands. The sight and smell and touch of his blood had affected his mind, made him impotent to plan, to look ahead. Hamed had given him an address in the Arab Quarter where he could hide. Perhaps in twenty-four hours, if he kept his mind together and didn't grow too weak, he could risk leaving the cave—an old, bent-backed, limping Rabbi. Or was he kidding himself? Was he finished this time? He tried to consider the possibility coldly, calmly. If so, he didn't want to die in this burrow, like a cornered rat, drowning in his own blood. He wanted to be in the open. Only time would tell if he had a chance . . .

He lay on his side on the hard stone and cursed his luck. Another few seconds would have done it. He had left himself open, sure he could finish the job. He had been careless. The bullet hitting his back had thrown him off balance and spoiled his aim, and the bomb had shot out about twenty degrees or several hundred yards off course. Now he would never see the dome exploding. But that had become too important to him. He had been too personally involved. His plan had really been ruined when he lost the German. He didn't have enough people then to carry it out efficiently. But killing the Pope was what mattered. Now it all depended on Ayad. He wondered where the young Palestinian was and if he was aware yet that the mortar attack had failed.

Ram checked with headquarters about the office building Judas had hit. The building wasn't occupied yet, but a laborer working there had been killed. Judas had taken another life, but, Ram reminded himself, hundreds more would have died if he had hit the church.

Ram stared down into Gehenna. Judas must have gone down into the valley, otherwise the soldiers would have seen him. Gehenna had never looked more sinister. It was a cruel, stony wilderness lying among the debris of centuries, not a place for human beings. Judas was down there somewhere.

Cousins, the CIA man, had come with the soldiers. He was studying a map of Gehenna.

"There are many subterranean tunnels and caves," he told Ram. "Excavations. Plenty of places he could hide."

Ram, pistol in hand, began to go down into the valley. Cousins followed him, breathing heavily. Ram felt very uneasy. Judas was capable of anything, and now he would be desperate.

32

Ayad waited in the square in front of the Damascus Gate for nearly an hour. He had made his way there through the side

alleys of the Old City as soon as he had sent up the Arab
firecracker. He couldn't relax during the long wait. He didn't
know if he would have to act or not. If the Pope appeared
at the Damascus Gate—still alive!—it meant that Judas' plan
had failed, and Ayad then would have to take over and kill
him. Ayad spent the long wait reciting passages from the
Koran and imagining the death of his parents who had died at
the hands of these people. He had to work himself up into the
right mood to kill a man who meant nothing to him.

The first warning he received was a low murmur in the distance that gradually grew louder until he recognized the sound
of cheering voices and clapping hands. Somebody was approaching past the welcoming crowd. It could mean only one
thing. The Pope had survived! The attack had failed!

He said to a Jewish-looking man standing nearby, "The
Pope—he come?"

"Any minute now," the man said heartily.

The noise increased until the people in the front of the
square began to applaud. The police lines across the massive
gateway parted, and there was the slight figure in black,
gently making the sign of the cross, blessing the faces massed
in front of him. There was the target!

Ayad felt a rush of concern for Judas. What had happened
to the Englishman? Ayad didn't have the empty, barren
feeling he had when someone was dead. But Judas must be in
great trouble, otherwise they wouldn't have been able to stop
him. Something had gone wrong, very wrong. The responsibility for success was his alone now. He couldn't fail.

Monsignor O'Malley had a sixth sense in matters concerning the Pope. Although he had been informed about the
foiled mortar attack, he still felt uneasy as David left the Old
City. There was something wrong. He sensed it as soon as
they came out through the Damascus Gate. The huge Monsignor moved as close to the slight figure of the Pope as he
could get. Orlando Moravia was by the Pope's side, then
came the popular, voluble Mayor of Jerusalem. O'Malley
towered gloomily over them, scanning the faces in the crowd,
his great fists clenched, waiting . . .

Ayad studied the slight figure approaching across the
square. The Pope presented a small target. He also had the
quick movements of a bird. The knife would have to hit him

when he was sure to be stationary—talking to someone, waiting to get in the limousine . . .

Ayad was prepared. He had climbed on the back of a truck belonging to a TV company. It gave him a grandstand view and was only a few yards from the Pope's limousine. During the long wait, he had ingratiated himself with the TV crew by helping them to lift heavy equipment. The police asked to see his passport, but otherwise didn't bother him; they probably assumed he was working for the TV crew.

As Pope David made his way slowly down the lane of religious and security people, Ayad touched the knife in his pocket. He would have to take it out and throw it in one quick movement. It was unlikely that he would escape. There were too many Israeli soldiers and police. He viewed his chances calmly, stoically. He would never know now what it was like to marry and rear children, but at least he should be able to carry out his orders—and that was enough for a warrior. He would hit the slight black figure in the center of the chest. His eyes concentrated on the target, and his fingers gripped the knife in his pocket, ready to touch the button that would spring the long blade . . .

Orlando Moravia, elegant and plump, wiped the sweat off his face with a large scented handkerchief as he waited at the Pope's limousine. He felt shaken. He had just overheard that an attack on the Pope in the Church of the Holy Sepulchre had been narrowly averted. They had all nearly been blown up as the Pope prayed before the Sepulchre. He heard the Jordanian Major, Falid, say the Russians were behind it. Moravia couldn't believe it. Collecting information, yes, even blackmail, but surely assassination wasn't the Russian style. He was surprised to find himself so angry about it. After all he had supplied them with, the risks he had run, his life had meant nothing to them. To assassinate David, they had been prepared to sacrifice him with the rest—assuming Falid Major was correct.

He watched the Pope. David seemed so calm, so serene in the middle of the crowd. Yet he must know of the attempt to blow up the Church of the Holy Sepulchre. He was a strong man. He would be a big loss—one the church couldn't afford at present.

David was shaking hands with a few Christian and Israeli dignitaries before getting into the limousine. As Moravia waited to follow him, his eyes idly scanned the faces of the crowd, the TV cameras . . . and then he froze with horror.

The sun flashed on naked steel.

A hand was holding a long, gleaming knife.

Fierce black eyes stared at David I.

The hand rose . . . the knife was aimed . . .

My God, Moravia thought, the Pope must not die.

The hand went back.

Instinctively Moravia knew what he must do.

Monsignor O'Malley, too, saw the knife. He moved extremely fast for such a big man, but the mayor of Jerusalem blocked his way. O'Malley, brushed the mayor aside, losing time, and charged forward trying to reach David before it happened, knowing despairingly that he would be too late . . .

"Tell me the worst," Ram said as the radio crackled on the hillside above Gehenna. It sounded like a submachine gun. Cousins closed in behind to listen.

"It was a knife attack," Feinberg reported. "A young Palestinian from Beirut—he was standing on a TV truck about twenty yards away when the Pope was getting into his limousine. It was a surprise attack—suicidal—"

"The Pope," Ram said impatiently. "What happened to the Pope?"

"He's okay—"

"Why the hell didn't you say so at the beginning?" Ram snapped, giving a great sigh of relief.

"Sorry, Marc. We're still trying to sort out the facts. Orlando Moravia must have seen the knife coming. He pushed the Pope aside and took it himself."

"How is he?"

"Dead. The knife struck Moravia high up in his throat and through the back of his skull."

"And the young assassin?"

"He's dead, too. Major Falid shot him."

"Ah, poor Falid," Ram said softly. "To have to kill a fellow Arab among the enemy in Israel—many will not forgive him." Ram stared down into the valley. "Now all we've got to do is find Judas. Make sure you don't relax your security screen around the Pope until we do," he told Feinberg.

* * *

Slowly, methodically, they covered the hillside. Cousins, with his amateur archaeologist's special knowledge of Gehenna, took them to every possible hiding place. His speed was amazing for such a fat man—amazing, too, was his ability to squirm into quite small tunnels and excavations of ancient burial places. Ram kept the soldiers back as a rearguard. Confronting Judas was a personal matter for him and Cousins.

It was almost dusk by the time they reached the cave. Cousins had checked so many places without success that his excessive caution at the start had relaxed. He entered the cave without waiting for Ram, his huge fat figure bent so that his buttocks bulged like the back of an elephant.

"Go easy," Ram shouted. "Remember, he's armed."

It was too late.

There was a sudden gunshot inside the cave that seemed to reverberate down into the valley. Cousins came out backwards, holding his great sagging belly, blood oozing between his fingers. He slowly sank to the ground.

"He's right at the back," Cousins panted.

Soldiers crept forward to carry him away. It took four of them.

Ram shot several times into the cave, holding the pistol at arm's length very firmly in his black-gloved hand. He thought he heard a low cry far back.

"Judas," Ram shouted, "throw your gun out first and then come out yourself with your hands up."

No answer.

"Your attempt at the Damascus Gate has failed," Ram shouted. *Take away any hope he has left.* "Your young Palestinian has been shot ... He's dead ..." *Expose him. Leave him with nothing.* "Come out, Judas, or should I say ... *Paul Brett?*"

There was no answer for several minutes, and then Ram heard a few stones being dislodged, the sound of slow, painful movements. Judas was coming out.

Ram waved the soldiers back and stood alone, facing the mouth of the cave.

Suddenly a grotesque figure reared out of the darkness. Judas was still in his rabbi's clothes, but he had lost his beard and sidelocks. There was dried blood on his face. He had difficulty in standing upright as the waves of pain from his wounds hit him. Only the strength of his tall, muscular body kept him on his feet. He held his long-barreled Beretta at his side, and stood glaring around him like a great blinded animal surrounded by enemies.

"Judas," Ram said simply to draw his attention.

Judas looked toward him—at the one arm. "Ram," he murmured, and the hand holding the Beretta twitched.

"Throw your gun away," Ram ordered, keeping him covered, hoping his steel hand hadn't been damaged in the helicopter crash and he could still press the trigger.

Judas stood there, swaying, still holding his pistol down.

Ram watched him, guessing what he intended to do.

The Beretta slowly rose. The bloodshot eyes seemed to be trying to focus.

He had come out to die.

The Beretta pointed unsteadily at Ram.

The soldiers raised their submachine guns. Ram gestured for them to stay out of it.

Judas tried to straighten up. The Beretta steadied. His finger tightened on the trigger, straining for the strength or the will to press.

Ram had waited long enough—almost too long. He squeezed his trigger at last and was surprised to feel no sense of triumph as his enemy fell backwards, knocked over by the force of the bullet and the sudden end of life.

Ram walked over slowly and stared sombrely down at the body. He had no need to check if Judas was dead. He had shot him deliberately in the region of the heart to make sure.

"Are you certain it's him?" a voice asked behind him.

It was Robert Miller. Judas looked different to the man he'd met at Amman airport.

"Let's see," Ram grunted.

He went down on one knee and opened Judas' shirt.

On his chest was the faded tattoo of a crucifix. The bullet had pierced the figure on the cross.

"The search is over," Robert Miller said.
desperate.

⚙ PART THREE ⚙

EASTER SUNDAY

33

Gina's cab took nearly two hours to reach Fiumicino Airport. She had witnessed many of the great Roman holidays, but she had never seen anything like this. Along the sixteen-mile route from the center of the city to the airport stretched a vast crowd estimated at close to two million people. The whole of Rome had turned out to welcome the Pope home.

It was a hero's welcome, Gina thought as she stared out of the cab at the massed faces blocking the roadway until the police moved them on, the unending lines of Romans waiting impatiently for the familiar Vatican limousine with the white and yellow flag.

"Everybody's out today," said the tanned young cab driver with a flashing smile. "Catholics, Communists, anarchists, atheists, businessmen, whores—*everybody!*"

He was right, Gina thought, and she knew why.

It wasn't only the news of the attempted assassination of the Pope; it wasn't only that Rome wanted to outdo Jerusalem in greeting David. It was more than that. Robert Miller's revelations about Judas and the Tolloni affair and Bellini's connection with it had been published in New York and then reprinted around the world. The Valeri caretaker government had allowed large extracts to be broadcast on Italian television and radio and to be published in the Italian newspapers. Her old boss, Inspector Scaglia, The Machine, had been arrested for his complicity in the murders of her father and Alberto Tolloni's widow. Romans—Italians from other parts of the country—Communists as well as Catholics—had turned out to stage a vast demonstration of repudiation, of rejection, of all that Sandro Bellini as Prime Minister and his henchmen had done in their name.

But, Gina told herself, it was more even than that. Easter Sunday morning, the morning of the Resurrection, was traditionally a happy time marking the end of winter to the sun-starved Romans. This immense crowd's mood was more than just tumultuous joy on this fine sunny morning. There was a definite feeling of affection here, too. The Romans *liked* David I, and they had nearly lost him.

LONG LIVE DAVID was on many of the banners held by people along the route. A group of lively teenagers even displayed one that read: David 2, Goliath 0.

On the cab radio, an Italian journalist named Mario Lepecci—wasn't he a friend of Roberto's?—was discussing the attempted assassination, referring to other popes who had died violently: "Of the 265 popes since Linus I succeeded St. Peter in A.D. 67, forty-five did not survive a year after their election. Six were murdered. One died of wounds received in the course of the Guelph-Ghibelline civil wars. Benedict V was deposed by the Holy Roman Emperor in 964 after a month. Benedict VI, the Emperor's papal candidate, was thrown into prison in 974 by the Roman noble family, the Crescentii, who set up an anti-pope, Boniface VII, and had Benedict strangled in prison. Another pope, John XXI, was killed by a falling ceiling in 1277. Fourteen popes didn't serve even as long as David I has so far. Thirteen served even a shorter time than John Paul I who was found dead in bed after a reign of only 34 days in 1978 . . ."

The cab driver grinned back at Gina. "Dangerous job the Pope's, huh?"

"There have been assassination attempts before in recent times," the voice on the radio continued. "A man, for example, attempted to kill Pope Paul VI on one of his foreign tours. But there has never been a professionally planned attempt on such an international scale as Operation Goliath.

Pope David was a target in the political game involving the Soviet Union, the Middle East nations, and the West ..."

Gina stared out of the window at the happy crowd. Why couldn't she be like them? Usually she found it easy to identify with a Roman crowd's mood. It was Easter Sunday and there was cause for rejoicing. She was as relieved as anyone that the Pope hadn't been killed. And yet she was in a bad mood. She felt depressed. And she knew why. It concerned Roberto and herself. She had fallen in love with the American reporter. But now she faced the possibility of losing him, just as she had lost her father.

Prime Minister Valeri had sent her a pass for the VIP section at the airport. The large room overlooking the main runways was crowded with famous and powerful Romans—she recognized several of her father's friends from the party and from the Quirinale palace, a prominent industrialist, a movie actress who was married to a Greek ship owner ... Valeri, in a formal dark suit, broke off a conversation with President Moltani to greet her. She noted the change in him. This was no longer the professor in his ivory tower above the battle. This was the politician who had successfully engineered the defeat of Sandro Bellini. He was brisker in manner, more self-confident, easily dominating the large room.

"It's good to see a Communist prime minister welcoming a pope," Gina said jokingly.

Valeri smiled down at her from his great height. "You have seen the great crowds, my dear. The people have spoken."

"They will speak again on election day, Valeri," said a voice behind them. It was Ignazio Silvieri, the silver-maned leader of the Christian Democrats.

"Ah, yes," said Valeri calmly, "but we don't yet know what they will say on election day, do we, Silvieri?"

There was a sudden rush to the long viewing windows. The Alitalia jet airliner leased by the Vatican was arriving from Amman. Valeri went out on the tarmac to greet the Pope. The red carpet had been weighted down against the cold wind that had been forecast, but contrary to prediction, it was a calm sunny day when the slight figure of Pope David appeared. He had changed from his Good Friday mourning into clothes more befitting Easter Sunday—a flat red hat, a long white topcoat, and red shoes. Despite the strain of the last few days, he looked serene and fresh and never lost his air of gaiety as he stepped forward to shake hands with Valeri and President Moltani. Cardinal Garonne behind him and even huge Monsignor O'Malley showed obvious signs of fatigue, but David seemed completely rested and relaxed as he waved to the cheering crowd behind the rows of Italian dignitaries. As he gave a general blessing with a large sign of the cross, Gina noticed that several of the Communist leaders, including Valeri, made a display of not bowing their heads.

Before the Pope started on his triumphant drive into Rome, he drew Monsignor O'Malley aside.

"Go to see Orlando Moravia's family," he said quietly. "I shall attend the requiem mass for him. There is no need for the truth to come out—even if we're sure what it was at the end. Who knows what state of mind he died in?"

The Pope walked over to speak to his father, who was waiting patiently in his wheelchair.

"I thank God, my son, you are still alive," John O'Neill whispered in his strangled voice.

"You don't kill an Irishman so easily," David said lightly. "Why don't you ride in the limousine with me?"

The paralyzed millionaire's eyes lit up gratefully. "I would like that very much," he said, "but I can ride only in a car fitted specially for my wheelchair."

The Pope hesitated. "Then I'll ride in your car with you." He turned to Monsignor O'Malley. "You can ride in the limousine, Joe."

"Signor Silvieri wondered if he could also ride with you," Monsignor O'Malley said.

"No," the Pope replied firmly. "If the Christian Democrats are to win the election, they must do it on their own."

"Is that wise?" his father murmured. "Don't you want the Communists to be defeated?"

"I want the people to make a free choice," the Pope said. "Valeri has been fair in allowing all the facts about Bellini to be published and broadcast. That should be enough to defeat the Communists."

"Can you be sure?" O'Neill asked his son.

"That won't be the only reason for their defeat," Pope David said confidently. "Valeri is a man of limited integrity. He must have known what was happening long before he acted. Never forget he still believes in a system that has no respect for the individual or for spiritual values. If he wins— and I don't think he can—it will only be because we Christians have fallen so far short of our ideals. We have allowed people to become disillusioned with us. Communism has played on their fears. We have a lot of ground to recover and very little time to do it. To win against a godless materialistic philosophy, our faith must be as real as the hills of Jerusalem or the grey rock of Calvary in the Church of the Holy Sepulchre. I believe I was given the experience of being nearly assassinated in the Holy City to open my eyes wider . . ."

At that moment the Pope had almost a visionary look. Watching him, O'Neill was moved to tears for perhaps the first time in his life. David gently touched his father's trembling hand. "Don't cry, Father. For we are blessed to have found each other, and this is a day to rejoice."

Robert Miller rushed off the media's chartered jet to find Gina. She was waiting for him just beyond the runway. He sensed her hesitation.

"What the hell's the matter with you?" he demanded gruffly, kissing her and then inspecting her at arm's length.

She had prepared an elaborate speech, but now it came out in a rush: "I'm pregnant, Roberto."

"You're sure?"

"I've been to the doctor."

Miller was silent, and she thought she knew what that meant.

"*You* don't need to worry about it," she said.

"There's no worry," he said with a grin. "Abortion's legal in Italy now."

"I'm not going to have an abortion," she said.

"You're going to have the baby?"

"I don't agree with abortion. It's part of the whole trend of our times to make individual life seem valueless."

"You're going to overpopulate the globe then."

"This may be the only baby I'll ever have."

He grabbed her by the arms and lifted her off the ground. "No, we're going to have a whole tribe of them."

"What do you mean, Roberto?" She couldn't follow his change of mood.

"We must get married as soon as possible, Gina. Our baby mustn't be a Roman bastard. There are too many already."

Her eyes brightened. "This is a proposal, Roberto?"

"I feel we're married already, Gina, but I guess we'll have

to go through the legal formalities." He smiled at her. "Sure it's a proposal. I'm a good prospect now—I'm going to replace Hammond as the Roman bureau chief. I'm settling down! I'll get a raise in time for the wedding. But don't forget we probably can't get married in one of your churches. I'm a divorced man."

"If the Catholics won't marry us, then the Communists will," Gina said playfully.

"You're whichever suits you at the moment, is that it? Catholic or Communist?"

"I'm a typical Italian, Roberto," she said lightly. "A typical human being. Do you know where I want to go for a honeymoon?"

"Tell me."

"Jerusalem. I want to see where it all happened."

Miller pulled her close. The last few days had had a tremendous effect on him. No longer did he want to be a loner—a solitary drifter with a typewriter. He was in love. His marriage would work this time. This he knew.

Cardinal Garonne sat with Monsignor O'Malley in the Vatican Mercedes. They came directly behind John O'Neill's specially designed Cadillac limousine, which had its roof open with Pope David standing up to wave to the crowds along the way.

Cardinal Garonne looked out at the cheering, happy faces and was full of admiration for the Pope's astuteness. David I had had this in mind when he decided to go to Jerusalem, the Cardinal thought. It was his answer to the Communists. But surely he hadn't guessed someone would try to kill him. That had given the crowd's welcome its unique intensity—its affectionate tone.

"He is one American who understands us Italians," Cardinal Garonne told Monsignor O'Malley. "I was wrong not to vote for him. Please look after him for us."

"We nearly lost him in Jerusalem," O'Malley replied ruefully. "Danger seems to follow him everywhere, but then so does God."

Between masses in Turin, old Cardinal Bracca watched on television the Pope's triumphant ride into Rome to the Vatican. The open Cadillac limousine was stopped several times when the crowd broke through the barriers. A crowd of factory workers on the outskirts of Rome presented David with a white lamb . . .

"Good," said the old Cardinal, "the people recognize a good man." He turned to his secretary. "Remember, it was my change in the Conclave that led to his election. I feel a responsibility. I'm afraid now he won't take my dream seriously. But it was meant as a warning! I thought it was a warning that *he* must not go to Jerusalem. But now I see its true meaning. The Vatican mustn't go to Jerusalem or dire things will happen! It must stay in Italy, come what may from the Communists! I must go to Rome to warn him . . ."

He stood on the red-draped central balcony of St. Peter's giant basilica, a slight lonely figure overlooking the immense crowd that stretched from the colonnade through the Piazza San Pietro down to the Tiber and beyond.

Gradually the great waves of cheering slackened. There were shouts of "Long live the Pope!" in many languages, and people knelt on the cobblestones and made the sign of the cross.

At last the vast gathering of the faithful stared upward, waiting.

It was an awe-inspiring few moments of silence among so many hundreds of thousands of people.

Then suddenly the familiar intense voice spoke out over the loudspeakers.

"Easter Sunday," David said slowly as if he were thinking aloud, "is a day of rejoicing—and never more so than today. Both in Rome and Jerusalem, we have seen the defeat of evil, of men who wished to control our lives, who had no respect for the individual. But they lost—both here and in the Holy City. We have gained a little time." He paused for a moment and then added quickly: "We must use it well. One of my first acts will be to sign an agreement formally recognizing the state of Israel . . ." A great roar went up from the crowd. No one missed the symbolic importance of the Pope's announcement—it was almost like signaling the end of anti-Semitism to the world.

His hands began to shake with the intensity of his feelings as he told the great crowd: "On the day Jesus rose triumphantly from the dead, we celebrate the strength of our individual faith—and our faith in the individual. We are each of us unique. Whatever our beliefs, we all belong to the human family. And so I will wish all people a Happy Easter in their own language ..."

David I moved to the very edge of the balcony and leaned over, as if to get as close as possible to the mass of faces below.

The hushed crowd listened intently as he spoke out in Albanian, Arabic, Armenian, Bulgarian, Chinese, Croatian, Czech, Finnish, French, Gaelic, German, Hebrew, Hindi ... On and on in more than forty languages, his voice echoed across the Piazza San Pietro, across the nation, across the world, in a universal message of love that everyone could understand.

Marc Ram was listening to the radio when Major Falid arrived in his small back office in The Knesset. Ram turned up the volume. A great roar filled the room.

"That's the crowd in St. Peter's Square. The Pope has just finished speaking ..."

Ram turned off the radio.

"Thank God he's safely back in Rome," Ram said. "He was a pain in the neck from a security point of view. No cooperation at all." But inwardly Ram had been strangely touched by the young Pope's recognition of his beloved homeland. He didn't want to show it, though, in front of Falid. "How was Cousins, Major?" Major Falid had just come from visiting the CIA agent in the hospital.

"Better than I expected. Those stomach wounds can do a lot of damage."

"Have you finished your business with us now?"

"Yes, Colonel, I'm through. I've provided a report about my shooting of the young Palestinian, Ayad. I have a copy of your report about the shooting of Judas for my files. It's all mere police formalities. The Don Paolo case is officially closed."

"One duty remains," said Ram. He touched an old tobacco jar on his desk. "Nobody wanted to claim Judas' remains. Like all intelligence services, the British A-7 accepted no responsibility for him and wouldn't pay the cost of flying the body to London. I think they were worried they might be implicated in the attempted assassination. The cousin who inherited the Brett estate wouldn't even recognize Judas as one of the family. He wasn't interested in the body. And who else was there? So I had the poor devil cremated here. I was the only mourner. Now I want to dispose of the ashes and I'd like a witness."

"Very well," said Major Falid.

The two men drove to Mount Zion and walked down into Gehenna. A slight mist came up like smoke from the valley. The ground seemed more arid than ever. Halfway down the hillside, Ram stopped. His black-gloved hand flicked the top off the tobacco jar. He waited for a gust of wind, and then tilted the jar and let the ashes go. The wind picked them up and carried them down into the valley, scattering Judas' remains over Gehenna.

"The end of Goliath," Ram grunted. More cheerfully he added, "Now, Major, let's go and get a strong drink at the King David Hotel. I think we've earned it."

"We Moslems do not drink alcohol," said the Major, "but it will be my pleasure to have coffee with you."

The two men, the Israeli and the Jordanian, climbed back up the hillside with the familiarity of old friends. At the top, the old walled city lay before them. The sun was now coming through the morning mist. As they stood together gazing down, the eroded tawny stones were transformed into a golden wonder, timeless, seemingly unravaged by all the violence of the past. It was as if they were seeing not the mere ancient buildings but the very spirit of Jerusalem—unchanging, unchangeable—the spirit of the divided peoples with opposing faiths who had come together here within the same walls. We are all One. Both men felt it at that moment, but they remained silent.

ABOUT THE AUTHOR

W. J. WEATHERBY is an Englishman living in the United States. He is a reporter and one-time foreign correspondent for the *Manchester Guardian*. Mr. Weatherby's first novel was written under a pseudonym and won the Mystery Writers of America Edgar Award several years ago for Best Mystery of the Year.

WATCH FOR
THE "THRILLER OF THE MONTH"

Every month, beginning with FALSE FLAGS, Bantam will publish a highly acclaimed adventure thriller. They will be available wherever paperbacks are sold.

FALSE FLAGS by Noel Hynd

Six silicone chips from an American computer are found in a Soviet diplomat's apartment. These miniscule dots can be programmed to do anything—and yet they are blank. So why do the Russians want them? Ex-CIA agent Bill Mason is enlisted for a daring mission through a maze of intrigue and fallen bodies to find the answers.

THE DANCING DODO by John Gardner

A wrecked World War II plane is discovered in an English marsh containing six bodies all wearing dogtags of men very much alive. Who were they? What was their mission? Why have the crash investigators been stricken with a strange illness uncommon to England? The climax is a race to prevent a catastrophe.

MOSCOW 5000 by David Grant

July 1980—the 5000 meter race at the summer Olympics brings together the most spectacular and troubled field ever presented. And in the stands CIA agents use the games as a cover to rescue one of their men. The KGB is trying desperately to prevent disaster as a terrorist bomb threatens the entire stadium.

THE 65TH TAPE by Frank Ross

A deathbed confession forces our hero to find the whereabouts of one tape, made in Nixon's office, that proves a gigantic conspiracy by some top officials to run their own man for president and take over the country. Only two men can stop this—our hero and Richard M. Nixon. "Knife-edge suspense," says *Publishers Weekly*.

THE WATCHDOGS OF ABADDON by Ib Melchior

A page-turner about a retired Los Angeles cop and his son who stumble on a Nazi plot which, 33 years after Hitler's death, is within weeks of deadly fruition. Their investigations uncover a fiendish plan to set off a nuclear blast and start the Third Reich. By the author of *The Haigerloch Project*.

PARTY OF THE YEAR by John Crosby

Chosen by *The New York Times* as one of the best of the year, this fast-paced story centers on a wealthy international jet set in spite of terrorist warnings. An woman who decides to give an elegant party for the ex-CIA man tries to defuse the situation which could erupt in a shocking bloodbath.

WHAT IF . . .

Fires, floods, air disasters, political intrigue. Events that could happen . . . and do in these exciting best-sellers. Guaranteed to keep you on the edge of your seat.

☐	20062	AIRPORT *Arthur Hailey*	$3.50
☐	13028	OVERLOAD *Arthur Hailey*	$2.95
☐	13017	THE CHINA SYNDROME *Burton Wohl*	$1.95
☐	11708	JAWS 2 *Hank Searls*	$2.25
☐	13880	RAISE THE TITANIC! *Clive Cussler*	$2.75
☐	12810	VIXEN 03 *Clive Cussler*	$2.75
☐	13707	RUNWAY ZERO-EIGHT *Arthur Hailey*	$2.50
☐	13169	SEVEN DAYS IN MAY *Knebel & Bailey*	$2.50
☐	14136	THE SEVEN LAST YEARS *Carol Balizet*	$2.75
☐	14455	ICEBERG *Clive Cussler*	$2.75
☐	14033	ICE! *Arnold Federbush*	$2.50

Buy them at your local bookstore or use this handy coupon for ordering:

Bantam Books, Inc., Dept. DI, 414 East Golf Road, Des Plaines, Ill. 60016

Please send me the books I have checked above. I am enclosing $_____ (please add $1.00 to cover postage and handling). Send check or money order —no cash or C.O.D.'s please.

Mr/Mrs/Miss_____

Address_____

City_____State/Zip_____

DI—4/81

Please allow four to six weeks for delivery. This offer expires 10/81.